PRINCE OF THE NORTH

HARRY TURTLEDOVE

Copyright © 1994 by Harry Turtledove

A Baen Books Original

Baen Publishing Enterprises
P.O. Box 1403
Riverdale, NY 10471

ISBN: 0-671-87606-6

Cover art by Larry Elmore

Map by Eleanor Kostyk

First printing, June 1994

Distributed by Paramount Publishing
1230 Avenue of the Americas
New York, NY 10020

Printed in the United States of America

"OUT SWORDS AND AT THEM!"

In such dreadful weather, bows were useless. Gerin stooped to pick up a stone the size of a goose egg. He flung it at the oncoming monsters, then yelled, "Out sword and at them!" A moment later, his own blade slid from its scabbard.

A stone flew past his head. One of the creatures, at any rate, had wit enough to think of it as a weapon. Then the fight was at close quarters, the savagery and strength of the monsters against the armor and bronze weapons of Gerin's warriors.

With his long, heavy spear, better made for use afoot than from a chariot, Van had an advantage over his monstrous foes: he could thrust at them long before they closed with him. But when he sank the leaf-shaped point into the belly of one screaming creature, another seized the spearshaft and wrenched it out of his hands. He shouted in shock and dismay; long used to being stronger than any man he faced, having an opponent who could match him in might came as a jolt.

The monster dropped the spear; it preferred its natural weapons to those made by art. But when it sprang at Van, he stove in its head with an overhand blow from his mace. He needed no second stroke; the fight with the creature the day before had warned him to put all his power into the first one.

Baen Books by Harry Turtledove

The Case of the Toxic Spell Dump
Agent of Byzantium
Werenight
Prince of the North
A Different Flesh (*forthcoming*)

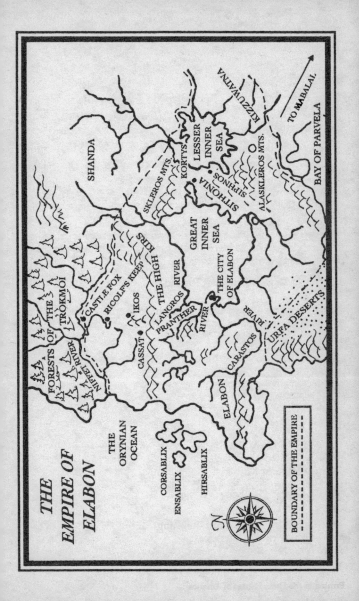

THE
EMPIRE OF
ELABON

BOUNDARY OF THE EMPIRE

I

Gerin the Fox eyed the new logs in the palisade of Fox Keep. Even after five years' weathering, they were easy to pick out, for they'd never been painted with the greenish glop the wizard Siglorel had concocted to keep Balamung the Trokmê mage from burning the keep around him. The stuff worked, too, but Balamung had slain Siglorel even so. Gerin knew something of magecraft himself, but he'd never been able to match Siglorel's formulation.

In front of those new logs, a handful of the Fox's retainers sat on their haunches in a circle. Gerin's four-year-old son Duren ran from one of them to the next, exclaiming, "Can I roll the dice? Will you let me roll them now?"

Drago the Bear held the carved cubes of bone. Rumbling laughter, he handed them to Duren, who threw them down in the middle of the gamblers' circle. "Haw! Twelve! No one can beat that," Drago said. He scooped up his winnings, then glanced toward Gerin. "The boy brings luck, lord."

"Glad to hear it," Gerin answered shortly. Whenever he looked at his son, he couldn't help thinking of the boy's mother. When he'd wed Elise, he'd been sure the gods had granted him everlasting bliss. He'd thought so right up to the day, three years ago now, when she'd run off with a traveling horseleech. Only the gods knew where in the shattered northlands she was these days, or how she fared.

The Fox kicked at the dirt. Maybe if he'd noticed she

1

wasn't happy, he could have done things to make her so. Or maybe she'd just tired of him. Women did that, and men, too. "The great god Dyaus knows it's too late to do anything about it now," he muttered.

"Too late to do anything about what, Captain?" Van of the Strong Arm boomed as he came out of the stables. The outlander overtopped Gerin's six feet by as many inches, and was nearly twice as thick through the shoulders, too; the red-dyed horsehair plume that nodded above his helmet only made him seem taller. As usual, he kept his bronze corselet polished almost to mirror brilliance.

"Years too late for us to do anything about getting imperial troopers up here," Gerin answered. He was the sort who guarded private thoughts even from his closest friends.

Van spat on the ground. "That for imperial troopers. It was too late for those buggers five years ago, when the carrion-stinking Empire of Elabon shut all the passes into the north sooner than help us keep the Trokmoi out."

"Dyaus knows we could have used the imperials then," Gerin said. "We could use them still, if they'd come and if—"

"If they'd keep their hands off what's yours," Van finished for him.

"Well, yes, there is that," Gerin admitted: he was given to understatement.

Van wasn't. He snorted, back deep in his throat. "Honh! 'There is that,' he says. You think the Emperor of Elabon would be happy with the title you've gone and taken for yourself? You know what he'd do if ever he got his hands on somebody who styled himself the Prince of the North, don't you? He'd nail you to the cross so the ravens could sit on your shoulders and pick out your eyes, that's what."

Since Van was undoubtedly right, Gerin shifted the terms of the argument. He did the same thing whenever he and his friend wrestled, using guile to beat strength and weight. In wrestling as in argument, sometimes it worked and sometimes it didn't. He said, "I'm not the only one in the northlands with a fancy new title since Elabon abandoned us. I'd have company on the crucifying grounds."

"Aye, so you would," Van said. "What's Aragis the Archer calling himself these days? Grand Duke, that's it. Honh! He's just a jumped-up baron, same as you. And there's two or three others of your Elabonian blood, and as many Trokmoi who came south over the Niffet with Balamung and stayed even after the wizard failed."

"I know." Gerin didn't like that. For a couple of centuries, the Niffet had been the boundary between the civilization of the Empire of Elabon—or a rough, frontier version of it, at any rate—on one side and woodsrunning barbarians on the other. Now the boundary was down, and Elabon's abandoned northern province very much on its own.

Van tapped Gerin on the chest with a callused forefinger. "But I tell you this, Captain: you have the loftiest title, so he'd nail you highest."

"An honor I could do without," the Fox said. "Besides, it's quarreling over shadows, anyhow. Elabon's not coming back over the mountains. What I really need to worry about is the squabbles with my neighbors—especially Aragis. Of the lot of them, he's the ablest one."

"Aye, he's near as good as you are, Captain, though not so sneaky."

"Sneaky?" Since Gerin's devious turn of mind was what had earned him his Fox sobriquet, he couldn't even deny that. He changed the subject again: "You're still calling me 'Captain' after all these years, too. Is that the sort of respect the Prince of the North deserves?"

"I'll call you what I bloody well please," Van retorted, "and if one fine day that doesn't suit your high and mightiness, well, I'll up and travel on. I sometimes think I should have done it years ago." He shook his head, bemused that after a lifetime of wandering and adventure he should have begun to put down roots.

Gerin still did not know from what land his friend had sprung; Van never talked of his beginnings, though he had yarns uncounted of places he'd seen. Certainly he was no Elabonian. Gerin made a fair representative of that breed: on the swarthy side, long-nosed and long-faced, with brown eyes and black hair and beard (now beginning to be frosted with gray).

Van, by contrast, was blond and fair-skinned, though tan; his bright beard was that improbable color between yellow and orange. His nose had been short and straight. These days it was short and bent, with a scar across the bridge. His bright blue eyes commonly had mischief in them. Women found him fascinating and irresistible. The reverse also applied.

"Roll the dice?" Duren squealed. "Roll the dice?"

Van laughed to hear Gerin's son say that. "Maybe we'll roll the dice ourselves later on, eh, Captain? See who goes to Fand tonight?"

"Not so loud," Gerin said, looking around to make sure their common mistress wasn't in earshot. "She'll throw things at both of us if she ever finds out we do that sometimes. That Trokmê temper of hers—" He shook his head.

Van laughed louder. "A dull wench is a boring wench. I expect that's why I keep coming back to her."

"After every new one, you mean. Sometimes I think there's a billy goat under that cuirass, and no man at all," Gerin said. Van might have settled in one place, but his affections flew wild and free as a gull.

"Well, what about you?" he said. "If her temper doesn't suit you, why don't you put her on a raft and ship her back over the Niffet to her clansfolk?"

"Dyaus knows I've thought about it often enough," Gerin admitted. After Elise left him, he'd thought about swearing off women forever. No matter what his mind said, though, his body had other ideas. Now he laughed, ruefully. "If either of us truly fell in love with her, we'd be hard-pressed to stay friends."

"Not so, Captain," Van answered. "If one of us fell in love with her, the other would say take her and welcome. If we both did, now—"

"You have me," Gerin admitted. He kicked at the dirt, annoyed at being outreasoned even in something as small as this. But if you couldn't grant someone else's reason superior when it plainly was, what point to reasoning at all?

Van said, "I think I'll roll the dice myself for a while. Care to join?"

"No, I'm going to take another pass at my sorcery, if you know what I mean," Gerin said.

"Have a care, now," Van said. "You're liable to end up in more trouble than you know how to get out of."

"Hasn't happened yet," Gerin answered. "I have the measure of my own ignorance, I think." He'd studied a bit of magic in the City of Elabon as a young man, back in the days when people could travel back and forth between the northlands and the heart of the Empire, but had to give up that and history both when the Trokmoi killed his father and elder brother and left him baron of Fox Keep.

"I hope you do," Van said. Pulling broken bits of silver from a pouch he wore on his belt, he made for the dice game. Before he could sit down, Duren sprang at him like a starving longtooth. He laughed, grabbed the boy, and threw him high in the air three or four times. Duren squealed with glee.

Gerin made for a little shack he'd built over in a back corner of the courtyard. It was far enough from the palisade that, if it caught fire, it wouldn't burn down the castle outwall along with itself. Thus far, he hadn't even managed to set the shack ablaze.

"Maybe today," he muttered. He was going to try a conjuration from a new grimoire he'd bought from a lordlet to the southwest whose grandfather might have been able to read but who was himself illiterate and proud of it. As with most spells in grimoires, it sounded wonderful. Whether results would match promises was another question altogether.

The codex of the grimoire had silverfish holes on several of its pages, and mice had nibbled its leather binding while it lay forgotten on a high shelf in a larder. The spell in which Gerin was interested, though, remained unmutilated. In a clear hand, the mage who'd composed it had written, "A CANTRIP WHICH YIELDETH A FLAMING SWORD."

That *yieldeth* had made Gerin suspicious. Along with wizardry and history, he'd studied literature down in the City of Elabon. (*And where*, he wondered, *will Duren be able to learn such things, if he should want to?* The answer was mournfully clear: *in the northlands, nowhere.*) He knew Elabonian hadn't used those archaic forms for hundreds of years, which meant the author was trying to make his work seem older than it was.

But a flaming sword . . . false antique or no, he reckoned that worth looking into. Not only would it make ferocious wounds, the mere sight of it should cast terror into the hearts of his foes.

He hefted the bronze blade he'd use. It was hacked

and notched to the point where it would almost have made a better saw than sword. Bronze was the hardest, toughest metal anyone knew, but it wasn't hard enough to hold an edge in continued tough use.

Gerin had the crushed wasps and bumblebees and the dried poison oak leaf he'd need for the symbolic element of the spell. Chanting as he worked (and wearing leather gauntlets), he ground them fine and stirred them into melted butter. The grimoire prescribed olive oil as the basis for the paste, but he'd made that substitution before and got by with it. It was necessary; the olive wouldn't grow in the northlands, and supplies from south of the High Kirs had been cut off.

He was readying himself for the main conjuration when someone poked his head into the hut. "Great Dyaus above, are you at it again?" Rihwin the Fox asked. His soft southern accent reminded Gerin of his student days in the City of Elabon every time he heard it.

"Aye, I am, and lucky for you at a place where I can pause," Gerin answered. If anyone had to interrupt him, he preferred it to be Rihwin. The man who shared his ekename knew more magic than he did; Rihwin had been expelled from the Sorcerers' Collegium just before his formal union with a familiar because of the outrageous prank he'd played on his mentor.

He walked into the hut, glanced at the sword and the preparations Gerin had made for it. He'd stopped shaving since he ended up in the northlands, but somehow still preserved a smooth, very southern handsomeness. Maybe the big gold hoop that glittered in his left ear had something to do with that.

Pointing to the wood-and-leather bucket full of water that stood next to the rude table where Gerin worked, he said, "Your precautions are thorough as usual."

Gerin grunted. "You'd be working here beside me if

you took them, too." Rihwin had been rash enough to summon up Mavrix, the Sithonian god of wine also widely worshiped in Elabon, after Gerin had earned the temperamental deity's wrath. In revenge, Mavrix robbed Rihwin of his ability to work magic, and left him thankful his punishment was no worse.

"Ah, well," Rihwin said with an airy wave of his hand. "Dwelling on one's misfortunes can hardly turn them to triumphs, now can it?"

"It might keep you from having more of them," Gerin replied; he was as much given to brooding as Rihwin fought shy of it. He'd concluded, though, that Rihwin was almost immune to change, and so gave up the skirmish after the first arrow. Bending over the grimoire once more, he said, "Let's find out what we have here."

The spell was no easy one; it required him to use his right hand to paint the sword blade with his mixture while simultaneously making passes with his left and chanting the incantation proper, which was written in the same pseudoarchaic Elabonian as its title.

He suspected the mage of deliberately requiring the left hand for the complex passes to make the spell more difficult, but grinned as he incanted: being left-handed himself, he was delighted to have his clumsy right doing something simple.

The painting and passes done, he snatched up the sword and cried, "Let the wishes of the operator be accomplished!"

For a moment, he wondered if anything would happen. A lot of alleged grimoires were frauds; maybe that was why this one had sat unused on a shelf for a couple of generations. But then, sure enough, yellow-orange flames rippled up and down the length of the blade. They neither looked nor smelled like burning butter; they seemed more the essence of fire brought down to earth.

"That's marvelous," Rihwin breathed as Gerin made cut-and-thrust motions with the flaming sword. "It—"

With a sudden foul oath, Gerin rammed the sword into the bucket of water. A hiss and a cloud of steam arose; to his great relief, the flames went out. He cautiously felt the water with a forefinger. When he discovered it remained cool, he stuck in his hand. "Cursed hilt got too hot to hold," he explained to a pop-eyed Rihwin. "Oh, that feels good."

"Which, no doubt, is the reason we fail to find blazing blades closely clenched in the fierce fist of every peerless paladin," Rihwin answered. "Many a spell that seems superb on the leaves of a codex develops disqualifying drawbacks when actually essayed."

"You're right about that," Gerin answered, drying his hand on the thigh of his baggy wool breeches. Everyone in the northlands wore trousers; the Trokmê style had conquered completely. Even Rihwin, who had favored southern robes, was in breeches these days. Gerin inspected his left palm. "I don't think that's going to blister."

"Smear butter or tallow on it if it does," Rihwin said, "but not the, ah, heated mixture you prepared there."

"With the poison oak leaves and all? No, I'll get rid of that." Gerin poured it out of its clay pot onto the ground. After a bit of thought, he scooped dirt onto the greasy puddle. If the sole of his boot happened to have a hole, he didn't want the stuff getting onto his skin.

He and Rihwin left the shack. Shadows were lengthening; before long, no one would want to stay outdoors. Ghosts filled the night with terror. A man caught alone in the darkness without sacrificial blood to propitiate them or fire to hold them at bay was likely to be mad come morning.

Gerin glanced to the sky, gauging the hour by the

moons. Nothos' pale crescent hung a little west of south; golden Math, at first quarter looking like half a coin, was about as far to the east. And ruddy Elleb (pinkish white now, washed out by the late afternoon sun), halfway between quarter and full, stood well clear of the eastern horizon. The fourth moon, quick-moving Tiwaz, would be a waning crescent when the serfs went out to work just after sunrise tomorrow.

As if Gerin's thinking of the serfs he ruled had brought them to new life, a mournful horn blew in the village close by Fox Keep, calling men and women in from the fields.

Gerin looked at the moons again, raised one eyebrow in a characteristic gesture. "They're knocking off early today," he remarked. "I think I may have to speak to the headman tomorrow."

"He'll not love you for making him push the other peasants harder," Rihwin said.

Who does love me, for any reason? Gerin wondered. His mother had died giving birth to him; maybe because of that, his father had always been distant. Or maybe his father simply hadn't known what to do when he got himself a thinker instead of a brawler.

His son Duren loved him, aye, but now it was his turn to have trouble returning that love, because whenever he saw Duren, he thought of Elise. She'd loved him for a while, until passion cooled . . . and then just disappeared, with only a note left behind begging him not to go after her. It was, in fact, very much the way she'd fled with him from her father's keep.

He didn't feel like going into any of that with Rihwin. Instead, he answered, "I don't care whether Besant Big-Belly loves me or not." That, at least, was true. "I do care that we grow enough to get through the winter, for if we don't, Besant will be big-bellied no more."

"He would say, did he dare, that all the peasants would be bigger-bellied did they not have to pay you a fourth of what they raised," Rihwin observed.

"He could say it to my face, and well he knows it," Gerin returned. "I'm not a lord who makes serfs into draft animals that happen to walk on two legs, nor do I take the half some barons squeeze from them. But if I took nothing, who would ward them from the chariot-riding wolves who'd swoop down on them?"

He waited for Rihwin to say something like, "They could do it for themselves." He was ready to pour scorn on that idea like boiling water splashing down from the top of a palisade onto the heads of attackers. Farmers didn't have the tools they needed to be fighters: the horses, the chariots, the swords, the armor. Nor did they have the time they needed to learn to use those tools; the endless rhythms of fields and livestock devoured their days.

But Rihwin said, "My fellow Fox, sometimes you don't know when you're being twitted."

Denied his chance to rend Rihwin with rhetoric, Gerin glared. He walked around to the front of the castle. Rihwin tagged along, chuckling. As they went inside, another horn sounded from a more distant village, and then another almost at the edge of hearing. Gerin said, "You see? If one village knocks off early, they all do it, for they hear the first horn and blow their own, figuring they don't want to work any harder than the fellows down the trail."

"Who *does* like to work?" Rihwin said.

"No one with sense," Gerin admitted, "but no one with sense will avoid doing what he must to stay alive. The trouble is, not all men are sensible, even by that standard."

"If you think I'll argue with that, you're the one who's not sensible," Rihwin said.

❖ ❖ ❖

The great hall of the castle occupied most of the ground floor. A fire roared in the stone hearth at the far end, and another, smaller, one in front of the altar to Dyaus close by. Above the hearth, cooks basted chunks of beef as they turned them on spits. Fat-wrapped thigh-bones, the god's portion, smoked on the altar. Gerin believed in feeding the god well; moreover, after his brush with Mavrix, he figured he could use all the divine protection he could get.

Two rows of benches ran from the doorway to the hearth. In winter, seats closest to the fire were the choice ones. Now, with the weather mild, Gerin sat about half-way down one row. A couple of dogs came trotting through the rushes on the rammed-earth floor and lay at his feet, looking up expectantly.

"Miserable beggars," he said, and scratched their ears. "I don't have any food myself yet, so how can I throw you bones and scraps?" The dogs thumped their tails on the ground. They knew they got fed sooner or later when people sat at those benches. If it had to be later, they would wait.

Van and Drago the Bear and the other gamblers came in, chattering about the game. Duren frisked among them. When he saw Gerin, he ran over to him, exclaiming, "I rolled the dice a lot, Papa! I rolled double six twice, and five-and-six three times, and—"

He would have gone down the whole list, but Van broke in, "Aye, and the little rascal rolled one-and-two for me, and sent me out of that round without a tunic to call my own." He shook a heavy fist at Duren in mock anger. Duren, safe beside his father, stuck out his tongue.

"The dice go up, the dice go down," Drago said, shrugging shoulders almost as wide as Van's. From him, that passed for philosophy. He was a long way from the brightest of Gerin's vassals, but a good many more clever men managed their estates worse. Since Drago never tried anything new, he discovered no newfangled ways to go wrong.

Gerin called to one of the cooks, "We have enough here to begin. Fetch ale for us, why don't you?"

"Aye, lord prince," the man answered, and hurried down into the cellar. He returned a moment later, staggering a little under the weight of a heavy jar of ale. The jar had a pointed bottom. The cook stabbed it into the dirt floor so the jar stood upright. He hurried off again, coming back with a pitcher and a double handful of tarred leather drinking jacks. He set one in front of everybody at the table (Duren got a small one), then dipped the pitcher into the amphora, pouring and refilling until every jack was full.

"Take some for yourself, too," Gerin said; he was not a lord who stinted his servants. Grinning, the cook poured what looked like half a pitcher down his throat. Gerin slopped a little ale out of his mug onto the floor. "This for Baivers, god of barley," he intoned as he drank.

"This for Baivers," the others echoed as they poured their libations. Even Van imitated him: though Baivers was no god of the outlander's, the deity, whose scalp sprouted ears of barley instead of hair, held sway in this land.

Rihwin made a sour face as he set down the mug. "I miss the sweet blood of the grape," he said.

"Point the first: the grape doesn't grow in the northlands and we've lost our trade south of the High Kirs," Gerin said. "Point the second: when you drink too much wine, dreadful things happen. We've seen that again and again. Point the third: wine lies in Mavrix's province, and have you not had your share and more of commerce with Mavrix?"

"True, all true," Rihwin said sadly. "I miss the grape regardless."

The cooks came round with bowls of bean-and-parsnip porridge, with tiny bits of salt pork floating in it to give it flavor. Like everyone else, Gerin lifted his bowl to his lips, wiped his mouth on his sleeve when he was done. South of the High Kirs, they had separate squares of cloth for cleaning your face and fingers, but such refinements did not exist north of the mountains.

Off the spit came the pieces of beef. While one cook carved them into man-sized portions, another went back to the kitchen and came out with round, flat, chewy loaves of bread, which he set in front of each man at the table. They'd soak up the juices from the meat and get eaten in their turn.

Gerin patted the empty place between Van and him. "Put one here, too, Anseis. Fand is sure to be down before long."

"Aye, lord prince," the cook said, and did as he was asked.

Duren started tearing pieces from his round of bread and stuffing them into his mouth. Gerin said, "If you fill yourself up with that, boy, where will you find room for your meat?"

"I'll put it someplace." Duren patted his stomach to show the intended destination.

Just as the cook who was carving the beef started loading steaming gobbets onto an earthenware tray, Fand did come down from Castle Fox's living quarters into the great hall. Gerin and Van glanced over at each other, smiled for a moment, and then both waved her to that place between them.

"Och, you're still not after fighting over me," she said in mock disappointment as she came up. Beneath the mock disappointment, Gerin judged, lay real disappointment.

She might have resigned herself to their peacefully sharing her, but she didn't like it.

Hoping to get her off that bloodthirsty turn of thought, Gerin called for a servant to pour her a jack of ale. He handed it to her himself. "Here you are."

"I thank you, sure and I do." Her Elabonian held a strong Trokmê lilt. She was a big, fair woman, not too much shorter than the Fox, with pale skin dusted with freckles wherever the sun caught it, gray-blue eyes, and wavy, copper-colored hair that tumbled past her shoulders. To Gerin, men of that coloring were enemies on sight; he still sometimes found it odd to be sharing a bed with a woman from north of the Niffet.

Not odd enough to keep me from doing it, though, he thought. Aloud, he said to Fand, "Should I have put you on a boat across the river after all?"

"'Twould have been your own loss if you had," she retorted, tossing her head so the torchlight glinted in her hair. One thing she had was unshakeable self-confidence—and why not, when two men such as they danced to her tune?

Gerin said, "My guess is still that you stuck a knife into the fellow who brought you south over the Niffet."

"I've told you before, Gerin dear: I brought my own self over, thinking life might be more lively here. Och, and so it has been, not that I reckoned on yoking myself to a southron—" she paused to half turn and make eyes at Van "—let alone two."

"*I'm* no Elabonian," Van boomed indignantly, "and I'll thank you not to call me one. One fine day I hitch a team to a chariot or just go off afoot—"

"How many years have you been saying that?" Gerin asked.

"As many as I've been here, no doubt, less maybe one turn of the fastest moon." Van shook his head, forever bemused he could stay in one place so long. "A tree, now, has need of growing roots, but a man—?"

"A man?" Fand said, still trying to stir up trouble. "You'll quarrel over whether you're a southron or no, but not over me? What sort of man is that after making you?"

"You should remember well enough from last night what sort of man I am." Van looked like a cat that had fallen into the cream pitcher.

Fand squeaked indignantly and turned back to Gerin. "Will you be letting him speak to me so?"

"Aye, most likely I will," he said. If she got fed up and left them both, he'd be sorry for a while, but he knew he'd also be relieved. He didn't feel like a screaming fight now, though, so he said, "Here comes the meat."

That distracted her. It distracted him, too. He drew his dagger from his belt and started carving strips off the bone in front of him and popping them into his mouth.

The dagger, like the rest of his personal gear, was severely plain, with a hilt of nothing more splendid than leather-wrapped bone. But it had good balance, and he kept the edge sharp; sometimes he used plainness to conceal effectiveness.

Van, by contrast, had the hilt to his knife wrapped in gold wire, with a big topaz set into the pommel. For him, flamboyance served the same purpose self-effacement did for Gerin: it disguised the true warrior beneath. Being dangerous without seeming so, Gerin had found, made the danger double.

Thinking thus, he glanced over at Fand, who was slicing with her own slim bronze blade. Was she disguising something? He snorted and took a long pull at his ale. No, concealment wasn't in her nature. But he'd thought as much about Elise, and where had that got him?

Duren said, "Papa, will you help me cut more meat?"

He had a knife, too, but a small one, and not very sharp. That helped keep him from getting cut, but it also kept him from eating very fast.

Gerin leaned over and sliced off several strips for him. "Splash water on your face when you're done," he said. He remembered how surprised and delighted he'd been to discover the elaborate hot and cold baths the City of Elabon boasted. North of the High Kirs, as best he knew, there was only one tub, and it wasn't at his holding. Not without a pang, he'd gone back to being mostly dirty most of the time.

Fand made eyes first at Van, then at him. "Och, a woman gets lonely, that she does."

"If you're lonely with the two of us to keep you warm at night, would you try a bandit troop next?" Van said.

She cursed him in the Trokmê language, Elabonian not being satisfying enough for her. Van swore back in the same tongue; he'd traversed the gloomy forests of the Trokmoi before he swam the Niffet (towing his precious armor behind him on a makeshift raft) and splashed up inside Gerin's holding.

"Will you be letting him speak to me so?" Fand demanded of the Fox once more.

"Probably," he answered. She picked up her drinking jack and threw it at him. She had more fury than finesse. It splashed down behind him and sprayed ale onto a couple of the hounds quarreling over bones. They separated with a yelp. Fand sprang to her feet and stomped upstairs.

"Not often dull around here," Van observed to no one in particular.

"It's not, is it?" Gerin said. "Sometimes I think I'd find a bit of dullness restful." He hadn't known much, not since he came back over the Kirs to take over his father's holdings and especially not since the Trokmoi and their wizard Balamung invaded the northlands. Balamung was dead now, without even a grave to hold him, but too many Trokmoi still raided and settled on this side of the Niffet, adding one more volatile element to already touchy politics.

Gerin emptied his own jack in a fashion more conventional than Fand's, went over to the amphora, and poured it full again. Some of his vassals were already swilling themselves into insensibility. *If I want dull,* he thought, *all I need do is listen to the talk around this table.* Dice, horses and chariots, crops, women . . . no new ideas anywhere, just old saws trotted out as if they were fresh-minted from pure gold. He longed for the days when he'd sat in students' taverns, arguing sorcerous techniques and the shape of the historical process.

Rihwin the Fox knew the pleasures of intellectual conversation, but Rihwin also knew the pleasures of the wine jar or, that failing, the ale pot. He might complain about having to pour down ale, but that didn't stop him from doing quite a lot of it. And, at the moment, he had a serving girl on his lap. He would have done a better job of fumbling at her clothes had his hands been steadier.

Van knew his letters; he'd made a point of learning them when he discovered Elabonian could be written. He even spoke well of its alphabet; Gerin gathered he'd run across other, more cumbersome ways of noting down thoughts in his travels. But learning his letters did not make him interested in quoting poetry, except for informational content, let alone analyzing it.

As for Gerin's own vassal barons, most of them thought reading a vaguely effeminate accomplishment (he wondered why; even fewer women than men were literate). They'd learned better than to say so to him, and had learned he was a good fighting man in spite of having a room that stored several dozen scrolls and codices. But that didn't mean they grew interested in thinking, too.

Gerin sighed and drank more ale himself. Sometimes he thought slipping back into near barbarism easier than trying to maintain the standards of civilization he'd learned south of the High Kirs. *Which is the way civilization falls apart,* said the part of him that had studied history.

After one more jack of ale, he didn't feel like arguing with that part any more. Rihwin and the girl had wandered off. Drago the Bear snored thunderously on the floor, and took no notice when one of the dogs walked over him. Duren was asleep, too; the little boy had curled up, catlike, on his bench.

Van, on the other hand, was wide awake and looked more sober than Gerin felt. The Fox raised an eyebrow at him. "What would you?" he asked. "Shall we roll the dice after all?"

"For the lass, you mean?" Van shook his massive head. "You go to her tonight, if you've a mind to. She'd sweeten up for me in a bit, I expect, but I haven't the patience to get through the shouting that'd come first. I'll drink a bit more and then maybe sleep myself."

"All right." Gerin lifted Duren off the bench. His son wriggled a little, but did not wake. As he carried Duren upstairs, the Fox was grateful for the banister he'd added to the stairway when he came back from the south. With it, he was much less likely to trip and break not only his neck but the boy's.

He set Duren on the bed in his own chamber, hoping his son would wake up if he had to piddle in the night. Otherwise, the mattress would need some fresh straw.

With Duren in his arms, the Fox hadn't been able to carry a lamp or a taper up to the bedchamber with him. That left it black as a bandit's heart inside. He stumbled over some wood toy or other that he'd carved for Duren and almost fell on his face. Flailing his arms, he managed to keep himself upright and, with a muttered curse, went out into the hallway.

A couple of failing torches cast a dim red light there, enough, at least, to let him see where he put his feet. The walk to the next chamber was a matter of just a few steps. He rapped on the door, wondering if Fand had fallen asleep. If she didn't answer, he'd go back to his own bed.

But she did: "Which of you is it, now?"

Maybe it was the ale, but Gerin felt mischievous. He deliberately deepened his voice and put on a slight guttural accent: "Which d'you think?"

He heard her take three rapid strides toward the door. She threw it open and blazed, "Van of the Strong Arm, if you're after thinking y'can—" Then, by the torchlight and the brighter flame of the candle beside her bed, she realized it wasn't Van standing there. She scowled at Gerin. "You're a right devil to befool me so, and I ought to be slamming the door on the beaky nose of you."

He looked down that member at her. "Well?" he said when she didn't do as she'd threatened.

"Well, indeed," she said, and sighed. "Must be I'm the fool, for taking up with a southron man—worse, for taking up with a southron man and his great galoon of a friend, the both of them at once. Often enough I've said it, but—" Her face softened. "Since I am the fool, you may as well come in."

She stood aside to let him pass, closed the door behind him. She kept the room scrupulously neat; it was, by all odds, the cleanest part of the castle. Gerin knew the tunics and skirts and drawers in the cedar chest against the wall would all be folded just the same way. Beside that chest, her sandals and shoes stood in precise pairs. He lavished that much care only on his weapons, where it could be a matter of life or death.

Fand must have been mending a tunic when he knocked: it lay on the wool coverlet to her bed. Candlelight glistened from the polished bone needle she'd used. She picked up the tunic, set it on the chest. She nodded toward the candle. "Shall I blow it out?"

"Please yourself," he answered. "You know I like to look at you, though."

That won him a smile. "You southrons are sweeter in the tongue than men of my own folk, I'll say so much for you. Maybe there's the why of my staying here. A Trokmê chief, now, he'd just tell me to be after spreading my legs and waste no time about it."

Gerin's skeptical eyebrow rose. "My guess is that any man who told you such a thing would be likelier to get a knife in the brisket than anything else."

"Sure and that's the very thing he got, the black-hearted omadhaun," she said. "Why d'you think a puir lone woman would come to your keep at sunset, seeking shelter from the ghosts? Had his kin caught me, they'd have burned me in a wicker cage, that they would."

He knew she was right—that or some other equally appalling fate. South of the High Kirs, they crucified their miscreants. He reckoned himself merciful: if a man needed killing, he attended to it as quickly and cleanly as he could. But he'd killed his share and more, these past few years.

His other thought was that Fand calling herself a poor lone woman was about as accurate as a longtooth claiming it was a pussycat. At need, she likely could have shouted down the ghosts.

She cocked her head to one side, sent him a curious look. "What is it you're waiting for? I've no knife the now, nor even a needle."

"And a good thing, too, I say." He took a step toward her, she one toward him. That brought them together.

Her face lifted toward his, her arms went round his neck.

She was cross-grained, quarrelsome, cantankerous—Gerin had never settled on just the right word, but it lay somewhere in that range. On the wool coverlet, though . . . she bucked like a yearling colt, yowled like a catamount, and clawed his back as if she were part wolverine.

In a way, it was immensely flattering. Even when he'd pleased Elise, which hadn't been all the time (nor, in the end, nearly often enough), she'd given little sign. With Fand, he had no room for doubt there. But a passage with her sometimes put him more in mind of riding out a storm than making love: the pleasure he felt afterwards was often tempered with relief for having got through it.

Their sweat-slick skins slid against each other as he rolled off her. "Turn over," he said.

"Turn over, is it?" she said. "Why tell me that? You're not one of those who-do-you-call-thems—Sithonians, that's it—who like boys and use their women the same way. And I'm not one for that, as well you know." But, the warning delivered, she did roll onto her belly.

He straddled the small of her back and started rubbing her shoulders. The warning growls she'd let out turned to purrs. Her flesh was warm and firm under his hands. "Is that too rough?" he asked as he dug in with his thumbs.

She grunted but shook her head; her bright hair flipped back and forth, with a few shining strands covering his fingers and the backs of his hands. "You've summat here we never found north o' the Niffet," she said. "Sure and there may be more to this civilization you're always after prating of than I thought or ever I came to Fox Keep."

He wondered if he should tell her the best masseur he'd ever known, down in the City of Elabon, was a

Sithonian who would have been delighted to do more with him than merely rub his back. He decided against it: the more people in the northlands who cherished civilization, for whatever reason, the better off the war-torn country would be.

As Gerin's hands moved from her shoulders down her spine, he moved down, too. After a bit, Fand exclaimed sharply, "I told you, I'm not one for—" She broke off, then giggled. "What a sneak of a man y'are, to put it in the right place from the wrong side." She looked back at him over her shoulder. "Different this way."

"Better? Worse?" Even in such matters, even at such a time, he liked to know exactly how things went.

But she laughed at him. "How can I tell you that, when we've hardly begun?" They went on, looking for the answer.

Gerin woke the next morning when Duren got out of bed to use the chamber pot. The light in the bedchamber was gray. The sun hadn't risen yet, but it would soon. Gerin got out of bed himself, yawned, stretched, and knuckled his eyes: the ale he'd drunk the night before had left him with a bit of a headache.

"Good morning, Papa," Duren said.

"Good morning," Gerin answered, yawning again; he woke up slowly. He tousled the boy's hair. "I'm glad you're using the pot. Are you finished? My turn, then." When he was through, he pulled on the tunic and trousers he'd tossed on the floor after he came back from Fand's room. They didn't have any new spots he could see, so what point in changing? People were more fastidious on the other side of the High Kirs, but not much.

Duren underfoot like a cat, Gerin walked down the hall to the stairs. Snores came from Fand's chamber. Louder snores came from Van's, one door further down.

In the great hall of the keep, some of the Fox's vassals were already up and stirring; others lay bundled in blankets on straw pallets. The fire in the altar still burned, holding night ghosts at bay.

The doors that led out into the yard stood open, to give the great hall fresh air and clear out some of the smoke from the cookfires. Gerin picked his way through the warriors and went outside. In the east, Tiwaz's thin crescent stood low in the brightening sky. The other three moons had set.

Torches smoked along the palisade. Even so, Duren, who had followed his father into the yard, whimpered and said, "I don't like the ghosts yelling in my ears, Papa."

To Gerin, the cries of the night spirits were not yells but whimpers and faint wails, none of them understandable. As he had fires lit and had given the ghosts blood in the great hall, they were not likely to do him or Duren harm. He set his jaw and endured the cries he heard only with his mind's ear. Children, though, were supposed to be more sensitive to the spirits than adults.

A couple of minutes later, the first rays of the rising sun touched the top of the tall watchtower that stood above the keep. The ghosts sounded frightened for an instant, then vanished back into whatever gloomy haunt was theirs while the sun ruled the sky.

"A new day," Gerin said to Duren. "This is the time for living men to go abroad in the world." He patted the boy's back, heartening him against the terror that fluttered with the ghosts.

Van of the Strong Arm came out a few minutes later, whistling loudly but off-key. Smoke poured from windows and doorways as the cooks built up the fire to heat the morning porridge. Van squinted as a strand of smoke stung his eyes. "There ought to be a way to cook your food without smoking everyone who eats it as if he were a sausage," the burly outlander complained.

Gerin narrowed his eyes, too, but not at the smoke. *There ought to be a way* was a phrase that always set him thinking. Sometimes nothing came of it, but sometimes things did. He said, "Remember the newfangled footholders Duin the Bold came up with so he wouldn't go over his horse's tail if he tried to ride? Maybe we could find a new way to get rid of smoke, too."

"Remember what happened to Duin? He got himself killed with his newfangled scheme, that's what. Me, I'd sooner fight from a chariot any day." For all his wandering, for all the strange things he'd seen and done, Van remained at heart a profoundly conservative man.

Gerin had more stretch to him. "I think this business of riding to war will end up coming to something: a horse alone can cross terrain where a chariot can't go. But you have a special trouble there—where will you find a beast to bear your bulk?"

"I've never been small; that's a fact," Van said complacently. "From the rumbles in my belly, though, I'll be thin if I don't put something in there soon. They'll have bread and meat from last night to go with the porridge, won't they?"

"If they don't, they'll be looking for a new master by this time tomorrow," Gerin answered. Van clapped his big hands together and hurried back inside.

The morning proved busy. Gerin always kept someone in the watchtower. Life had been dangerous enough before the Trokmoi swarmed south over the Niffet. Now danger could come from any direction at any time. When the lookout's horn blew, men up on the palisade reached for their weapons; the gate crew got ready to pull up the drawbridge and defend Castle Fox against barbarians or men of Elabon.

But after he winded the horn, the watchman cried,

"'Tis but a single man approaching—a trader, by the look of him."

Sure enough, the fellow was no harbinger of a ravening horde: he drove a two-horse team from a small, neat wagon. "Dyaus give you a good day, sir," Gerin greeted him when he rolled into the courtyard. The Fox glanced at the sun. "To get here so early in the day, you must have spent last night in the open."

"That I did, lord prince," the man answered. He was small and neat himself, with a shortsighted gaze and hands with long, slim fingers. "I bought a couple of chickens from a peasant—likely a serf of yours—and their blood in a trench warded me against the ghosts. Otes son of Engelers I am, maker and purveyor of jewelry of all descriptions, and also ready to do tinker's work if you have pots and such that need patching."

"Aye, we have a few of those," Gerin said. "If you know the secret of proper soldering, you'll make a bit of silver before you leave here. I've tried, but without much in the way of luck. But jewelry, now—hmm." He wondered if he could find a piece Fand would like at a price that didn't make his own thrifty soul quail.

Van came up to the wagon and, from the thoughtful look on his face, might have had the same idea. But what he said was, "You're not the least brave man I ever met, Master Jeweler, if you take your wares through this bandit-raddled countryside alone."

Otes Engelers' son dipped his head to the outlander. "You are gracious, sir. I traveled up into the Fox's lands from those of Aragis the Archer. Few bandits try to make a living in your holding, lord Gerin, or in his—few who aren't vassals styling themselves barons, at any rate." He smiled to show that was meant as a joke.

"Aye, Aragis is a strong man." Gerin let it go at that. One of these days, he and Aragis were liable to fight a war. The prospect would have bothered him less had he been less afraid he might lose.

"Show us these jewels of yours," Van boomed.

Otes, as he'd said, had adornments of all descriptions, from polished copper with "gems" of glass paste to gold and emeralds. Before he'd opened all his little cedar chests to display the baubles inside, Fand came out of the castle to admire them with her two men. Suddenly she pointed to a brooch. "Isn't that pretty, now?" she breathed. "Sure and it must be Trokmê work. It fair puts me in mind of my auld village on the far side of the Niffet, that it does."

Smiling, the jeweler picked it up and held it in the palm of his hand. It was a circular piece, about three fingers broad, decorated with spirals half silver and half inlaid, polished jet. "As a matter of fact, my lady, I made this one myself, and I'm as Elabonian as they come," Otes said. "That it is from a northern pattern, though, I'll not deny."

"'Twould suit the very tunic I have on me," Fand said, running a hand across the dark blue woad-dyed linen. She looked from one of her paramours to the other.

Van, who'd quarreled with her the night before, weakened first. With a cough, he said, "Master Otes, perhaps you'll be good enough to tell me what outrageous price you're asking for this chunk of tin and dirt."

"Tin?" Otes screeched. "Dirt? Are you blind, man? Are you mad? Feel the weight of that metal. And look at the care and the workmanship I put into the piece, shaping the tiny slivers of jet one by one and slipping each into its place—"

"Aye, tell me more lies," Van said.

Sensing that the dicker would go on for some time, Gerin took his leave. He figured he had time to walk out to the village by Fox Keep, talk with Besant Big-Belly about knocking off too early, and be back before Van and Otes had settled on a price. He knew how stubborn Van could be, and the jeweler looked to have mule's blood in him, too.

But before the Fox could walk out over the drawbridge, the lookout in the watchtower winded his horn again. He called down, "A chariot approaches, lord Gerin, with what looks to be a Trokmê chieftain and two of his men."

"Just a chariot?" Gerin shouted up. "No army attached?"

"I see only the one, lord," the lookout answered. A moment later, he added, "The chieftain is holding up a green-and-white striped shield: he comes under sign of truce."

Gerin called to the gate crew, "When you spy him, give him sign of truce in return. We'll see what he wants." Before the invasions, he'd have attacked any northerners he caught on his holding. Now the Trokmoi were powers south of the Niffet. However much it galled him, he had to treat with them.

"Who comes?" one of the men at the gate called to the approaching chariot.

"It's Diviciacus son of Dumnorix I am, liegeman to himself himself, the great chief Adiatunnus son of Commus, who's fain to have me bring his words to Gerin the Fox," the chieftain answered in Elabonian that lilted like Fand's. "No quarrel, no feud, stands between us the now."

The Trokmoi had slain Gerin's father and brother. As far as he was concerned, that put him eternally at feud with them. Moreover, he reckoned them deadly dangerous to the remnants of civilization that survived in the northlands after Elabon had cut the province loose. But in a narrow sense, Diviciacus was right: no active fighting went on between Adiatunnus' men and those of the Fox.

Dropping into the Trokmê tongue, Gerin said, "If it's the Fox you're seeking, I am he. Aye, I grant the truce between your chief and my own self. Come sit yourself by my hearth, drink a stoup of ale, and tell me Adiatunnus' words at your comfort and leisure."

Diviciacus beamed. He was a tall, thin, pale man with a lean, wolfish face, clean-shaven but for a straggling mustache of bright red. He wore a checked tunic and baggy wool trousers tucked into boots; a long, straight bronze sword hung from his belt. The other warrior in the chariot and its driver might have been poured into the same mold as he, save that one of them had sandy hair and mustache, the other blond.

Inside the smoky great hall, Diviciacus gulped down his first jack of ale, wiped his mouth on his sleeve, belched loudly, and said, "Sure and you're after living up to the name you have for hospitality, lord Gerin, that y'are."

Gerin could take a hint. He filled the Trokmê's drinking jack again, then said, "And what would Adiatunnus wish with me, pray?" The northern chieftain controlled several holdings a fair distance south and west of Fox Keep. Of all the Trokmoi who'd settled south of the Niffet, he was probably the most powerful, and the most adept at riding—and twisting—the swirling political currents of the northlands.

Diviciacus came to the point with barbarous directness: "Himself wants to know if you're of a mind to join forces with him and squeeze the pimple called Aragis off the arse of mankind."

"Does he?" Gerin said. In a way, that was logical: Aragis blocked Gerin's ambitions no less than Adiatunnus'. In another way . . . "Why wouldn't I be more likely to combine with a man of my own blood against an invader?"

"Adiatunnus says he reckons you reckon Aragis more

a thorn in your side than his own self." Diviciacus smiled at the subtlety of his chief's reasoning, and indeed it was more subtle than most northerners could have produced. The envoy went on, "Forbye, he says that once the Archer is after being cut into catmeat, you can go your way and he his, with no need at all for the twain of ye to clomp heads like bull aurochs in rutting season."

"He says that?" Gerin didn't believe it would work so; he didn't think Adiatunnus believed it, either. Which meant—

He was distracted from what it meant when Duren came in and said, "I'm bored, Papa. Play ball with me or something."

"A fine bairn," Diviciacus said. "He'd have, what—four summers on him?" At Gerin's nod, the Trokmê also nodded, and went on, "Aye, he's much of a size with my youngest but one, who has the same age."

Gerin was so used to thinking of Trokmoi as warriors, as enemies, that he needed a moment to adjust to the notion of Diviciacus as a fond father. He supposed he shouldn't have been taken aback; without fathers, the Trokmoi would have disappeared in a generation (and the lives of all the Elabonians north of the High Kirs would have become much easier). But it caught him by surprise all the same.

To Duren, he said, "I can't play now. I'm talking with this man." Duren stamped his foot and filled himself full of air, preparatory to letting out an angry screech. Gerin said, "Do you want my hand on your backside?" Duren deflated; his screech remained unhowled. Convinced his father meant what he said, Duren went off to look for amusement somewhere else.

"Good on you for training him to respect his elders, him still so small and all," Diviciacus said. "Now tell me straight how you fancy the notion of your men and those of Adiatunnus grinding Aragis between 'em like wheat in the quern."

"It has possibilities." Gerin didn't want to say no straight out, for fear of angering Adiatunnus and of giving him the idea of throwing in with Aragis instead. The Fox reckoned Aragis likely to be willing to combine with the Trokmê against his own holdings; no ties of blood or culture would keep Aragis from doing what seemed advantageous to him.

"Possibilities, is it? And what might that mean?" Diviciacus demanded.

It was a good question. Since Gerin found himself without a good answer, he temporized: "Let me take counsel with some of my vassals. Stay the night here if you care to; eat with us, drink more ale—by Dyaus I swear no harm will come to you in Fox Keep. Come the morning, I'll give you my answer."

"I'm thinking you'd say aye straight out if aye was in your heart," Diviciacus said dubiously. "Still, let it be as you wish. I'll stay a bit, so I will, and learn what you'll reply. But I tell you straight out, you'll befool me with none o' the tricks that earned you your ekename."

Since persuading the Trokmê not to leave at once in high dudgeon was one of those tricks, the Fox maintained a prudent silence. He suspected Diviciacus and his comrades would use the day to empty as many jars of ale as they could. *Better ale spilled than blood*, he told himself philosophically.

Fand came in, wearing the silver-and-jet brooch just above her left breast. Diviciacus' eyes clung to her. "My leman," Gerin said pointedly.

That recalled to Diviciacus the reason he'd come. "If you've allied with us so, why not on the field of war?" he said, hope for success in his mission suddenly restored.

"As I said, I'll talk it over with my men and tell you in the morning what I've decided." Gerin went out to the courtyard, where Van was practicing thrusts and parries with a heavy spear taller than he was. The outlander, for all his size, moved so gracefully that he made the exercise seem more a dance than preparation for war.

When Gerin told him what Adiatunnus had proposed, he scowled and shook his head. "Making common cause with the Trokmê would but turn him into a grander threat than Aragis poses."

"My thought was the same," Gerin answered. "I wanted to see if you saw anything on the other side to change my mind." Van shook his head again and went back to his thrusts and parries.

Gerin put the same question to Drago. The Bear's response was simpler: "No way in any of the five hells I want to fight on the same side with the Trokmoi. I've spent too much time tryin' to kill them buggers." That made Gerin pluck thoughtfully at his beard. Even had he been inclined to strike the bargain with Adiatunnus, his vassals might not have let him.

He went looking for Rihwin to get one more view. Before he found him, the lookout called, "Another man approaches in a wagon."

"Great Dyaus, three sets of visitors in a day," Gerin exclaimed. Sometimes no one from outside his holding came to Fox Keep for ten days, or twenty. Trade—indeed, traffic of any sort—had fallen off since the northlands went their own way. not only did epidemic petty warfare keep traffic off the roads, but baronies more and more either made do with what they could produce themselves or did without.

"Who comes?" called a warrior up on the palisade.

"I am a minstrel, Tassilo by name," came the reply—in, sure enough, a melodious tenor. "I would sing for my supper, a bed for the night, and whatever other generosity your gracious lord might see fit to provide."

Tassilo? Gerin stood stock-still, his hands balling into fists. The minstrel had sung down at the keep of Elise's father, Ricolf the Red, the night before she went off with Gerin rather than letting herself be wed to Wolfar of the Axe. Just hearing Tassilo's name, and his voice, brought those memories, sweet and bitter at the same time, welling up in the Fox. He was anything but anxious to listen to Tassilo again.

But all the men who heard the minstrel name himself cried out with glee: "Songs tonight, by Dyaus!" "Maybe he'll have ones we've not heard." "A lute to listen to—that'll be sweet."

Hearing that, Gerin knew he could not send the man away. For his retainers, entertainment they didn't have to make themselves was rare and precious. If that entertainment made him wince, well, he'd endured worse. Sighing, he said, "The minstrel is welcome. Let him come in."

When Tassilo got down from his light wagon, he bowed low to the Fox. "Lord prince, we've met before, I think. At Ricolf's holding, was it not? The circumstances, as I recall, were irregular." The minstrel stuck his tongue in the side of his cheek.

"Irregular, you say? Aye, there's a good word for it. That's the business of a minstrel, though, isn't it?—coming up with words, I mean." Being moderately skilled in that line himself, Gerin respected those who had more skill at it than he. He eyed Tassilo. "Curious you've not visited Fox Keep since."

"I fled south when the Trokmoi swarmed over the Niffet, lord prince, and I've spent most of my time since then down by the High Kirs," Tassilo answered. He had an open, friendly expression and looked as much like a fighting man as a singer, with broad shoulders and a slim waist. In the northlands, any traveling man had to be a warrior as well, if he wanted to live to travel far.

"What brought you north again, then?" Gerin asked.

"A baron's daughter claimed I got her with child. I don't think I did, but he believed her. I thought a new clime might prove healthier after that."

Gerin shrugged. He had no daughter to worry about. He said, "The men look forward to your performance tonight." Lying a little, he added, "Having heard you those years ago, so do I." The minstrel could sing and play, no doubt about that. The Fox's memories were not Tassilo's fault.

After a few more pleasantries, Gerin strode out over the drawbridge and headed for the peasant village a few hundred yards away. Chickens and pigs and skinny dogs foraged among round huts of wattle and daub whose thatched conical roofs projected out far enough to hold the rain away from the walls. Children too young to work in the fields stared at Gerin as he tramped up the muddy lane that ran through the middle of the village.

He stuck his head into Besant Big-Belly's hut, which was little different from any of the others. The headman wasn't there, but his wife, a scrawny woman named Marsilia, sat on a wooden stool spinning wool into thread. She said, "Lord, if you're after my man, he's out weeding the garden."

The garden was on the outskirts of the village. Sure enough, Besant was there, plucking weeds from a patch of vetch. Not only did he have a big belly, he had a big backside, too, which at the moment stuck up in the air. Resisting the urge to kick it, Gerin barked, "Why have you been blowing the horn with the sun only halfway down the sky?"

Besant jerked as if Gerin had kicked him after all. He whirled around, scrambling awkwardly to his feet. "L-lord Gerin," he stuttered. "I didn't hear you come up."

"If you don't want more unexpected visits, make sure you work the full day," Gerin answered. "We'll all be hungrier come winter for your slacking now."

Besant gave Gerin a resentful stare. He was a tubby, sloppy-looking man of about fifty in homespun colorless save for dirt and stains here and there. "I shall do as you say, lord prince," he mumbled. "The ghosts have been bad of late, though."

"Feed them more generously, then, or throw more wood on the nightfires," Gerin said. "You've no need to hide in your houses from an hour before sunset to an hour past dawn."

Besant nodded but still looked unhappy. The trouble was, he and Gerin needed each other. Without the serfs, Gerin and his vassal barons would starve. That much Besant Big-Belly knew. But without the barons, the little villages of farmers would be at the mercy of Trokmoi and bandits: peasants with pitchforks and scythes could not stand against chariots and bronze armor and spears and swords. The headman did his best to ignore that half of the bargain.

Gerin said, "Remember, I'll be listening to hear when you blow the horn come evening." He waited for Besant to nod again, then walked off to see how the village fared.

The gods willing, he thought, the harvest would be good. Wheat for bread, oats for horses and oatmeal, barley for ale, rye for variety, beans, peas, squashes: all grew well under the warm sun. So did row on row of turnips and parsnips, cabbage and kale, lettuce and spinach. Gardens held vetch, onions, melde, radishes, garlic, and medicinal herbs like henbane.

Some fields stood vacant, the grass there lengthening for haymaking. Cattle and sheep grazed all the way out to the edge of the trees in others. A couple of lambs butted heads. "They might as well be barons," Gerin murmured to himself.

The peasants were hard at it as usual: weeding like Besant, repairing wooden fences to keep the animals where they belonged, unbaling straw to repair a leaky roof—all the myriad tasks that kept the village going. Gerin stopped to talk with a few of the serfs. Most seemed content enough. As overlords went, he was a mild one, and they knew it.

He spent more time in the village than he'd intended; the sun was already sinking toward the treetops when he headed back to Fox Keep. *No, Besant won't blow the horn early tonight, not with me here so long*, he thought. *We'll have to see about tomorrow.*

When he returned to the castle, the cooks were full of praise for the way Otes son of Engelers had fixed half a dozen pots. The Fox nodded approvingly. The large sale the jeweler had made to Fand (or rather, to Van) hadn't kept him from doing the other half of his job. On seeing Otes himself, Gerin invited him to stay for supper and pass the night in the great hall. By the way he grinned and promptly accepted, the neat little man had been expecting that.

In the great hall, Tassilo was fitting a new string to his lute and plucking at it to put it in proper tune. Duren watched him in pop-eyed fascination. "I want to learn to do that, Papa!" he said.

"Maybe you will one day," Gerin said. Stored away somewhere was a lute he'd had as a boy. He'd never been much good with it, but who could say what his son might accomplish?

After supper, Tassilo showed what he could do. "In honor of my host," he said, "I shall give you some of the song of Gerin and the dreadful night when all the moons turned full together." He struck a plangent chord from the lute and began.

Gerin, who had lived through that dreadful night five years before, recognized little of it from the minstrel's description. Much of that had to do with the way Tassilo composed his song. He didn't create it afresh from nothing; that would have overtaxed even the wits of Lekapenos, the great Sithonian epic poet.

Instead, like Lekapenos, Tassilo put his song together from stock bits and pieces of older ones. Some of those were just for the sake of sound and meter; the Fox quickly got used to hearing himself called "gallant Gerin" every time his name was mentioned. It saved Tassilo, or any other poet, the trouble of having to come up with a new epithet every time he was mentioned in the story.

And some of the pieces of old songs were ones Gerin had heard before, and which didn't perfectly fit the tale Tassilo was telling now. The bits about battling the Trokmoi went back to his boyhood, and likely to his grandfather's boyhood as well. But that too was part of the convention. More depended on the way the minstrel fit the pieces together than on what those pieces were.

All the same, Gerin leaned over to Van and said, "One thing I remember that Tassilo isn't saying anything about is how bloody frightened I was."

"Ah, but you're not a person to him, not really," Van replied. "You're gallant Gerin the hero, and how could gallant Gerin be afraid, even with every werebeast in the world trying to tear his throat out?"

"At the time, it was easy," Gerin said, which won a laugh from Van. He'd been through the werenight with

Gerin. "Bold Van," Tassilo called him, which was true enough, but he hadn't been immune to fear, either.

And yet, the rest of Tassilo's audience ate up the song. Drago the Bear, who'd gone through his own terrors that night, pounded on the table and cheered to hear how Gerin had surmounted his: it might not have been true, but it sounded good. Duren hung on Tassilo's every word, long after the time he should have been asleep in bed.

Even the Trokmoi, whose fellows had been on the point of putting an end to Gerin when the chaos of the werenight saved him, listened avidly to the tale of their people's discomfiture. Well-turned phrases and songs of battle were enough to gladden them, even if they came out on the losing side.

Tassilo paused to drink ale. Diviciacus said to Gerin, "Give me your answer now, Fox, dear. I've not the patience to wait for morning."

Gerin sighed. "It must be no."

"I thought as much," the Trokmê said. "Yes is simple, but no needs disguises. You'll be after regretting it."

"So will your chief, if he quarrels with me," the Fox answered. "Tell him as much." Diviciacus glared but nodded.

When Gerin, who was yawning himself, tried to pick up Duren and carry him off to bed, his son yelled and cried enough to make the Fox give it up as a bad job. If Duren wanted to fall asleep in the great hall listening to songs, he'd let him get away with it this once. Gerin yawned again. *He* was tired, whether Duren was or not. With a wave to Tassilo, he headed for his bedchamber.

What with Fand and Van in the next room, the noise up there proved almost as loud as what the minstrel made, and even more distracting. Gerin tossed and turned and grumbled and, just when he finally was on the point of dropping off, got bitten on the cheek by a mosquito. He mashed the bug, but that woke him up again. He lay there muttering to himself until at last he did fall asleep.

Because of that, the sun was a quarter of the way up the sky when he came back down to the great hall. Van, who was just finishing a bowl of porridge, laughed at him: "See the slugabed!"

"I'd have gotten to sleep sooner if someone I know hadn't been making such a racket next door," Gerin said pointedly.

Van laughed louder. "Make any excuse you like. You outslept your guests, no matter what. All three lots of them are long gone."

"They want to get in as much travel as they can while the sun's in the sky. I'd do the same in their boots." Gerin looked around. "Where's Duren?"

"I thought he was with you, Captain," Van said. "Didn't you take him up to bed the way you usually do?"

"No, he wanted to listen to Tassilo some more." Gerin dipped up a bowl of porridge from the pot over the fire, raised it to his mouth. After he swallowed, he said, "He's probably out in the courtyard, making mischief."

In the courtyard he found Drago the Bear pouring a bucket of well water over the head of Rihwin the Fox. Both of them looked as if they'd seen the bottoms of their drinking jacks too many times the night before.

"No, I've not seen the boy all morning," Drago said when Gerin asked him.

"Nor I," the dripping Rihwin said. He added, "If he made as much noise as small boys are in the habit of doing, I'd remember seeing him . . . painfully." His eyes were tracked with red. Yes, he'd hurt himself last night.

Gerin frowned. "That's—odd." He raised his voice. "Duren!" He put two fingers in his mouth, let out a long, piercing whistle that made Rihwin and Drago flinch.

His son knew he was supposed to come no matter what when he heard that call. He also wasn't supposed to go by himself too far from Castle Fox to hear it. Wolves and longtooths and other wild beasts roamed the woods. So, sometimes, did wild men.

But Duren did not come. Now Gerin began to worry. Maybe, he thought, the boy had gone off to the peasant village. He'd done that alone once or twice, and got his backside heated for it. But often a boy needed a lot of such heatings before he got the idea. Gerin remembered he had, when he was small.

He walked over to the village, ready to thunder like Dyaus when he found his son. But no one there had seen Duren, either. A cold wind of dread in his belly, Gerin went back to Castle Fox. He sent men out in all directions, beating the bushes and calling Duren's name. They came back scratched by thorns and stung by wasps, but without the boy.

Duren was missing.

II

Gerin paced between the benches in the great hall, making Rihwin and Van and Drago move out of the way. "One of those three must have snatched him," he said: "Diviciacus or Tassilo or Otes. I can't believe Duren would go wandering off where we couldn't find him, not of his own accord."

"If you're right, Captain, we've eaten up a lot of the day looking around here," Van said.

"I know," Gerin answered unhappily. "I'll go out and send others in chariots as well, even so; if Dyaus and the other gods are kind, one of us will catch up with our— guests." He spat the last word. Guest-friendship was sacred; those who violated it could expect a long, unhappy time in the afterlife. Unfortunately, though, fear of that didn't paralyze all rogues.

"Who'd want to steal a little boy?" Drago the Bear growled. His big hands moved in the air as if closing round a neck.

Gerin's more agile wits had already started pursuing that one. "Diviciacus might, to give Adiatunnus a hold on me," he said. "I don't think Adiatunnus would have ordered it—who could guess ahead of time if the chance would come up?—but I don't think he'd turn down a gift like that if it fell into his lap."

"Duren might give him a hold for now, but he'd get nothing but grief from you later," Van said.

"Aye, but since I turned him down for a joint move on Aragis, he's liable to think he'd get only grief from me anyhow," the Fox answered, thinking, *He's liable to be*

41

right, too. Aloud, he went on, "Speaking of Aragis, Otes the jeweler came from his lands. And Aragis might not turn down a hold on me, either."

"You're right there, too," Drago said, making more choking motions.

"You're leaving out Tassilo," Van said.

"I know." Gerin kicked aside a dog-gnawed bone. "I can't think of any reason he'd want to harm me."

"I can," Rihwin the Fox said.

"Can you indeed?" Gerin said, surprised. "What is it?"

Rihwin coughed; his smoothly handsome face went a couple of shades pinker than usual. "You'll recall, lord, that when last you made the acquaintance of this Tassilo, I was in the process of, ah, disqualifying myself from marrying the fair Elise. I hadn't tasted wine in too long, you understand."

"Disgracing yourself is more like it," Van said, blunt as usual. Gloriously drunk, Rihwin had stood on his head on a table at Ricolf the Red's and kicked his legs in the air . . . while wearing a southern-style toga and no drawers.

He coughed again. "Perhaps your word is more accurate, friend Van, though not calculated to make me feel better about the incident or myself. Be that as it may, I resume: Elise having found you no more to her taste, lord Gerin, than her father did me, she might possibly have engaged the services of this minstrel to rape away the boy for her to raise."

Gerin bit down on that like a man whose teeth closed on a worm in an apple. Ever since Elise left him, he'd done his best not to think about her; whenever he did, it hurt. He had no idea where in the northlands she was, whether she was still with the horse doctor with whom she'd gone away, or even whether she still lived. But what Rihwin said made enough sense that he had to ask himself those questions now.

Slowly, he answered, "Aye, you're right, worse luck; that could be so." He plucked at his beard as he weighed odds. "I still think the Trokmoi are likeliest to have stolen Duren, so Van and I will go southwest after them. Which way did Tassilo fare?"

"West, toward the holding of Schild Stoutstaff, or that's where he told the gate crew he was heading," Drago answered.

Gerin grunted. If Tassilo had Duren with him, he might well have lied about his chosen direction. Or he might not have. Schild had been the leading vassal to Wolfar of the Axe. He wasn't a deadly foe to Gerin, as Wolfar had been, but he was no great friend, either. Though he'd acknowledged the Fox his suzerain after Gerin killed Wolfar, he forgot that whenever convenient. He might shelter Tassilo, or at least grant him safe passage.

"All right, Rihwin," Gerin said. "You ride west to Schild's border, and past it if his guards give you leave. If they don't—" He paused for effect. "Tell them they, and their overlord, will have cause to regret it."

Rihwin nodded. "As you say."

"Now, Otes," Gerin said.

Again, Drago answered: "He said he was heading east along the Emperor's Highway, to see if Hagop son of Hovan had tinker's work for him. He didn't think he'd sell Hagop much in the way of jewelry: 'skinflint' was the word he used, I think."

"For Hagop, it's a good one," Gerin said judiciously. "All right, you go after him, then."

"I'll do that, lord," Drago said, and strode out of the great hall. Gerin was as sure as if his eyes could follow that Drago was heading for the stables to hitch his team to his chariot, and that he'd ride out after Otes the minute the job was done. To Drago, the world was a simple place. His liege lord had given him an order, so he would follow it. Gerin sometimes wished he couldn't see all the complications in the world around him, either.

Van said, "You'll want me to ride with you, eh, Captain? We'll need a driver as well, if we're to take on Diviciacus and his friends on even terms."

"You're right on both counts," Gerin said. He thought about adding another chariot and three-man team of warriors, too, but decided against it. Van was worth a couple of ordinary men in a fight, and the Fox did not denigrate his own skill with his hands. And Raffo Redblade, who'd been driving for them for years, hadn't earned his ekename by running from fights. The Fox added, "And we'll send Widin Simrin's son south to ask what Aragis knows. Van, find him—he'll be in the courtyard somewhere—and get him moving, too."

The decision made, Gerin took his armor down from the wall and put it on: bronze greaves first, then leather cuirass faced with scales of bronze, and last of all a plain pot of a helmet. None of it was polished; none of it looked the least bit fancy—the Fox left that to Van. But his own gear was sound. It did what he wanted it to do: it kept edged and pointed metal from splitting his flesh. As far as he was concerned, nothing else mattered.

He slung his quiver over his shoulder, took down his bow, and then grabbed his shield. That was a yard-wide disk of leather and wood, with bronze edging to keep swordstrokes from chewing it up.

Most Elabonian warriors had gear much like the Fox's. Some men went in for gold or silver ornamentation, but he wanted nothing of the sort: curlicues and inlays could catch and hold a point, while rich armor made a man a special target on the battlefield.

With his outlandish armor, Van of the Strong Arm was always a target on the battlefield, but no one yet had been able to strip his crested helm and two-piece corselet from him. Along with his spear, he carried a sword, a mace, and several daggers. He was also a fine archer, but did not use the bow in combat, affecting to despise slaying foes from afar as unmanly.

"Foolishness," Gerin said, as he had many times before. "As long as you're alive and the other fellow isn't, nothing else matters. You get no points for style, not in war you don't."

Van brandished his spear. "Captain, that's never been a problem." His grin showed only a couple of broken teeth, more evidence (as if more were needed) he was more dangerous with weapons in hand than anyone he'd run up against.

Practical as usual, Gerin went into the kitchens and filled a leather sack with twice-baked bread that would keep indefinitely (and that needed someone with good teeth to eat it) and strips of smoked mutton even tougher than the bread. If he had to fight from the chariot, the sack would go over the side. If he didn't, he and Van and Raffo could travel for a few days without worrying about supplies.

Gerin shouldered the bag and carried it out to the stables. Raffo, a gangling young man with pimples along the margin of his beard, looked up from hitching the horses to either side of the chariot shaft. "Be good to get out on the road, lord Gerin," he said, getting the animals into the double yoke and securing them to the shaft with straps that ran around the front of their necks.

"It would be better if we were going out for a different reason," Gerin said heavily. Raffo's face fell; he'd forgotten that. The Fox had given up on expecting tact from his men. They were, he sometimes thought with something approaching despair, only a couple of steps more civilized than the Trokmoi. Improving that was a matter for generations, not just years; even keeping them from falling back into barbarism often seemed none too easy.

He stowed his shield on the brackets mounted on the inside of the car. It made the side wall higher. Van walked into the stables then. His place in the chariot was on the right side. He set his shield into its stowage place, too, and grunted approvingly when he saw the sack of supplies.

"That's good," he said. "Now we'll just need to buy a fowl from the peasants if we camp out in the open, or bleed out our prey if we go hunting: have to give the ghosts something, after all."

"Aye." Gerin's voice was abstracted. "The chase won't be easy. Diviciacus and his friends have half a day's start on us, and more than one road they can choose to go back to Adiatunnus—and we don't even know they have my boy." He wanted to scream in rage and fear. Instead, he grew more quiet and withdrawn than ever; he was not one to show worry on the outside.

"Only one way to find out," Van said.

"True, true." Gerin turned to Raffo. "Are you done harnessing the beasts?" By way of answer, the young driver vaulted into the car. The Fox clapped him on the back. "Good. Let's travel."

The six-spoked wheels began to spin. The bronze tires on those wheels rattled and clattered as they bounced over pebbles. Gerin felt every tiny thing the wheels went over, too. Had he not needed the most speed he could get, and had he not thought he might have to fight to get Duren back, he would have taken a wagon instead. But the chariot it had to be.

"A day of standing in this car and we'll wobble on

solid ground like sailors coming off a ship long at sea," he said. The chariot rumbled out through the gateway, over the drawbridge, and away from Fox Keep.

"Speak to me not of sailing," said Van, who had done his share of it. "You're not likely to get seasick in the car here, and that's a fact—a fact you can thank the gods for, too. I've puked up my guts a time or three, and I've no wish to do it again."

"South and west," Raffo said musingly. "Which road would they have taken, lord Gerin? Would they have fared south down the Elabon Way and then gone straight west toward Adiatunnus' castle? Or do you think they went along the lesser roads that run straighter between here and there?"

The Fox rubbed his chin as he considered. At last he said, "If they're going down the Elabon Way, Widin will come on them, for he's taking that road toward Aragis' holding."

"He'd be one against three," Van pointed out.

Gerin grimaced. "I know. But he wouldn't be foolish enough to attack them. If they have Duren, and he finds out about it, he'll get word back to the keep. We can plan what to do next—go to war with Adiatunnus, I expect."

"I didn't think you wanted to do that yet, lord Gerin," Raffo said.

"I don't," Gerin answered, "but I will. But if we go the same way Widin has, we narrow the search more than I want. I aim to throw my net as wide as I can, hoping to catch something in one strand of the mesh."

"Aye, makes sense to me," Van said, which eased the Fox's mind somewhat: his burly friend had a keen eye for tactics, though Gerin reckoned himself more adept in planning for years ahead.

Raffo steered the team down a way that headed

toward Adiatunnus' lands. Within a couple of minutes, the clearing where Gerin's serfs scratched their living from the soil disappeared behind the chariot. Forest closed in on either side of the road, which, but for the ruts from wagons and chariots, might have been a game track. Branches reached out and tried to slap the Fox in the face.

He held up an arm to turn them aside. Whenever he went down a back road like this one, he was struck by how lightly civilization rested on the northlands. The stink of the castle midden, and the bigger one in the peasant village, were out of his nostrils now; the woods smelled green and growing, as if man with his stinks had never come this way. In the virgin pines and elms, robins sang sweetly, chickadees twittered, and jays cried their harsh, metallic calls. A red squirrel flirted its tail as it clambered up a tree trunk.

But Gerin knew better than to idealize the forest, as some Sithonian poets (most of whom had never set foot outside the City of Elabon) were wont to do. Wolves ranged through the woods; in hungry winters they'd go after flocks or the herders who tended them. Longtooths would take men as they would any other prey, winter or summer. And the aurochs, the great wild ox of the forest, was nothing to take lightly—a few years before, Gerin had almost died under the horns and trampling hooves of a rogue bull.

He motioned for Raffo to stop the chariot. With a puzzled look, the driver obeyed. But for the bird calls and the soft purling of a stream somewhere off out of sight, silence closed down like a cloak. To the Fox, who was comfortable with only himself for company, it felt pleasant and restful.

Van, though, quickly started to fidget. He pulled a baked-clay flute from a pouch on his belt and began playing a tune whose notes ran in no pattern familiar to Elabonian music. "That's better," he said. "Too bloody quiet here."

Gerin swallowed a sigh and tapped Raffo on the shoulder. "Let's get going again. I'd sooner listen to jingling harness than to Van's tweedles."

"Aye, lord Gerin. Now that you mention it, so would I." Raffo flicked the reins. The horses snorted resentfully—they'd started cropping the grass that grew between the ruts—and trotted down the road.

At the next village, Gerin asked the serfs if they'd seen the chariot full of Trokmoi come past. They all shook their heads, as if they'd not only not seen such a thing but never heard of it, either.

The Fox scowled. "We're too far north or too far south, and Dyaus only knows which: that or they've gone down the Elabon Way as Raffo feared." He pounded his fist on the chariot rail in frustration.

"Too far north'd be my guess," Van said. "The track we were on curved, I think, till it ran nearer west than southwest."

"I didn't note that myself, but you're most often right about such things," Gerin said. "Raffo, the next road we come on that heads south, you take it till it crosses one leading in the direction we really want to go." *Or until it peters out*, he thought: not all paths connected to others.

The peasants watched as their overlord rode out of the village. Though still on land he ruled directly rather than through one of his vassal barons, he seldom came here save when collecting what was due him each fall. He wondered what the serfs thought of this unexpected appearance. Most likely, they were relieved he hadn't demanded anything of them.

Shadows lengthened as the chariot rattled and rumbled through woods that seemed to grow ever thicker. "I wonder if this road ever does join up with anything else," Van said.

"If it doesn't pretty bloody soon, we're going to have to turn back and head for that last village to buy a couple of chickens," Gerin said. "I don't want to have to count on just fire to keep the ghosts away."

Raffo pointed with his free hand. "Looks like more light up ahead, lord Gerin. Might be only a meadow, mind you, but it might be fields, too, and fields mean another village."

It was fields; Gerin felt like cheering. No sooner had the chariot emerged from the woods than the quitting horn called the peasants in from their labor. The Fox looked around. "Yes, I know this place—Pinabel Odd-Eyes is headman here. I'm used to coming here from the west, though, not out of the north."

Pinabel's left eye was blue, his right brown. Brown and blue both widened when Gerin rolled into the center of the village. Pinabel bowed very low. "L-lord prince, what brings you here?" he stammered.

The nervousness he showed made Gerin wonder what sort of cheating he was doing, but he'd have to worry about that later. "My son's been kidnapped," he announced baldly. Pinabel and the other serfs who heard exclaimed in dismay; family ties mattered to them, not least because those were almost all too many of them had. He went on, "I think three Trokmoi who visited Fox Keep yesterday may have taken him."

That brought more murmurs from the peasants. They were even more afraid of the Trokmoi than of night ghosts, and with reason: the ghosts could be propitiated, but the woodsrunners ravaged as they pleased. But when Gerin asked if Pinabel and the others in the village had seen the chariot Diviciacus and his comrades were riding, they all denied it.

He believed them, much as he wished he thought they were lying. Pinabel said, "They might have gone through by way of the next road south. It's very great, I hear, though I have never traveled far enough to see it."

"Maybe." Gerin didn't have the heart to tell the headman that next road was just another muddy track. Like most serfs, Pinabel had never traveled more than a few hours' walk from where he was born.

"Will you stay with us till morning, lord prince?" Pinabel asked. "Night comes soon." He gestured to the east, where Elleb, only a day before full, had already risen. Math hung halfway up the sky, while Nothos, almost at first quarter, showed near enough where south lay. And in the west, the sun was near the horizon. When it set, the ghosts would come out.

But Gerin shook his head. "I want to push on as long as I may—every moment may prove precious. Sell me two chickens, if you would, so I can give the ghosts blood when they come."

"Aye, lord prince." Pinabel hurried away. He returned a couple of minutes later with a pair of hens, their legs tied with strips of rawhide. Gerin gave him a quarter of a silverpiece for them: probably more than they were worth, but the smallest bit of money he had in the pouch at his belt. Pinabel Odd-Eyes bowed himself almost double.

As the chariot bounced away, Raffo observed, "Most lords would have said, 'Give me two chickens' there."

That hadn't occurred to Gerin. He said, "Those birds aren't remotely part of the dues Pinabel's village owes on its land. I have no right just to take them from him."

"Neither does any other Elabonian lord with his serfs, if I understand your ways aright," Van said. "The thing of it is, most wouldn't let that stop 'em."

"You're probably right," Gerin said with a sigh. "But

the way I see it, I owe my peasants fair dealing, just as they do with me. If I don't give it, how can I expect to get it in return?"

"Often enough you won't get it in return, no matter what sort of dealing you give," Van said.

"You're right." The Fox sighed again. "But when I don't, I'm not soft on that, either." Gerin was scrupulously fair. Anyone who thought him weak on that account soon regretted it.

"If I don't stop now, lord Gerin, we'll not have time to make ready to meet the ghosts," Raffo said, pointing to the western skyline. The sun, red as hot copper, had to be just on the point of setting.

Gerin thought about pushing on for another furlong or two, but regretfully decided Raffo was right. At his nod, the driver reined in. Gerin jumped down and gouged out a trench in the soft dirt by the side of the road. That did the edge of his dagger no good, but it was the only digging tool he had. Van handed him the trussed fowls. He cut off their heads, one after the other—the knife was still sharp enough for that—and let their blood spill into the trench.

None too soon: he still held the second hen over the hole when the ghosts came. They were, as ever, indistinct; the eye would not, could not, grasp their shape. They buzzed round the blood like carrion flies, soaking up vitality from it. Because he'd given them the gift, they were not fierce and angry and terrifying as they would have been otherwise, but tried to give him good advice in return.

He could not understand them. He had never been able to, save on the werenight, when his brother's shade managed to deliver a message of truly oracular obscurity—though he'd been able to use it later to destroy Balamung just when the opposite result looked far more likely.

Van bent over a firebow, twirling a stick with a rawhide lace to start a blaze for the evening. He shook his head like a man bedeviled by gnats. "I wish they'd quit yowling in my mind," he grumbled, but then he grunted in satisfaction. "Here we go, Raffo—feed me tinder, a bit at a time. You know how."

"Aye." Raffo had been crumbling dry leaves. He poked some into the hole where the stick from the firebow spun. Van breathed gently on the sparks he'd started, hoping to fan them rather than blowing them out. "You have it!" Raffo said, and gave him more tinder to feed the new little flames. With the fire well and truly started, he passed Van larger twigs to load on. Soon the thick chunk of branch on which the outlander had used the firebow would also catch.

"I wish it were that easy all the time," Van said. "Gut those birds, Fox, and pluck 'em, so we can get ourselves outside them. They're better fare than what we brought with us."

"You're right there." The plucking job Gerin gave the hens was quick and decidedly imperfect. He didn't care; he was hungry. He picked out the birds' hearts, livers, and gizzards from the offal to roast them over the fire, then threw the rest of the guts into the trench with the blood.

He, Raffo, and Van drew stems of grass for the night watches. Few bandits dared the ghosts to travel by night, but Gerin was not the sort to take unnecessary chances— the necessary ones were quite bad enough. And the beasts of the forest, being without souls themselves, took no notice of the night spirits. They usually did not attack travelers encamped in the woods, but you never could tell.

Van drew the short stem, and chose the first watch. Gerin and Raffo drew again. This time Raffo won, and picked the watch that led to dawn. "Since I get to have my sleep broken up, I may as well take what I can get of it," Gerin said, and wrapped himself in a blanket—as much to keep off the bugs as for warmth, for the night was mild.

Van shook him awake with the cheerful insouciance of a man who'd already done his share of a job. "Nothing much doing, Captain," he said while Gerin tried to break free of the fog that shrouded his wits. Van took off the helm, corselet, and greaves he'd worn through his watch, cocooned himself in his blanket, and was snoring by the time the Fox began to think himself awake.

Gerin put on his own helmet and sword, but did not bother with his cuirass. He paced back and forth, not willing to sit down until he was sure he wouldn't doze off. The fire had died into embers. He fed it twigs and then branches and brought it back to briskly crackling life. That drove away some of the ghosts flittering near, and reduced their murmur in his mind.

By the time he'd taken care of that, he felt more confident he could stay awake. He walked to the edge of the circle of firelight and sat down with his back to the flames. His night vision, almost ruined when he'd stoked them, slowly returned.

The moons had wheeled a good way through the sky. Nothos was nearing the western skyline, Math well west of south—when her golden gibbous disk sank below the horizon, it would be time for the Fox to rouse Raffo. Elleb, looking like a bright new bronze coin, neared the meridian.

Here and there in the forest, birches mingled with ash and oak and pine. By the light of the moons and the nightfire, their pale trunks seemed almost to gleam against the darker background.

Gerin wished his ears could grow more sensitive to

the dark the way his eyes did. Off in the distance, a barn owl hooted. The Trokmoi thought the souls of dead warriors inhabited the pallid night birds. The Fox had his doubts about that, but he'd never tried a sorcerous experiment to find out one way or the other. He spent a while trying to figure out how such an experiment might be run, and what he could do if he found the Trokmoi were wrong. Making the arrogant woodsrunners doubt themselves in any way was likely to be worthwhile.

"You know," he said to himself in a low voice, "the midwatch isn't so bad after all. I don't get enough time of my own, with no one havering at me to do this or decide that right this moment." In small—or sometimes not so small—doses, he relished solitude.

Perhaps three parts of his four-hour watch had gone by when a coughing roar not far away roused him from contemplation, or rather jerked him out of it by the scruff of the neck. No one could ignore a longtooth's hunting cry; a man's blood knew it meant danger. One of the horses let out a frightened snort. The Fox found his left hand on the hilt of his sword without conscious memory of how it had got there—not that a sword would stop one of the great hunting cats if it chose to hunt him.

The longtooth, to his vast relief, came no closer to the campsite. "Well," he muttered, "I'm not sleepy now." He felt as if he'd had ice water splashed over him. When a nightjar swooped down to grab one of the moths fluttering around the fire, he almost jumped out of his skin.

He woke Raffo as soon as Math set. The driver looked toward the west, saw the moon was down, and nodded in approval. "No one ever said you weren't one for right dealing, lord," he said blurrily around a yawn.

Gerin wrapped himself in his blanket once more. He kept an eye on Raffo to make sure the younger man wouldn't go back to sleep as he almost had. Raffo, though, took watch-standing seriously, and paced about as the Fox had. Gerin feared he himself would have trouble dozing off again but, in spite of his worries, quickly drifted away.

The rising sun made him rise, too. His eyes came open just as the ghosts vanished for the day. He got to his feet, feeling elderly. Van was still snoring. Gerin roused him cautiously; the outlander's first waking act—especially when he was disturbed—was usually to grab for a weapon.

This time, though, he seemed to remember where he was, and came to himself without violence. He headed for the forest, saying, "Either I go off behind a bush or I burst where I stand."

"I watered the grass on watch, so I don't have that worry," Gerin said, buckling on his right greave. Raffo harnessed the horses.

The chicken bones and guts were already beginning to stink. The travelers moved upwind before they gnawed on bread and smoked meat. "Are we ready?" Raffo asked, looking around the little camp to make sure nothing had been forgotten. Gerin looked, too; if they had left something behind, he would have blamed himself.

They climbed into the chariot, Raffo driving, Gerin behind him on the left, Van on the right. Raffo flicked the reins. The horses started forward. When they came to a stream, Raffo let the animals have a brief drink. Gerin scooped up some water in the palm of his hand, too, and freshened what he carried in the waterskin at his belt.

At the next road that ran west, Raffo swung the chariot onto it. A little village lay not far from the crossroads. The appearance of their lord so early in the day was a prodigy for the peasants. When he asked if they'd seen Diviciacus and his comrades the day before, one of the men nodded. "Aye, just before noon it were," he said. A couple of other people nodded.

The Fox scowled; he was on the right track, aye, but no closer to the Trokmoi than when he'd set out. If they were traveling hard, maybe they had a reason. "Did they have a boy with them?" he asked, and then amplified that: "My son, I mean."

The serfs looked at one another. "Didn't see no boy, lord," answered the fellow who'd spoken before.

That wasn't what Gerin wanted to hear. Had the Trokmoi cut Duren's throat as if he were some sacrifice to the night ghosts, then dumped the corpse by the side of the road? Horrid dread filled him: his father, his brother—now his son, too? If that was so, he vowed he'd not rest till every red-mustached robber south of the Niffet was dead or routed back to the northern woods. Even as he made it, he knew the vow to be impossible of fulfillment. He spoke it in his mind, all the same; it would give his life a target.

"Take everything you can from the horses," he told Raffo, his voice harsh. "Now we have to catch them before they win back to Adiatunnus' lands."

"Aye, lord Gerin." But Raffo sounded doubtful. "They have a long lead, though. Gaining enough ground won't be easy, the more so as we may have to keep casting about for the road they took."

"I know that," Gerin growled. "But I'll have answers from them if I have to wring out each word with hot pincers."

Van thumped him on the shoulder. "Easy, Captain, easy. We don't even know they ever had the lad, mind you."

"But they must have—" Gerin stopped, shook his head. Assuming something was so because you thought it had to be was one of the flaws in logic that made the savants in the City of Elabon laugh. He took a deep breath and said, "You're right. We *don't* know they had him."

He wondered if he ever would, or could, know. Had Diviciacus and his crew killed Duren and tossed his body into the woods, scavengers would make short work of it (he knew too well that his son had only a little meat on his bones). When he'd charged out after the Trokmoi, he'd figured he or Drago or Rihwin or Widin would catch up with Duren's kidnappers, rescue the boy, and return in triumph to Castle Fox. Now he realized he'd been making assumptions there, too. Uncertainty, in a way, felt even worse than being sure of Duren's death would have. How long could he go on wondering without going mad?

Then he thought that, after a while, he wouldn't be uncertain any more. He'd have to reckon Duren dead if he wanted to keep on living himself.

"Push them," he said to Raffo. This time, the driver did not answer back. He flicked the whip over the horses' backs. They leaned into the harness, pushed their pace up to a fast trot.

The chariot rolled through another peasant village and then drove by the small keep of Notker the Bald, one of Gerin's vassal barons. "Aye, lord Gerin," Notker called from the palisade, "they came by here yesterday, sometime past noon, but they showed shield of truce, just as they had on the way to your castle, so I thought no more about it."

"Did they have Duren with them?" Gerin asked. Two sets of serfs had already answered no to that, but the Fox put the question again anyhow. Maybe, he thought with what he knew to be irrationality, a noble would have noticed something the serfs had not.

But Notker shook his head. "Your son, lord?" he said. "No, I saw him not. What then? Is it war between the woodsrunners and us despite the truce sign?"

"By the gods, I wish I knew." Gerin tapped Raffo on the shoulder to drive on before Notker asked any more questions he couldn't answer.

Toward the middle of the afternoon they passed the boundary stone that had marked the border between Gerin's holdings and those of his southwestern neighbor, Capuel the Flying Frog. No one had seen Capuel since the werenight; Gerin sometimes wondered if his ekename had been a clue to a were strain in his family and he'd turned toad when all the moons rose full together. More likely, though, the Trokmoi had slain him.

The boundary stone lay on its side these days, ruining the charms for peace and prosperity that had been carved into it. Whether that was cause or effect Gerin did not know, but Capuel's former holding knew no peace these days. None of his vassals had been able to take any kind of grip on the land. The Fox held some of it himself, Trokmoi had overrun a couple of keeps, and the rest was given over to banditry.

The first peasant village the chariot passed was only a ruin, some of the houses burned, the rest falling to pieces from lack of care. Some grain grew untended in weed-choked fields, but before another generation passed no sign would be left that man had ever lived here.

"Captain, we may need to stop to hunt toward sunset, and I don't mean for the Trokmoi," Van said. "Who's going to sell us a chicken in country like this?"

Gerin didn't answer. He knew Van was right but didn't want to admit it, even to himself. Stopping to slay an animal with whose blood to propitiate the ghosts would make him lose time on Diviciacus, not gain it.

The next village was still inhabited, but that did the travelers no good. Only a handful of people remained in what had been a fair-sized hamlet. When one of them spotted an approaching chariot, he let out a yell full of fear and desperation. Everyone—men, women, children—fled from fields and houses into the nearby woods.

"Wait!" Gerin shouted. "I just want to ask you a couple of questions." No one paid him any attention.

He looked helplessly to Van. The outlander said, "You ask me, Captain, these poor buggers have got themselves trampled too often lately to take chances when somebody who looks like a warrior comes by."

"No doubt you're right," the Fox answered, sighing. "Doesn't say much for the state the northlands are in, does it?"

"Your serfs don't run from you, lord Gerin," Raffo said.

"That's so," Gerin said, "but there's more to the northlands than my holdings—and if I took in these lands, I'd do it by war, so the peasants here wouldn't get the chance to learn I treat them decently. They'd just go on running when they saw me coming."

Raffo didn't answer. Unless he should be involved in fighting to gain control of land beyond Gerin's holding, it was too remote to matter to him. That made him typical, not otherwise, which saddened Gerin: he tried to think in larger terms.

Van said, "You're not the only baron—excuse me, Captain: prince—the serfs don't flee. What Aragis does to the ones who run that he catches makes all the others think three times before they try it."

"He's a hard man," Gerin agreed. "Harder than need be, I think. But it may be that hard times require a hard man. Who can tell for certain?"

"Do you know what your trouble is, Captain?" Van said.

"No, but I daresay you're going to tell me," the Fox answered, raising that eyebrow of his. Every so often, Van found a flaw in him, rarely the same one twice. The infuriating thing was that more often than not he had a point.

"Your trouble, Captain, is that you're so busy trying to understand the other fellow's point of view that you don't give enough heed to your own."

Gerin clutched his chest and lurched in the chariot, as if pierced by an arrow. Van's chuckle rumbled deep in his chest. That was a hit, though, and the Fox knew it. He said, "Understanding the other fellow has its uses, too. Sometimes he may even be right."

"And what does that have to do with the price of tin?" Van said. "All you really need worry about is that he does what you have in mind."

"Are you sure you're not really a Trokmê after all?" Gerin asked mildly. That earned him the glare he'd expected.

The chariot rattled past a burned-out keep. Perched atop one of the charred logs sat a fat bustard. Van tapped Raffo on the shoulder, pointed. The driver pulled back on the reins; the horses stopped and began to graze. Van reached for Gerin's bow. "I saw the bird—will you let me do the hunting?" he asked.

"Go ahead," the Fox answered. Van might think slaying men with the bow an effete way to fight, but he was a fine archer nonetheless.

The outlander strung the bow. Gerin handed him an arrow. He dropped down from the chariot and slid toward the bustard, light on his feet as a stalking longtooth. The bustard grubbed under its wing for mites. Van got to within twenty paces before he stood still, nocked the shaft, drew the bow, and let fly.

The arrow hit the bustard just below where it had been scratching. It let out a startled squawk and tried to fly, but tumbled off its log into the ditch that had not served to protect the palisade. Van scrambled in after it.

When he came out again, he carried the bird by the feet and wore an enormous grin.

"Well shot," Gerin said, pleased the hunt had been so successful—and so brief. "Blood for the ghosts and supper for us."

"The very thing I was thinking," Van said.

Before long, sunset forced the travelers to a halt. Gerin and Van got out of the chariot and, one with sword, the other with spear, moved cautiously through the woods on either side of the road until Gerin came upon a small clearing screened off by trees. He hurried back to the dirt track, whistled to let Van know he'd found what he was after.

"You've got a place to keep us away from prying eyes, do you?" the outlander said, slipping out from between a couple of oaks. Despite his bulk, he moved so quietly that Gerin had not heard him till he spoke.

"Indeed I do. In my own lands, I wasn't much worried about making a fire out where anyone could see it. Here, though, it might draw serfs on the run, bandits—who knows what? Why take the chance?" The Fox turned to Raffo. "Unharness the horses. We can lead them back to the clearing, too; the way's not badly overgrown."

"Aye, lord Gerin." Raffo freed the animals from the central shaft; he and the Fox led them away to tether them in the clearing.

Van joined them a few minutes later. "I dragged the chariot off the road and into the bushes," he said. "It won't be so easy to see now."

"Good." Gerin nodded. "And if one of the horses goes lame, now we know we can hitch you to the shaft in its stead. Maybe we'll let the horse ride in your place in the car."

"I thank you, Captain," Van said gravely. "Always good to see how you look out for the welfare of them that serve you, so it is."

Suspecting he'd come off worse in that exchange, Gerin dug a trench to hold the blood from the bustard Van had killed earlier in the afternoon. When the bird had bled out, he frowned. "I hope that will be enough," he said. "We'd better build the fire bigger than we would have otherwise, or we'll have dreadful dreams all through the night."

After the sun went down, the ghosts did buzz gratefully around the offering the travelers had given them, but they rose from it faster than the Fox would have liked to see, as if they were men getting up from the table still hungry. They also braved the light and heat of the fire to gain more vital essence from the cut-up chunks of bird Gerin, Van, and Raffo were roasting.

The Fox drew first watch. After he woke Raffo for the middle stint, he fell asleep almost at once. His dreams *were* dreadful: monsters rampaging over the northlands, with men in desperate and what looked like losing struggle to drive them back. At first, in one of those almost-conscious moments dreams sometimes have, he thought he was harking back to the werenight. But he soon realized that was not so; these monsters seemed more appalling than mere wild beasts armed with the remnants of human wit that still clung to them.

When Van shook him awake at sunrise, he rose with such alacrity that the outlander gave him a curious look and said, "You're not apt to be so cheerful of a morning."

"Bad dreams," Gerin muttered, sliding a foot into a sandal.

"Aye, I had 'em, too." Van shook his head. "All manner of horrid creatures running loose—the gods grant I had a sour stomach or some such, to make me see such phantoms in my sleep."

The Fox paused with the sandal strap still unfastened. "That sounds like the same dream I had," he said slowly.

"And I," Raffo agreed. "I wouldn't have minded spending more time on watch and less in my blanket, and how often do you hear me say something like that?"

They hashed it out over breakfast, each recounting what he remembered of his dreams. As best Gerin could tell, they were all the same. "I don't like that," he said. "The omen is anything but good." His fingers shaped a sign to turn aside ill luck. The sign worked well enough for small misfortunes. Whatever misfortune lay ahead, he feared it would not be small—with Duren missing, it was already large. He offered the sign as a man without food in his house will offer a neighbor a stoup of water: not much, but the best he can do.

Van said, "If it is an omen, we won't be able to escape it, whatever it may prove to mean. One way or another, we'll get through." He seized his spear, made a sudden, savage thrust, as if to dispose of any troublesome foretellings.

The Fox wished he could match his friend's confidence. Van had never found anything, even the werenight, he couldn't overcome with brawn and bravery. Gerin trusted his own power less far. He said, "Let's get on the road."

They passed another couple of mostly deserted villages that day, and a wrecked keep. And, about noon, the Fox saw on a distant hill a building that wasn't quite a keep but was far stronger and more elaborate than anything a serf would need. Raffo saw it, too, and scowled blackly. "If that's not a bandits' nest, you can call me a Shanda nomad."

"That's what it is, all right, and right out in the open, too." Gerin spat into the dirt of the road to show what he thought of it. "Everything's going to the five hells when bandits set themselves up like barons."

"Who do you think the first barons were?" Van said.

"Bandits who got rich, most likely. That's how it was a lot of places, anyhow."

"Insulting my ancestors, are you?" Gerin said. "I'd be angrier if I didn't know you were probably right. Even so, one fine day we're going to come down here and burn these bandits out before they get the chance to turn into barons."

"We're getting close to the lands Adiatunnus holds," Raffo said. "He's liable not to like that."

"Aye, he might have in mind to use these buggers, whoever they are, as a buffer between him and me," Gerin agreed. "That he has it in mind, though, doesn't mean it will happen so."

The sun had slid more than halfway down toward the west when the chariot clattered up to a new border stone standing by the side of the road. The boulder was carved not with Elabonian designs or letters, but rather with the fylfots and spirals the Trokmoi favored. In the roadway itself stood a couple of red-mustached northerners, one with a spear, the other with a sword. The one with the spear called in lilting Elabonian, "Who might you be, coming to the lands of the great chief, Adiatunnus his own self?"

"I might be anyone. I am Gerin the Fox," Gerin answered. "Did Adiatunnus' liegeman Diviciacus pass this way?"

"He did that." The border guard gave Gerin a look more curious than hostile. "And I'm after thinking it's fair strange, Fox, for you to be after him so. Have you changed your mind, now, over the matter anent which Diviciacus was sent forth for to talk with you?"

"I have not," Gerin answered at once, which made both Trokmoi scowl. "But neither am I at feud with Adiatunnus, nor with any of his. Does peace hold between us, or not?" He reached for the bronze-headed axe in its rest on the side wall of the chariot. Van hefted his own spear, not in a hostile way but thoughtfully, as if to find out how heavy it was.

It certainly made the Trokmoi thoughtful. The man who had spoken before said, "Sure and you've no need to be fighting us, now. For all Diviciacus ranted and carried on about what a black-hearted spalpeen you were, Fox—these are his words, mind, and none o' my own— he said not a whisper of faring forth to fight."

"As I told him I had no quarrel with Adiatunnus," Gerin agreed. "But tell me this—when Diviciacus rode through here, did he have with him in the chariot a boy of four summers? Not to put too fine a point on it, did he have my son? Before you answer, think on this: if you lie, we shall be at feud, and to the death."

The two northerners looked at each other. This time, the one who had the sword replied: "Fox, by Esus, Taranis, and Teutates I swear he did not." That was the strongest oath the Trokmoi used, and one they did not swear lightly. The fellow went on, "If we aimed to go to war with you, we'd up and do it. Stealing a child, now?" He spat. "Bad cess to any man who's after trying such a filthy thing."

"Aye," the other warrior said. "Did one of ours do such to you, Fox, we'd hand him back nicely tied and all, for you to do with him as you thought best. You could make him last days so, and wish every moment he'd never been born. I've two lads and a girl of my own, and I'd use the same way any ogre of a man who so much as ruffled a hair on their heads without my leave."

His anger and sincerity were unmistakable. Maybe Adiatunnus had set him and his friend here just because they lied so well, but Gerin couldn't do anything about that, not without an army at his back. He said, "I shall believe you, but remember what I said if you've not spoken truth."

"Och, but we have, so we've nought to fear," the fellow with the sword said. "I hope you find the bairn safe, Fox."

His friend nodded, adding, "Since you're apt to be spending the night in the open, would you want to buy a hen from us, now?"

"You probably stole it," Gerin said without rancor. "That's what all you Trokmoi south of the Niffet are—just a bunch of damned chicken thieves."

"Indeed and we're not," the northerner with a spear answered indignantly. "We came south because you Elabonians are after having so many things better and better than chickens to steal."

Since that was nothing but the truth, Gerin could not even argue with it. He tapped Raffo on the shoulder. His driver slewed the chariot in the narrow roadway and started east, back toward Castle Fox. "Sensible," Van said. "This set of woodsrunners seemed friendly enough, but we'll want to put some distance between them and us all the same. One of their higher-ups is liable to decide we're worth hunting through the night."

"My thought exactly," Gerin agreed. "Raffo, go by back roads while the day lasts, so long as they lead north or east. If we stay on the main track, I think we're asking for trouble."

"Aye, lord Gerin," Raffo said, and then, after a moment, "I'm sorry we didn't find your son."

Gerin sighed. "So am I. I have to pray that Rihwin or Drago or Widin had better luck than we did." He tried not to think about what might be happening to Duren. Too many of the pictures his imagination came up with were black ones.

"We were so sure the Trokmoi had run off with him, too," Van said. Another man might have put that, *You were so sure*— Like any proper friend, the outlander shared responsibility as well as credit.

"We'll know more when we get back to the castle," the Fox said, wondering how he'd keep from going mad till then.

Rihwin the Fox spread his hands. "Lord Gerin, Schild Stoutstaff's border guards declined to give me leave to pass into their overlord's land. For whatever it may be worth, they say Tassilo did enter that holding, but that they saw no sign of any small boy with him."

"For whatever it may be worth," Gerin repeated. "If he had Duren trussed up in the back of the wagon, it may be worth nothing at all. Or, on the other hand—" He gave up, shaking his head in frustration and dismay. He'd hoped he'd find answers at Fox Keep, not just more questions, but questions seemed in better supply. Turning to Widin Simrin's son, he asked, "Any luck with you?"

Widin was a young man, but wore his beard long and forked, an antique style. He shook his head. "The same as Rihwin, lord prince. Aragis' borderers say they'd not seen Rihwin—nor Tassilo nor Otes, either—but would not give me leave to enter their lord's land."

Drago the Bear said, "As for Otes son of Engelers, lord Gerin, far as I can tell he's just vanished off the face of the earth. No trace of him eastwards, that's certain."

"Well, what happened to him?" Gerin growled. But he knew that could have a multitude of answers, too. The jeweler might have run into bandits, he might have been taken ill and laid up at some little peasant village which Drago had gone right past, or he might have decided not to fare east after all. No way to be certain, especially now that Drago the Bear had decided to give up the trail and return to Fox Keep. Gerin might have wished for more diligence from him, but he'd done what he was told, which was about what he was good for.

As if uneasily aware his overlord was dissatisfied with

him, Drago tried to change the subject: "Lord Gerin, you shouldn't let Schild get by with the insolence he shows you these days. He bent the knee and set his hands in yours after you slew Wolfar, but you'd never know it by the way he acts. He has his nerve, he does, keeping your vassals off his land when he's properly a vassal his own self."

"In law, you're right," Gerin said. "Trouble is, we haven't much law north of the High Kirs. So long as he hasn't warred on me or attacked my lands when I was busy elsewhere, I've always had more important things to do than forcing him to heel."

"But when it's your son, lord prince?" Widin asked softly.

Gerin sighed. "Aye, now it's my son—not that Tassilo seems to have had him. I'll send Schild a courier with a letter: his border guards won't hold back a courier under my orders to take the message to their lord."

"They'd better not, anyhow," Drago said. "'Twould be against all polite usage." Down in the heart of the Empire, Gerin thought, Drago would have made a perfect man of law: he lived in a world where precedent bulked more real and larger than reality. That often served him well—it saved him the trouble of thinking, which was not his strength, anyhow. But when he had to confront something new and unusual, he might as well have been unarmed.

Rihwin the Fox said, "I hope the mere sending of a letter will not offend Schild's, ah, delicate sensibilities."

"You mean, will he get angry because my courier can read and he can't?" Gerin asked. Rihwin nodded. Gerin said, "It shouldn't be a problem. Schild may not have much in the way of learning, but he doesn't hate people who do—unlike some I could name." *Some who are my vassals*, he thought.

"If you did want to make him worry about you, Captain, you could use one of those serfs you've taught their letters," Van said.

"Makes me worry, too," Drago muttered, just loud enough to let Gerin hear.

"No, I try not to let word of that leak out of the holding," Gerin said. "The time's not ripe, not yet."

"Still don't know why you started that crazy business anyhow, lord," Widin said.

"Why? Because there's too much ignorance running around loose in the northlands, that's why," Gerin said. Widin and Drago both stared at him in incomprehension. Van shook his massive head; he'd known what the Fox was up to for years, and hadn't complained about it, but that didn't mean he approved.

Even Rihwin, who was himself not only literate but possessed of a formal education better than Gerin's, seemed dubious. "One of the things of which the serfs remain cheerfully ignorant is their own miserable lot," he remarked. "Let them learn to think, to reason, and they will surely wonder at the justice of an order which keeps them in their huts and the barons who rule them in grand keeps like this one."

"They wonder at that anyhow," Gerin said. "The northlands have never been free from peasant revolts, and that's only grown worse since the Trokmoi came over the Niffet. But my serfs, among them the ones I've taught, have stayed loyal where those of other lords rose."

"Belike that's so—for now," Van said. "But often, too, it works out that a man who's too hungry and worn to rise up will go on working where even a pack mule would drop dead. Give that same man a bit of hope, now, and a full belly, and then try to crack the whip on him . . . well, you'd better have a good place to hide, is all I have to tell you."

Gerin clicked his tongue between his teeth. That had some truth to it; his own reading of history said as much. But he answered, "I have to take the chance. If I don't, this whole land will slide back into barbarism in two generations' time, and the only way you'll be able to tell Elabonians from Trokmoi will be by black mustachios in place of red."

"I'm not ignorant," Drago said indignantly. "Hearing I am all the bloody time wears thin, lord Gerin. I know how to war and raise horses and keep order in my own holding. What else do I need?"

"Suppose there's a drought and you need magic done to get some rain?" Gerin asked.

"I hire a mage, of course."

"Where do you suppose the mage learned his art? If he's any good, at the Sorcerers' Collegium down in the City of Elabon. But northlands mages can't do that any more—we're cut off, remember. If we want to have another set of mages come along to replace the ones who die, we'll just have to find some way to train them ourselves. That means reading and writing, too, you know."

Drago scowled. "You don't argue fair, Fox."

"There I must disagree," Rihwin said. "Lord Gerin's arguments strike me as logical enough—and logic also seems to me to be a civilized appurtenance worth preserving. The question is whether the risks inherent in seeking to make civilized men of serfs outweigh the benefits to be gained from that course if successful."

Gerin abruptly sickened of the dispute. "A murrain on it," he growled. "The only thing that truly matters now is who has Duren and what they're doing to him. I said the same thing before we all set out searching, but I hoped we'd know something when we came back to Fox Keep. Instead, here we are sitting along this same cursed table five days later, and just as ignorant as the moment we set out."

Rihwin gave him a sidelong glance. "Where chariots rumbling down roadways and men beating bushes fail, sorcery might serve. I speak purely in the abstract, you understand, my own abilities along those lines having been raped away by the angry god, but the possibility deserves mention."

"It would deserve more mention if I were more of a wizard." Gerin sighed. "Oh, aye, you have the right of it, and I'll try, but I've essayed such magics before, and never yet found what I was looking for. And by the time we can find a proper mage and bring him here, the trail will have grown cold."

"Attempting a spell while convinced it will fail is the surest way to guarantee such failure," Rihwin said.

"I know that, too, but I find optimism hard to come by when I see no good reason for it." The Fox wished he could cast aside his gloom. As Rihwin had said, he would have been a better wizard—*though never a good one*, he thought—without it. But it was as much a part of him as the scar over his left eye.

Just then, Fand came into the great hall. She pointed to Rihwin and Widin and Drago. "I know they had no luck," she said. "Are you after finding your lost boy, and him so small and all?"

"No," Gerin said, and the one word pressed the weight of defeat and despair more heavily onto his shoulders.

"Och, the black shame of it, to be snatching children," Fand said. She meant it, Gerin judged, but hers was a nature that held the troubles of others in mind for only a little while before returning to her own concerns: "And fair lonely I was, too, with both my men off on a sleeveless errand. Still and all, though, they might have brought something back with them to make amends for being gone so long." She looked hopefully from Gerin to Van.

The outlander answered first: "Maybe I should bring my hand across your greedy backside. Does that seem fair, when you think on what we were about?"

When Van spoke in that rumbling tone of warning, as if he were an earthquake about to happen, sensible men walked soft. But Fand was nothing if not spirited herself. She shouted, "Greedy, is it, to be asking a simple question of you? Often enough there's a question you ask of me, aye, and with the understanding my answer had better be yes, too, or I'd be sorry for it. And you call me greedy? A pox take you!"

"If a pox did take me, where would I likely get it?" Van retorted.

"You've been staying with me too long," Gerin murmured. "That's the sort of crack I'm apt to make."

Fand didn't hear him. She let her wrath fall on Van: "You? Who knows where you'd be likely to come by the pox? You think I don't know you'll cover anything with a slit, like a billy goat in the springtime? I've more to fear from your wanderings than you from mine. Go on, now, tell me I'm a liar."

Van turned the color of the embers smoldering on the hearth. "That's the way of a man," he sputtered. Drago, Rihwin, and Widin nodded. So did Gerin, though he was less inclined to make a tomcat of himself.

"Och, I know that." Fand tossed her head in fine disdain. "But since it is, why blame me for what'd be the fault of your own self?"

Gerin worked so hard to choke down laughter that he had a coughing fit. Van wasn't the only one who'd spent a lot of time with him. No toga-wearing Sithonian sophist could have done a neater, more logical job of punching holes in the outlander's gibe than Fand just had.

Van looked his way. "Will you not come to my aid?" he asked plaintively, as if alone on the field and beset by a host.

"I think our lady here was greedy, too, but as for the rest, you got yourself into it, and you can get yourself out." Gerin rose and headed for the stairs. "As for me, I'm going to see what sort of search spells I can use to try to find my son."

Bass and alto shouts, like angry kettledrum and horn, followed him up to his library. He knew of no greater hoard of books anywhere in the northlands, yet he also knew how inadequate the collection was. There were hundreds of grimoires, for instance, but he owned fewer than ten. With them he had Lekapenos' epics, a few codices of history, a couple on natural philosophy, a treatise on horsemanship, another on war, a school set of Sithonian plays (many of them crumbs from Lekapenos' banquet)—and that was all. So much knowledge stored away in volumes he would never see, let alone own . . . thinking of his own ignorance saddened him.

He went through the grimoires one after another, looking for a spell that would let him see either who had taken Duren or where his son was now. He found a fair number of them, but had to dismiss most out of hand. Some were beyond his limited abilities as a mage. Some required ingredients he could not hope to obtain: dried sea-cow flipper from the Greater Inner Sea, for instance.

And too many needed wine. Even if it hadn't been unavailable, he would have been afraid to use it. The last thing he wanted was to attract the angry notice of Mavrix.

"I wonder if ale would do?" he muttered, running a finger down the closely written column of a cantrip that looked promising except for prescribing a silver bowl full of wine as the scrying medium.

A sentence near the end of the spell leaped out at him: *Whereas the aspect of Baivers god of barley is dull, sodden, and soporific, whilst that of Mavrix lord of the sweet grape (to whom the cry of Evoii! rings out) sparkles with wit and intelligence, the ill-advised operator who seeks to substitute ale for wine will surely have cause to regret his stupidity.*

"It was only an idea," the Fox said, as if talking things over with the author of the grimoire. That author was a Sithonian; though the Fox's copy was an Elabonian translation, he'd already found several scornful references to the westerners who had conquered and then been all but conquered by the more anciently civilized land, and equally short shrift given to other Elabonian gods.

Gerin plucked at his beard as he thought. Substituting butter for olive oil had worked out well enough. No matter what this snooty Sithonian said, using ale in place of wine could also succeed. And he was and always had been on good terms with Baivers. He picked up the grimoire, saying, "I'll try it."

He had a silver bowl; it had been at Fox Keep since his grandfather's day. He'd been thinking about melting it down along with the rest of the odd bits of silver in the keep and starting his own coinage. Now he was glad he'd never got round to doing that. And ale, of course, was easy to come by.

He took the bowl and a pitcher of the strongest brew in his cellar out to the shack where he essayed his magics. Before he began the conjuration, he took a while studying the text of the spell, making sure he could slip in Baivers' name and standard epithets for those of Mavrix. He nodded to himself: that ought to work. He didn't think he'd need to modify any of the mystical passes that accompanied the charm.

"I bless thee, Baivers, god of clear sight, and call upon

thee: lift the darkness of night," he intoned, and poured the silver bowl half full of golden ale. He smiled a little when he thought of that; mixing gold and silver, even symbolically, ought to make the spell work better.

As often happened, the sound of his chanting drew Rihwin, who stood in the doorway to see what he was up to. Gerin nodded to him and set a finger to his lips to enjoin silence. Rihwin nodded back; he knew a man working magic did not need and sometimes could not tolerate distraction.

Again, the wizard who had written the grimoire made the operator perform the more difficult passes with his left hand. Again, Gerin gratefully accepted that, because it made the spell easier for him. Soon, he thought, the ale would turn clear as crystal and he would be rewarded with a glimpse of Duren's face, or at least of his surroundings.

He caught himself yawning in the middle of the spell. *What's wrong?* he thought. He couldn't say it aloud; he was in the middle of the chant. As if from very far away, he watched his sorcerous passes grow languid, listened to his voice turn fuzzy. . . .

"Lord prince! Lord Gerin!"

With a great effort, the Fox opened his eyes. Anxious faces crowding close blocked light from the smoking torches that lit the great hall. Gerin's eyebrows came down and together—last he remembered, he hadn't been in the great hall, and torchlighting was hours away.

"What happened?" he croaked. He discovered he was lying in the rushes on the floor. When he tried to sit up, he felt as if he'd forgotten how to use half his muscles.

Among the faces peering down at him was Rihwin's. "Would that you could tell us, lord Gerin," the southerner answered. "You fell asleep, or perhaps your spirit left your body—however you would have it—in the middle of the spell you were using. We've tried from that time to this to rouse you, but to no avail till now."

"Aye, that's the way of it," Drago agreed. "We didn't know what in the five hells to do next—stick your foot in the fire, maybe."

"I'm glad it didn't come to that," Gerin said. From Rihwin, the suggestion might have been a joke. Drago, though, had neither the wit nor the temperament for jokes. When he said something, he meant it.

That odd, unstrung feeling was fading. Gerin managed to get to his feet. Van, ever practical, gave him a jack of ale. "It's not enchanted, Captain, but it's pretty good," he said.

Gerin gulped down half the jack before he choked and spluttered. "That's it," he said. "That's what went wrong. This time, the chap who wrote the grimoire was smarter than I am. He warned that Baivers' influence on the spell was soporific, and that's just what he meant."

"The Elabonian pantheon is so dismayingly stodgy," Rihwin said. Like many of his educated countrymen, he preferred the Sithonian gods to those native to Elabon.

But Van said, "Honh! Remember how much joy you had of Mavrix." Rihwin flinched but was honest enough with himself to nod, acknowledging the justice of the hit.

"Never mind any of that," Gerin said; his wits were beginning to work more clearly again, and his body to seem as if it might be fully answerable to him after all. "I've learned something from this escapade, which may in the long run make it worthwhile."

"What's that?" Van asked, a beat ahead of the rest.

"That whatever magic I can do isn't going to let me find my son. And find him I will." Gerin counted stubbornness a virtue. If you kept hitting at a problem, sooner or later it was likely to fall down. He went on, "Using ale

for wine in the spell might have knocked me out, but, by
Dyaus, there are eyes that never sleep."

"Not by Dyaus," Drago said. "By Biton, you mean, or
do I mistake you?"

"No, you have the right of it," Gerin said. "I'll fare
forth to the Sibyl at Ikos. Her verse will tell me what I
need to know." He hesitated, then added, "If I can
understand it, of course."

III

After the Empire of Elabon conquered the land between the High Kirs and the Niffet, the Elabonians pushed an all-weather highway, the Elabon Way, north from the town of Cassat to the river so they would always be able to move troops against invaders or rebels.

No large numbers of imperial troops had been seen in the northlands for generations before Elabon severed itself from its province north of the Kirs, but the highway remained: far and away the best land link the northlands boasted. Even barons who did little else maintained the stretch of the Elabon Way that ran through their territory: if for no other reason, then to make sure they collected tolls from travelers along the road.

"Hard on the horses' hooves," Van remarked as the wagon rumbled onto the flag-paved roadbed.

"So it is," Gerin said. "Nothing to be done about it, though, unless you want to throw away the road whenever it rains for more than two days straight. Getting a wagon through hub-deep mud isn't much fun."

"Can't argue with that," Van agreed. "Still, we don't want the animals lamed or stonebruised, either."

"No. Well, we won't push them hard, not when it's a five days' run to Ikos," Gerin said. "As a matter of fact, the horses aren't what worries me most."

"You always have something to worry about—you'd be worried if you didn't," Van said. "What is it this time?"

"Ricolf the Red's would be a logical place to stop for the third night," the Fox answered. "Or it would have been the logical place—" His voice trailed away.

"—if Ricolf weren't Elise's father. If Elise hadn't up and left you," Van finished for him. "Aye, that does complicate your life, doesn't it?"

"You might say so," Gerin agreed dryly. "Ricolf's not my vassal. When Elise was with me, there seemed no need, and afterwards I hadn't the crust to ask it of him. Nor has he ever sought my protection; he's done well enough on his own. When Elise was with me, I had a claim on his keep once he died. Now that she's gone, I suppose Duren is the rightful heir: she's Ricolf's only legitimate child, and none of his bastard sons lived."

"Which means Duren is Ricolf's only grandson, too," Van said. "He'll need to know about the boy disappearing. Or let me put it another way—he'd have cause to quarrel with you if you rode by without saying so much as a word."

Gerin sighed. "I hadn't thought about it quite like that, but I fear you're right. I'm his guest-friend from years gone by, but it'll be bloody awkward just the same. He thinks Elise never would have run off if I'd done . . . Dyaus, if I'd known what I should have done, I'd have done it. He won't think better of me for letting Duren be kidnapped, either."

"Captain, you feel bad enough about that all by yourself—you won't hardly notice anyone else piling on a little more."

"Only you would think of making me feel better by reminding me how bad I feel now." The method was, Gerin admitted to himself, nicely calculated to suit his own gloomy nature.

Sitting beside him on the wagon's bench, Van stretched and looked about with an almost childlike delight. "Good to be out on the road again," he said. "Fox Keep's all very well, but I like having new things to see every minute or every bend in the road—not that the Elabon Way had many bends in it, but you take my meaning."

"So I do." The Fox looked eastward. Quick-moving Tiwaz, now a day past first quarter, had raced close to Nothos, whose pale gibbous disk was just rising over the tree-covered hills. He shook his head. Just as Tiwaz gained on Nothos, so troubles seemed to gain on him with every day that passed, and his own pace was too slow to escape them.

"There's a pleasant thought," Van said when he spoke his conceit aloud. "Tell you what, Fox: instead of sleeping in the open tonight, what say we rest at the next serf village we come upon? They'll have ale there, and you'll be better for drinking yourself drunk and starting off tomorrow with a head that thumps like a drum. Then at least you'll know what ails you."

"I know what ails me now," Gerin said: "Duren's missing. What I don't know is what to do about it, and that eats at me as much as his being gone." Nevertheless, he went on reflectively, "Headman at the next village south is Tervagant Beekeeper. His ale doesn't have the worst name in the lands I hold."

Van slapped him on the back, nearly hard enough to tumble him out of the wagon. "The very thing. Trust me, Captain, you'll be better for a good carouse."

"That's what Rihwin thought, and he ended up with his robe round his ears and his pecker flapping in the breeze."

Even so, the Fox reined in when they rolled up to Tervagant's village. The headman, a nervous little fellow who kept kneading the front of his tunic with both hands as if it were bread dough, greeted the arrival of his overlord with ill-concealed alarm. "W-what brings you so far south, l-lord prince?" he asked.

"My son's been stolen," Gerin answered flatly.

Tervagant's eyes widened. The news, the Fox saw, had not reached the village till this moment. He set it forth for the headman and the crowd of listeners—mostly women and children, for the men still labored in the fields—who gathered round the wagon.

"Lord prince, I pray the gods give you back your boy," Tervagant said. Everyone else echoed his words; noble and peasant shared the anguish a missing child brought. The headman's hands fell away from his tunic. His face, which had been pasty, gained color. *Another one who's glad I'm not looking into his affairs*, Gerin thought. He wondered just how many village headmen had little schemes of their own in play. One of these days, he'd have to try to find out.

Not today, though. Tervagant ducked into his hut, came out with a ram's-horn trumpet. He glanced at Gerin for permission before he raised it to his lips. The Fox nodded. Tervagant blew a long, unmusical blast. Some of the peasants looked up from their work in surprise: the sun was low in the west, but not yet brushing the horizon. The men came in happily enough, though.

"Shall we kill a pig, lord prince?" the headman asked.

"Aye, if you can without hurting yourselves," Gerin answered. The thought of fat-rich pork made spit rush into his mouth. He added, "The blood from the beast will give the ghosts what they want, too."

"Some of the blood," Tervagant corrected thriftily. "The rest we'll make into blood pudding." In good times, serfs lived close to the edge. In bad times, they—and the nobles they supported—fell over it. They could afford to waste nothing.

The pig, like any other, was half wild, with a ridge of hair down its back. Tervagant lured it to him with a turnip, then cut its throat. He had to spring back to keep it from tearing him with its tushes. Blood sprayed every which way as the beast ran through the village until it fell over and lay kicking.

"That'll keep the ghosts happier than if the blood went into a nice, neat trench," Van said.

The fire the villagers made was big enough to hold a fair number of ghosts away by itself. They butchered the pig, baked some of it in clay, and roasted the rest. Living up to his ekename, Tervagant went into his hut, came out with a pot full of honey, and glazed some of the cooking meat with it. The delicious aroma made Gerin hungrier than he had been before.

Along with bread, ale, and berries preserved in more of Tervagant's honey, the pork proved as good as it smelled. A sizable pile of rib bones lay in front of Gerin when he thumped his belly and pronounced himself full. Van had found a pointed rock and was cracking a leg bone to get at the marrow.

"More ale, lord prince?" one of the peasant women asked.

"Thank you." He held out the cup they'd given him. She smiled as she filled it for him. She was, he noticed, not bad-looking, with light eyes that told of a Trokmê or two in the woodpile. She wore her hair long and unbraided, which meant she was unmarried, yet she was no giggling maid.

When he asked her about that, her face clouded. "I had a husband, lord prince, you're right, I did, but he died of lockjaw year before last."

"I'm sorry," Gerin said, and meant it—he'd seen lockjaw. "That's a hard way to go."

"Aye, lord prince, it is, but you have to go on," she said.

He nodded solemnly; he'd had quite a bit of ale by then. "What's your name?" he asked her.

"Ethelinda, lord prince."

"Well, Ethelinda," he said, and let it hang there. Now she nodded, as if he'd spoken a complete sentence.

After supper, Tervagant waved Gerin and Van into a couple of huts whose inhabitants had hastily vacated them. "The gods grant you good night, lord prince, master Van," he said.

"Me, I intend to give the gods some help," Van said. While he'd been sitting by the fire and eating, a couple of young women had almost come to blows over him. Now he led both of them into the hut Tervagant had given him. Watching that, Gerin shook his head. Too bad no one could find a way to put into a jar whatever the outlander had.

And yet the Fox was not altogether surprised to find Ethelinda at his elbow when he went into the hut the headman had set aside for him. "You've no new sweetheart?" he asked her. Some lords took peasant women without thinking past their own pleasure. Along with hunger, though, that was the sort of thing liable to touch off an uprising. As usual, Gerin was careful.

But Ethelinda shook her head. "No, lord prince."

"Good." Gerin had to duck his head to get into the hut. It was dark inside, and smelled strongly of smoke. He shuffled in, found a straw-filled pallet with his foot. "Here we are."

The straw rustled as he sank down onto it, then again when Ethelinda joined him there. She pulled her long tunic off over her head; that was all she wore. Gerin took a little longer getting out of his clothes, but not much. By the way she clung to him, he guessed she'd been telling the truth about having no sweetheart; he didn't think anyone had touched her so for a long time.

That made him take care to give her as much pleasure as he could. And, at the last moment, he pulled out and spurted his seed onto her belly rather than deep inside her. He thought he would make her grateful, but she said, "What did you go and do that for?" in anything but a happy voice.

"To keep you from making a baby," he answered, wondering if she'd made the connection between what they'd just done and what might happen most of a year later. Every time he thought he had the measure of serfs' ignorance, he ended up being startled anew.

Ethelinda knew that connection, though. "I wanted to start a baby," she said. "I hoped I would."

"You did?" Gerin rolled off her and almost fell off the narrow pallet. "Why?"

"If I was carrying your baby, I could go up to Fox Keep and you'd take care of me," she answered. "I wouldn't have to work hard, at least for a while."

"Oh." Gerin stared through the darkness at her. She was honest, anyhow. And, he admitted to himself, she was probably right. No woman had ever claimed he'd put a bastard in her; he was moderate in his venery and, to keep such things from happening, often withdrew at the instant he spent. But he would not have turned away anyone with whom he'd slept.

Maybe you shouldn't have pulled out, the darker side of him murmured. *With Duren gone, you're liable to need an heir, even if he is a bastard.*

He shook his head. Sometimes he got trapped in his own gloom and lost track of what needed doing. He couldn't let that happen, not now. His son depended on him.

Ethelinda sat up and reached for her tunic. "Do you want me to go away, lord prince?" she asked.

"We'll be crowded on this bed, but stay if you care to," Gerin answered. "The night's not so warm that we'd be sticking to each other wherever we touched."

"That's so," she agreed. "I always did like having somebody in a bed with me. That's how I grew up, with all my brothers and sisters and my father and my mother while she was alive, all packed tight together. Sleeping just by yourself is lonely." She tossed the tunic to the dirt floor. "And besides, who knows what might happen later on?"

What happened was that Gerin slept the night through and didn't wake up till after sunrise, when Ethelinda rose from the pallet and finally did put her tunic back on. When she saw his eyes open, she gave him a scornful glance, as if to say, *Some stallion you turned out to be.*

He bore up under that without getting upset; unlike Van, he didn't wear some of his vanity in his trousers. He looked around the peasant hut for a chamber pot. When he didn't see one, he got up, dressed quickly, and went off into the bushes by the village to relieve himself. The reek that rose from those bushes said he was but following the peasants' practice.

When he came back, Van was standing outside the hut he'd been given, tweedling away on his flute. The two women who'd gone in there with him both clung to him adoringly. His grin was smug. The Fox felt like throwing something at him, but contented himself with saying, "Time we got moving. We can eat as we travel."

"As you will." Van walked over to the horses, which were tethered to the low branches of a maple. "You harness the leader, then, and I'll see to the off beast. You're so hot to be on the road, the two of us together'll get us on our way in a hurry."

That afternoon, the wagon rolled into the holding of Palin the Eagle. Palin, who had Trokmoi on his western flank, acknowledged Gerin as his suzerain and, because he'd needed the Fox's help more than once against the woodsrunners, was more sincere about his submission than Schild Stoutstaff.

Not far into Palin's land, Gerin and Van came upon a

belt of devastation: for several miles, the Elabon Way and the land to either side of it had been cratered by Balamung's destructive sorcery. Now that weeds and shrubs had had five years to spread over the craters, they looked less raw and hideous than they had when they were new, but the ground remained too broken for farmers to work.

The Elabon Way itself was in fair repair. That was at Gerin's order; he did not want the main road south from Fox Keep to remain a ruin. The repairs, he knew, did not come up to the standard the Elabonian Empire had set when it pushed the highway north to the Niffet. With the resources of a realm behind them, the imperial artisans had built to last, with a deep bed of gravel and stone, stone flags cemented together, and good drainage to either side of the roadway.

With peasant levies working in time snatched from their fields, the Fox hadn't had a prayer of matching such construction. Cobblestones and gravel did give the rebuilt stretch of the Elabon Way a surface that, while it was hard on hooves, did not turn into gluey mud whenever rain fell.

"Strange," Gerin said as the wagon jounced along over the uneven surface: "Whenever I travel this stretch of road, I remember trying to fight my way north over it just before the werenight."

"You're not likely to forget that," Van agreed. "Me, I find it strange to travel the same stretch of road more than once. I'm too used to seeing something new every day to be easy with the idea of going back and forth, back and forth. Boring to see the same hills on the skyline every day. I want to find out what's on the other side of them."

"Those hills?" Gerin pointed west. "They shelter Trokmoi and bandits."

"Not what I meant," Van said. "Captain, you've no poetry in you, and that's a fact."

"I suppose not. I do the best I can without it, that's all."

Toward evening, they passed the keep of Raff the Ready, where they'd guested on their last trip south to Ikos. No guesting at Raff's tonight; the keep had fallen to the Trokmoi, and nothing but tumbled ruins remained. Gerin shook his head, remembering the fine meal Raff had fed him. Tonight it would be hard bread and sausage and sour beer and whatever they managed to hunt up to keep the ghosts happy.

A red fox scurried across the road in front of the wagon. It paused by a clump of hound's-tongue, sitting up on its haunches with its own tongue lolling out as it watched the horses and men. Van tapped Gerin on the shoulder. "Rein in. Let me grab the bow and we'll have our evening's offering."

"What? Where?" Gerin said.

Van pointed to the fox. "Right there. Are you blind, not to see it?"

Gerin stared, first at the fox, then at his friend. "You're enough like a brother to me that I often forget you're not Elabonian born. It's not our custom to kill the animals that give us our ekenames. All my luck, such as it is, would run away if I tried to slay a fox."

"You wouldn't," Van said. "I would."

"I'd be abetting you." Gerin shook his head. "In the spirit world, it would count for the other."

"The spirit world will do more than count if we don't find something with blood in it pretty soon," Van grumbled. "Looks like all the peasants hereabout have fled, and a night in the open with only a fire to hold the ghosts at bay is nothing to look forward to."

"Something will turn up." Gerin sounded more confident than he felt. But hardly more than a minute after he'd spoken, he spotted a big, fat gray squirrel sitting on the topmost branch of an oak sapling that really should have been cleared away from the side of the road. Now he did rein in. Van had seen the squirrel, too; he was already reaching into the back of the wagon for the bow.

The bowstring thrummed as he let fly. The squirrel toppled out of the little tree and lay feebly kicking on the mossy ground below. It had stopped moving by the time Van walked over and picked it up. He hefted it in his hand. "It should serve," he said.

"Not a whole lot of meat, but what there is will be tasty baked in clay," Gerin said. "If you'd shot at the fox, the gods might not have put the squirrel in our path."

"If they're so grateful for me being good, why didn't they put a nice fat buck in that tree instead of a rat with a fuzzy tail that won't give us two good bites apiece?"

"Abandoned scoffer," Gerin said, though he had to fight to get words past the laughter that welled up when he pictured an antlered stag perched atop a sapling. "Show some respect for the gods of Elabon."

"I give them as much as they deserve and not a bit more," Van said. "I've done enough traveling, seen enough gods to know they're stronger than I am, but I'll be switched if I can see that some of 'em are a whole lot smarter than I am."

Gerin grunted, remembering Mavrix's long, pink tongue flicking out like a frog as the deity had mocked him and taken away Rihwin's sorcerous ability. "You may have something there, though you'll not be happier for it if some god hears what you've said."

"Ifsobe that happens, I'll just go on to someplace else where the writ of Elabonian gods doesn't run," Van said. "The thing about gods is, they're tied to the lands of those that worship them, and me" —he thumped his chest— "I'm not."

"Just like you to be so sure you'd get away," Gerin said, but then something else occurred to him. "Gods can travel, though, as their worshipers do—look at the way the Sithonian deities have taken hold in Elabon. And, I fear, we'll have Trokmê gods rooting themselves here in the northlands now that the woodsrunners have made homes south of the Niffet."

"You're likely right; I hadn't thought of that," Van said. "Not a crew I'd be happy with as neighbors: their yen for blood is as bad as the one the Trokmoi have themselves. I should know; the woodsrunners were all set to offer me up till I got free of them."

"Yes, you've told that tale," Gerin said. He shook his head. "One more thing to worry about." Trouble was, he seemed to add to that list almost every day. He halted the wagon. As long as he and Van had an offering for the ghosts for tonight, he wouldn't worry about any of the things on that list till tomorrow.

Splitting the night into two watches rather than three left the Fox and Van yawning as they started traveling a little past sunrise. "I'm slower than I should be, and that's not good," Gerin said. "When we cross Bevon Broken-Nose's holding, we'll need all our wits about us."

"Bevon Broken-Land would be a better name for him, that's certain," Van said.

"Can't argue with you there," Gerin replied. Bevon's sons had been squabbling over their father's holding five years before. Bevon himself was still alive, but universally ignored beyond a bowshot from his keep.

Gerin pointed ahead. "There we are. That's progress, if you like."

"Your fort, you mean? Aye, I expect so. It's about the only thing that keeps the Elabon Way open through Bevon's lands, anyhow."

Despite a wooden palisade, the building wasn't a keep in the proper sense of the word: no stone castle sat inside the wall, only a blockhouse also of wood. Gerin had run up the fort and put a garrison in it less than a year after the werenight, to make sure the road stayed clear. Bevon and all four of his sons had protested furiously, but couldn't unite even to get rid of the Fox's men.

"One day soon, Captain, you'll just quietly claim the land along the road as part of your own holding, won't you?" Van said. "Without your patrols, it'd be the howling wilderness it was before you put your men here—and it's like you to let the facts talk before you open your mouth yourself."

"That has been in my mind lately, as a matter of fact." Gerin gave his friend a look half respectful, half annoyed. "I like it better when no one else can pick out what's in my mind."

"Live in a keep for a while with a man and he will rub off on you." Van added, "However much he doesn't care to," in the hope—which was realized—of making Gerin scowl.

A three-chariot patrol team came north up the Elabon Way toward the fort. Seeing the wagon, they made for it instead, to see who was on the road. Gerin waved to one of the men in the lead car. "Hail!" he called loudly. "How fares the road, Onsumer?"

"Lord Gerin!" the bulky, black-bearded man called back. "I thought that was your wagon, though I'm just now close enough to be sure. We had a quiet run down to Ricolf's border and back, so the road is well enough." His face clouded. "But what of you? Is this the business Widin Simrin's son spoke of?"

"My son being stolen, you mean? Yes," Gerin said. "All my searches went awry, those after the men who might have taken him and the one round Fox Keep as well. I'm off to Ikos, to learn if the Sibyl can see farther than I did."

"Dyaus and Biton grant it be so," Onsumer said. The driver and warrior who shared the car with him nodded vigorously.

"I can but hope," Gerin said. "Widin told me he learned nothing new on his run down here. Have you had word of anything unusual from Bevon's sons? One of them, I suppose, could have arranged to kidnap Duren, though I'd not have thought any of them had the wit to plan such a thing."

Onsumer shook his head. "No, lord Gerin, nothing of the sort. I think the lot of them are too busy trying to slaughter one another to worry about outsiders, even ones they hate. We haven't had an attack on the fort in close to a year, but the strife among the brothers never ends."

"You're probably right," Gerin said. "All the barons in the northlands squabbled among themselves and didn't pay heed to the Trokmoi till it was too late. I wonder if we Elabonians learned the joys of faction fighting from Sithonia."

"I wouldn't have the faintest idea about that," Onsumer said. He was a good enough soldier, and far from stupid, but all he knew of the wider world he'd heard in minstrels' songs.

He got the horses moving again. "Good luck to you," Onsumer called as the wagon rolled by. His comrades waved to Gerin. Then they turned around and headed back toward the fort.

An hour or so later, Van pointed to a column of black smoke rising in the distance. "Somebody's burning his neighbor out there, or I miss my guess."

"Better they battle each other than my men," Gerin said, "but better still if they didn't battle at all."

"Honh! What are the odds of that?"

"On the face of it, not good," Gerin admitted. "Still, it used to happen. Elabon, not so long ago, was a single empire stretching from the Niffet east past the Lesser Inner Sea into the seething river plains of Kizzuwatna. Now it's falling apart. When the Emperor and his court think more of putting gold in their own belt pouches now than worrying about where the Empire will be a generation hence, that happens."

"It's not just the ones at the top," Van said. "It's everyone who's strong, out to get rich off the ones who aren't and to put a fist in his strong neighbor's eye."

"Aye, that's the way of it," Gerin said. "In the early days, they say, Elabonian warlords would go back to the plow once they'd won a war." He grinned wryly. "Of course, who knows what tales of those early days are worth?"

Near the southern edge of Bevon's unhappy holding lay another belt of devastation from Balamung's sorcery. As before, the wagon bounced roughly over the equally rough repairs Gerin had had the local peasants make. Van said, "Remember how Bevon's sons tried to stop you from fixing the road, each of them screaming he'd do it himself?"

"Oh, yes." The Fox's laugh was less than mirthful. "And if I'd waited for that, I'd be waiting still, and so would Duren's grandson."

When Gerin had come into Ricolf the Red's holding five years before, only a couple of guards kept watch at the border. Now a fort like the one he'd built on Bevon's land stood strong to keep out bandits—and perhaps to keep out his own men as well. The thought saddened him.

A guardsman strode out from the open gateway of the fort to ask his business. The fellow started slightly when he recognized Gerin and Van. Gerin started slightly, too; he had no idea what this warrior's name was, but he'd been at the border on that other journey, too. The Fox remembered those first days when he'd known Elise and snuck her out of her father's keep as vividly as if they were just past. Now that only ashes lay between him and her, he often wished he could forget. Somehow that only made him remember more intensely.

"Lord prince," Ricolf's man said, his voice polite but wary. "What brings you to the holding of Ricolf the Red? Is it the matter your vassal—what was his name?—spoke of some days past?"

"Widin Simrin's son," Gerin supplied. "Yes, it has to do with my son—Ricolf's grandson. We've had no luck finding him—I'm for the Sibyl at Ikos, to see if Biton will grant her sight of where the boy might be."

"May it prove so," the guard said. "Since it's but you and your comrade here, and no host in arms behind you, pass on, lord prince."

"No host in arms behind me?" Gerin said angrily. "Does Ricolf look for one? I've no quarrel with him, but I may, by Dyaus, if he keeps thinking that way."

"You had no quarrel with Bevon, either, yet your men stay on his land against his will. We don't want that happening here."

"Ricolf ought to get down on his knees and thank me for that," Gerin ground out. "If my men didn't keep order along the Elabon Way, you'd have more trouble spilling into this holding than you dream of. But Ricolf keeps his own house quiet, and needs no help from me."

"Just pass on," the guard said.

Gerin flicked the reins so violently, the horses sprang forward with startled snorts. Van said, "A good thing we're away. I thought you were going to jump down and murder that fellow."

"For a counterfeit copper, I would have." Gerin rubbed at the scar over his eye. He was sure it was white now; it always went dead pale when he got furious. "Worst of it is, the fool's only echoing what Ricolf says."

"Would you sooner we didn't stop of Ricolf's holding, then?" Van asked.

"Now that you mention it, yes." But the Fox sighed. "Has to be done, though—as you say, Duren's his grandson, after all. I expect I'll get through it. I wouldn't show my face in his holding if I thought he seriously meant me harm—not without that host in arms behind me, anyhow."

"The gods grant it doesn't come to that."

"Yes." Gerin wasn't thinking of the gods alone. If he ever did have to take on Ricolf, his former father-in-law was only too likely to call on Aragis the Archer for aid. Having Aragis extend his power northward was the last thing Gerin wanted. For that reason as well as for Duren's sake, he'd speak softly to the older baron. So he told himself, anyhow.

The sun tinged the western sky with colors like the belly of a salmon. Gerin imagined he felt the ghosts stir, though they would not truly emerge until after sunset. And from the castle ahead came a boy's cry from the watchtower: "Who comes to the holding of Ricolf the Red?"

All was so much as it had been five years before that the hair on Gerin's arms tried to prickle up. He felt himself caught in time, like an insect in the sticky sap of a pine tree. Insects so stuck rarely got loose. The Fox knew the trouble here lay in his own mind, but knowing did little to help him get free, either.

He shouted back toward the keep, giving his own name and Van's—just as he had then. But then Ricolf had been eager to let him in; they'd become friends on Gerin's earlier journeys south. Now? Who could say what Ricolf thought now?

Whatever it was, the drawbridge lowered, thick bronze chains rattling and squealing over the spokes of the winch as the gate crew turned it. The horses' hooves drummed like thunder when they walked across the timbers over the moat. Water plants added touches of green there, but the smell said that Ricolf's men used the barrier to empty their slop jars.

Ricolf the Red stood in the bailey near the gate, waiting to greet Gerin. He was a broad-shouldered, thick-bellied man heading toward sixty, his manner still vigorous and his hair still thick, though now mostly white rather than the Trokmê-like shade that had given him his sobriquet. When he opened his mouth to speak, Gerin saw he'd lost a front tooth since the last time they'd met.

"Guest-friendship is a sacred trust," Ricolf said, his deep voice younger than his years. "With that trust in mind, I greet you, Fox, and you also, Van of the Strong Arm. Use my keep as your own while you stay here."

"You are gracious as always," Gerin said. Ricolf hadn't sounded particularly gracious; he sounded more like a man doing a duty he didn't much care for. Gerin thought more of him for that, not less. Sometimes his own sense of duty was all that kept him going.

"Pah! This for graciousness." Ricolf kicked at the dirt. "I hear something's amiss with my grandson, and I want to know everything there is to know about it. First Elise, now Duren—" He shook his big, hard-featured head. "I wasn't the luckiest man born, to link my family to you."

"That's not what you thought when you gave me your daughter," Gerin answered as steadily as he could; as always, anger and longing surged in him when Elise came to the front of his mind. He went on, "The gods know I am not a perfect man. Will you entertain the notion that Elise may not have been a perfect woman?"

"The notion does not entertain me." Ricolf kicked at the dirt again. "Well, we'll speak of that later. What's your pleasure for supper? We killed a sheep this afternoon, so there's mutton, or we can chop a couple of hens down to size if the two of you would rather."

"Mutton," Gerin and Van said in the same breath. The Fox added, "We've been traveling a good deal these past few days, and mostly supping on the fowls we've killed as blood-offerings for the ghosts."

"Thought as much," Ricolf answered, "but I figured I owed you the choice." He was indeed meticulous in observing the rituals of guest-friendship.

Inside Ricolf's great hall, fat-wrapped bones smoked on Dyaus' altar. At the cookfire, servants roasted ribs and chops. A big bronze pot boiled busily above it. Van stabbed a finger toward it. "That'll be the tongue and tripe, the lungs and lights?" he asked.

"Aye," Ricolf said. "Which of the dainties do you care for most?"

"The tongue," the outlander answered at once. "Have you got any rock salt to scatter on it?"

"I do that," Ricolf answered, a Trokmê turn of phrase he probably would not have used before he got woodsrunners for neighbors. "The holding has several good licks, one of them near big enough to mine salt from."

Had Ricolf's holding been Gerin's, he suspected he would have mined salt and sold it to his neighbors. The only concern Ricolf had beyond his own borders was foes who might come at him. Past that, he was content with his land as he found it. Gerin wondered if he himself would ever be content with anything.

Bread and ale and meat distracted him from such

worries. He gnawed roasted mutton from ribs, then tossed them to the dogs. Tripe was slippery and gluey under his knife, chewy in his mouth. The kidneys' strong smell cut through the smoke that filled the hall and foretold their flavor.

He stuffed himself full, but Van outdid him. Ricolf watched the outlander with awe tinged by alarm. He said, "Dyaus, I'd forgotten how you put it away. You could eat a man out of his barony."

"There's a deal of me to keep fed," Van replied with dignity. "Would you pass me the pitcher of ale? Ah, thank you, you're very kind." He poured from the pitcher into a delicately carved rhyton, part of the great stock of southron goods Ricolf had laid on to impress the band of suitors for Elise's hand. Elise was gone. The drinking horns, the even more elaborately carved bathtub, and other such things remained, and probably lacerated Ricolf's spirit whenever he saw or used them.

Van poured the horn of ale down his throat, hardly seeming to swallow. He filled it again, drained it with the same ease. By the look Ricolf gave him, the older man expected him to slide under the table at any moment. Instead, he got up and spoke softly to one of the young women who'd fetched food. Gerin listened to her giggle and was not surprised when, a little later, she and the outlander went upstairs together.

The Fox wished he could have gone upstairs, too, even alone, but Ricolf's eyes held him. The white-haired baron said, "Your harvests must have been good in spite of everything, or you'd not be able to afford to keep him around."

"I don't begrudge him his appetites," Gerin answered. "Not any of them. The rest of his spirit is in proportion."

"As may be, as may be." But Van was not what Ricolf wanted to talk about, and Gerin knew it. Ricolf stared down at his own drinking horn for a while before he went on, "Well, Fox, what in the five hells happened?"

"With Duren, you mean? You've heard everything I know about that," Gerin answered. "Someone snatched the boy, and when I find out who he was, he'll be sorry for the day his father woke up with a stiff one in his breeches."

"Oh, no doubt." Ricolf drank, smacked his lips, brought his fist down onto the table. "You'll track the whoreson down and make him pay. You're bloody good at all that sort of thing. Prince of the North these days, are you? I'll not deny you've earned the title. You hold more land—or control it, which amounts to the same think—than anyone else in the northlands save maybe Aragis and one or two of the cursed Trokmoi, and you run it better, too."

"You're generous." The Fox also took a pull at his ale. He could feel it buzzing inside his head. Maybe that was what made him burst out, "I wish I were shut of the whole business, and just left to be what I'd like."

"So do we all," Ricolf said. "But you do it well, like it or no. Which brings me to what I'd truly learn: how was it you didn't do as well by Elise?"

Gerin wished he were drunk enough to fall asleep— or a good enough mime to pretend he was that drunk. But he wasn't, not either one—and he knew he owed Ricolf an answer. He drank some more, as much to give himself time to think as for any other reason. Ricolf waited, patient and stubbornly unmoving as a boulder.

"I suppose part of it was that her life at Fox Keep wasn't as different as she'd hoped from what she had here," Gerin said slowly. He snorted air out through his nose. Wherever Elise was now, she'd surely found a different life. Whether it was better was a different question altogether.

"Go on," Ricolf said.

"You know what the first flush of passion is like," Gerin said. "It masks everything bad or even boring about whomever it lights on. After a while, though, you can wake up and realize this isn't what you had in mind. I—suppose that's what Elise did."

"None of it your fault, eh?" Ricolf's rumbling baritone flung sarcasm as a catapult flung stones.

"I didn't say that," Gerin answered. "Looking back, I guess I took a lot for granted. I figured everything was all right because she didn't complain out loud—and I've always been one who doesn't necessarily expect things to be perfect all the time, so I didn't worry so much when they weren't. I think perhaps Elise did after we fell in love, and when things got rocky, they looked worse to her than maybe they really were. If I'd realized that sooner . . . oh, who knows what I'd have done?"

Ricolf chewed on that with the air of a man finding something on his plate other than what he'd expected. Now he drank and thought a while before he spoke: "I respect that knack you have, Fox, for looking at yourself and talking about yourself as if you were someone else. Not many can do it."

"For this I thank you," Gerin said.

"Don't." Ricolf held up a big-knuckled hand. "The trouble with you is, you don't know how to do anything *but* stand back from yourself, and from everybody around you. You talked about how my daughter might have felt after passion cooled, but what about you? Did you go back into that keep inside your head, the one you mostly live in?"

"You shame me," Gerin said quietly.

"Why? For asking a question?"

"No, because the answer is so likely to be yes, and you know it very well." If sarcasm had stung, truth cut like a knife, the more so for being unexpected.

Ricolf yawned. "I'm getting old to sit around drinking half the night," he said. "Come to that, I'm getting old for anything else, too. Only a handful of serfs on this holding who were born before I was. One winter not so far from now lung sickness will get me, or I'll fall over with an apoplexy. That wouldn't be too bad—quick, any-how."

"You're strong yet," Gerin said, alarmed for his host. Few men spoke so openly of death, lest a god be listen-ing. "If you do go out, you'll go fighting."

"That could happen, too," Ricolf said. "I'm not as fast nor as strong as I was, and there's plenty of fighting around. And what becomes of the holding then? I'd hoped to last long enough to pass it on to Duren, but now—"

"Aye, but now," Gerin echoed. If Ricolf died heirless, his vassal barons would brawl over the holding, just as Bevon's sons had been doing for so long further north. And Ricolf's neighbors would be drawn in, Aragis com-ing up from the south, the Trokmoi from the west per-haps biting off a chunk . . . and the Fox did not see how he could stand aloof. He even had a claim of sorts to the barony.

As if picking that from his head, Ricolf said, "Aye, a couple of my vassals might think well of you because you were wed to Elise. More of 'em, though, are likely to think less of you because she ran off. And if she ever came back here wed to a man with a fighting tail of his own—"

Gerin upended his drinking horn, poured the last draft down his throat. That thought, or rather night-mare, had crossed is mind, too, most often of nights when he was having trouble sleeping. He said, "I have no notion how likely that is, nor what I'd do if it happened.

A lot would depend on who and what the fellow was."

"On whether you thought you could use him, you mean." Ricolf spoke without rancor. He drained his own rhyton, then pushed to his feet. "I'm going up to bed. Do you want to come along, so I can show you the chamber I've set aside for you? The keep's not packed with suitors now; I don't have to give you one of the little rooms down here off the kitchens."

"I'll come," Gerin said, and rose, too. Ricolf carried a lamp as they went up the stairs. He didn't say anything. The Fox counted that something of a minor triumph. He'd been dreading this interview since the day Elise left him, and he seemed to have got through it.

Ricolf opened a door. As Gerin walked through it into the little bedchamber the lamplight revealed, the older man asked quietly, "Do you miss her?"

Another knife in the night. Gerin said, "Yes, now and then. Quite a lot, sometimes." He stepped into the room and shut the door before Ricolf could stab him with any more questions.

South of Ricolf's holding, the land grew debatable once more. Gerin and Van traveled in armor, the Fox keeping his bow ready to hand. The Elabon Way seemed all but deserted. That suited Gerin fine: the fewer people he saw, the fewer people who saw him. He knew too well how vulnerable the wagon was to a good-sized band of raiders.

The roads that ran into the Elabon Way from east and west were dirt tracks like the ones up in the Fox's holding. Pieces of the Elabon Way were just dirt here, too; peasants had prised up the paving stones for the houses, and maybe barons for their keeps, too. That hadn't been so the last time Gerin visited Ikos, five years before.

He said, "Taking stones from the roadway used to be a crime that would cost a man his head or put him up on a cross. A good law, if you ask me; roads are a land's lifeblood."

"No law left up here but what comes from the edge of a sword," Van said. "Most lands are like that, when you get down to it."

"South of the High Kirs, Elabon isn't, or wasn't," Gerin said. "Law counted for more than might there, for a lot of years. It was even true here for a while. No more, though. You're not wrong about that."

They rolled slowly past another connecting road. At the crossroads stood a granite boulder carved with pictures showing where the road led: a crude keep surrounded by farms and horses. "That's not the one we want, eh, Captain?" Van said.

"No. We're looking for an eye with wings—that's Biton's mark. We're not far enough south to come to it yet, I don't think. I hope it will still be there; some of the crossroads stones I thought I remembered from my last trip to the Sibyl aren't here any more."

"You were paying attention to stones?" Van shook his head in disbelief. "Far as I could see, you were so busy panting over Elise, you didn't have eyes for anything else."

"Thank you, my friend. I needed that just now, I truly did," Gerin said. The visit with Ricolf had left him glum enough. If Van was going to rub salt in the wounds, they'd sting even worse.

But Van, perhaps mercifully, kept quiet after that. Like Gerin's, his eyes went back and forth, back and forth. Every time the wagon went by a clump of bushes or some elm saplings growing closer to the road than they should have, he shifted the reins to his left hand so he could grab his spear in a hurry if he needed it.

The Fox soon became certain some crossroads stones

were missing: he and Van rolled past a hollow in the ground that showed where one had recently been removed—so recently the grass hadn't filled in all the bare dirt. "Someone's losing trade on account of that," he said sadly. "I wonder if he even knows."

About halfway between noon and sunset, Gerin spied the winged eye he sought. "I'd have guessed it'd be there," Van said. "You steal it, you're fooling with a god, and what man with a dram of sense does that?"

"How many men have sense?" Gerin returned, which made his comrade grunt. He added, "Not only that, how many are wise enough to realize they're stealing from Biton and not just from some petty lordlet?"

"They don't know beforehand, they'll find out pretty soon," Van said, which was likely enough to be true that Gerin had to nod. The farseeing god looked after what was his.

The wagon swung east down the road that led to the Sibyl and her fane. Gerin remembered the lands away from the Elabon Way as poorer than the baronies along the main north-south route. They didn't seem so now. That wasn't because they'd grown richer. Rather, the holdings along the chief highway had suffered more from the Trokmoi and from the nobles' squabbles among themselves.

When Elabon conquered and held the northlands, the road that bore the Empire's name had also been one of the chief routes along which colonists had settled. Farther from the Elabon Way, the folk native to the land were more in evidence. They were dark like Elabonians, but slimmer and more angular, their faces full of forehead and cheekbones.

Old customs lingered away from the highway, too. Lords' castles grew scarce; most of the peasant villages held freeholders, men who owed no part of their crop to a baron. Gerin wondered how they'd fared when Trokmê raiders swooped down on them: they had no lords to ride to their defense, either.

The freeholders measured him and Van with their eyes when the travelers paused in a village to buy a hen before evening caught them. "You're for the Sibyl, then?" asked the man who sold it to them. His Elabonian had a curious flavor to it, not quite an accent, but old-fashioned, as if currents of speech had swept up the Elabon Way, too, but never reached this little hamlet.

"That we are," Gerin answered.

"You've rich gear," the peasant observed. "Be you nobles?"

Van spoke first: "Me, I'm just a warrior. Anyone who tries taking this corselet off my back will find out what kind of warrior I am, and won't be happier for knowing, either."

"I can take care of myself, too," Gerin said. Peasants without lords had to defend themselves, which meant they needed weapons and armor. Robbing people who already had them seemed a likely way to acquire such.

If that was in the peasant's mind, he didn't let on (*but then, he wouldn't*, Gerin thought). He said, "Aye, the both of you have that look. Go on, then, and the gods watch over you through the night."

As soon as they were out of earshot, Gerin spoke to Van, who was driving: "Put as much space between that village and us as you can. If you find a side road just before sunset, go up it or down it a ways. We'll want to camp where we can hide our nightfire."

"Right you are," Van said. "I'd have done the same thing without your saying a word, mind, but I'm glad you have the same thoughts in mind as I do. On your watch, sleep with your bow, your sword, and your shield and helm where you can grab them in a hurry."

"If I thought I could, I'd sleep in armor tonight," the Fox said. Van grunted out a short burst of laughter and nodded.

They traveled until the ghosts began to wail in their ears. Then, setting his jaw, Gerin sacrificed the hen to calm the spirits. A boulder shielded the light of the fire from the little track down which they traveled to get off the main road to Ikos.

Gerin had the first watch. Nothos and Tiwaz stood close together, low in the east at sunset: both were approaching full, though swift-moving Tiwaz would reach it a couple of days sooner than Nothos. Math would not rise until almost halfway through his watch, and Van alone could commune with Elleb, for the ruddy moon would stay below the horizon till after midnight.

The Fox moved as far away from the fire and the blood-filled trench near it as the ghosts would allow: he wanted to be sure he could spot trouble coming down the road from the village where he'd bought the chicken. His bow was strung, his quiver on his back and ready for him to reach over his shoulder and pull out a bronze-tipped shaft.

Sure enough, just about the time when golden Math began peeping through the leaves of the trees, he heard men coming along the road from the west. They weren't trying very hard to keep quiet; they chattered among themselves as they ambled eastward.

They all carried torches, he saw when they came to the crossroads. Even so, the ghosts bothered them. One said, "This havering is fair to drive me mad. An we don't find them soon, I'm for my hut and my wife."

"Ah, but will she be for you in the middle of the night?" another asked. The lot of them laughed. They paused at the narrow track down which Gerin and Van had gone. A couple of them peered toward the Fox. He crouched lower behind the bush that concealed him, hoping the light of three moons would not betray him to the peasants. Maybe their own torchlight left them nightblind, for they did not spy him. After some muttered discussion, they kept heading east down the main road.

Perhaps half an hour later, they came straggling back. Now their torches were guttering toward extinction, and they hurried on toward their village. "Mayhap 'tis as well we found the whoresons not," one of them said; Gerin recognized the voice of the fellow who'd sold him the hen. "They'd have slain some or ever we overcame them."

"We need arms," somebody answered.

"Belike, but we need men to wield them, too," the hen-seller replied. "You were in the fields, and saw them not: a brace of proper rogues, ready for aught. We'd have given the ghosts our own blood had we broiled ourselves with them, I tell you."

As the peasants withdrew, the argument got too low-voiced for Gerin to follow. The peasant who'd sold him the chicken was right; he and Van would have sold their lives dear. Even so, he was nothing but glad the farmers or robbers or whatever they reckoned themselves to be hadn't found him and his comrade. No matter how dearly you sold your life, you could never buy it back.

The Fox drew back down the path toward his camp. He didn't think the locals would come out again, and he proved right. When Math had traveled a little more than halfway from the horizon to the meridian, he woke Van and told him what had passed.

"Expected as much," the outlander answered, setting his crimson-crested helm on his head and adjusting the cheekpieces. "They had that look to 'em, so they did. Not likely they'll be back, not so late in the night."

"No." Gerin got out of armor as Van donned it. "Wouldn't do to count on that, though."

"Hardly." Van's rumbling chuckle had next to no breath behind it. "Tell you something else, Captain: on the way home, we make sure we roll through this place around noontime, so we're none too close to it the night before or the night after."

"Can't argue with you." Gerin yawned enormously. "Haven't the wit to argue with anything right now. I just want to sleep. If I get killed while you're on watch, I'll never forgive you."

"Nor have the chance, either," Van said, chuckling again. Gerin crawled under the blanket, conceding him the last word.

He awoke unmurdered the next morning to the savory smell of toasting sausage. Van had built the fire up from embers and was improvising breakfast. The flames sputtered and hissed as grease dripped down into them. Gerin accepted a sharp stick with a length of hard sausage impaled on it, burned the roof of his mouth when he tried to take a bite while it was still too hot to eat, swore, and then did manage to get the meat down.

Van finished before he did, and harnessed the horses while he was getting into his cuirass and greaves. A jay perched on a branch of a spruce seedling screeched at the outlander all the while. He pointed at it. "You'd best be quiet—some lands I've been through, the folk reckon songbirds good eating." As if it understood him, the jay shut up.

"Elabonians eat songbirds now and again," Gerin said. "We catch 'em with nets, usually, not with bow and arrow."

"Aye, that makes sense," Van said. "They're so small and swift, you'd need to be a dead shot to hit 'em, and you'd waste a slew of arrows." He fastened a last strap. "Come along, Captain. Let's be off."

The forest deepened and took on a new aspect as they rolled on toward Ikos. Perhaps, Gerin thought, taking

on an old aspect was a better way of describing it.
Elabonian traders and explorers, back in the days before
Ros the Fierce brought the northlands under imperial
control, described them as almost unbroken forest from
the High Kirs to the Niffet and all the way west to the
Orynian Ocean.

Around the Sibyl's shrine at Ikos, that ancient forest
survived undisturbed. Some of the gnarled oaks and deep
green pines might have been saplings when the men
round what would become the City of Elabon were still
unlettered barbarians. Some of them might have been
saplings before the Kizzuwatnans in their river valleys
scratched the world's first letters onto clay tablets and
set them in an oven to bake.

Maybe the shaggy beards of moss hanging from many
of those trees helped muffle sound, or maybe some lingering power clung to the forest: some of the trees that
grew there, at any rate, Gerin had never seen outside
these confines. Whatever the reason, the woods were
eerily still. Even the squeak and rattle of the wagon's
ungreased axles seemed diminished. Far above the roadway, branches from either side interlaced, cutting off a
good part of the daylight and turning the rest cool and
green and shifting.

"If we could drive the wagon under the sea, it might
look like this," Gerin said.

"Maybe so." Van kept craning his neck, looking up,
down, all around. "I don't like this place—and I don't
think it likes people, either. It wishes we weren't here,
and so do I."

"I'd argue with you, if only I thought you were wrong."
Gerin kept not quite hearing things pacing alongside the
road as if tracking the wagon, not quite seeing them no
matter how quickly he turned his head toward what he
hadn't quite heard.

Van mused, "I wonder what would happen if, come a dry summer, some lord sent his peasants in here with axes and torches."

Gerin wondered if the forest and the things that dwelt in it understood Elabonian. He feared they did, for all at once the cover of branches over the road grew thicker and lower, while most of those branches suddenly seemed full of thorns. The very roadway narrowed, with trees—many of them full of thorns, too—crowding close, as if ready to reach out and seize the intruders. Once or twice he was sure he saw eyes staring balefully at him from behind the leaves, but he never got a glimpse of the creatures to which they were attached.

Nervously, he said, "You were just joking there, weren't you, my friend?"

"What? Oh, aye." Van was more than bold enough against any human foe, but how could even the boldest man fight a forest? Eyeing the growing number of encroaching branches, he went on, "All this lovely greenery? In truth, it would be a dreadful shame to peel even one leaf off its stem."

For a long moment, nothing happened. But just when Gerin was about to grab for his sword and start slashing away at the aroused trees and bushes, everything returned to the way it had been. The sun played through breaks in the overhead canopy, the road widened out again, and the trees went back to being just trees. Whatever had been moving along with the wagon went away, or at least became altogether silent.

"Whew!" Van muttered under his breath. "Place must have decided I was just joking after all—which I was, of course." He added that last in a much louder voice.

"Of course you were," Gerin agreed heartily. Then his voice fell: "All the same, we'll spend tonight in one of the lodgings round Ikos, not in this wood. That will further prove we mean no harm to the powers here."

Van's eyes met his. The two men shared one thought: *It will also keep anything in the forest that's still angry from coming down on us.* The words hung unspoken in the air. Gerin didn't want to give any of those possibly angry things ideas they didn't have already.

The sun was low in the west behind Gerin and Van when they topped a rise and looked down into the valley wherein nested Biton's gleaming white marble shrine and, leading down from within it, the rift in the earth that led to the Sibyl's chamber.

"Last time we came this way, we camped in the woods," Van said. "As you say, though, better to pay the scot at one of the inns down there tonight." A little town had grown up in front of the Sibyl's shrine, catering to those who came to it seeking oracular guidance.

"Aye, you're right." Gerin sighed. He didn't like silver going without good cause. Come to that, he wasn't over-fond of paying silver even with good cause. But he did not want to spend a night in these uncanny woods; they were liable to shelter worse things than ghosts. He twitched the reins and urged the horses forward.

When he'd visited Ikos before, the town in front of the shrine had been packed with Elabonians from both the northlands and south of the High Kirs, Sithonians, Kizzuwatnans, Trokmoi, Shanda nomads, and other folk as well. A big reason Gerin had preferred to camp in the woods then was that all the inns had bulged at the seams.

Now, as the wagon rolled into town, he found the dirt streets all but empty. Several of the inns had closed; a couple of them, by their dilapidated look, had been empty for years. The innkeepers who survived all rushed from their establishments and fell on him and Van with glad cries. Gerin hardly needed to haggle with them; they bid against one another until he got his lodging, supper, and a promise of breakfast for half what he'd expected to pay.

The taproom in the inn was all but deserted. Apart from Gerin and Van, only a couple of locals sat at the tables, drinking ale and telling stories they'd probably all heard a thousand times. The innkeeper brought ale and drinking jacks to his new guests. "And what would your pleasure for supper be?" he asked, bowing as low as if the Fox had been Hildor III, Emperor of Elabon.

"Not chicken," he and Van said, much as they had at Ricolf's.

"You've traveled some way, then, and spent nights in the open." The innkeeper pursed his lips to show he sympathized. "I killed a young pig this afternoon. I was going to smoke and salt down the flesh, but I do some lovely chops flavored with basil and thyme and wild mushrooms. It's a splendid dish, if I say so myself, and one I don't have the chance to prepare as often as I'd like these days. True, the cooking of it takes a while, but where have you gentlemen to go in the meantime?"

Gerin and Van looked at each other. They nodded. The Fox said, "Your trade has fallen off since the Trokmoi swarmed over the Niffet and the Empire shut the last passage up from the south."

"Good my sir, you have no idea." The innkeeper rolled his eyes. "Sometimes I think all of us left here make our living by taking in one another's washing. The shrine has fallen on hard times, that it has, and every one of us with it."

"Does the old Sibyl still live?" Gerin asked. "I'd not expected to find her breathing when I was last here five years ago. Now nothing would surprise me."

"No, Biton took her for his own last year," the

innkeeper answered. "The god speaks through a younger woman now. 'Tis not that the quality of oracle has suffered that's cost us trade" —he made haste to reassure the Fox— "only that fewer folk now find their way hither."

"I understand." Gerin drained his jack dry. The innkeeper hastened to refill it. Gerin drank again, sighed with something close to contentment. "Good to relax here, away from the ghosts, away from robbers in the night, with only the worries that brought me here to carry on my shoulders."

"That my humble establishment is able to ease your burdens does my heart good," the innkeeper declared.

"To say nothing of your coin hoard," Gerin said dryly.

The innkeeper turned his head to one side and coughed, as if mention of money embarrassed him. Then he paused, plainly listening over again to what Gerin had said a moment before. "Robbers in the night, good my sir? So men begin to hold the ghosts at bay and the gods in contempt?"

"Men on the very road that leads here," the Fox said, and told of the free peasants who'd looked to arm themselves at his and Van's expense. "They didn't come on us, for which Dyaus be praised—and Biton, too, for watching over us—but they weren't out there in the darkness just for the journey. I heard them speak; I know what I'm talking about."

"Sometimes I think the whole world is guttering down toward darkness, like a candle on the last of its tallow," the innkeeper said sadly. "Even my dreams these days are full of monsters and pallid things from the underground darkness. At night in my bed I see them spreading over the land, and poor feeble men powerless to do aught against them."

Gerin started to nod: here was another man who shared his gloomy view of the world. Then he gave the innkeeper a sharp look. "I too have had dreams like that," he said.

"And I," Van put in. "I tell you the truth—I mislike the omen."

"Maybe the Sibyl will shed light on it." Gerin did his best to sound hopeful, but feared his best was none too good.

IV

The horses were curried till their coats gleamed and hitched to the wagon waiting when Gerin went out to the stables to reclaim them. He tipped the groom who'd cared for them, saying, "You did more here than was required of you."

"Lord, you're generous beyond my deserts," the fellow answered, but Gerin noticed he did not decline the proffered coin.

Every other time Gerin had visited the Sibyl's shrine, the area around the fenced forecourt had been packed with wagons, chariots, and men afoot, and with all the visitors passionately eager to put their questions to Biton's oracle as soon as possible. The only way to get in quickly—sometimes the only way to get in at all—was to pay off one of the god's eunuch priests.

The Fox had prepared himself for that eventuality. At his belt swung two medium-heavy pouches, one an offering for the temple, the other (though the word would not be used in public) a bribe for the priest who would conduct him to the shrine.

He soon discovered he was going to save himself some money. When he and Van came to the gate in the marble outwall, only three or four parties waited ahead of them. Just a few more rolled up behind the wagon. Instead of shouting, cursing chaos, the oracle-seekers formed a single neat line.

Van recognized what that meant, too. "Let's see the priests try to squeeze anything past their due out of us today," he said, laughing.

To their credit, the priests did not try. They took the suppliants one group at a time, leading away their animals to be seen to while they consulted the Sibyl. Everything ran as smoothly as the turning spokes of a chariot wheel. Gerin wished all his visits had gone so well. He also wished this particular visit hadn't been necessary.

A plump, beardless fellow in a robe of glittering cloth of gold approached the wagon. Bowing to Gerin and Van, he said, "Gentles, you may call me Kinifor. I shall conduct you to the Sibyl and escort you from her chamber once the god has spoken through her." His voice was pleasant, almost sweet, not a man's voice but not a woman's, either.

Thinking of the mutilation eunuchs suffered, Gerin always felt edgy around them. Because the mutilation was not their fault, he always did his best to conceal those feelings. He swung a plump leather sack into Kinifor's equally plump hand. "This is to help defray the cost of maintaining your holy shrine."

The eunuch priest hefted the bag, not only to gauge its weight but to listen for the sweet jingle of silver. "You are generous," he said, and seemed well enough pleased even without any special payment straight to him; Gerin wondered if the temple would see all the money in the leather sack. The priest went on, "Descend, if you will, and accompany me to the temple."

As Gerin and Van got down from the wagon, another priest, this one in a plainer robe, came over and led the horses away. The travelers followed Kinifor through the gate and into the fenced-off temenos surrounding the shrine. The first thing the Fox saw was a naked corpse prominently displayed just inside the gateway; hideous lesions covered the body. Gerin jerked a thumb at it. "Another would-be temple robber?"

"Just so." Kinifor gave him a curious look. "Am I to infer from your lack of surprise that you have seen others Biton smote for their evil presumption?"

"Another, anyhow," Gerin answered. "With the chaos that's fallen on the northlands since the last time I was here, though, I wondered if your god was up to the job of protecting the treasures here from everyone who'd like to get his hands on them."

"This is Biton's precinct on earth," Kinifor said in shocked tones. "If he is not potent here, where will his strength be made manifest?"

Perhaps nowhere, Gerin thought. When the Elabonians conquered the northlands, they'd taken Biton into their own pantheon, styling him a son of Dyaus. But the Trokmoi brought their own gods with them, and seemed to care little for those already native to the land. If they prevailed, Biton might fail for lack of worshipers.

Van cast an appraising eye on the treasures lavishly displayed in the courtyard before the temple: the statues of gold and ivory, others of marble painted into the semblance of life or of greening bronze, the cauldrons and mixing bowls set on golden tripods, the piled ingots that reflected the sun's rays in buttery brilliance.

The outlander whistled softly. "I wondered if I misremembered from last time I was here, but no: there's a great pile of stuff about for your god to watch over, priest."

"The farseeing one has protected it well thus far." One of Kinifor's hands shaped a gesture of blessing. "Long may he continue to do so."

The white marble temple that housed the entrance to the Sibyl's cave was in a mixed Sithonian-Elabonian style, a gift of Oren the Builder to win the favor of Biton's priesthood—and the god himself—not long after the northlands came under Elabonian sway. The splendid fane, elegantly plain outside and richly decorated within, was surely magnificent enough to have succeeded in its purpose.

Seemingly out of place within all that gleaming stone, polished wood, and precious metal was the cult image of Biton, which stood close by the fissure in the earth that led down to the cavern wherein the Sibyl prophesied. The temple was a monument to Elabonian civilization at its best, to everything Gerin labored to preserve in the northlands. The cult image was . . . something else.

As he had the last time he visited the shrine, the Fox tried to imagine how old the square column of black basalt was. As he had then, he failed. This was no realistic image of the god, carved with loving care by a Sithonian master sculptor or some Elabonian artist who had studied for years in Kortys. The only suggestions of features the column bore were crudely carved eyes and a jutting phallus. Yet somehow, perhaps because of the aura of immeasurable antiquity that clung to it, the cult image carried as much impact as any polished product of the stonecutter's art.

"Seat yourselves, gentles," Kinifor said, waving to the rows of pews in front of the basalt column, "and pray that the lord Biton's sight reaches to the heart of your troubles, whatever they may be."

The eunuch sat beside Gerin, bowed his head, and murmured supplications to his god. The Fox also prayed, though unsure how much attention Biton paid to petitioners' requests. Some gods, like Mavrix, seemed to listen to every whisper addressed to them, even if they did not always grant requests. Others, such as Dyaus the father of all, were more distant. He didn't know where in that range Biton fell, but took no chances, either.

As soon as he finished his prayer, he glanced up at the cult image. Just for a moment, he thought he saw brown eyes staring back at him in place of the almost unrecognizable scratches on the basalt. He shivered a little; he'd had that same odd impression on his last visit to the shrine. Biton's power might not reach far, but it was strong here at its heart.

Puffing a little, a plump eunuch priest climbed up out of the fissure in the earth that led down to the Sibyl's chamber. Behind him came a grizzled Elabonian with a thoughtful expression on his face. With a nod to Gerin, he strode out of the temple and away to reclaim his team and vehicle.

Kinifor said, "Nothing now prevents us from seeking the wisdom Biton imparts through his sacred Sibyl. If you will please to follow me, stepping carefully as you descend—"

On his previous visit, Gerin had had to fight for his life against Trokmoi dissatisfied with what they heard from the oracle. He looked down to see if bloodstains still remained in the cracks between the tesserae of the mosaic floor. He saw none, which pleased him.

Kinifor stepped into the cave mouth. Gerin followed. Darkness, illuminated only by torches not nearly close enough together, swallowed him. The air in the cave felt altogether different from the muggy heat he'd endured in the temple: it was damp but cool, with a constant breeze blowing in his face so that the atmosphere never turned stagnant.

Kinifor's shadow, his own, and Van's swooped and fluttered in the torchlight like demented birds. Flickering shadows picked out bits of rock crystal—or possibly even gems—embedded in the stone of the cave walls. One glint came red as blood. "Was that a ruby we just passed?" Gerin asked.

"It could be so," Kinifor answered. "Biton has guided us to many treasures underground."

"Is it your god or your greed?" Van asked. Kinifor spluttered indignantly. The outlander laughed at the priest's annoyance. Just then they came to a branch of the cave that had been sealed up with stout brickwork. "What about that? Didn't you have to wall it up because your prying roused things that would better have been left asleep?"

"Well, yes," Kinifor admitted reluctantly, "but that was long ago, when we were first learning the ways of this cave. The bricks say as much, if you know how to read them."

Gerin did. Instead of being flat on all sides, the bricks bulged on top, as if they were so many hard-baked loaves of bread. That style had come out of Kizzuwatna in ancient days, not long after men first gathered together in cities and learned to read and write and work bronze. He took a long look at those bricks. They couldn't possibly reach back so far in time . . . could they?

After that first long look came a second one. Loaf-shaped bricks had not held their popularity long in Kizzuwatna: they required more mortar to bind them together than those of more ordinary shape. Some of the mortar on these, after Biton only knew how many centuries, had begun to crack and fall away from the bricks; little chips lay on the stone floor of the cave.

The Fox pointed to them, frowning. "I don't remember your wall there falling apart the last time I came this way."

"I hadn't noticed that," Kinifor confessed. "Some evening, when no suppliants seek the Sibyl's advice, we shall have to send down a crew of masons to repair the ravages of time." His laugh was smooth and liquid, like the low notes of a flute. "If the barrier has sufficed to hold at bay whatever lies beyond it lo these many years, surely a few days one way or the other are of scant import."

"But—" Gerin held his tongue. The eunuch priest was bound to be right. And yet—this wasn't a slow accumulation of damage over many years. Unless he and Kinifor were both wrong, it had happened recently.

The rift wound deeper into the earth. Kinifor led Gerin and Van past more spell-warded walls. Several times the Fox saw more loose mortar on the ground. He would have taken oath it had not been there when he'd last gone down to the Sibyl's chamber, but forbore to speak of it again. Kinifor, plainly, did not intend to hear whatever he had to say.

The priest raised a hand for those who accompanied him to halt. He peered into the chamber that opened up ahead, then nodded. "Gentles, you may proceed. Do you seek privacy for your question to the Sibyl?"

Privacy would have cost Gerin an extra bribe. He shook his head. "No, you may hear it, and her answer, too. It's no great secret."

"As you say." Kinifor sounded sulky; most people who thought a question important enough to put to the Sibyl also thought it so important that no one other than Biton and his mouth on earth could be trusted with it. Gerin had been of that opinion on his latest visit. Now, though, he did not mind if the priest listened as he enquired about his son's fate.

Kinifor stepped aside to let the Fox and Van precede him into the Sibyl's underground chamber. As before, Gerin marveled at the throne on which she sat. It threw back the torchlight with glistening, nacreous highlights, as if carved from a single black pearl. Yet contemplating the oyster that could have birthed such a pearl sent his imagination reeling.

"It *is* a new Sibyl," Van murmured, very low.

Gerin nodded. Instead of the ancient, withered crone who'd occupied this chamber on all his previous journeys to Ikos, on the throne sat a pleasant-faced woman of perhaps twenty-five in a simple white linen dress that fastened over her left shoulder and reached halfway between her knees and ankles. She nodded politely, first to Kinifor, then to those who would question her.

But when she spoke, she might have been the old Sibyl reborn. "Step forward, lads," she said to Gerin and Van. Her voice was a musical contralto, but it held ancient authority. Though the Fox and the outlander were both older than she, they were not merely lads but babes when measured against the divine power she represented. Gerin obeyed her without hesitation.

Coming to the crone on that seat had seemed natural to him. Finding a new, young Sibyl there made him think for the first time of the life she led. Biton's mouth on earth was pledged to lifelong celibacy: indeed, pledged never even to touch a whole man. Here far below the ground she would stay, day upon day, the god taking possession of her again and again as she prophesied, her only company even when above the earth (he assumed—he hoped— she was allowed out of the chamber when no more suppliants came) eunuchs and perhaps serving women. Thus she would live out however many years she had.

He shivered. It struck him more as divine punishment than reward.

"What would you learn from my master Biton?" the Sibyl asked.

Gerin had thought about how to ask that question all the way south from Fox Keep. If the god got an ambiguous query, the questioner was liable to get an ambiguous reply; indeed, Biton was famous for finding ambiguity even where the questioner thought none lurking. Taking a deep breath, the Fox asked, "Is my son alive and well, and, if he is, when and where shall we be reunited?"

"That strikes me as being two questions," Kinifor said disapprovingly.

"Let the god judge," Gerin answered, to which the priest gave a grudging nod.

Biton evidently reckoned the question acceptable. The mantic fit came over the young Sibyl, harder than it had with the old. Her eyes rolled up in her head. She thrashed about on the throne, careless of her own modesty. And when she spoke, the voice that came from her throat was not her own, but the same powerful baritone her predecessor had used—Biton's voice:

> *The Sibyl's doom we speak of now*
> *(And worry less about the child):*
> *To flee Ikos, midst fearful row*
> *(Duren's fate may well be mild).*
> *All ends, among which is the vow*
> *Pledged by an oracle defiled.*

The god left his mouth on earth as abruptly as his spirit had filled her. She slumped against an arm of the throne in a dead faint.

Kinifor said, "Gentles, the lord Biton has spoken. You must now leave this chamber, that the Sibyl may recover and ready herself for those who come here next."

"But the Sibyl—or Biton, if you'd rather—said next to nothing about the question I asked," Gerin protested. "Most of that verse had more to do with you, by the sound of it, than with me."

"That is neither here nor there," Kinifor said. "The god speaks as he will, not as any man expects. Who are you, mortal, to question his majesty and knowledge?"

To that Gerin had no answer, only frustration that he had not learned more from the query over which he'd pondered so hard on the journey down from his keep.

He took what coals of comfort he could: Biton had urged him not to worry. But what if that was because Duren was already dead, and so beyond worry? Would the god have mentioned him by name if he was dead, especially when Gerin had not named him? Who could say what a god would do? Where the Fox had done his best to prevent ambiguity, it had found him out. Dismayed, he turned to go.

Van pointed to the Sibyl, who remained unconscious. "Should the lass not have come back to herself by now? You'd not bring new folk down here if they were to find her nearer dead than alive."

Kinifor opened his mouth, perhaps to say something reassuring. But before he did, he too took another look at the Sibyl. A frown crinkled the unnaturally smooth skin of his face. "This is—unusual," he admitted. "She should be awake and, if a priest is here with her, asking what the god spoke through her lips."

Gerin started to take a step toward her, then remembered the conditions under which she served Biton: any touch from him, no matter how well-meaning, brought defilement with it. He wondered if that was what the last line of her prophecy meant, then stopped worrying about prophecy while she sprawled unconscious. He asked Kinifor, "Do you want to tend to her while we make our own way back up to the temple?"

He might as well have suggested burning down the fane. "That cannot be!" the eunuch priest gasped. "For one thing, you might well lose your way, take a wrong turning, and never be seen again. For another, some turns lead to treasures not displayed above ground. No one not connected with the cult of Biton may turn his eyes upon them."

"I know what Biton does to those who would be thieves," Gerin protested, but Kinifor shook his head so vehemently that his plump jowls wobbled.

Van, as usual, spoke to the point: "Well, what about the wench, then?"

Kinifor went over to her, put a hand in front of her nose and mouth to make sure she was breathing, felt for her pulse. When he straightened, his face held relief as well as worry. "I do not believe she will perish in the next moments. Let me guide you back to the surface of the earth, after which she shall, of course, be properly seen to."

"Honh!" Van said. "Seems to me you care more about Biton's gold and gauds than about his Sibyl."

Kinifor answered that with an injured silence which suggested to Gerin that his friend had hit the target dead center. But this was the priest's domain, not his, so he let Kinifor lead him out of the Sibyl's chamber and back up the length of the cave to Biton's temple. Still grumbling and looking back over his shoulder, Van reluctantly followed.

To give Kinifor his due, he hurried along the stony way, pushing his corpulent frame till he panted like a dog after a long run. Surprisingly soon, light not from torches showed ahead, though the priest's body almost obliterated it as he climbed out of the cave mouth. Gerin came right after him, blinking until his eyes grew used to daylight once more.

"About time," rasped the tough-looking fellow who waited impatiently for his turn at the oracle. "Take me down there, priest, and no more nonsense."

"I fear I cannot, sir," Kinifor answered. "The Sibyl seems to have suffered an indisposition, and will not be able to reply to questioners at least for some little while."

That brought exclamations of dismay from the other eunuchs within earshot. They hurried to Kinifor to find out what had happened. He quickly explained. Two of

Biton's servitors hurried down into the cave mouth. "If she has not yet returned to herself, we shall bring her out," one of them said as he disappeared.

The Elabonian warrior whose question was delayed shouted, "This is an outrage!" When no one paid any attention to him, he shouted viler things than that. His face turned the color of maple leaves in fall.

Gerin looked down his long, straight nose at the man. "Do you know what you remind me of, sirrah?" he said coldly. "You remind me of my four-year-old son when he pitches a fit because I tell him he can't have any honied blueberries till after supper."

"Who in the five hells do you think you are, to take that tone with me?" the fellow demanded, setting his right hand on the hilt of his sword.

"I'm Gerin the Fox, Prince of the North," Gerin said, matching the gesture with his left hand. "You should be thankful I don't know your name, or want to."

The red-faced man scowled but did not back down. Gerin wondered if he would have to fight in Biton's shrine for the second time in two visits. The temple complex had guards, but most of them were outside the fane keeping an eye on the treasures displayed in the courtyard and on any visitors who, careless of Biton's curse, might develop itchy fingers.

Then, from the entrance to the shrine, someone called, "Any man who draws his blade on Gerin the Fox, especially with Van of the Strong Arm beside him, is a fool. Of course, you've been acting like a fool, fellow, so that may account for it."

The angry Elabonian whirled. "And what do you know about it, you interfering old polecat's twat?" he snarled, apparently not caring how many enemies he made.

The newcomer strode toward him. He was a tall, lean man of perhaps forty, with a forward-thrusting face, a proud beak of a nose, and dark, chilly eyes that put Gerin in mind of a hunting hawk's. He said, "I'd be the fool if I didn't make it my business to learn all I could of Gerin the Fox. I am Grand Duke Aragis, also called the Archer."

The angry color drained from the face of the impatient warrior as he realized he'd caught himself between the two strongest men in the northlands. With a last muttered curse, he stomped out of the temple, though he took care to step wide around Aragis.

"Well met," Gerin said. He and Aragis were rivals, but not open enemies.

"Well met," Aragis answered. He turned his intent gaze on the Fox. "I should have thought I might find you here. After word of your son, are you?"

"Aye," Gerin said stonily. "And you?"

"On business of my own," Aragis said.

"Which is none of *my* business," Gerin suggested. Aragis nodded—once; he was not a man given to excess. Gerin said, "Have it as you wish. Whatever your question is, you may not be able to put it to the Sibyl, any more than that big-mouthed ruffian was."

"Why not?" Aragis asked suspiciously. The idea that Gerin should know something he didn't seemed to offend him.

Before the Fox could answer, the two priests who had gone down to see how the Sibyl fared came back up into the temple. They carried her between them, her face white and her arms dangling limply toward the ground. "Does she live?" Gerin called to them in some alarm.

"Good sir, she does," one of the eunuchs answered. "But since her senses do not return to her, we'll take her to her own dwelling" —he nodded his head to show in which direction from the shrine that lay— "and minister to her there. At the very least, she can rest more comfortably in her bed than in the underground chamber.

Surely, though, the lord Biton will aid in her recovery."
That would have come out better had it sounded more
like assertion and less like prayer.

"Why should the lord Biton care?" Van asked, blunt
as always. "Down below there, he sounded like he was
getting out of the prophecy game."

"You rave, good sir, and tread the edge of blasphemy
as well," the priest answered. He looked for support to
Kinifor, who had heard the Sibyl's last prophecy.

The eunuch who had accompanied Gerin and Van
made a strange snuffling sound, almost one a horse would
produce, as he blew air out through his lips. Slowly, he
said, "The verses may lend themselves to the interpreta-
tion proposed. Other interpretations, however, must be
more probable."

Even such a halfhearted admission was enough to
shock the other two priests. Clucking to themselves, they
carried the unconscious Sibyl away.

Kinifor said, "I begin to fear there will be no further
communing with the lord Biton this day. Perhaps everyone here would be well advised to return to his inn, there
to await the Sibyl's return to health. We shall send word
directly that occurs, and shall seek no further fee for
your inquiries."

"You'd better not." Aragis put as much menace into
three words as Gerin had ever heard. "And if the wench
ups and dies, I expect my silver back."

The eunuch twisted his hand in a gesture to turn aside
the evil omen. "The lord Biton would not summon two
Sibyls to himself in such a short span of time," he said,
but his words, like the other priest's, lacked confidence.

People filed out of the shrine, muttering and grumbling to themselves. Kinifor went out to let those who
waited in the courtyard know they would be disappointed
in their hope for an oracular response. Their replies, like

those in the temple, ranged from curious to furious.

With rough humor, Aragis turned to Gerin. "What did you ask her, anyway, to put her in such a swivet? To marry you?"

Gerin growled down deep in his throat and took a step toward the Archer. Unlike the fellow who'd started to move on him, though, he mastered himself. "I ought to just tell you it's none of your cursed business," he said, "but since you already know why I'm here, what's the point? I asked after my son, as you've figured out for yourself."

"That's a bad business," Aragis answered. "The whoreson who did it may come to me, seeking advantage from it. By Dyaus, if he does, I'll run up a cross for him, and you'll have the boy back fast as horses can run. I swear it."

"If it happens so, I'll be in your debt," the Fox said. "I'd be lying if I told you the idea that you had something to do with it was never in my mind."

Aragis scowled. "Because we're the two biggest, we circle round each other like a couple of angry dogs—I don't trust you, either, as you know full well. But I did not have my hand in this, and I will not seek to profit from it, come what may. Would you, were it my lad?"

"I hope not," Gerin said. Aragis chewed on that, then slowly nodded. He looked sincere, but his face, as Gerin had already seen, showed what he willed it to, not necessarily what he felt. That was useful for a ruler, as Gerin knew—his own features were similarly schooled.

Van said, "All right, Archer, if you don't care to circle and watch and not trust, suppose you do tell us why you came up to Ikos, so long as it's not life or death for your holding that we know."

For a moment, Aragis was nonplussed. Gerin hadn't been sure he could be. Then his usual watchful expression returned as he considered the outlander's words. At last he said, "Fair enough, I suppose. I rode here because I've had bad dreams; I hoped—I hope still—the Sibyl could put meaning to them."

"What sort of dreams?" Gerin's curiosity was as dependable as the changing phases of the moons.

Aragis hesitated again, perhaps not caring to show a rival any weakness. But after another pause for thought, he murmured, "If I can't understand them, you bloody well won't, either." He raised his voice to answer the Fox: "They've been filled with horrid things, monsters, call them what you will, overrunning my lands—overrunning the rest of the northlands, too, for all I could tell." He grimaced and shook his head, as if talking about the visions made him see them again.

"I too have had this dream," Gerin said slowly.

"And I," Van agreed.

"And the innkeeper from whom we've taken rooms," Gerin said. "I did not like the omen when it was Van and I alone. Now with four—" He checked himself. "Four I know of, I should say—I like it even less."

"Wherever else we rub, Fox, I'll not argue with you there." Aragis ran a hand down to the point of his graying beard. "Did the Sibyl say anything to you of this before she had her fit? What verse did she speak?"

"Why don't you ask him how big his is, as long as you're snooping?" Van said.

Like most men, Aragis seemed a stripling when set against the burly outlander. But he had no retreat in him. He reached for the sword that hung on his belt. Before Van could grab any of the lethal hardware he carried, Gerin held up a hand. "Hold, both of you," he said. "Aragis, you know what the question was. The answer has nothing to do with you, so I can give it without fear you'll gain from it." He repeated the oracular response.

Aragis listened intently, still rubbing his chin and now and then plucking at his beard. When Gerin was done, the other noble gave a grudging nod. "Aye, that's nought to do with me, and might even hold good news about Duren mixed in there. But what of the rest? I've never heard—or heard of—a reply so filled with doom. No wonder the Sibyl wouldn't wake up after she delivered it."

"I wonder if it's got summat to do with the dreams we've had," Van said.

Aragis and Gerin both looked at him. As if animated by a single will, their hands formed the same sign to turn away evil. "Off with you, omen," Aragis exclaimed. The Fox nodded vehemently.

Van said, "It's not much of an omen talk and finger-twitching'll turn aside."

"The little vole will turn and bite in the eagle's claws," Gerin answered. "One time in a thousand, or a thousand thousand, he'll draw blood and make the bird drop him. With omens, you never know which ones you can shift, so you try to shift them all."

Now it was Van's turn to look thoughtful. "Might be something to that, I suppose. I know what I'd sooner do, though, now that the Sibyl's not going to give you what you're after."

"And what's that?" Gerin asked, though he thought he knew the answer.

Sure enough, Van said, "Go back to the inn and hoist enough beakers of ale that we don't care about omens or Sibyls or anything else."

"If there's nothing for us here, we should head straight off to Fox Keep," Gerin said, but he sounded doubtful even to himself.

Van looked at the sun. "You want to start up the road just a bit before noon, so we can camp for the night in the middle of the haunted wood? Begging your pardon, Captain, that's the daftest thought you've had in a good-ish while."

Gerin prided himself on his ability to admit mistakes. "You're right, it is. And if we're stuck with spending another day at the inn, how better to pass it than with a carouse?"

He looked doubtfully at Aragis. Polite talk with his main rival in the northlands was one thing, a day of drinking with him something else again. Aragis studied him with the same question on his face. The Fox realized that, while he and the self-styled grand duke were very different men, their station gave them common concerns. That was disconcerting; he hadn't tried mentally putting himself in Aragis' shoes before.

After a moment of awkward silence, the Archer resolved the problem, saying, "The way back to my hold-ing is straight enough, and I'll be free of the woods well before sunset if I start now, so I think I'll head south."

He stuck out his hand. Gerin clasped it. "Whatever comes, I hope we get through it without trying to carve each other's livers," he said. "The only one who'd gain from that is Adiatunnus."

Aragis' eyes grew hawk-watchful again. "I hear he sent to you. You were worried whether his men stole your boy. You're telling me you didn't join forces with him."

"That's just what I'm telling you," Gerin answered. "The five hells will vomit forth the damned before I join hands with a Trokmê."

He waited for Aragis to say something like that. Aragis didn't. He only nodded to show he'd heard, then walked off to reclaim the chariot or wagon in which he'd come to Ikos.

"Cold fish," Van said judiciously. "Not a man who makes an easy enemy, though, or I miss my guess."

"You don't," the Fox answered. "We've met only a couple of times before, so I don't have his full measure as a man, but what he's done in building up his holding speaks for itself. And you heard what he had done after his men hunted down a longtooth that had been taking cattle from one of his villages?"

"No, somehow I missed that one," Van said. "Tell me."

"He had an extra strong cross raised, and nailed and lashed the beast's carcass to it as a warning to others of its kind—and, more to the point, as a warning to any men who might have thought about trifling with him."

"Mm. It'd make me think twice, I expect," Van said. "Well, let's amble after him and get back our animals."

The beasts and the vehicles they drew waited outside the walled courtyard around the temple. By luck, the low-ranking priest who'd taken the wagon by the gate stood close to it now; that meant Gerin didn't have to convince someone else he wasn't absconding with the property of another. As he climbed in, he pointed to a thatch-roofed wooden cottage not far away. "Is that where the Sibyl lives when she's not prophesying?" he asked.

"So it is, good my sir," the priest answered. His smooth face held worry. "I saw her carried there not long since, and heard rumors and tales so strange I know not what to believe: even those who brought her seemed confused. Did the mantic trance take her for you?"

"It did. In fact, she lost her senses just afterwards, and did not get them back again as she usually does." Without repeating the oracular verse, Gerin told the priest what had happened in the underground chamber.

The corners of the eunuch's mouth drew down even further. "Biton grant she recover soon," he exclaimed. "Never has the good god seen fit to call two Sibyls to himself so quickly. The temple suffers great disruption while the search for a new maid to speak his words goes on."

"To say nothing of the fees you lose when the oracle is quiet," Gerin said, remembering sacks of silver he'd pressed into priests' pudgy palms.

But, in injured tones, the eunuch replied, "I did say nothing of those fees." Perhaps he was genuinely pious. Stranger things had happened, Gerin supposed. He twitched the reins, urging the horses back toward the inn.

The innkeeper and the head groom met him in front of it. "You'll honor my establishment with another night's custom?" the innkeeper asked eagerly, adding, "I trust all went well for you with the Sibyl? I gather there was some sort of commotion in the temple?" Like anyone else, he delighted in gossip.

"Not in the temple—under it," Van said. Gerin let him tell the tale this time. The outlander was a better storyteller than he, anyhow. When Gerin told what he knew, he did it baldly, laying out facts to speak for themselves. Van embellished and embroidered them, almost as if he were a minstrel.

When he was through, the innkeeper clapped his hands. Bowing, he said, "Good my sir, if ever you tire of the life you lead, which I take to be one of arms, you would be welcome to earn your bread and meat here at my inn, for surely the stories you spin would bring in enough new custom to make having you about a paying proposition."

"Thank you, sir, but I'm not quite ready yet to sit by the fire and tell yarns for my supper," Van said. "If you'll fetch Gerin and me a big jar of ale, though, that'd be a kindness worth remembering."

Seeking to be even more persuasive, Gerin let silver softly jingle. The innkeeper responded with alacrity. He shouted to his servants as Gerin and Van went inside and sat in the taproom. Grunting with effort, two men hauled a huge amphora up from the cellar. Right behind them came another fellow with a flat-bottomed pot full of earth. The Fox wondered at that until the two men stabbed the pointed base of the amphora down into the pot.

"It won't stand by itself on a wooden floor, don't you see?" the innkeeper said. "And if the two of you somehow empty it, you won't be able to stand by yourselves, either."

"Good. That's the idea," Van boomed. "You have a dipper there, my friend, so we can fill our jacks as we need to? Ah, yes, I see it. Splendid. If we do come to the point where we can't walk, you'll be kind enough to have your men carry us up to our beds?"

"We've done it a few times, or more than a few," said one of the men who'd lugged in the amphora. "For you, though, we ought to charge extra, seeing as you're heavy freight." He looked ready to bolt if Van took that the wrong way, but the outlander threw back his head and laughed till the taproom rang.

The innkeeper hovered round Gerin like a bee waiting for a flower to open. The Fox didn't take long to figure out why. He'd jingled silver, but he hadn't shown any. Now he did. The innkeeper bowed himself almost double as he made the coins vanish—no easy feat, for he was almost as round as some of the temple eunuchs.

Once paid, he had the sense to leave his guests to themselves. Van filled two jacks, passed one to Gerin. He raised on high the one he kept. "Confusion to oracles!" he cried, and poured the red-brown ale down his throat. He let out a long sigh of contentment: "Ahhhh!"

Gerin also drank, but more slowly. Halfway through, he set down his jack and said, "The poor Sibyl seemed confused enough already. I hope she's come back to herself."

"Well, so do I," Van admitted. He clucked impatiently. "Come on, Captain, finish up there so I can pour you full again. Ah, that's better." He plied the dipper. Before upending his own refilled jack, he went on, "I wonder if, for a woman with juice in her like the new Sibyl looks to have, letting the god fill you makes up for long years without a man to fill you. Not a swap I'd care to make, anyhow."

"I had the same thought myself, when I saw her in the chamber in place of the crone who'd been there time out of mind," Gerin answered. "I don't suppose Biton would speak to anyone who wasn't willing to listen, though."

"Mm, maybe not." Van kicked him under the table. "What shall we drink to this round?"

Without hesitation, Gerin raised his jack and said, "Dyaus' curse, and Biton's, too, on whoever kidnapped Duren." He emptied the jack in one long pull, his throat working hard. Van shouted approval and drank with him.

After a while, they stopped toasting with each round and settled in for steady drinking. Gerin felt at the tip of his nose with thumb and forefinger. It was numb, a sure sign the ale was beginning to have its way with him. Suddenly, half drunk, he decided he didn't feel like sliding sottishly under the table.

Van filled his own jack, lowered the dipper into the amphora, and brought it, dripping, toward Gerin's. When he turned it so the dark amber stream poured into the jack, it quickly overflowed. He scowled at the Fox. "You're behindhand there." Only the care with which he pronounced "behindhand" gave any clue to how much he'd poured down himself.

"I know. Go on without me, if you've a mind to. If I drink myself stupid today, I'll drink myself sad. I can feel it coming on already, and I have plenty to be sad about even with my wits about me."

The outlander looked at him with an odd expression. Gerin needed a moment to recognize it; he hadn't often seen pity on his friend's blunt, hard-featured face. Van said, "The real trouble with you, Captain, is that you don't let go of your wits no matter how drunk you get. Me, I'm like most folk. After a while, I just stop thinking. Nice to be able to do that now and again."

"If you say so," Gerin answered. "I've lived by and for my wits so long now, I suppose, that I'd sooner keep 'em about me all the time. I'd feel naked—worse than naked—without 'em."

"Poor bastard." Van had drunk enough to make his tongue even freer than it usually was. "I tell you this, though: a long time ago I learned it was cursed foolishness to try and make a man go in a direction he doesn't fancy. So you do what you feel like doing. Me, I intend to get pie-eyed. Tomorrow morning I'll have a head like the inside of a drum with two Trokmoi pounding on it, but I'll worry about that then."

"All right," Gerin said. "You've touched wisdom there, you know."

"Me? Honh!" Van said with deep scorn. "I don't know from wisdom. All I know is ale feels good when it's inside me, and I feel good when I'm inside a wench, and a nice, friendly fight is the best sport in the world. Who needs more?"

"No, really." The Fox had enough ale inside him to make him painfully earnest. "So many folk aren't content to let their friends" —he almost said *the people they love*, but knew with accurate instinct that that would have been more than Van could put up with— "be what they are. They keep trying to make them into what they think they're supposed to be."

Van grunted. "Foolishness," was all he said. He plied the dipper yet again, then burst into raucous song in a language Gerin didn't know.

The outlander went to the jakes several times over the course of the afternoon as the ale extracted a measure of revenge. When he came back from the latest of those visits, he zigzagged to the table like a ship trying to tack into port against a strong wind. His chair groaned when he threw his bulk into it, but held.

Even after more drinking, he was able to paste an appreciative smile on his face when a servitor brought over flatbread and a juicy roast of beef. He used his eating knife to carve off a chunk that would have done a starving longtooth proud, and methodically proceeded to make it disappear, lubricating the passage with ale.

After so many years' comradeship, the outlander's capacity no longer amazed Gerin, even if it did still awe him. The innkeeper watched Van eat and drink with amazement, too: glum amazement that he hadn't charged more, if the Fox was any judge. Gerin did his best to damage the roast, too, but, beside Van's, his depredations went all but unnoticed.

Twilight faded into night. Torches, their heads dipped in fat for brighter flames, smoked and crackled in bronze sconces. Gerin drained his jack one last time, set it upside down on the table, and got to his feet. He moved slowly and carefully, that being the only sort of motion he had left to him. "I'm for bed," he announced.

"Too bad, too bad. There's still ale in the jar," Van said. He got up himself, to peer down into it. "Not a lot of ale, but some."

"Don't make me think about it," the Fox said. "I'm going to have a headache in the morning as is; why bring it on early?"

"You!" Van said. "What about me?" Pity showed on

his face again, this time self-pity—he had indeed drunk titanically, if he'd managed to make himself maudlin.

Gerin climbed the stairs as if each were a separate mountain higher than the last. Triumph—and a bellyful of ale—surged in him when he got to the second story. The floor seemed to shift under his feet like the sea, but he reached the room he shared with Van without having to lean against the wall or grab at a door. That too was triumph of a sort.

He rinsed out his mouth with water from the pitcher there, though he knew it would be a cesspit come morning anyhow. Then he undressed and flopped limply onto one of the beds. He pulled off his sandals, hoping Van wouldn't choose the same bed and squash him when— if—the outlander made it upstairs.

Sometime in the middle of the night, the Fox sat bolt upright in bed, eyes staring, heart pounding. His head was pounding, too, but he ignored it. The horror of the dream that had slammed him out of sodden slumber made such merely fleshly concerns as hangovers meaningless by comparison.

Worst of all, he couldn't remember what he'd seen— or perhaps the darkness of the dream had been so absolute that even imaginary vision failed. Something dreadful was brewing somewhere in the dark.

The room in which he lay was dark, too, but not so dark that he could not see. Light from all the moons save Elleb streamed in through the window, painting crisscrossing shadows on the floor. In the other bed, Van snored like a bronze saw slowly cutting its way through limestone.

Just as Gerin tried to convince himself the dream, no matter how terrifying, had been only a dream and to go back to sleep, the outlander stirred and moaned. That he could move at all amazed the Fox; the room reeked of stale ale.

Van shouted—not in Elabonian, not in words at all, but like an animal bawling out a desperate alarm. One of his big hands groped for and found a knife. He sprang to his feet, naked and ferocious, his eyes utterly devoid of reason.

"It's all right," Gerin said urgently, before that mad gaze could light on him and decide he was the cause of whatever night terror Van faced. "It's only a dream. Lie down and sleep some more."

"A dream?" Van said in a strange, uncertain voice. "No, it couldn't be." He seemed to shrink a little as consciousness came back. "By the gods, maybe it was at that. I can hardly believe it."

He set the knife back on the floor, sat down at the edge of the bed with a massive forearm across his eyes. Gerin understood that; now he noticed his own throbbing head, and Van's had to be ten times worse. The outlander stood again, this time to use the chamber pot. Gerin also understood that. "Pass it to me when you're done," he said.

"I thought I was lost in a black pit," Van said wonderingly. "Things were looking at me, I know they were, but I couldn't see even the shine of their eyes— too dark. How could I fight them if I couldn't see them?" He shuddered, then groaned. "I wish my head would fall off. Even the moonlight hurts my eyes."

"I had a dark dream, too, though I don't remember as much of it as you do," Gerin said. Analytical even hung over, he went on, "Odd, that. You've drunk much more than I have, yet you recall more. I wonder why."

"Captain, I don't give a—" Van's reply was punctuated by a frightened wail that came in through the window with the overbrilliant moonlight. The Fox recognized the innkeeper's voice, even distorted by fear.

More than his headache, more than his own bad

dream, that fear kept him from falling back to sleep. Van said nothing but, by the way he tossed and fidgeted, he lay a long time wakeful, too.

Breakfast the next morning was not a happy time. Gerin spooned up barley porridge with his eyes screwed into slits against the daylight. Van drew up a bucket of water from the well outside the inn and poured it over his head. He came back in dripping and snorting, but turned aside with a shudder from the bowl of porridge the innkeeper offered him.

The innkeeper did his best to seem jolly, but his smiles, although they stretched his mouth wide, failed to reach his eyes. Little by little, he stopped pretending, and grew almost as somber as his suffering guests. "I have some word of the Sibyl, good my sirs," he said.

"Tell us," Gerin urged. "You'll give me something to think about besides my poor decrepit carcass." Van did not seem capable of coherent speech, but nodded—cautiously, as if afraid the least motion might make his head fall off.

The innkeeper said, "I hear she still lies asleep in the bed where the priests put her, now and again thrashing and crying out, as if she has evil dreams."

"I wonder if hers are the same as mine and Van's," Gerin said: "darkness and unseen things moving through it."

"I saw—or rather, did not see—the same last night." The innkeeper gave a theatrical shiver. His eyes flicked over to Dyaus' altar by the fireplace. The king of the gods might hold the ghosts at bay, but seemed powerless against these more frightening seemings that came in the night.

Van made a hoarse croaking noise, then said, "I wonder what Aragis dreamt last night." He didn't quite whisper, but used only a small piece of his big voice: more would have hurt him.

"Are you sure you won't eat something?" Gerin asked him. "We'll want to do a lot of traveling today, to get beyond the wood and also past that peasant village where they hunted us in the night."

"I'm sure," Van said, quietly still. "You'd make a fine mother hen, Captain, but if I put aught in my belly now, we'd just lose time stopping the wagon so I could go off into the woods and unspit."

"You know best," the Fox said. The porridge was bland as could be, but still sat uncertainly in his own stomach, and lurched when he stood up. "I do think we ought to go upstairs and don our armor, though. However much we hurt, we're liable to have some handwork ahead of us."

"Aye, you're right," Van answered. "I'd be happier to sit here a while—say, a year or two—till I feel I might live, or even want to, but you're right." With careful stride, he made his way to the stairs and up them. Gerin followed.

The rasps and clangs of metal touching metal made the Fox's head hurt and, by Van's mutters, did worse to him. "Don't know how I'm supposed to fight, even if I have to," Gerin said. "If I could drive somebody away by puking on him, I might manage that, but I'm not good for much more."

"I feel the same way," Van said, "but no matter how sick I am, if it's a choice between fighting and dying, I expect I'll do the best job of fighting I can."

"Can't argue with that," Gerin said. "If you think I'll be looking for a fight today, though, you're daft."

"Nor I, and I'm a sight fonder of them than you are," Van said. "The thing of it is, a fight may be looking for you."

"Why do you think I'm doing this?" Gerin shrugged

his shoulders a couple of times to fit his corselet as comfortably as he could, then jammed his bronze pot of a helm over his head. Sighing, he said, "Let's go."

"Just a moment." Van adjusted the cheekpieces to his own fancy helm, then nodded. By his pained expression, that hurt, too. Anticipating still more future pain, he said, "And we'll have to listen to the cursed wagon wheels squeaking all the rest of the day, too."

Gerin hadn't thought of that. When he did, his stomach churned anew. "We've got to do something about that," he declared.

"Stay here a while longer?" Van suggested.

"We've stayed too long already, thanks to you and your carouse. Curse me if I want to spend another useless day here because you drank the ale jar dry—and I helped, I admit it," the Fox added hastily. He plucked at his beard. Thinking straight and clear through a pounding headache was anything but easy, but after a few seconds he snapped his fingers. "I have it! I'll beg a pot of goose grease or chicken fat or whatever he has from the innkeeper. It won't be perfect, the gods know, but it should cut the noise to something we have hope of standing."

Van managed the first smile he'd risked since he woke up. He made as if to slap Gerin on the back, but thought better of it; perhaps he imagined how he would have felt had someone bestowed a similar compliment on him in his present delicate condition. "By the gods, Captain, it can't hurt," he exclaimed. "I was thinking we'd have to suffer the whole day long, and no help for it."

"No point in suffering if you don't have to," Gerin said. "And I can't think of a better way to use wits than to keep from suffering."

The innkeeper produced a pot of chicken fat without demur, though he said, "There's a cure for a long night I never ran across before."

"Aye, that's just what it is, but not the way you mean." The Fox explained why he wanted the fat. The innkeeper looked bemused, but nodded.

Gerin crawled under the wagon and applied a good coat of grease to both axles. When he came out and stood up again, Van said, "We'll draw flies."

"No doubt," Gerin said. "After a while, it'll go bad and start to stink, too, and somebody will have to scrub it off. For today, it'll be quieter. Wouldn't you say that's worth it?"

"Oh, aye, you get no quarrel from me there." Van's laugh was but a faint echo of his usual booming chortle, but it served. "Thing of it is, I'm usually the one with no thought but for today and you're always fretting about tomorrow or the year after or when your grandson's an old graybeard. Odd to find us flip-flopped so."

The Fox considered that, then set it aside. "Too much like philosophy for early in the day, especially after too much ale the night before. Shall we be off?"

"Might as well," Van said. "Can I humbly beg you to take the reins for the first part of the go? I don't think you hurt yourself as bad as I did."

"Fair enough." Gerin clambered onto the seat at the front of the wagon. The reins slid across the calluses on his palms. Van got up beside him, moving with an old man's caution.

"The lord Biton bless the both of you, good my sirs," the groom said.

Gerin flicked the reins. The horses leaned forward against their harness. The wagon rolled ahead. It still rattled and creaked and jounced, but didn't squeak nearly as much as it had. Van looked wanly happy. "That's first rate," he said. "With even a bit o' luck, I'll feel like living by noon or so."

"About what I was hoping for myself," Gerin said. He

drove out of the stable yard and around to the front of the inn. The wagon wasn't as quiet as all that, but it was enough quieter than it had been to satisfy him.

The innkeeper stood by the entryway and bowed himself double as the wagon passed him. "The lord Biton bless the both of you," he said, as the groom had. "May you come again to Ikos before long, and may you recall my humble establishment with favor when you do."

"They didn't used to act like that before the Empire blocked the last pass through the Kirs," Gerin murmured. "Then they had guests up to the ceiling and sleeping in the horses' stables, and they hardly knew or cared whether they saw anyone in particular again."

"Reminds me of a story, Captain, indeed it does," Van said, a sure sign he was feeling better. "Have I told you how they get the monkeys to pick pepper?"

"No, I don't think I've heard that one," Gerin answered. "How do they—"

He got no further, for the horses gave a snort of alarm and reared in terror. Trying to fight them under control, Gerin thought their unexpected motion the reason the wagon swayed beneath his fundament as if suddenly transformed to a boat bobbing on a choppy sea. Then Van shouted "Earthquake!" and he realized the whole world was trembling.

He'd felt earthquakes once or twice before, years ago. The ground had twitched, then subsided almost before fear could seize him. This quake was nothing like those. The shaking went on and on; it seemed to last forever. Through the roar of the ground and the creaking of the buildings in the town of Ikos, he heard cries of fear. After a moment, he realized the loudest of them was his own.

A couple of inns and houses did more than creak; they collapsed into piles of rubble. And when the Fox looked down the street toward the temple of Biton, he saw with horror that the gleaming marble fane was also down, along with great stretches of the wall that protected the holy precinct.

When the earth finally relented and stood still, Gerin realized his hangover was gone; terror had burned it out of him. He stared at Van, who stared back, his usually ruddy face fishbelly white. "Captain, that was a very bad one," the outlander said. "I've felt quakes a time or two here and there, but never any to compare with that."

"Nor I," Gerin said. The ground shook again, just enough to send his heart leaping into his mouth. He scrambled down from the wagon and ran toward the nearest fallen building, from which came pain-filled shouts. Van ran right beside him. Together they pulled away timbers and plaster until they could haul out a fellow who, but for a couple of cuts and a mashed finger, had taken miraculously little hurt.

"All the gods bless you," the man said, coughing. "My wife's in there somewhere." Careless of his own injuries, he began clawing at the wreckage himself. Gerin and Van worked with him. Men and women also came running from buildings that had stayed upright.

Then someone screamed, "Fire!" Flames born in the hearth or on Dyaus' altar or of some flickering lamp were loose and growing. Black smoke, thin at first but all too quickly thicker, boiled up to the sky—and not just from the downfallen inn where the Fox labored. Every wrecked building was soon ablaze. The shrieks of those trapped under beams rose to a new and dreadful pitch.

Along with everyone else, Gerin fought the fires as best he could, but there were not enough buckets, not enough water. Flames grew, spread, began to devour buildings the earthquake had not tumbled.

"Hopeless," Van said, coughing and choking against the smoke that now streaked his face with soot. "We don't get away, we're going to cook, too, and the wagon and horses with us."

Gerin hated to retreat, but knew his friend was right. He looked again toward Biton's overthrown temple. "By the gods," he said softly, and then shivered when, as if the gods were listening, the ground shook again. "I wonder if the Sibyl foresaw this when she prophesied yesterday."

"There's a thought." Van's face lit up. "And here's another: with the wall down and the temple guards likely either squashed or scared to death, what's to keep us from scooping a wagonload of gold out of the holy precinct?"

"You're braver than I am if you want to chance Biton's curse," Gerin said. "Remember the corpses we've seen of those who tried stealing from the temenos?" By Van's expression, first sulky and then thoughtful, he hadn't remembered, but did now. Gerin went on, "But let's head over there anyhow. We ought to see if we can do anything for the poor Sibyl. If I know those greedy priests, they'll be so worried over the temple and their treasures that they're liable to forget her—and she may not even be aware to remind them she's alive." The thought of her lying in the rubble, trapped and unconscious and perhaps forgotten, raised fresh horror in him: he could not imagine a lonelier way to die.

"Right you are, Captain." Now Van got into the wagon and took the reins without hesitation; maybe the shock of the earthquake had made him forget his morning-after pains, too. Gerin scrambled up beside him. The horses snorted, both in fear and from the billowing smoke. The Fox counted himself lucky that they hadn't bolted when the fires started. He was anything but sorry to get away from the flames himself.

Along with so much else, the gold-and-ivory statues

of Ros and Oren had fallen in the earthquake—fallen and shattered into the pieces from which they were made. Oren's head, its features plump and unmemorable but decked with a crown heavy with gold and sparkling with rubies, sapphires, and emeralds, had bounced or flown out beyond the overthrown marble wall that delimited Biton's precinct.

Gerin and Van looked at each other, the same thought in both their minds. So much gold—Whispering a prayer of propitiation to Biton, the Fox leaped down from the wagon. He seized the image of the dead Emperor's head, ready to cast it aside at the first sign of the curse striking home (and devoutly hoping that would be soon enough). Grunting at the weight of gold, he picked up the head and crown and chucked them into the back of the wagon.

"We won't need to fret about money for a bit," Van said, beaming, and even the abstemious Fox could only nod.

The quake struck so early in the day that hardly anyone had yet come in hope of hearing the Sibyl's prophetic verse. Only one wagon and one chariot had their horses tethered out in front of the dwelling the Sibyl used as her own. The cottage still stood, while chunks of the marble wall around the temple precinct had come down with gruesome result on the priest who the day before had tended Gerin's team.

Seeing the Sibyl's dwelling intact made the Fox hesitate. "Maybe we should just head for home," he said doubtfully. "Those fellows over there will be able to take care of her without violating ritual." He pointed through a gap in the wall toward figures running around by the ruined temple.

Van looked that way, too. His eyes were sharper than Gerin's, perhaps because, unlike the Fox, he spent no time peering at faded script in crumbling scrolls. He grabbed the mace off his belt. "Captain, you'd better look again. Whatever those things are, you don't want 'em tending the Sibyl."

"What are you talking about? They must be priests, and they—" Gerin's voice broke off as, squinting, he did take another look. He saw priests, all right, but they were down on the ground, not one of them moving. Over them bent pallid shapes hard to make out against the white marble of the temple. They didn't quite move or look like men, though.

One of them raised his head and saw the wagon. The bottom of his—its?—face was smeared with red. Gerin didn't think the thing was hurt. The blood around its mouth likelier said it had been—feeding.

As Van had seized the mace, so Gerin grabbed for his bow. The pale, bloodstained figure loped toward the wagon. The Fox remained unsure whether it was man or beast. It carried itself upright on two legs, but its forehead sloped almost straight back above the eyes (which were small and themselves blood-red) and its mouth was full of teeth more formidable than anything Gerin had seen this side of a longtooth.

Ice ran down his back. "The quake must have knocked down the underground walls, the warded ones," he exclaimed. "And these are the things the wards held back."

"Belike you're right," Van answered. "But whether you are or not, don't you think you'd better shoot that one before it gets close enough to take a bite out of us? Whatever it was eating before doesn't seem to have filled it."

Staring at the pallid monster, Gerin had almost forgotten he was holding his bow. He pulled an arrow from his quiver, nocked, drew, and let fly in one smooth motion. The monster made no effort to duck or dodge; it might never have seen a bow before. The arrow took it in the middle of its broad chest. It clawed at the shaft, screaming hoarsely, then crumpled to the ground.

The scream drew the attention of a couple of other monsters. *How many of them had lived underground?* Gerin wondered. *And for how long?* Whatever the answer was, the things were above ground now, and looked to be out for revenge against the men who had forced subterranean life on them for so long—and on any other men they could sink their teeth into.

Before the monsters rushed the wagon, a charge by a squad of temple guards distracted them. They attacked the guardsmen with the ferocity of wild beasts. The guards had spears and swords and armor of bronze and leather. The monsters looked to be faster and stronger than anyone merely human.

Gerin got but a brief glimpse of the fight, which looked to be an even match. "If we mix ourselves up in that, all we'll do is get killed," he said to Van. "More of those cursed things keep swarming up out of what's left of the temple."

"Well then, let's snatch the Sibyl and get out of here before they find her and figure she'd make a tasty snack," Van said. In other circumstances, that would have seemed rough humor. Remembering the blood round the mouth of the monster he'd shot, Gerin thought the outlander was just stating a probability.

He jumped down from the wagon when Van reined in by the Sibyl's dwelling. The door stood ajar, perhaps knocked open by the earthquake. Gerin ran inside.

Had the quake not thrown pots from shelves and lamps from tables, the cottage would have reminded the Fox of one inhabited by a prosperous peasant. Tapestries enlivened whitewashed walls; the furniture looked better made than most. That hadn't kept stools from falling down, though, or the clay oven in one corner of the cottage from cracking.

The Sibyl lay on her bed, unconscious still, in the midst of chaos. As Gerin stepped toward her, the ground trembled beneath his feet once more. That was almost enough to send him fleeing out of the cottage in terror of offending Biton. But, he reasoned, earthquakes were not in the province of the farseeing god. Had he angered Biton, the deity would have shown his displeasure more directly.

He stooped beside the Sibyl, who still wore the thin linen dress she'd had on in the chamber beneath the ruined temple. He wondered if his touch would bring her to herself. She stirred and muttered as he lifted her, but her eyes stayed closed. He hurried back out through the doorway.

"Good thing the monsters are still battling in there," Van said when he returned. "A wench in your arms is pleasant even if you're not having her, but worthless to fight with."

"Scoffer," Gerin said. But the rising noise of combat inside the temple precinct warned him he had no time to swap banter with Van. As gently as he could, he set the Sibyl in the back of the wagon. Again she muttered but did not wake. He took his seat beside Van, snatched up his bow and quiver once more. Nocking another arrow, he said, "Let's get out of here."

"Right you are." Van twitched the reins. The horses bolted ahead, glad to have an outlet for their fear. As the wagon rattled past a gap in the fence, a monster came through. Gerin shot it. It fell with a roar. Van pushed the horses up to a gallop. Skirting the burning town of Ikos, the wagon plunged into the old woods.

V

Not long after noon, the Sibyl came back to herself. By then, the travelers were more than halfway through the strange forest that guarded the road to Ikos. Gerin had expected trees fallen across that road, perhaps other signs of upheaval from the earthquake. He discovered none. As far as the woods were concerned, the temblor might never have happened.

"Good," Van said when he remarked on that. "Maybe the trees'll swallow up those creatures, too, when they come swarming out of Ikos."

"Wouldn't that be lovely?" Gerin said. "Likely too much to hope for, though, because—" He broke off as the wagon shifted under his fundament. It wasn't, as he'd first feared, yet another quake: rather, he found when he looked back into the bed of the wagon, the Sibyl had gone from lying to sitting up. He nodded to her. "Lady, I bid you good day."

Her eyes showed nothing but confusion. "You are the pair for whom I prophesied just now," she said, her voice also halting. Though it suited her appearance well, hearing it once more gave Gerin a small shock: after Biton had spoken through her, he'd almost forgotten she had a voice of her own.

"Not 'just now,'" he said, wondering how he could let her know what had happened while she lay unconscious. "That was yesterday; you've been in Biton's trance for more than a whole day."

"Impossible. It never takes me so," she said angrily. But a moment later, she looked confused again. "Yet if

152

you do not speak truth, why am I on the point of bursting? Halt a moment, I pray you." Van reined in. The horses, glad of a breather, began nibbling grass by the side of the road.

Gerin got down and went around to the back of the wagon. He held out a hand. "Here, lady, I'll help you down so you can ease yourself."

She recoiled as if he'd proposed helping her down so he could ravish her. "Are you mad?" she demanded in a voice like winter. "I may have no contact whatever with any entire man. Were I to do so, I'd be Sibyl no longer."

The Fox sucked in a long breath. She hadn't figured out how she'd got into the wagon. He could hardly blame her, but it didn't make what he had to say come any easier: "Lady, I fear that to save your life I had to touch you. The gods know I'm sorry for it, but I saw no other way." He repeated the oracular verse she had given him, and explained the morning's horrors.

The more he talked, the paler the Sibyl grew. "Lies," she whispered. "It must be lies. You've ruined me, and now you seek to twist my own words against me and make me believe you did it for my own good?" Her head whipped around like a hunted animal's; her eyes lit on the gold and ivory head of Oren the Builder. Gerin had thought she was already white as could be, but discovered he was wrong. "You—took this?" she demanded. "And the lord Biton did not strike you dead?"

A flip answer came to Gerin's mind; he stifled it before it passed his lips. "Lady, he did not. When I took it, it lay outside the bounds of the holy precinct. As I said, the earthquake knocked everything into confusion. The temple itself no longer stands. What happened to the chamber where you prophesied I could not say, but the quake must have knocked down the warded walls that kept those monsters from coming to the surface."

Van turned and said, "For all you know, Fox, it might have been the other way round. Remember the bits of mortar we saw at the base of those walls when Kinifor led us down to the lady? The things might have been trying for years to breach the magic that held 'em in check, and when they finally did it, that could've made the earth shake."

"You're right; it could have happened so," Gerin agreed. "But whichever way it was doesn't matter." He gave his attention back to the Sibyl. "Lady—have you a name, by the way?"

She'd been listening to him and Van talk back and forth as if they were madmen whose madnesses by chance coincided. She snapped back to herself when the Fox asked her that question, but needed a moment to find an answer for it. At last she said, "I was called . . . Selatre. They took the name from me when I became Biton's mouth, but I recall it was mine." The bitter curve of her lips was anything but a smile. "I may as well wear it again, for thanks to you I'll serve the god no more. If all you say is true, better you should have left me to die there."

"Lady . . . Selatre . . . I pray I'm wrong, but I don't think I am, when I tell you the only things left alive in Ikos by sunset tonight will be the ones that came out from under Biton's fane. How deep and wide the caves run, how many monsters there are—I know none of that. But I couldn't leave you in your cottage to perish from their teeth and claws, not when the question I put to you was what made you swoon away," Gerin said.

Selatre said, "If you think saving me was a favor, you're wrong. Lost, polluted . . . how can I hope to make my way in the world again, now that you've taken away my reason for being?"

"You made your way in it before you were Sibyl," Van said roughly. "And plenty of people go on living who've taken worse hurts than you. Go into the woods, water the ferns, and come back and we'll feed you bread and sausage and ale. Things always look cheerier with food in your belly, and you must be hungry as a longtooth after sleeping the day around."

Selatre sniffed at the homely advice, but, perhaps because nothing better occurred to her, nodded after a moment. Gerin started to offer his hand again, but the first motion made her shrink back with such dismay that he stopped before it was well begun. Instead, he ostentatiously stepped away from the wagon and let her clamber down by herself.

"What do we do if she tries to run to Ikos on her own?" he whispered to Van when she walked in among the bushes by the side of the road.

"If the jade's that foolish, let her go," the outlander answered. "Me, I don't think she is."

Gerin got out the food Van had promised the Sibyl. She took longer to come back than he'd expected, and he wondered if she had slipped away. The idea of pursuing her through the uncanny forest was far from appealing. But just when he was beginning to worry he might have to, she returned, her face unreadable. He pointed to the meal he'd fixed from the travel supplies, but did not try to give it to her. If she didn't want to be touched, that was her affair.

She did manage a quiet word of thanks, then fell on bread and sausage and onions and ale as if she'd gone without food for ten or twenty days, not just one. She was still eating when, faintly, from far down the road to the west came a snarling roar that wasn't bear or longtooth or wolf or any beast Gerin had heard before. The hair on his arms and the back of his neck prickled up even so.

Van said, "That's one of the things from the caves, if you ask me."

Selatre put down the piece of bread she'd been gnawing. "A terrible sound," she said, shuddering. "I've heard it in my nightmares. Now, perhaps, I begin to believe you."

The innkeeper had said she seemed to be having evil dreams. *That was this morning*, Gerin thought, amazed. It seemed an age ago, in a different world. Given all that had changed between then and now, maybe it was.

The Fox said, "We've seen monsters in our dreams, too—and seen them in the flesh today, in the temple compound."

"And if we don't want to see more of them in the flesh, I think we'd better get rolling again," Van said. "If I had to guess, I'd say they're likely not after us in particular right now, just out exploring, finding out what aboveground is like after being down below so long. But if they come on us, I don't think they'd stop with a cheery good day, if you take my meaning."

Gerin stood aside to let Selatre scramble into the wagon by herself. Getting her back to Fox Keep was going to be awkward if she thought any accidental bump the equivalent of a violation. Of course, if that was how she felt, she was already convinced he'd violated her, and he couldn't do anything about it. He chewed on the inside of his lower lip. No time to worry about any of that now. Once they were safe away from Ikos would be soon enough.

He said to Van, "I'll drive for a while now. You can rest your head."

"It's all right," the outlander answered. "Since the

ground started shaking, I haven't hardly noticed my poor aching noodle."

"The same with me," Gerin said. "It's not the cure for a long night of drinking I'd choose, though."

"Nor I, Fox, nor I." Van started to laugh, but broke off: another one of those snarling roars cut through the stillness of the woods. The outlander yanked on the reins, then reached around behind him into the wagon for the whip. He cracked it just above the horses' backs. Gerin thought that was laying it on thick; the animals seemed alarmed enough to run hard just from the fierce sound of the roar.

Selatre said, "Have a care, please. You almost touched me when you were groping back here." She sat huddled in a far corner, as if certain Van had intended to grope her.

"Lady—Selatre—we're not out to do you harm or throw you down in the roadway and have you or anything of the sort." The outlander sounded as if he were holding on to his patience with both hands. "For one thing, Gerin and I both prefer willing wenches. For another, or if you think I'm lying about the first, we could have had our way with you four times each before you woke up."

"I know that," she answered quietly. "Any touch, though, pollutes me, not just a lewd one. Lord Gerin, I grant you meant well when you plucked me from my cottage, but I'd sooner you had not done it. To lose that sense of union with the god, to know he will never speak through me again because I am his pure vessel no more . . . life stretches long and empty ahead of me."

The Fox exhaled through his nose in impatient anger. "Lord Biton would have spoken through you no more whether we came to your dwelling or not. If we hadn't, you'd have been monster fodder before another hour went by. And that, if you ask me, is a short and empty life, save perhaps when speaking about a monster's belly, which would have been quite comfortably full."

He twisted around to see how Selatre took that. He didn't want to flay her with words; after all, she was suddenly cast into a situation she'd never imagined and for which she'd never prepared. If he'd hit too hard, he was ready to backtrack and apologize.

But, to his surprise, she returned the ghost of a smile. "Next to being devoured, I suppose rescue may be a better choice. Very well; I do not blame you for it—much."

"Lady, I thank you." He could have—given his nature, he easily could have—freighted that with enough sarcasm to make it sting. This time, though, it came out sincere. The Sibyl—no, the ex-Sibyl—was trying to adjust; he could at least do the same.

Shadows were lengthening when they came out of the haunted forest that surrounded Ikos and into woods like those in the rest of the northlands. The transition point was easy to spot: as soon as they returned to the normal woods, the earthquake showed its effects again, not least with a couple of toppled trees stretched across the roadway.

Moving those trunks would have taken half a village of serfs. Van drove around them through the undergrowth. As he did so, he said, "Wouldn't have wanted to try this back a ways. You go in there, who knows if you come out again?"

"I like that," Selatre said. "You were willing enough to send me off into those woods when I needed to make water. Did you hope you would be rid of me?"

Van coughed and spluttered. "No, lady, nothing like that at all. If I thought of it at all, I thought you were holy enough to have nothing to fear."

"So I may have been, once," Selatre said, gloom returning. "No more."

They rode on a while in silence after that. Eyeing the sinking sun, Gerin said, "We might do well to look for that spot after we came through the free peasant village. They won't know what we're about until we roll past them early tomorrow morning."

"If they're not all downfallen from the quake," Van added. "Only thing I worry about there, Captain—not counting the ghosts, for we've little to give 'em—is monsters on our trail."

"The ghosts will keep them from traveling at night. . . ." Gerin's voice trailed away. "I hope," he finished, realizing he had no way of knowing what—if anything—the ghosts could do to the horrid creatures from the caves.

"*We* can't go on traveling all night," Van said. "Whether the ghosts let us or not, we'd ruin the horses, maybe kill 'em. So stopping's still our best plan, and I think you picked a good place for it."

To the Fox's admiration, Van recognized the little side road down which they'd turned a few nights before. Gerin recognized it, too—once he was on it. But the landmarks looked different coming west from the way they had going east, and he might well have driven right past the junction.

The outlander got busy making a fire. Bow in hand, Gerin walked through the woods in search of a blood offering for the ghosts. When the light began to fade alarmingly before he'd found either bird or beast, he began turning over stones and pieces of bark. He grabbed a fat, long-tailed lizard before it could scuttle back into hiding. It twisted in his grasp and bit his finger hard enough to draw blood from him, but he held on and, swearing, carried the creature to camp.

Van gave it a dubious look. "That's the best you could

come up with?" he asked, and made as if to get up himself. But the sun was down by then, and the ghosts beginning to haver. Scowling against their cries, he said, "Cut its throat, quick. It has to be better than nothing."

Gerin made the sacrifice, then flipped away the lizard's writhing body. He peered down into the trench he'd dug. The blood seemed hardly enough to dampen the dirt at the bottom. He wondered if he should have kept hunting till he found a creature with more to give the ghosts.

But in spite of the paltry offering, the night spirits seemed no more vicious than they had at other times when he'd camped in the open. Mildly puzzled but not inclined to complain at his good fortune, he pulled a sack of supplies from the back of the wagon. Selatre accepted the small loaf of hard-baked bread he held out to her, but was careful not to let her fingers brush his when she took it.

He forgot to be irked, exclaiming, "Lady, I wonder if the holiness you bring from Ikos—the last holiness left of Ikos, I fear—isn't helping hold the ghosts at arm's length."

"I am holy no more," she answered bleakly.

"You're the Sibyl no more, true," Gerin said, "but I wonder if the other is so. You didn't abandon Biton; he chose to leave you. How could that be your fault?"

She looked startled, and did not answer. She looked startled again when Gerin and Van drew straws to see who would take first watch and who second, but shook her head at her own foolishness. "Of course that's needful here," she said, half to herself. "Who would do it for you?"

"We didn't bring any temple guards along, that's certain," Van said. He got up and paced about; Gerin had won his choice, and decided to sleep through the first watch. The outlander went on, "Here, lady, you can take my blanket till I wake up the Fox; then I expect he'll let you have his."

"You're generous, both of you," the Sibyl said, watching Gerin nod. Even so, she made sure she placed herself on the far side of the fire from him before she wrapped the checked square of wool around her and settled down for the night.

Van needed to shake and prod and practically pummel Gerin before he'd wake. The outlander pointed over across the embers to Selatre. With a grin, he said, "She's human enough—she snores." The grin disappeared. "Now how am I supposed to wake her and get my blanket back without making her think I've got rape on my mind? That's what she thinks of touching, plain enough."

"You can have mine if you like," Gerin said.

"Too small for my bulk; you know mine's bigger than the usual," Van said. "I'll take it if I have to, but I'd really like to roll up in my own."

Gerin did some thinking. With his wits midnight-slow, it wasn't easy. At last, though, he said, "Here, I have it." He rose creakily and poked around under a tree until he found a long, dry stick. Then he went over to the Sibyl and tapped her with it until she jerked awake and sat up.

"How dare you lay hands on—" she began. Then she realized Gerin hadn't laid hands on her. Faint firelight and the beams of all the moons but Elleb (which hadn't yet risen) showed her confusion. "I see," she said at last, inclining her head to Gerin. "Your friend wants his blanket back, not so? And you found a way to let me know without touching me. I wonder if I would have done as well." She unwrapped herself and stood. "Here you are, Van of the Strong Arm."

As Van came to strip off his armor and claim the blanket, Selatre stepped back to make sure they didn't bump even by accident. She looked away till he was settled. Then, instead of taking Gerin's blanket at once, she said, "Let me walk off into the woods for a moment first."

She didn't go far because of the ghosts (whose wails seemed to Gerin to get worse while she was away), and came back as fast as she'd promised, but Van was snoring by the time she returned. He'd said Selatre snored, too, but the Fox doubted she came anywhere close to the thunderous buzz he produced.

The former Sibyl wrapped herself in Gerin's blanket and wiggled around on the ground, trying to find a comfortable position. She kept squirming for some time, while Gerin walked back and forth waking up. Finally Selatre said, "I can't sleep right now."

"Nothing too out-of-the-way about that, I suppose, not when you lay in your bed through the day and the night and into the next day again," Gerin said.

"I can still hardly believe that." Selatre looked up into the sky. After a moment, Gerin realized she was studying the moons. When she spoke again, her voice held wonder: "Tiwaz is closer to Math than he should be, and has sped farther past golden Nothos. What you say there must be so, which argues for the truth of the rest of your tale."

"Lady, I told you no lies, nor did Van." The Fox was nettled; here he'd risked his life to save her, and she still wondered if he was nothing more than a kidnapper? That irritation came out in the sneer with which he said, "I trust you don't find yourself polluted by mere talk with a man?"

She flinched as if he'd slapped her. "By no means," she answered tonelessly. "However—" She turned her back on him and started to wrap his blanket around her once more.

"I'm sorry," he said, scraping a shallow trench in the

ground with the hobnailed sole of his sandal. "I shouldn't have said that. Talk all you care to; I'll listen."

He wondered if she'd pay any attention to him; he would not have blamed her for ignoring him after that gibe. But, slowly, she turned back to him, eyeing him with the same grave attention she'd given the moon not long before. "You will forgive me when I say that (knowing little of men in general and barons in particular) you strike me as unusual?" she asked.

His laugh held little mirth. "Since everyone in the northlands says as much, why should you be any different?"

"I meant no insult," Selatre said. "The word of you that came to Ikos after Biton laid his hand on me and made me Sibyl held no reproach: indeed, you were on the whole well thought of for trying to hold to the standards of the Empire of Elabon even after Elabon abandoned the northlands."

"Nice to know someone somewhere had some notion of what I was about," Gerin said. "More than my vassals do, I think." With a deliberate effort of will, he forced his thoughts from that gloomy track and changed the subject: "How did it happen that Biton chose you through whom to speak?"

"I'd known he might since I became a woman," Selatre answered. "For though I was normal in every other way, my courses never began, which is a sign of the farseeing one's notice in the villages round his shrine. But Biton's mouth on earth had served him so long I never dreamt he might one day call her to himself at last—or that his eye would fall on me to take her place."

"How did you know you were the one he wanted?" Gerin asked.

"He came to me in a dream." Selatre's eyes went far away, looking through the Fox rather than at him. Slowly, she continued, "It was the realest dream, the most life-like, you can imagine. The god—touched me. I may say no more. I've never felt anything like that dream for realness, save, very much the opposite way, with horror rather than delight, the evil dreams I've had of late."

Gerin nodded. "I've had those myself. They're worse than any I've known before, that's the truth." He wondered if she experienced them even more vividly because of her intimate contact with Biton and things of the spirit generally. Not knowing any way to find an answer to that, he chose a different question: "Did you go and proclaim yourself at the temple, then?"

"No. I would have, but the very next day the priests came to my village instead. Biton had sent some of them dreams of me, and they sought me out."

"Ah," the Fox said. Had the dream come to Selatre alone, he might have thought it sprang from her imagination, but if the priests also knew the farseeing god had chosen her to succeed the ancient Sibyl, not much room was left to doubt Biton had sent it.

Endlessly curious, the Fox found a chance to put a question he'd never expected to be able to ask: "What is it like when Biton speaks through you? What do you feel or think or whatever the word is?"

"It's not—like—anything else I know," Selatre answered. "When the mantic fit takes hold of me, of course, I know nothing at all; I always have to ask the priest, if one is there with me, what my response was. But while the god's power is coming over me, before he takes me fully—" She didn't go on, not with words, but she shivered, and her eyes were full of longing. At last she added, "And now no more, never again. No more."

Her voice wept. Suddenly Gerin believed in his belly that she would sooner have died than be rescued at the cost of losing that link with Biton; it struck him as almost like losing a lover or a husband. But with the temple cast down and monsters loose on the northlands, the link was surely lost anyhow. Had he not believed that, he would have drowned in guilt.

Maybe Selatre conceded the point, however reluctantly, for she said, "And now that it is to be no more, what, lord Gerin, do you see life holding for me at Fox Keep? What would you have me do?"

Gerin had his mouth open to reply before he realized he had no idea what to say. What place had he, had the keep, for Biton's former Sibyl? Serving woman, apt to be pawed by his vassals and his guests? Could she return to peasant life after time spent with the god? He doubted it.

And then, just as he was about to confess ignorance, inspiration struck. "Do you have your letters?" he asked.

"No—Biton spoke to me direct, not through scribblings," she answered. "But I always thought I might like to learn."

"I'd be glad to teach you," he said. "One of the things that goes into keeping up the standards of the Empire of Elabon, as you called it, is having a grasp of time and place that goes farther than what you—or I, or anyone— can keep in your head. The more people who read and write, the more who can get that wide knowledge civilization needs. I teach as many folk as I can."

"As may be," Selatre said. "But what has it to do with whatever my life at Castle Fox would become?"

"I have a fair store of books at the keep," Gerin answered. "Oh, any bibliophile south of the Kirs would laugh himself silly to hear it called such, but I do have several dozen scrolls and codices, and I get new ones— old ones other folk don't care about, most of the time— now and again. I had in mind for you, if you think it would suit, to take charge of them, learn what's in them and where it can be found, make new copies as they're needed or if someone asks for such: not likely, I admit, in the state the northlands are in, but stranger things have happened. What say you?"

She was silent a long time, so long he began to fear he'd somehow insulted her after all, even if he'd just intended to find her a place where she could be useful and one that might keep her from some of what she would surely see as indignities. Then, at last, she said, "I am not ashamed to tell you I must apologize, lord Gerin."

"Why?" he asked, startled. "For what?"

"In spite of everything you've said, you have to understand I had trouble fully crediting your reasons for snatching me from Ikos," she answered. "Once you had me back at Fox Keep, who could guess what you might do with me? In truth, I could guess, and my guesses frightened me." Her laugh came shaky, but it was a laugh. "And instead of putting me in your bed, you'd put me in your library. Do you wonder that I needed a moment before I found a way to answer you?"

"Oh," Gerin said. "Put that way, no." He too took a while groping for words before he went on, "Lady, enough women are willing that forcing one who's not has always struck me as more trouble than it's worth. But folk who have wits and can use them are precious as the tin that hardens copper to bronze. I judge you may be one of that sort. If you are, by Dyaus, I'll use you."

"Fair and more than fair," she said, then seemed to surprise herself with a yawn. "Perhaps I shall sleep more, after all. My heart is easier than I thought it could be."

"I'm glad of that," Gerin said as she wrapped herself in his blanket again. She seemed to have forgotten the creatures still issuing from the cave under Biton's temple. He remembered, but forbore to remind her. Let her rest easy while she could.

❖   ❖   ❖

The free peasant village whose men had hunted Gerin and Van through the night on their way to Ikos was a sorry place when they and Selatre rode up to it at midmorning the next day. Half the houses had fallen down in the earthquake; several bodies lay sprawled and stiff on the grass, awaiting burial.

"If they'd built stronger, they'd have come through better," Van said, unwilling to waste much sympathy on folk who would have robbed and maybe murdered him.

"Maybe so," Gerin said, "but maybe not, too. Stronger houses might still have fallen—look at Biton's temple. And if they did, they'd have crushed whoever was inside them. This way, a lot of people probably managed to crawl out of the wreckage."

"Mm, something to that, maybe," Van admitted. "All the same, I won't be sorry to see this place behind me." He started to urge the horses up from a walk to a trot.

"No, wait," Gerin said, which made the outlander grunt in surprise and send him a disbelieving look. He explained: "The lady there has but the one linen dress, which is all very well for prophesying in but not what you'd want to wear day in and day out. I was thinking we might stop and buy another here, something of sturdy wool that would do until we got back to Castle Fox."

"Ah. There's sense to you after all. There usually is, but this time I wondered." Van reined in.

Several of the villagers were in the fields; earthquake or no, tragedies or no, the endless routine of tillage had to go on. The women and children and few men who stayed by the houses swarmed toward the travelers' wagon. "Noble sirs, spare us such aid in our misfortunes as you can give," a woman cried. Others said the same thing in different words.

The Fox stared down his nose at them. "By Dyaus,

you're better disposed to us now than you were when you came after us in the night to take our armor and swords."

"And mace," Van added, hefting the viciously spiked weapon in question. If the peasants had any thoughts of trying to attack now, the blood-red reflections of the sun off those bronze spikes did a good job of dissuading them.

The older man who'd sold the travelers a hen spoke for his people: "Lords, we all have to live as best we can, so I shan't go grizzling out I'm-sorries, though I expect you wish the five hells would take us. But would you see us cast down like this?"

"You don't have it as bad as some," Gerin said: "The temple at Ikos crashed in ruins yesterday." The peasants wailed, some in genuine horror and distress, others, Gerin judged, in fear that, with the temple ruined, no one would ever again use the road from the Elabon Way to Ikos. That was, he thought, a good guess. He went on, "In aid of which, I present to you the lady Selatre, who was till yesterday the Sibyl at Ikos, and whom we rescued from the wreckage of the place."

The villagers gasped and exclaimed all over again. The Fox got down from the wagon to let Selatre descend without—the gods forfend!—touching him; Van shifted on the seat to make her way out easy. The peasants stared at her and muttered among themselves. At last one of them called to her, "Lady, though the temple be fallen, why did you not stay and wait for its repair?"

Selatre cast down her eyes and did not answer. Gerin looked for some gentle way to break the news of the eruption of the monsters from the caves below the fane. While he was looking, Van, who minced few words, said, "If she'd stayed, she'd have been eaten. The same is liable to happen to the lot of you in the next few days, so you'd better listen to what we have to say."

He and Gerin, as was their way, took turns telling the tale of what had happened back at Ikos. When they were through, the fellow from whom they'd bought the chicken, who seemed to be a village spokesman, said, "If you didn't have the Sibyl with you, I'd reckon you were makin' up the tale to pay us back with a fright for wanting to lift the bronze off you."

"And since the lady is here, what do you believe?" Gerin demanded in no small exasperation. "You'll find out soon enough whether we lie, I can tell you that. You've made a point of getting arms and armor, however you do it. When those creatures come, you'll need them. Don't leave them sitting wherever you've got them hidden; wear the mail, and take the spears and swords out into the fields with you."

"Take bows, too," Van said. "These monsters aren't what you'd call clever, from the little we saw of 'em. They don't know arrows. Every one you kill from long range is one you won't have to fight up close. I'd say they're stronger and faster than people, and they have nasty teeth."

The details the Fox and Van gave were enough to begin to convince the villagers they weren't just trying to frighten them. "Maybe we'll do as you say," the old man said after looking over his comrades.

"Do whatever you bloody well please," Gerin said. "If you don't care about your necks, don't expect me to do your worrying for you. All I'd like to do before I get out of here is buy a proper wool dress for the lady. I'll pay silver for it, too, though the gods alone know why I'm dealing justly with folk who aimed to deal unjustly with me."

When he said "silver," three or four women ran into their houses—those that still stood—and brought out dresses. None of them seemed to the Fox to stand out from the others; he turned to Selatre. She felt of them and examined the stitching with the air of a woman who had done plenty of her own spinning and weaving and sewing. Gerin remembered she had been a peasant before she was Sibyl: she knew of such things.

"This one," she said at last.

The woman who'd produced it tried to set a price more or less equal to its weight in silver. Gerin, who parted with precious metal reluctantly at best, let out a loud, scornful laugh. "We don't have to buy here," he reminded her. "Other villages must have seamstresses who've not been stricken mad." After that, she quickly got more reasonable; he ended up buying the dress with only a slight wince.

"Have you also a pair of drawers you might sell?" Selatre asked.

The woman shook her head. "Don't wear 'em but in winter, to help keep my backside warm." Selatre shrugged; likely it had been the same where she grew up, too.

"Do you want to put the dress on here, where you'll have more in the way of privacy?" Gerin asked her.

"I'd not thought of that," she said. "Thank you for doing it for me." She ducked into one of the peasant huts, soon returning wearing the wool dress and with the linen one under her arm. Some of the aura of the Sibyl's cave left her with the change of clothes; she seemed more intimately a part of the world around her, not so much a waif cast adrift by circumstance. Maybe she felt that, too; she sighed as she stepped around Gerin to stow the linen dress in the wagon. "It's as if I'm putting away part of my past."

"The gods willing, you have long years left ahead of you," Gerin answered. He meant it as no more than a polite commonplace, but it set him wondering. With monsters not only loose on the world but emerging from the ruins of Biton's temple, who could judge the will of the gods?

Van spoke to the villagers: "Remember what we told you, now. How sorry you'll be in a few days depends on whether you listen to us or not. You take no notice today, you won't have the chance to be sorry and wish you'd paid heed."

"And the lot of you, you're just driving away and leaving the trouble behind your wheels," said the older peasant who spoke for the peasants.

He had some reason to sound bitter. Peasants stayed with their land; a journey to the next village was something strange and unusual for them. But Gerin said, "If what I fear is true, you'll just see the creatures before us; there may well be enough to torment all the northlands."

He did not convince the peasant, who said, "Aye, but you're a lord; you can hide behind your stone walls." He gestured to the buildings of the village, some of them fallen and even those still standing none too strong. "Look at the forts we have."

To that the Fox found no good reply. Once Selatre was aboard the wagon, he climbed in, too. Van clucked to the horses and flicked the reins. The animals snorted and began to walk. The wagon rolled out of the peasant village.

When they'd gone a couple of furlongs, Selatre said, "The man back there was right. He and his have no way to shelter against the creatures that come forth against them."

"I know," Gerin answered sadly. "I have nothing I can do about it, though. Did I stay to fight, I'd die, and so would they, and so I'd do them no good, and myself only harm."

"I saw as much," Selatre said. "Otherwise I'd not have

waited to speak until the villagers could not hear. But that's a callous way to have to look at the world."

"Lady, the world's a hard place," Van said. "Begging your pardon, but I'm thinking you've not seen a whole lot of it. Well, now you will, and much of what you see, I fear, will leave you less than joyful."

Selatre didn't answer. Gerin couldn't tell whether that was because she disagreed with Van but was too polite to say so or because she agreed but didn't care to admit it. His opinion of her good sense had risen a notch, though, for the way she'd held her tongue where speaking out would have embarrassed him.

They returned to the Elabon Way that afternoon. Selatre exclaimed in pleasure at seeing Biton's mark on the stone that marked the side road. Then, remembering what had happened back at Ikos, she sobered once more. Gerin said, "I'm sorry the stone reminded you of the temple, but I must say you're taking it bravely."

"In part, I suppose, what happened back there still seems unreal, not least because I wasn't awake to see and feel it myself," she answered. "And I lived most of my life in a village not much different from the one we went through. I know life can be hard."

Van urged the horses onto the stone slabs of the Elabon Way. The drum of their hoofbeats, so different from the muffled clopping they'd made on the dirt side road, caught Selatre's notice. She exclaimed in wonder: "Here's a marvel! Who would have thought you could cover over a roadway and use it the whole year around? No mud here."

"That's why they made it so," Gerin agreed. "You catch on fast."

"The work it must have taken," Selatre said. "How far does it run?"

"From the Kirs up to the Niffet," the Fox said. "In the old days, they could command and have folk heed." He clicked his tongue between his teeth, remembering the troubles he had keeping the stretch of the Elabon Way under his control even partly and poorly repaired.

Van said, "Seems to me, Captain, every time we come north toward your holding, we're in the midst of trouble. Last time, we were heading into the teeth of the Trokmoi, and now we're stormcrows ahead of those—things— coming out of Ikos."

"We'd better stay ahead of them, too," Gerin said. "Otherwise we won't make it back to Fox Keep." He pointed to the horses. "We have to get the best we can from them without making them break down. Getting stuck somewhere could prove downright embarrassing."

"That's one word for it," Van said, "and a politer one than I'd choose, too."

Gerin had hoped to reach some lordlet's castle by nightfall; all at once, the idea of sleeping behind walls too high to be easily climbed developed a new and urgent appeal. But the approach of sunset found the wagon on the road with no keep in sight, only a peasant village. The Fox glumly bought a chicken and pushed the horses forward until the first stirrings of the ghosts reluctantly made him stop.

"No sooner than we start out tomorrow, we'll ride past three keeps," he grumbled as Van spun his firebow. The outlander made fire with his usual skill; Gerin killed the fowl, drained its blood as an offering, then gutted it and did a hasty job of plucking before he cut it in pieces for cooking.

"That's the way of things, Captain, so it is," Van agreed. He turned to Selatre. "Ah, thank you, lady—is that wild basil you've found?"

"Yes." She set the herb on the ground so he could pick it up and rub the chicken with it before he put the meat over the flames.

Gerin drew first watch. Selatre curled up in his blanket and tonight fell asleep almost at once. When she began to snore (something Van had mentioned, but not a noise the Fox had thought to associate with someone a god sometimes possessed), the outlander sat up. Gerin jerked in alarm. "I thought you were gone, too," he said reproachfully.

"I nearly was, before I thought of something that woke me right up again," Van said. "Mind you, Fox, I'm not saying a word against aught you've done since the earthquake—you'd best understand that. But—"

"What is it?" Gerin asked, suspicion in his voice. Anyone who prefaced his remarks by denying he was going to criticize always ended up doing just that.

"Well, Captain, all well and good we rescued the Sibyl here, even if she won't let herself be touched by the likes of us. All well and good—better than well and good—you've figured out a place for her at Castle Fox if she picks up her letters as you hope. But we're bringing back with us a lass who's young and not the least comely I've seen—*and what will sweet Fand say to that?*"

"Oh, father Dyaus." Gerin didn't know in detail the answer to that question, but contemplating it was plenty to make his head start aching. "She'll wonder which of us aims to throw her out of the keep, and she won't think a finger's breadth past that—which will end up tempting me to throw her out even if the notion hadn't crossed my mind till now."

"Just what I was thinking, Captain. Hard to have lustful thoughts about a woman who'd turn blue if you brushed her hand while you passed her a drumstick, but will Fand see it the same way? I ask you."

"Not likely." One of the serfs in Besant's village was a decent potter, not for any fancy ware but for serviceable cups and jars. Gerin had the feeling he'd be busy soon:

when Fand got upset, crockery started flying. The Fox scowled at his friend. "Thank you so much. I wasn't going to have any trouble staying awake through my watch anyhow. Now I wonder if I'll ever sleep again."

Van started to bark laughter, then abruptly stopped. "Might not be safe sleeping in the same bedchamber, and that's a fact, seeing how she stuck a knife into that Trokmê."

"Mm—there is that." Gerin tried to look on the bright side: "Maybe she'll take it all in good part, or maybe she'll be so offended when we bring in Selatre that she'll get up on her hind legs and take the next boat over the Niffet."

"Since when did Fand ever make anything easy, outside the bedroom, I mean?" Van said. He didn't wait for an answer—which was as well, for Gerin had none to give him—but lay down again and soon began to snore loud enough to drown out Selatre.

After a while, what precisely had happened at Ikos began to blur in Gerin's mind with the tale he told of it at every peasant village and lord's holding up along the Elabon Way. The disbelief he met was so strong that sometimes he began to doubt his own memory. Only when he looked to the former Sibyl at his side was he reassured he hadn't imagined it all.

"They're a pack of fools," Van said after the travelers rolled out of the keep of one of Ricolf's vassals.

"Oh, I don't know," Gerin answered resignedly. "Had someone come to Fox Keep with our tale, would you have believed it?"

"They'll find out soon enough whether we're telling the truth," Van said. "And they'll be sorry they think we aren't."

The outlander's pique lasted through a midday meal

at the holding of Ricolf himself. Van, though, so loved to spin stories that telling Ricolf about what had happened at Ikos restored his good humor. Ricolf said, "Aye, we felt the quake here, and lost crockery in it, but I'd not looked for word so weighty as what you bring."

Seeing his former father-in-law at least willing to take him seriously, Gerin said, "You'd be wise to start thinking of ways to keep your peasants safe from the monsters as they spread, either by making sure they have a keep they can flee to or by posting armed men among 'em."

"Ah, Fox, you should have been a schoolmaster after all," Ricolf said, smiling not quite enough to take the sting from his words. "You're so good at telling everyone else what he should do; if only you'd try telling yourself as well."

"What's that supposed to mean?" Gerin said.

Instead of answering directly, Ricolf got up from the table and walked out of the long hall into the courtyard. Gerin followed him. Ricolf paused by the well. Gerin started feeling foolish as he walked up to him; if the older baron wanted to make a pleasantry at his expense, he should have ignored it. But he hadn't, and now he'd lose more face by turning around and walking away than by going on.

"What did you mean by that?" he repeated.

"I believe you may not know, so I'll answer straight," Ricolf said. "Anything at all can happen to a person once; the gods delight in keeping us confused so we remember we're not so wise nor so strong as they are. But when a man does something twice, that says more about him than about the way the knucklebones fall."

"You call that a straight answer?" Gerin said. "Dyaus preserve me from a twisty one, then—or Biton, if you aim to take the Sibyl's station now that she's let go of it."

"The Sibyl enters in, sure enough," Ricolf answered, leaning back against the stonework of the well. "This is the second time now, Fox, you've snatched away women you had no proper business taking, Elise being the first."

Gerin exhaled in annoyance. "What was I supposed to do, Ricolf? Leave the Sibyl to be devoured by those— things? If I'd come here with that tale, you'd have found some other way to connect it to your daughter . . . and to blame me for it. It's not as if I'm in love with Selatre."

"As I recall, you weren't in love with Elise, either, not when you took off with her," Ricolf said. "You were just bearing her to her uncle south of the Kirs. But those things have a way of changing."

"Ricolf, however our holdings have sometimes rubbed these past few years, have I ever used you with less than the courtesy any man owes the father of his wife?" Gerin asked. He waited for Ricolf to shake his head before he went on, "Then within that courtesy, I have to tell you you've got your head stuck right in the dung heap."

He took a wary step back. If Ricolf drew blade on him, he wanted room in which to fight. He had no great worries about holding off the older baron, but he wanted to be able to hold him off in a way which suggested to Ricolf's warriors that he wasn't trying to murder their overlord, merely protect himself.

Ricolf stared as if he doubted his own ears. A flush turned his face as red as his hair had once been (Elise had had skin like that, the Fox remembered—transparent as a Trokmê's). Then, to Gerin's relief, a snort escaped his lips and turned into a guffaw. "All right, Fox, you win that one," Ricolf wheezed, but he added, "For now, anyhow. A year or two down the road, we'll see who laughs last."

"Oh, go howl," Gerin said.

"I'm done, I'm done." Ricolf pacifically held up his

hands. "Dyaus forbid I should try to tell you anything when you already know all that's been written or thought by every wise man since the gods decided they'd like to have a ball they could kick around and made the world to give themselves something interesting to do: besides swiving one another, I mean, and if that gets stale for a man after a while, it likely does for the gods, too."

"Not by the tales that are told of them," Gerin answered, but he let it go at that; Ricolf waxing philosophical struck him as unlikely enough to make a challenge unwise.

And indeed, Ricolf's next words were utterly mundane: "With all this hurrah behind you, you'll be all in a sweat to get back to Fox Keep, so I don't suppose you'll stay the night. You'll be wanting a trussed fowl, then, or some such, to hold the ghosts out of your head."

"Aye, that would be kind of you," the Fox agreed. "Do you know, though, Selatre seems to calm them—not altogether, but partway—by herself. I suppose it's because she was Biton's intimate for so long."

"Does she?" Ricolf's tone irked Gerin, but not enough to make him rise to it. The older baron shrugged and said, "I'll see what sort of bird the kitchen crew can scare up for you."

Instead of a hen, Ricolf's cooks presented Gerin with a trussed duck that tried to bite his hand and quacked furiously when he stowed it in the back of the wagon. It kept quacking, too. "Can't say as I blame it," Van remarked as he got onto the wagon's seat himself. "I wouldn't be happy if anybody did that to me, either."

"Can you tie something around its beak?" Gerin asked Selatre when the duck went right on making a racket after the wagon rolled out of Ricolf's keep and headed up the Elabon Way once more.

"Oh, let it squawk. What else can it do, poor thing?"

Selatre said. Since she was in the back of the wagon with it and had to endure more of the noise than Gerin did, and since Van had already said more or less the same thing, the Fox let her have her way. Nonetheless, by the time the sun neared the western horizon, he looked forward to lopping off the duck's head for more reasons than just keeping the ghosts happy.

When they stopped to camp for the night, he steered the wagon off the road to a little pond that had enough saplings growing close by to screen it away from the casual glance of anyone on the road by night. Van got down and began gathering dry leaves and twigs for tinder.

Gerin descended, too. He went around to the back of the wagon and said to Selatre, "Hand me out that pestiferous duck, if you please. We'll eat him tonight, but he's already had his revenge. My head aches."

The ex-Sibyl seemed merely practical, not oracular, as she picked up the duck by the feet and held it out to Gerin, warning, "Be careful as you take him. He'll do his best to bite; he won't just quack."

"I know." Trying to take the duck from Selatre without touching her as he did so didn't make things any easier for Gerin, but he managed, and didn't bother mentioning the extra awkwardness. If that was how Selatre was going to be, he'd accept it as best he could.

Once he had the duck, he set it on the ground. He made himself stand by and not offer Selatre a hand as she got down from the wagon, wondering all the while how long he'd need before not offering aid became automatic for him. Then Selatre stumbled over a root, exclaimed, and started to fall. Altogether without thinking, Gerin jumped forward and steadied her.

"Thank you," she said, but then stopped in confusion and jumped back from him as if he were hot as molten bronze.

"I'm sorry," he said, though apologizing for having kept her from hurting herself struck him as absurd.

She shivered as she looked down at the arm he'd grabbed, then nodded with the same sort of deliberation Gerin had shown when he kept himself from helping her down a few moments before. "It's all right," she said. "However much I try to stay away from them, these things will happen now that I'm so rudely cast into the world. I may as well do my best to get used to them."

The Fox bowed. "Lady, on brief acquaintance I thought you had good sense. Everything you do—this especially—tells me I was right."

"Does it?" Selatre's laugh came shaky. "If that's so, why do I feel as if I'm casting away part of myself, not adding on anything new and better?"

"Change, any change, often feels like a kick in the teeth," Gerin answered. "When the Trokmoi killed my father and my elder brother and left me lord of Fox Keep, I thought the weight of the whole world had landed on my shoulders: I aimed to be a scholar, not a baron. And then—" He broke off.

"Then what?" Selatre asked.

Gerin wished he'd managed to shut up a few words earlier. But he'd raised the subject, so he felt he had to answer: "Then a few years ago my wife ran off with a horseleech, leaving me to raise our boy as best I could. His kidnapping was what made me come to Ikos."

"Yes, you've spoken of that." Selatre nodded, as if reminding herself. "But if you hadn't come, by everything else you've told me, the creatures that dwelt in the caves under Biton's temple would have killed and eaten me after the earthquake."

"If the earthquake would have happened had I not come," Gerin said, remembering the words of doom in the last prophecy Biton had issued through Selatre's mouth.

Van came around the wagon. "I've already got the fire going," he announced. "Are you going to finish off that duck, or do you aim to stand around jabbering until the ghosts take away what few wits you have left?" He turned to Selatre. "Take no notice of him, lady, when he gets into one of his sulks. Give him a silver lining, as you did, and he'll make a point of looking for its cloud."

"To the hottest of the five hells with you," Gerin said. Van only laughed. The nettle he'd planted under Gerin's hide stung the worse for bearing a large measure of truth.

The Fox dug a trench in the ground with his dagger, then drew sword and put an end to the duck's angry squawking with a stroke that might have parted a man's head from his shoulders, much less a bird's. He drained the duck's blood into the trench for the ghosts. Van took charge of the carcass. "It'll be greasy and gamy, but what can you do?" he said as he opened the belly to get rid of the entrails.

"Gamy or no, I like the flavor of duck," Selatre said. "Duck eggs are good, too; they have more taste than those from hens."

"That's so, but hens are easier to care for—just let 'em scavenge, like pigs," Gerin said. He glanced around. "Even though we were slow with the offering, the ghosts are still very quiet. Lady, I think that's your doing, no matter that we happened to touch again."

Selatre cocked her head to the side, listening to the ghosts as they wailed and yammered inside her head. "You may be right," she said after she'd taken their measure. "I remember them louder and more hateful than this when I was still living in my village, before Biton made me his Sibyl. But I am Sibyl no more; the god himself said as much, and your touch sealed it—" She shook her head in confusion; the dark hair that had spilled over one shoulder flew out wildly.

Gerin said, "I don't think holiness is something you can blow out like a lamp. It doesn't so much matter that I touched you—certainly I didn't do it with lust in my heart, or aiming to pollute you. What matters is that the god touched you. My touch is gone in an instant; Biton's lingers."

Selatre thought about that and slowly nodded, her finely molded features thoughtful. Watching her in the firelight, Gerin decided Van had been right: she was attractive enough to make Fand jealous. Was she more attractive than the Trokmê woman? Their looks were so different, the comparison didn't seem worthwhile. But that it had even crossed his mind made him wonder if Ricolf hadn't been wiser back at his keep than the Fox had thought at the time.

He scowled, angry at himself for so much as entertaining that notion. Selatre said, "What's wrong? You look as if you just bit into something sour."

Before he could come up with anything plausible, Van saved the day, calling, "Come over here by the fire, both of you, and bite into something that's going to be gamy and greasy, like I said before, but better all the same than a big empty curled up and purring in your belly."

The duck was just as Van had predicted it would be, but Gerin fell to gratefully even so. A full mouth gave him the excuse he needed for not answering Selatre's question, and a full belly helped him almost—if not quite—forget the thoughts which had prompted that question in the first place.

The wagon came out from behind the last stand of firs that blocked the view toward Castle Fox. "There it is," Gerin said, pointing. "Not a fortress to rival the ones the Elabonian Emperors built in the pass south of Cassat, but it's held for many long years now; the gods willing, it'll go on a bit longer."

Selatre leaned forward in the rear of the wagon to see better, though she was still careful not to brush against the Fox or Van. "Why are most of the timbers of the palisade that ugly, faded green?" she said.

Van chuckled. "The lady has taste."

"So she does." Gerin refused to take offense, and answered the question in the spirit in which he hoped it had been asked: "It was a paint a wizard put on them, to keep another wizard from setting them afire."

"Ah," Selatre said. Thin in the distance—Gerin did not allow trees and undergrowth to spring up anywhere near the keep; if anyone set ambushes, he'd be that one— a horn from the watchtower said the wagon had been seen.

He twitched the reins and rode forward with a curious mixture of anticipation and dread: seeing his comrades again would be good, and perhaps some of them had word of Duren. But the trouble he expected from Fand cast a shadow over the homecoming.

"We were free peasants in the village where I grew up; we owed no lord service," Selatre said. "Not much of what we heard about Elabonian barons was good, and I came to have a poor opinion of the breed. You tempt me to think I may have been wrong."

Gerin shrugged. "Barons are men like any others. Some of us are good, some bad, some both mixed together like most people. I'm bright enough, for instance, but I worry too much and I'm overly solitary. My vassal Drago the Bear, whom you'll meet, isn't what you call quick of wit and he hates anything that smacks of change, but he's brave and loyal and has the knack of making his own people like him. And Wolfar of the Axe, who's dead now, was vicious and treacherous, if you ask me, but he'd never shrink from a fight. As I say, we're a mixed bag."

"You speak of yourself as if you were someone else," Selatre said.

"I try sometimes to think of myself that way," the Fox answered. "It keeps me from making too much of myself in my own mind. The fellow who's sure he can't possibly go wrong is usually the one who's likeliest to."

A couple of men came out of the gate and waved to the approaching wagon: squat Drago with slim Rihwin beside him. "Any luck, lord?" Drago called, raising his voice to a shout.

"What did the Sibyl say?" Rihwin asked, also loudly.

"We're still the ripple of news furthest out from where the rock went into the pond," Van said.

"So we are." Gerin nodded, adding, "I like the picture your words call to mind." Behind them and in every other direction, others would also be spreading word of what had happened at Ikos. Soon the whole of the northlands would know. But for now, there was a dividing line between those who did and those who didn't, and he and Van were on it.

He raised his voice in turn to answer his vassals: "By your leave, I'll tell the tale in the great hall and not sooner. That way I'll have to retell it only once, and there's a good deal to it."

"Is that Duren in the wagon behind you?" Rihwin asked.

Drago's sight had begun to lengthen as he aged. Today, that served him well. "No, loon," he said. "That's a man grown. No, I take it back—a woman?" The Fox didn't blame him for sounding surprised.

Rihwin's agile wits let him leap to a conclusion that wouldn't have occurred to Drago. "You've caught up with

Elise?" he said loudly. "Did she steal the boy away, lord Gerin?" That his wits were agile, of course, didn't necessarily mean he was right.

At that moment, Gerin wished he'd kept quiet. The rumor would be all over the keep, all over the serf villages, and would spread faster than the truth could follow it. "No, it's not Elise," he said, even louder than Rihwin had spoken. "This is the lady Selatre, who up till bare days ago was Biton's Sibyl at Ikos."

Warriors up on the palisade, who'd already begun to gossip about Rihwin's speculation, abruptly fell silent. Then they started buzzing again, more busily than before. Maybe Rihwin's wild guess wouldn't go everywhere after all, Gerin thought: the truth was so much stranger that it might take precedence.

He drove the wagon over the drawbridge and into the keep, then got down from it. Van slipped off from the other side. They both stood back to let Selatre descend with no risk of touching either of them.

Gerin introduced his vassals to her one by one. He wondered how good she'd be at matching unfamiliar names to equally unfamiliar faces; that often gave him trouble. But she coped well enough, and showed she knew who was who when she spoke to the men. The Fox was impressed.

Widin Simrin's son asked the question they all had to be thinking: "Uh, lord Gerin, how did you come to have the holy Sibyl riding with you?"

"You felt the earthquake a few days past?" Gerin asked in turn.

Heads bobbed up and down. Drago said, "Aye, we did, lord. Like to scare the piss out of me, it did. We lost some pots, too, and spilled ale from a couple of broken jars." He sighed in sorrow at the misfortune. Then he scratched his head. "Has that aught to do with the lady here?"

"It has everything to do with the lady here," Gerin said. Van nodded, the crimson horsehair plume on his helm drawing eyes to him. The Fox went on, "Let's all go into the great hall. I hope not all the ale spilled." He waited until reassured on that before finishing, "Good, for I'll need a mug or two to ease my throat as I—and Van, and the lady Selatre—tell you what happened, and why she's here."

He waved toward the entrance to the castle. Drago and Widin and Rihwin and the rest hurried inside. Selatre waited till they'd gone through the door before she too went in. Even if she'd consciously decided not to let getting touched every once in a while bother her, she aimed to avoid it where she could.

Gerin did not go into the great hall until even Selatre was inside. He told himself that was politeness, and so it was, but it was also anxiety: he put off for a moment the likelihood of confronting Fand.

He knew that was foolish: putting off trouble, even for a little while, wasn't worth the effort, and often made it worse when it finally came. But knowing that and facing up to a screaming fight with Fand were two different things. At last, bracing himself as if walking into a winter wind, he walked into the great hall.

His stiff pose eased as his eyes adjusted to the gloom within: Fand had to be still upstairs. "Took you long enough," Van rumbled, though he no doubt had the same concern. "If you'd stayed out there much longer, the ale would've been drunk by the time you got around to joining us."

"Can't have that." Gerin went over to the jar and dipped a jack full. He wet his throat, then told what had happened on the way to Ikos and after he and Van had got there. His vassal barons muttered angrily when he spoke of the peasants who'd hunted him in the night.

He shook his head. "I was angry at the time, too, but it all fades away when you set it alongside what came later."

He spoke of the trip down to the Sibyl's cave and of the disturbing oracular response Biton had delivered through Selatre's lips. His listeners muttered again, this time with the same dread he'd felt when those doom-filled words washed over him. Selatre broke in, "I remember lord Gerin and Van coming into my underground chamber, but nothing after that, for the mantic trance had possessed me."

Gerin went on with the rest of the story: Selatre's continued and abnormal unconsciousness, the meeting with Aragis in the temple, the carouse afterwards (now that his hangover was gone, Van grinned in fond memory), and the earthquake the next morning.

Sometime while he was going through all that, Fand came down and sat beside Drago the Bear. Maybe the vassal baron's bulk kept Gerin from spotting her right away, or maybe he'd kept from looking toward the stairs on purpose. But she leaned forward when he spoke of the monsters that had emerged from the ruins of Biton's temple. Again, he had his listeners' complete and dismayed attention. Fand kept quiet while he spoke of the battle the creatures had had with the temple guards in the sacred precinct.

Then he said, "We'd gone back there, Van and I, because our innkeeper said the Sibyl still hadn't come to her senses. After the quake, we feared her cottage would burn like so many buildings in the town of Ikos. Since we'd been responsible for pitching her into the fit, we thought we should make amends for it if we could. As it happened, her dwelling hadn't caught fire, but the monsters would have made short work of her if we hadn't got there when we did."

Fand stirred but still did not speak. Selatre said, "I

woke up in their wagon some hours later, with my world turned all topsy-turvy."

Actually hearing Selatre seemed to draw Fand's notice to her. The Trokmê woman leaned forward, her chin on her hands, intently studying the former Sibyl. Then, to Gerin's dismay, she got to her feet and looked from him to Van. In a voice low but no less menacing because of that, she said, "And which of you was it, now, who was after wanting to trade me for the first new bit o' baggage you chanced upon, like a wandering tinker mending a pot in exchange for a night's rest and a bit o' bread in the morning?"

"Now, lass, didn't you listen to the Fox?" Van usually had no trouble with women, but now he sounded nervous, which didn't help. "It wasn't her body we had designs on, just saving her life."

"Likely tell," Fand snarled. "Sure and you'd have been just as eager to go back for her had she been old and toothless, not young and toothsome, sure and you would."

Gerin had thought himself the most sarcastic soul in the northlands; saying one thing and meaning another was a subtle art more often practiced south of the High Kirs. But wherever Fand had picked it up, she was dangerously good at it. And her furious question made the Fox ask himself if he would have headed back toward the fane to rescue Selatre's crone of a predecessor. He had to admit he didn't know, and that troubled him.

"Is this your wife, lord Gerin, thinking I'm some sort of menace to her?" Selatre asked. "I hope that is not so." Now she looked as if she doubted anew all the assurances she'd come to trust on the road north from Ikos.

"My leman, rather, and Van's," the Fox answered. Selatre raised an eyebrow at his domestic arrangements, but he ignored that; he'd worry about it later. Fand, as usual, was immediate trouble. To her, he said, "I'll thank you to keep a civil tongue in your head. By the gods, I did what I did for the reasons I said I did it, and if you don't fancy that, you can pack up and leave."

"Och, you'd like that, now wouldn't you?" Fand was low-voiced no more; her screech drove Drago from the seat close by her. "Well, lord Gerin the Fox—and you too, you overthewed oaf" —this to Van— "you'll not be rid of me so easy as that, indeed and you won't. Use me and cast me forth, will you?"

She picked up her drinking jack and threw it at Gerin. It was half full; a trail of ale, like a comet's tail, followed it as it flew. The Fox had been expecting it, so he ducked in good time—you needed battle-honed reflexes to live with Fand.

Van tried again. "Now, lass—"

She snatched the dipper out of the jar of ale and flung it at him. It clanged off the bronze of his cuirass. He was vain about his gear; he looked down in regret and anger at the ale that dripped to the floor.

"I ought to heat your backside for that," he said, and took a step forward, as if to do it on the spot.

"Aye, come ahead, thrash me," Fand fleered, and stuck out the portion of her anatomy he had threatened. "Then tomorrow or the day after or the day after that you'll be all sweet and poke that cursed one-eyed snake o' yours in my face—and I'll bite down hard enough to leave you no more'n a newborn wean has. D'you think I wouldn't?"

By the appalled look he wore, Van thought she would. He turned to Gerin for help in quelling this mutiny. The Fox didn't know what to say, either. He wondered if Fand would storm out of the castle, or if he'd have to throw her out. He didn't really want to do that; for all her hellish temper, he liked having her around, and not just because he slept with her. Till Duren was kidnapped, she'd watched over him as tenderly as if she'd given birth to him. Her wits were sharp, too, as he sometimes found to his discomfort.

Right now, though, he wouldn't have minded putting a hard hand to her behind, if only he'd thought that would make matters better. Unfortunately, he thought it would make them worse. If force wouldn't help and she wouldn't listen to reason, what did that leave? He wished he could come up with something.

Then Selatre got to her feet. She dropped a curtsy to Fand as if the Trokmê woman had been Empress of Elabon and said, "Lady, I did not come here intending to disrupt your household in any way: on that I will take oath by any gods you choose. I am virgin in respect of men, and have no interest in changing my estate there; as lord Gerin and Van of the Strong Arm both know, any touch from an entire man would have left me religiously defiled before—before Biton abandoned me." Her brief hesitation showed the pain she still felt at that. "I tell you once more, I am not one like to steal either of your men from you."

Where Gerin and Van had fanned Fand's fury, Selatre seemed to calm her. "Och, lass, I'm not after blaming you," she said. "By all 'twas said, you had not even your wits about you when these two great loons snatched you away. But what you intend and what will be, oftentimes they're not the same at all, at all. Think you I intended to cast my lot with southron spalpeens?"

"I'm no southron," Van said with some dignity.

"You're no Trokmê, either," Fand said, to which the outlander could only nod. But Fand wasn't screaming any more; she just sounded sad, maybe over the way her life had turned out, maybe—unlikely though that seemed to Gerin—regretting her show of temper.

"And what am I?" Selatre said. She answered her own question: "I was the god's servant, and proud and honored he had chosen me through whom to speak. But now he has left me, and so I must be nothing." She hid her face in her hands and wept.

Gerin was helpless with weeping women. Maybe that explained why he got on with Fand as well as he did—instead of weeping, she threw things. He knew how to respond to that. He hadn't known what to do when Elise cried, either, and suddenly wondered if that had been one of the things that made her leave.

He looked to Van, who made an art of jollying women into good spirits. But Van looked baffled, too. He jollied women along mostly to get them into bed with him; when faced with a virgin who wanted to stay such, he was at a loss.

Finally the Fox went into the kitchens and came back with a bowl of water and a scrap of cloth. He set them in front of Selatre. "Here, wash your face," he said. She gulped and nodded. Van beamed, which made Gerin feel good; he might not have done much, but he'd done *something*. It was a start.

VI

A chariot came pounding up the road toward Fox Keep. The driver was whipping the horses on so hard that the car jounced into the air at every bump, threatening to throw out him and his companion. "Lord Gerin! Lord Gerin!" the archer cried.

The Fox happened to be on the palisade. He stared down in dismay at the rapidly approaching chariot. He was afraid he knew what news the onrushing warriors bore. But he had been back in Fox Keep only five days himself; he'd hoped he might have longer to prepare. Hopes and reality too often parted company, though. "What word?" he called to the charioteer and his passenger.

They didn't hear him over the rattling of the car and the pound of the horses' hooves, or spy him on the wall. The chariot roared into the courtyard of the keep. The driver pulled back on the reins so sharply that both horses screamed in protest. One tried to rear, which might have overturned the chariot. The lash persuaded the beast to keep all four feet on the ground.

At any other time, Gerin would have reproved the driver for using the horses so; he believed treating animals mildly got the best service from them. Now, as he hurried down from the walkway across the wall, such trivial worries were far from his mind. "What word?" he repeated. "Tomril, Digan, what word?"

Tomril Broken-Nose tossed the whip aside and jumped out of the chariot. "Lord Gerin, I'm here to tell you I beg your pardon," he said.

"You didn't come close to killing your team for that," the Fox answered.

"Oh, but we did, lord prince," Digan Sejan's son said. "Tomril and I, we both thought you were babbling like a night ghost when you came up the Elabon Way warning folk of those half-man, half-beast things that were supposed to have gotten loose from under some old temple or other—"

"But now we've seen 'em, lord Gerin," Tomril broke in, his eyes wide. "They're ugly, they're mean, they've got a taste for blood—"

Now Gerin interrupted: "And they must be up at the bottom of Bevon's barony by now, or you wouldn't have seen them. What news do you have from Ricolf's holding?"

"About what you'd expect," Tomril answered. "They're loose there, too, the cursed things, and ripping serf villages to bits."

"Oh, a pestilence," Gerin said wearily. "If they're in Ricolf's holding, and Bevon's, they'll be here, too. How are the peasants supposed to grow crops if they're liable to be killed in the fields or torn to pieces in their beds?"

"Curse me if I know the answer to that one," Tomril said. "Things I've seen, things I've heard, make me think these creatures are worse than the Trokmoi, and harder to get rid of, too."

"They don't care a fart about loot, neither," Digan chimed in. "They just kill and feed and go away—and in the woods, they're clever beasts, and not easy to hunt."

"I hadn't thought of that, but you're right," Gerin said. "How many Trokmoi have we disposed of because they stayed around to plunder or loaded themselves down with stolen gewgaws till they couldn't even flee?"

"A good many, lord." Tomril touched the hilt of his sword in fond reminiscence. Then he scuffed the ground with a hobnailed sandal. "Won't be so with these monsters, though. They've got teeth and claws and enough of a man's cleverness to be more dangerous'n wolves ever dreamt of, but they aren't clever enough—I don't think so, anyways—to steal the things we make."

"Maybe they're too clever for that," Gerin said. His warriors stared at him in incomprehension. He didn't try to explain; struggling against the black depression that threatened to leave him useless took all he had in him. After he'd ridden out the Trokmê invasion, he'd begun, now and then, to have hope that he might keep something of Elabonian civilization alive north of the High Kirs. Now even a god seemed to have abandoned the land, leaving it open for these monsters from underground to course over it.

Rihwin came up in time to hear the last part of the exchange between Gerin and the two troopers. He said, "Lord Gerin, meseems these creatures, however horrific their semblance, should by virtue of their beastly nature be most vulnerable to magic: nor are they likely to have sorcerers of their own to help them withstand the cantrips we loose against them."

"The cantrips *I* loose against them, you mean," Gerin said, which made Rihwin bite his lip in embarrassment and nod. Gerin went on, "A really potent mage might be able to do what you say. Whether I can is another question altogether. I tell you frankly, I'm afraid of spells of bane, mostly because I know too well they can smite me instead of the ones at whom I aim them."

"A man who recognizes his limits is wise," Rihwin said, which made Gerin snort, for if he'd ever met a man who had no sense of limit whatever, that man was Rihwin.

Gerin paced up and down in the courtyard. At last he stopped and made a gesture of repugnance. "I won't try those spells," he said. "That's not just for fear of getting them wrong, either. Even if I work them properly, I'm liable to end up like Balamung, consumed by evil magic that's overmastered me."

Rihwin studied him judiciously. "If any man could work spells of bane without their corrupting him, I reckon you to be that man. But whether any man can do such is, I concede, an open question."

"Sometimes open questions are best left unopened," Gerin said. What he would do if faced by disaster complete and unalloyed he did not know; he muttered a silent prayer to Dyaus that he would not have to find out. Aloud, he went on, "What we need to do first, I think, is summon the vassals, fare south, and see if we can't teach those creatures fear enough to make them learn to stay away from lands I hold."

"As you say, lord prince," Rihwin agreed cheerfully. "I look forward to sallying forth against them." He mimed shooting a bow from the pitching platform of a chariot.

The Fox did not look forward to sallying forth. He felt harassed. He'd never wanted to be baron of Fox Keep, and once he became baron willy-nilly he'd never delighted in war for its own sake, as so many men of the northlands did. After the Empire of Elabon abandoned the northlands, his main aim had been to maintain its legacy in the lands he ruled. Fighting all the time did nothing to further that aim, but failing to fight meant dying, so what was he to do?

Rihwin said, "Of course, you also must needs take into account the possibility that the Trokmê clans north of the Niffet will seize the chance to strike south on learning of your deployment toward the opposite side of your holding."

"Thank you so much, bright ray of sunshine," Gerin said. "And I have to worry about Schild Stoutstaff, and Adiatunnus, and where in the five hells my son has disappeared to, and more other things than I have fingers and toes to keep track of."

"Lord Gerin, that's why the Sithonians devised counting boards," Rihwin said with a sly smile. Gerin stooped, picked up a clod of dirt, and flung it at him. Rihwin ducked. His smile got wider and even more impudent. "Ah, my fellow Fox, I see you've been taking lessons in deportment from your lady."

"Grinning and ducking won't save you now," Gerin exclaimed. "You'd better run, too." He chased Rihwin halfway round the keep, both men laughing like boys. Gerin finally stopped. "You're made of foolishness, do you know that?"

"Maybe I am," Rihwin said. "But ifsobe that's true, what does it make you?"

"Daft," Gerin answered at once. "Anyone who'd want to run a holding, let along the beginnings of a realm, has to be daft." He sobered quickly. "I'll have to send out word to my vassal barons to gather here with as many armed men as they can bring. That can't wait. If it does, we'll have other visitors than our warriors."

Fand stood in the doorway to her chamber and shook her head. "No, Fox, I don't care to have you in here this evening, so back to your own bed you can go."

Gerin scowled at her. "Why not? This is three times running you've told me no, and I know you've said aye to Van at least twice." One reason the two friends had stayed friends and not quarreled over Fand was that she'd always treated them pretty evenhandedly—till now.

"Because I don't care to, is why," she said, now tossing her head so her hair flew about in coppery ringlets. "And if that's not enough of an answer to suit you, why, to the corbies with you."

"I ought to—" he began.

"Ought to what?" she broke in. "Have me by force? Och, you can do it the once, belike; you're bigger nor I am, and stronger, too. But your back'd never be safe after that, nor had you better sleep but behind barred door. For that I'd take vengeance if it cost the life of me."

"Will you shut up, you idiot woman, and let me get a word in edgewise?" he roared in a startlingly loud voice—loud and startling enough to make Fand give back a pace. "I was trying to say, before you started screeching at me, that I ought to know what you think I've done wrong so I can figure out whether I really meant it or if I should try to make amends."

"Oh." Fand came as close to seeming subdued as she ever did. After a moment, she sighed. "It's not that you don't mean well, indeed and it isn't. But haven't you had enough to do with women to know that if you need to ask a question like that, the answer'll do you no good?"

Elise had said things like that, not long before she left him. He hadn't understood then, and didn't altogether understand now. "I don't fancy guessing games," he said slowly. "Usually you tell me whatever's in your mind—more than I want to hear, sometimes. Why not now?"

"Och, it's late at night, and I'd sooner sleep than have a row with you the now," Fand said. "Go on to your own bed, Fox. Maybe tomorrow I'll feel kinder toward you—who knows?" Then, because she was honest in her own fashion, she added, "Or maybe I won't."

Evasion made Gerin angry; when he wanted to know something, he kept digging till he found out. "Tell me what you're thinking," he growled. "If I've done something wrong, I'll find a way to make it right."

"You do try that, I'll own; you're just enough and to spare, for a fact," Fand said. "This time, though, 'twill not be so easy for you, I'm thinking." She shut her mouth tight then, and gave him a stubborn look that warned she'd say no more.

More than her words, the set of her face finally told Gerin what she meant. He clapped a hand to his forehead. "You're still sizzling because I brought Selatre to the keep," he exclaimed.

"And wouldn't you be, now, if I was after coming back here with a big-thewed, big-balled Trokmê man with a fine yellow mustache on him?" she said. "Och, puir fellow, by the side o' the road I found him, starving and all. Sure and I didn't fetch him back to sleep with him, even if he will be living in the castle from here on out." She did a wicked parody of his explanation of how he'd come to bring Selatre to Castle Fox, and topped it off by assuming an expression innocent and wanton at the same time.

Gerin hoped he managed to disguise his startled laugh as a cough, but wouldn't have bet money on it. "You have the tongue of a viper, do you know that?" he said. It pleased her, which wasn't what he'd had in mind. He went on, "By the gods, I haven't set a hand on her since she got here. I don't mean I haven't tried to take her to bed, I mean I literally have not touched her. So I don't know why you keep wanting to have kittens about it."

"Foosh, I know you've not touched her." Fand tossed her head in fine contempt. "But can you tell me so easy you've not wanted to?"

"I—" Gerin lied with few qualms when he dealt with his neighbors; only a fool, he reckoned, told the bald truth on all occasions. But lying to his leman was a different business. He ended up not answering Fand at all.

When she saw he wasn't going to, she nodded and quietly shut the door between them. The bar on her side did not come down; he could have gone in.

He stood in the hallway for a minute or so, then

muttered, "What's the bloody use?" He went back to his own chamber and lay down. He was still awake when pale Nothos rose in the east, which meant midnight had come and gone. Eventually he slept.

Van sang in the stables as Raffo readied the chariot to go out on campaign. Gerin had always looked on war as an unpleasant part of the business of running a barony, but now the idea of escaping from Castle Fox for a while suited him fine.

When he said as much, Van stopped singing and started to laugh. "What's so stinking funny?" the Fox asked irritably.

"You're that glad to get away from sweet Fand, are you?" Van said, laughing still. "This I tell you: she's as happy to have you gone as you are to be going. Not just her eyes are green; she's jealous enough to spit poison like some of the snakes they have in the jungles of the east."

"I already saw that for myself, thank you very much," Gerin said. He wished Van hadn't brought it up where Raffo and a good many other men as well could listen, but after a moment he realized that didn't matter: the only people in his holding who hadn't heard about how well Fand liked his coming back with Selatre were deaf, and their friends had probably drawn pictures in the dirt for them. Fixing the outlander with a baleful stare, he ground out, "And how is it she hasn't stayed angry with you? You had as much to do with getting Selatre here as I did."

"Oh, no doubt, no doubt," Van admitted. Just then Raffo climbed into the chariot. Van followed him, setting his shield in the bracket on his side of the car.

Gerin did the same on his side. "You were saying?" he prompted when Van showed no sign of going on.

"I was, wasn't I? Well, how do I put it?" Van fiddled with his weapons to give him time to gather his thoughts. Raffo flicked the reins and got the horses going. As they passed from the stable out into the courtyard, the outlander said, "I guess the nub of it is, she believes me when I tell her I'm not out to bed Selatre. You she's not so sure about."

"I don't know what I have to do," Gerin said wearily. "I've told Fand and I've told her—"

"Not that simple, Captain, and you likely know it as well as I do," Van said. "Me, I'm a wencher and not a lot more, and Fand, she suits me well enough, though the gods know I'd sooner she didn't have that redheaded temper of hers. You and Fand, though . . . but for bed, damn me to the hottest one of your five hells if I can see where the two of you fit together."

"She came to Fox Keep at the right time," Gerin answered.

"Oh, I know that," Van said. "After Elise up and left, any woman would have done you for a while, just to let you remember you're a man. But I'd not expected this to last so long." He laughed again. "I figured you'd sicken of quarreling with her and leave her all to me, not that I know whether I could stand that myself."

"You have all of her now, seems like, without my having any say at all," the Fox answered, less than delighted his friend had seen into him so clearly.

"So I do, and I still don't know whether I can stand it." The outlander sighed. "What made it work so well, the three of us I mean, is that Fand has more than enough venom for any one man, but she's bearable when she has two to spread it on. Of course, it helps that neither of us is the jealous sort."

"No." Gerin let it go at that. Had he cared more for Fand, he thought, he would have been more likely to be jealous, too, but he didn't care to say as much straight out. He did add, "Another thing that helps is that she's lickerish enough for the two of us together. I think she'd wear me out if I had to try to keep her happy by my lonesome."

"You're getting old," Van said, to which the Fox mimed throwing a punch, for his friend was no younger. Then Van sighed again, and went on, "One more thing to worry about." He stopped, seemed to listen to himself, and guffawed. "By the gods, I've been with you too long, Captain. I'm even starting to sound like you."

"Believe me, I like the idea even less than you do," Gerin answered, and Van pretended to wallop him. Up ahead at the reins, Raffo snickered.

The chariots rolled south down the Elabon Way in no particular order, now bunched together, now strung out in a long line. Sometimes the Fox's warriors sang or swapped jokes, sometimes they kept them to themselves. Gerin knew the Empire of Elabon had imposed stricter discipline on its soldiers when it was strong, but he didn't know how the trick was done. By all the evidence, Elabon didn't know anymore, either.

Even though he was still in his own holding, he kept a wary eye on the woods and brush to either side of the Elabon Way. If the monsters from Ikos had been seen in Bevon's holding (not that Bevon held much of it), they might be loose in Palin's lands, too—and they might have come farther north than that.

Serfs in the fields stared as the chariots bounced past them. A few took no chances, but dropped their hoes and stone-headed mattocks and ran for the safety of the trees. After the chaos the northlands had endured the past five years, that did not surprise the Fox, but it left him sad. Here he and his comrades fared forth to protect the peasants, and they seemed to feel they needed protecting from their overlords.

Thanks to Gerin's forethoughtfulness, the little army had several hens among the baggage. They also had enough axes to cut plenty of firewood for a good-sized blaze. Between the offering and the fire, the evening ghosts were hardly more than a distraction.

"We'll set pairs of sentries out all night long in a triangle," Gerin said. "I won't have us assailed without warning."

Van took charge of roasting the two chickens they'd sacrificed. He was the logical man for the job: not only was he as good a roadside cook as anyone else, he was also no one to argue with when he passed out pieces of meat, for there weren't enough to go around. Those who went without chicken made do with hard-baked biscuits and smoked meat, cheese, and onions. Everyone drank ale.

Gerin tossed a gnawed thighbone into the fire. He chewed at a biscuit about as tough as his own teeth. "I wonder if this came from Ros the Fierce's reign, or just Oren's," he said after he managed to get a mouthful down.

"You have no cause to make complaint against Oren the Builder," Rihwin said, "for the image of him you fetched back from the fane at Ikos leaves you perhaps the richest man in the northlands."

"Aye, gold is good to have, I'll not deny," Gerin said. "That's not the way I expected to come by it, but you hear no complaints from me."

Some of the warriors rolled themselves in their blankets as soon as they'd finished eating. Others stayed up a while to talk or roll knucklebones by the light of the fire. Van snarled in angry dismay when he lost three throws in a row; his luck usually ran better than that. Then he lost again, and stood up from the game. "Enough is enough," he declared.

"Well, if you won't gamble with us, what about a tale?"

Widin Simrin's son said. He had his own reasons for being willing to call off the game: a nice little pile of silver gleamed in front of him.

Everyone who heard the suggestion spoke up for it all the same, especially the men from outlying keeps who seldom got the chance to hear Van yarn. The outlander coughed and plucked at his beard. "Which tale shall I give you?" he asked. "You pick one for me."

"How about the one about how they teach the monkeys to pick pepper?" Gerin said. "You were going to start it a few days ago, but we got interrupted. And if I've not heard it, my guess is that few others here have."

From the way the warriors exclaimed, none of them knew the story. "So I've not told it in all the time I've been at your keep, eh, Captain?" Van said. "Nice to know I've not yarned myself dry, and that's a fact. All right, here goes: the tale of the way they teach monkeys to pick pepper."

Before he started the story, he paused to swig ale and lubricate his throat. That accomplished, he said, "This is what I saw in Mabalal, which is a hot, damp country a good ways east and south from Kizzuwatna. Take the muggiest summer day you've ever known here, imagine it ten times worse, and you'll start to know what the weather there is like.

"Now maybe it's on account of the weather, but a lot of the folk of Mabalal are what you'd have to call lazy. Some of 'em, I swear, would just as soon lie with their mouths open in the rain as get up and find themselves a cup to drink from—but that's no part of the tale.

"If you want to know what pepper trees are like, think of willows—they look much like 'em, right down to the clusters of fruit. The trouble with 'em is, they grow on the steepest hillsides and cliffs, so people have a beastly time getting to 'em to take away the pepper."

"Probably why it costs so much by the time it gets here," Gerin said.

"Likely so, Captain. Now the folk of Mabalal are lazy, like I said. If we had to hope for them to climb hillsides and cliffs to gather the pepper fruits, it'd cost more than it does, I tell you true. What they do instead is get the monkeys to work for 'em, or maybe trick 'em into it would be a better way to put it."

"What's a monkey?" asked a warrior from an isolated keep, a man who never went more than a couple of hours' walk from his holding unless on campaign.

"A monkey is a beast about the size of a half-year babe that looks like a furry, ugly little man with a tail," Van answered patiently. "They live in trees, and have thumbs on their feet as well as their hands. They're clever and mischievous, almost like children, and they cause a lot of trouble stealing things and ruining them.

"The other thing about monkeys is, they like to do what people do—and the folk of Mabalal, who live with 'em the same way we do with dogs and cats, know it. There are whole bands of these monkeys, mind you, that live in the rough country where the pepper trees grow. So when the Mabalali want to get themselves some pepper, what they do is this: they go down to the foothills below the rough country and pick all the fruit off some of the trees there. Then they dump piles of the fruit in little clearings they've made close by, and they pretend to up and leave.

"Now, all the while the monkeys have been watching them from the high ground. The monkeys go and they pick the fruits from the pepper trees, and then they come down and they drop them in the clearings just the same way they'd seen the men do it. Sometimes they'll steal the fruit the Mabalali have left, sometimes they won't. Either way, the Mabalali get the pepper, and they get it without having to do the hard work themselves. So you see, sometimes being lazy isn't such a bad thing after all."

The warriors buzzed appreciatively, as they would have at any tale well told. For them it was a pleasant way to pass the time and a story to remember so they could tell it in turn. Gerin also liked it on those terms, but it set him thinking in a different way, too. "I wonder how many useful things have come from men's being too lazy to keep on doing things the same old hard way," he mused.

"Give me a for-instance, Captain," Van said.

That made the Fox scratch his head. At last he said, "Take the fellow who thought of the wagon. Wouldn't you bet he was sick of hauling things on his back?"

"Ah, I see what you're saying," Van said. "Likely so."

"And the fellow who first brewed ale, what was he sick of?" Rihwin asked. With a grin, he answered his own question: "Seeing straight, I suppose."

Gerin and Van both laughed at that, but Drago the Bear drew in a sharp, disapproving breath. "No man first brewed ale," he said flatly. "'Twas the gift of the god Baivers, and any who don't want his anger had best remember it."

Rihwin opened his mouth for what Gerin was sure would be a reply taken straight from the philosophers of the City of Elabon. Before that reply could emerge, Gerin forestalled it: "Rihwin, my fellow Fox, I trust you do recall the difficulties you had with Mavrix god of wine not so long ago?"

"Well, yes, I do," Rihwin said reluctantly. "I did not believe, however, that you of all people in the northlands would stifle the full and open discussion of ideas of all sorts. I—"

Gerin took him by the arm. "Here, walk with me," he said in a tone that brooked no argument. When the two men were as far from the fire and the blood offering as the wailing of the ghosts would let them go, Gerin continued in a low voice, "For all your study, one thing you never learned: there's a time and a place for everything. If you want to start arguments about the nature and powers of the gods, don't do it when you're heading out on campaign. I want my men's thoughts focused on two things: working with one another and slaughtering any monsters they happen across. Does that make sense to you?"

"I suppose so," Rihwin said, though he sounded sulky. "Yet you would be hard-pressed to deny that in theory—"

Gerin cut him off again, this time with a sharp chopping gesture of his left hand. "Theory is wonderful," he said. "What we have here is fact—if the men quarrel among themselves, they won't fight well. You do anything more to make them fight worse than they would otherwise and I'll leave you behind at the first keep we come to, or at a peasant village failing that. Do you understand me?"

"Oh, indeed." Rihwin angrily tossed his head; firelight glinted from the gold hoop in his left ear. "You're a hard man when you take the field, lord prince Gerin the Fox." He loaded Gerin's title with scorn.

"War is too important a business to be slack with it," Gerin answered, shrugging. "Will you do as I say and not stir up disputes among the gods, or shall I leave you? Those are your choices, sirrah."

Rihwin sighed. "Let it be as you say. You'd do better, though, if you learned to ease men into doing your will rather than hammering them into it."

"No doubt." Gerin sighed, too. Rihwin had nothing wrong with his wits, only a dearth of common sense. "And you'd do better if you thought more before you started talking or doing things. We all try to be the best men we can, and we all fail in different ways. Which watch do you have tonight?"

"The middle one." Rihwin's mobile features assumed an expression of distaste.

"There, you see?" Gerin said. "If your head held as much sense as a cabbage, you'd be asleep already instead of standing here arguing with me. Go curl up in your blanket."

"The power of your reasoning ravishes me yet again," Rihwin cried. Gerin snorted and made as if to kick him in the backside. The transplanted southerner lay down and soon fell asleep. Gerin had the midwatch, too, but stayed awake a good deal longer.

When the Fox's chariots rolled down into Bevon's holding, all the local barons shut themselves up right in their keeps and prepared to stand siege. "You just want to bite out another piece of our land," one of them called from his palisade when Gerin came up to the wall.

"That's not so," Gerin answered, wondering if the white rag he bore would protect him from the lordlet's archers. As he had so many times before, he spoke of the monsters that had erupted from the caves beneath Biton's temple.

And, as had happened too many times before, he met only disbelief. The petty baron laughed scornfully. "You're supposed to be clever, Fox. I'd have thought you could come up with a better excuse than that to come down on your neighbors."

"Have it as you will." The Fox knew he sounded weary, but couldn't help it. "You'll find out soon enough whether I'm telling the truth. When you learn I am, maybe you'll remember some of what I've said." He turned and walked back to the chariot where Van and Raffo waited. No one shot at him, so he just rode on.

Down at the southern border of Bevon's holding, Ricolf's men were no longer wary of the force Gerin used to hold the Elabon Way open. They'd seen the monsters for themselves—seen more of them than the Fox had, as a matter of fact. He spent the first couple of hours after he arrived asking questions.

"Some of the creatures are smarter than others, lord prince, seems like," one of Ricolf's troopers said. "I've seen a couple carrying sword or axe, and one even with a helm on its ugly head. But others'll either charge or run off, just like wild beasts."

"Interesting." Gerin plucked at his beard. "How many of them are there, would you say, and how much damage have they done?"

"How many? Too many, that's sure," the trooper said. "As for damage, think how much fun wolves would be if they had more in the way of wits, and hands to let them get into things doors and gates keep them out of."

Gerin thought about it. He didn't like the pictures that painted themselves in his mind. Elabonians were in the habit of calling Trokmoi wolves because of their fierce raids, but they had humanly understandable motives: they were out for loot and captives as well as slaughter for its own sake. Beasts that hunted and killed without grasping, let alone using, the concepts of mercy and restraint were daunting in an altogether different way.

The Fox thanked Ricolf's man and went back to pass the word to his own warriors. "One thing's certain," he said when he'd given them the grim news: "These creatures won't act like a regular army of men. They aren't an army at all, not really. Instead of trying to storm up the Elabon Way in a mass, I look for them to spread through the woods by ones and twos and maybe packs—no larger groups or bands or whatever you want to call them."

"If that's so, lord Gerin, we might as well not have brung these here chariots," Widin Simrin's son said.

"For fighting, you're right," the Fox answered, letting his young vassal down easy. "But we'd have been another two or three days on the road if we'd footed it down here."

Widin nodded, abashed. Drago the Bear said, "What'll you have us do with the cars, then? We can't go into the woods with 'em, that's certain, and you say the woods is where we'll find these things." He shook his head in somber anticipation. "You're going to make foot soldiers out of us, I know you are."

"Do you see that I have any choice?" Gerin asked. "Here's what I'm thinking: we'll split up by chariot crews, with teams of three crews sticking together in teams. That'll give each team nine men, which should be enough to hold off even a pack of the creatures. At the same time, we'll have eight or ten teams spreading out along the border between Bevon's and Ricolf's holdings, and that ought to give us a chance to keep a lot of the beasts from slipping farther north."

"What about the ones that are already over the border?" Van asked. "How are you going to deal with them?"

"Bevon's vassals, or rather Bevon's sons' vassals, will slay some of them," Gerin said. "That should convince them the things are real and dangerous. As for the others, we'll just have to hope there aren't too many."

"Fair enough," Van said, to Gerin's relief. The Fox's great fear—one he didn't want to speak aloud to his followers—was that, like the Trokmoi, the monsters would permanently establish themselves in the northlands. If men couldn't rid the woods of wolves, how were they to be free of creatures cleverer and more vicious than wolves?

He divided his men into teams of nine, and appointed

a leader for each band. He had contrary misgivings about naming Drago and Rihwin: the one might miss things he ought to find, while the other got in trouble by being too inventive. But they were both better than anyone else in their bands, so he spoke their names firmly and hoped for the best.

He ordered half the teams to head east from the Elabon Way, the other half west. "We'll go out for three days, hunt for a day, and then come back," he said. "Anybody who's not back to the road in seven days' time and hasn't been eaten to give him an excuse will answer to me."

Eastbound and westbound forces headed out from the highway; the Fox and his chariot crew were in the latter. At first each half of the little army tramped along as a single body, the better to overawe any of the local nobles who might be tempted to fare forth against them. Men chattered and sang and, after a while, began to grumble about sore feet.

When morning had turned to afternoon and the sun sank toward the horizon, Gerin turned to the team headed by Widin Simrin's son. "You men go back and forth through the woods hereabouts," he said. "The rest of us will push on, then leave another team behind, then another, and another, so when we're through we'll have men all along the border. Do you see?"

"Aye, lord," Widin answered. "That means at the end of our reach, though, so to speak, we won't be able to search for as long as we will here closer to the Elabon Way."

"True enough," the Fox said, "but I don't know what we can do about it. Travel takes time, and there's no help for it." He nodded approvingly to Widin; that was a much better point than the one he'd raised before. Gerin hadn't worked the implications of his strategy through so logically himself. "When we get back to Fox Keep, would you be interested in learning to read and write?"

"No, lord prince," Widin replied at once. "Got better things to do with my time, I do—hunting and wenching and keeping my vassals and serfs in line." He sounded so sure of himself that Gerin subsided with a sigh and did not push the question.

With Widin's team left behind, the rest tramped on. They took a game track through a stand of oaks and emerged on the far side at the edge of cleared fields in which peasants labored. The peasants stared at them in horror, as if they were so many monsters themselves, then fled.

Their cries of terror made Gerin melancholy. "This holding has seen too much war," he said. "Let's push ahead without harming anything here: let them know not every warrior is out to steal what little they have."

"A wasted lesson if ever I heard one," Van said. "The next band through here, so long as it isn't one of ours, will treat them the way they expect us to." Gerin glared at him so fiercely that he hastened to add, "But we'll do it your way, Captain—why not?"

Evening came before the Fox reckoned the time ripe to detach another piece of his force. Along with the men he had with him, he tossed knucklebones to see who would stand watch through the night. He felt like cheering when he won the right to uninterrupted sleep. No sooner had he cocooned himself in his blanket and wriggled around a little to make sure no pebbles poked his ribs than he knew nothing of the world around him.

A hideous cry recalled him to himself: a wailing shriek part wolf, part longtooth, part madman. He sat up and looked around wildly, wondering for a moment where he was and what he was doing here. His gaze went to the heavens. Tiwaz, nearly full, stood high in the south; ruddy Elleb, a couple of days past fullness, was in the southeast. Crescent Math had set and Nothos not yet risen. That put the hour a little before midnight.

Then all such mundane, practical thoughts vanished from his head, for the dreadful call again rang through the woods and across the fields. Some men started up from their bedrolls, grabbing for bow or sword. Others shrank down, as if to smother the cry with the thick wool of their blankets. Gerin could not find it in himself to blame them; the scream made him want to hide, too.

In a very small voice, someone said, "Is that the cry these monsters make?"

"Don't know what else it could be." Van sounded amazingly cheerful. "Noisy buggers, aren't they? 'Course, frogs are noisy, too, and a frog isn't hardly anything but air and legs."

Gerin admired his friend's sangfroid. He also admired the way the outlander had done his best to make the creatures from the caves seem less dangerous; he knew they were a great deal more than air and legs.

The frightful cry rang out yet again. "How are we to sleep with that racket?" Widin Simrin's son said.

"You roll up in your blanket and you close your eyes," Gerin said, not about to let Van outdo him in coolness. "We have sentries aplenty; you won't be eaten while you snore."

"And if you are, you can blame the Fox," Van put in, adding, "Not that it'll do you much good then."

Off in the distance, almost on the edge of hearing, another monster shrieked to answer the first. That sent ice walking up Gerin's back, not from terror at the faraway cry but because it said the creatures that made those dreadful sounds were spreading over the northlands. Gerin wondered how many more were calling back and forth farther away than he could hear.

The one nearby kept quiet after that. Exhaustion and edgy nerves fought a battle over the Fox; exhaustion eventually won. The next thing he knew, the sun was prying his eyelids open. He got up and stretched, feeling elderly. His mouth tasted like something scraped off the bottom of a chamber pot. He walked over to a tree, plucked off a twig, frayed one end of it with the edge of his dagger, and used it to scrub some of the vileness from his teeth. Some of his men did the same, others didn't bother.

Rihwin, who'd grown up south of the High Kirs, was so fastidious that even frayed twigs didn't completely satisfy him. As he tossed one aside, he said, "In the City of Elabon they make bristle brushes for your mouth. Those are better by far than these clumsy makeshifts."

"If you like, you can teach the art to one of the peasants who makes big brushes for rubbing down horses," Gerin said. "We might be able to sell them through the northlands—not many southern amenities to be had here these days."

"My fellow Fox, I admire the wholeheartedness of your mercenary spirit," Rihwin said.

"Anyone who sneers at silver has never tried to live without it." Gerin looked around. "Where'd Van go?"

"He walked into the woods a while ago," Widin said. "He's probably off behind a tree, taking care of his morning business."

The outlander returned a few minutes later. He said. "When you're done breaking your fast, friends, I want you to come with me. I went looking for the spot where that thing made a racket last night, and I think I found it."

Several of the men were still gnawing on hard bread and sausage as they followed Van. He led them down a tiny track to a clearing perhaps a furlong from the camp. The carcass of a doe lay there. Much of the hindquarters portion had been devoured.

A scavenging fox fled from the carcass when the men came out of the woods. Van said to Gerin, "I hope your name animal hasn't ruined the tracks I saw. I'd be liable to think ill of it if it has, and I know you wouldn't like that." He walked over to the doe, grunted. "No, looks like we're all right. Come up a few at a time, all of you, and have a look at what the ground shows."

Gerin was part of the first small group forward. When he got close to the dead doe, Van pointed to a patch of bare, soft dirt by the animal. The footprints there were like none the Fox had ever seen. At first he thought they might be a man's, then a bear's—they had claw marks in front of the ends of their toes. But they didn't really resemble either. They were—something new.

"So this is the spoor we have to look for, is it?" he said grimly.

"Either that or someone's magicking our eyes," Van answered. "And I don't think anybody is."

The Fox didn't think so, either. He waited till all his men had seen the new footprints, then said, "They have claws on their hands, too. Now that we know what their tracks look like, let's get moving and see if we can't hunt down a few."

The warriors were quiet as they trooped back to the campsite. Now they had real evidence that Gerin and Van hadn't made up the tale about the monsters. They'd believed them already, likely enough, in an abstract way, but hearing about something new and terrible wasn't the same as seeing proof it was really there.

A couple of hours after they started tramping west, Gerin detached another band of men from his force to scour the area where they were. The rest slogged on; grumbles about aching feet got louder.

Around noon, Rihwin said, "Lord Gerin, something which may be of import occurs to me."

"And what is that?" Gerin asked warily. You never could tell with Rihwin. Some of his notions were brilliant, others crackbrained, and knowing the one bunch from the other wasn't always easy.

Now he said, "My thought, lord prince, is that these may in sooth be creatures of the night, wherein we heard the two of them giving cry. For does it not stand to reason that, having lived an existence troglodytic lo these many years, perhaps even ages, their eyes, accustomed as they must be to darkness perpetual, will necessarily fail when facing the bright and beaming rays of the sun?"

"Troglo—what?" Van said incredulously, no doubt speaking for a good many of the Fox's warriors.

Gerin was well-read and used to Rihwin's elaborate southern speech patterns, so he at least understood what his fellow Fox was talking about. "Means 'living in caves,'" he explained for those who hadn't followed. To Rihwin, he said, "It's a pretty piece of logic; the only flaw is that it's not so. Van and I saw the things fighting the temple guards in broad daylight the morning of the earthquake, and heard one behind us coming out of Ikos later that same day. Their eyes work perfectly well in sunlight."

"Oh, a pox!" Rihwin cried. "How dreadful to see such a lovely edifice of thought torn down by hard, brute fact." He sulked for the next couple of hours.

The Fox detached another team late that afternoon, and camped with his remaining two teams not long afterwards. The night passed quietly, much to his relief. Standing first watch was not so onerous—better that than being torn from sleep by a horrible screech, at any rate.

Early the next morning, he gave Rihwin's team their area to patrol. "Good hunting," he said, clapping his ekenamesake on the shoulder.

"I thank you, lord Gerin," Rihwin answered, and then,

"Do you know, there are times when I wonder how wise I was to cast aside my life of wealth and indolence in the southlands for an adventurous career with you."

"There are times when I wonder about that, too," Gerin said. "A lot of them, as a matter of fact. What you're saying now is that your heart wouldn't break if you didn't happen to run across any monsters?"

"Something like that, yes."

"I feel the same way, believe me," Gerin said, "but if we don't go after them, they'll end up coming after us. I'd sooner make the fight on my terms, and as far from my keep as I can."

"I understand the logic, I assure you," Rihwin said. "The argument takes on a different color, however, when it moves from the realm of ideas to the point of affecting one personally. Logicians who cling to abstract concepts seldom run the risk of being devoured."

"No matter how much they may deserve it," Gerin added, which won him a glare. He gave Rihwin another encouraging swat. For all the southerner's talk, Gerin didn't worry about his courage. His common sense was another matter, or would have been if he'd had any to speak of.

The Fox led his own team westward. Alarmed at their advance, a young stag bounded out of a thicket. Van pulled an arrow from his quiver, nocked, and let fly, all in close to the same instant. "That's a hit!" he shouted, and hurried forward to where the stag had been. Sure enough, blood splashed the grass. "Come on, you lugs," the outlander said to his companions. "With a trail like this to follow, a blind man'd be eating venison steaks tonight."

They ran the deer down about a quarter of an hour later. It lay panting on the ground, too weak to run any further; Van's arrow stood in its side, just back of the heart. It tried to struggle to its feet, but could not. Its large brown eyes stared reproachfully at the warriors. Van stooped beside it. With one swift motion, he jerked up its head and cut its throat.

Together, Van and Gerin tackled the gory job of butchering the stag. "Next stream we come to, I wash," Gerin declared.

"You may not need to wait for a stream, Captain," the outlander answered, pointing west. The weather had been fine, but clouds were beginning to roll in off the distant Orynian Ocean. "That could be rain."

"So it could." The Fox glowered at the clouds, as if he could hold them back by sheer force of will. "If it starts raining, how are we supposed to track anything? By the gods, how are we even going to keep fires going to help hold the ghosts at arm's length?" His rising bad temper even extended to Van. "And why couldn't you have killed this deer closer to sunset, so we could use its blood as an offering to the spirits?"

Van stood tall and glared down at him. "Are you going to complain that the grass is green instead of blue, too, or will you help me get the meat off this beast?" As usual, his comrade's bluntness showed Gerin where he'd stepped over the line from gloomy to carping. He nodded shamefacedly and fell to work.

Raffo said, "I have a thought, lord Gerin." He waited for the Fox to grunt before he went on, "What say we post ourselves in hiding around the offal there and see if it doesn't lure one of the creatures we're seeking? The stink of blood might draw 'em."

"We're already farther west than any of the other teams," Gerin said musingly. "It would mean pushing on a ways further tomorrow, but why not? As you say, the lure is good: might as well be a grub on a fish hook. Aye, we'll try it—but I still want to go and find water."

"And I," Van agreed. His arms were bloody to the elbows.

"We'll be back as soon as we may," Gerin said. "Set your ambush, but remember to know what you're shooting at before you let fly."

He and Van found a creek a couple of furlongs west of where the stag had fallen. Just as they came up to the bank, a kingfisher dove into the water, to emerge a moment later with a minnow in its bill. Something else— a frog or a turtle, Gerin didn't notice which—splashed into the creek from a mossy rock and didn't come out again.

The stag's blood had already started to dry; scrubbing it off wasn't easy. "We need some of the soap they make from fat and ashes south of the High Kirs," Gerin said, scraping one arm more or less clean with the nails of his other hand. "Maybe I'll try cooking a batch myself when we get home to Fox Keep."

"The stuff's too harsh for my liking," Van answered. "It takes off the top layer of your hide along with the dirt." He looked at Gerin. "You have a splash of blood by your nose, Fox. . . . No, on the other side. There, you got it."

"Good." Gerin gave a theatrical shiver. "That water's cold." He glanced westward again. The dirty gray clouds were piled higher there. "And before too long, more than my arms'll get wet. That does look like rain coming. The serfs will be glad of it, but I wish it would have held off till we were under a roof again."

"Weather won't listen, any more'n a woman will," Van said. "Let's head back and see if Raffo's brainstorm came to anything."

"We'd have heard if it did," Gerin answered. But he followed Van back toward the rest of their team. They could hold their ambush till it was time to set up camp for the night, he decided. Turning to his friend, he added, "It occurs to me now—too late, of course—that pile of guts might draw something besides monsters. If a longtooth decides it wants a meal, I hope they have sense enough to let it eat its fill."

"You're right," Van said. "I'm just glad Rihwin's not with us. He's a fine chap, mind you, but he hasn't the sense you need to cart guts to a bear, so why should a longtooth be any different? If you ask me—"

Gerin didn't have the chance to ask Van anything. A racket broke out ahead, the shouts of men and the hideous shriek they'd heard in the night. He jerked his sword out of its sheath, Van pulled the mace from the loop at his belt on which it hung, and the two of them pounded toward the tumult as fast as their legs would carry them.

"It's us!" Gerin yelled as he ran. "Don't shoot—we're not monsters." Whether any of the men was cool-headed enough to note and heed his cry was an open question.

Because he thought that way, the arrow that hissed between him and Van neither surprised nor infuriated him. He had a moment to be glad it had missed them both, then burst through the bushes into the little open space where the stag had died and been butchered.

Several of his men had already emerged from cover, too. "The thing went that way," Raffo exclaimed, pointing south. "We all shot at it, and hit it at least twice, maybe three times." What he'd seen suddenly seemed to sink in. His eyes went wide and staring. "Lord Gerin, forgive me that I ever doubted your words, I pray you. The creature is all you said it was, and more and worse besides."

"Yes, yes," Gerin said impatiently. "Enough jabbering—let's catch it and kill it. Lead on, Raffo, since you know the way."

Looking imperfectly delighted with the privilege he'd

been granted, Raffo plunged into the woods. The trail was easy to follow, blood and tracks both. Before long, Gerin could hear the monster crashing through the undergrowth ahead. "The things have weaknesses after all," Van panted. "They aren't woodswise like proper beasts, and they aren't what you'd call fast, either."

"You don't know about that," Gerin answered. "How fast and careful would you be with two or three arrows in you?" Van didn't answer, from which Gerin concluded he'd made his point.

With a roar, the monster sprang out from behind an elm tree. Four men shot arrows at it. Two of those missed; excitement could ruin anybody's aim. The creature screamed when the other two struck. But despite them, and despite the other shafts that pierced it, it rushed at its pursuers.

Its claws scraped against the bronze scales of Gerin's corselet. He could feel the force behind them, even if they did not wound; as he'd guessed, the monster was stronger than a man. He slashed with his sword. The thing screamed again.

Van clouted it with his mace. The blow would have crushed the skull of any man. It knocked the monster to the ground, but it got up again, blood streaming from the dreadful wound to the side of its head. Cursing in half a dozen languages, Van smote it again, even harder than before. This time it fell and did not rise again.

"Father Dyaus above," said a warrior named Parol and called Chickpea after a wart by his nose. Gerin's heart pounded in his chest. He felt as if he'd fought against a Trokmê rather than hunted a beast. The monster's strength, even badly wounded, accounted for some of that. More, though, came from how much the thing resembled a man.

"Will you look at it?" Raffo said in wondering tones.

"Take the ugliest scoundrel you've ever seen—old Wolfar, for instance—and make him five times as ugly as he really was, every which way, I mean, and you've just about got this thing here."

"Oh, not quite everything," Parol said. "I wouldn't mind being hung so good, and that's no lie."

That comment aside, Raffo's remark was to the point. Gerin had noted how manlike the monsters were from the moment he set eyes on them. Then, though, he hadn't had the leisure to examine one closely; he'd been more concerned about getting away from Ikos with his life and Van's and the Sibyl's.

Squat, muscular, hairy—the thing did resemble Wolfar, he thought, unkind to his old enemy though he'd killed him five years earlier. But Wolfar, except when he turned werebeast, had not been armed with claws on hands and feet both, and even as a werebeast his teeth had hardly matched the ones filling the monster's long, formidable jaws.

Above those jaws, its features were also a vicious parody of mankind's: a low nose with slit nostrils; large eyes set deep under heavy ridges of bone; thick hair, almost fur, rising to a crest on top of its head and nearly disguising how little forehead it had.

"There it is," Gerin said. "Dyaus above only knows how many of these things are spreading over the northlands."

"Are they all of the same sort as this one?" Raffo asked.

"Some of 'em are likely to be females or bitches or woman monsters or whatever the right name is," Parol put in.

"They're ugly enough so it'd only matter to another monster." Raffo made a gesture of distaste. "What I meant was, is this one pretty much like the others? You'd get a different notion of what people were like from Van's corpse and the one I'd like to make out of that weedy little jeweler who may have run off with Duren."

"Otes." Gerin heard the growl in his own voice as he supplied the name. How could he properly search for his son when catastrophe was overtaking all the northlands? More and more, he feared he'd never again see Duren alive. But Raffo's question raised a serious point. "I haven't had enough experience with them to answer that, though Ricolf's man said some seemed smarter than others," he said. "One way or another, we'll all find out before long."

The warriors trooped back to where they had slain the deer, leaving the monster's body where it lay. "We may as well camp, as Raffo said," Van remarked. "No point in pushing further in the little daylight left."

When evening fell, the ghosts were very quiet. "Likely gorging on the creature's blood," Gerin said. He looked up to the sky. Math should have been at first quarter, with Tiwaz and Elleb rising in the early hours after sunset, but he saw only clouds. The wind was picking up. "We'll have trouble gauging watches tonight, and it feels like rain, to boot."

"I'm not looking forward to tramping along through the mud," Van said. "We won't be able to do much in the way of looking for monsters, either, not with rain making it hard for us to see our hands when we stretch our arms out at full length."

"Aye, you're right," Gerin said morosely. "I hadn't thought so far ahead yet." The gobbet of venison on which he was gnawing suddenly lost a good deal of its flavor. How was he supposed to set a perimeter to keep the monsters out of his holding if they could shamble past fifty paces away without getting noticed?

For that matter, if other nobles in the northlands didn't fight them as hard as he would himself, how was he supposed to keep the monsters out of his holding at all? The most obvious answer to that was depressing: maybe he couldn't. He hadn't had much hope of besting Balamung, either, but he'd persisted and come through. He had to believe he could do the same again.

He stood an early watch, then rolled himself in his blanket and fell asleep at once in spite of his worries. When he woke, he looked around in confusion—why was everything still dark? Then a raindrop landed on the end of his nose, and another in his hair.

The rain started pattering down in earnest a few minutes later. Men swore sleepily and rigged makeshift tents from their blankets and saplings pressed into service as tent poles. In spite of those, the rest of the night was chilly, wet, and miserable.

Day came with rain falling steadily from a leaden sky. The fire had gone out. Some of the venison from the night before had been cooked; along with hard bread, it made a decent enough breakfast, but not as good as it would have been, hot and juicy from the flames.

The warriors donned their armor and squelched off westward. Gerin felt as if he were moving inside a circle perhaps a bowshot across; the rain curtained away everything beyond that distance. Every so often, he or one of his comrades would slip in the mud and get up covered with it. Little by little, the rain would wash him clean once more—until he slipped again.

Echoing what Van had said the night before, Raffo grumbled, "How are we supposed to search in this? We'll be lucky if we can keep track of ourselves, let alone the cursed monsters."

Gerin did not answer, for he feared his driver was right. With rain and clouds concealing sun and landmarks, he wasn't even altogether sure he was still heading west. "Have to wait to see which half of the sky gets dark first,"

Van said. "Then we'll have a notion of how to head back toward the Elabon Way, anyhow, if not just where we'll strike it."

Raffo said, "Poor old Rihwin. He could be sitting under one of those red tile roofs south of the High Kirs that he never gets tired of talking about, with wenches to fetch him meat and grapes and wine. And he was silly enough to trade all that for this life of luxury." He shook himself like a wet dog to show what he meant.

Just thinking of being dry made Gerin wish he were somewhere other than tramping through the mud. He said, "May the next puddle you step in be over your head." As if to turn his words into a magic-powered curse, he waggled his hands in mock passes.

He'd almost stopped paying attention to the circle of relatively clear vision in which he moved: one piece of damp, dreary ground seemed much like the next. Looking where he put his feet so he wouldn't go into a puddle over his head himself struck him as more important than anything else.

Then Raffo gasped, half in horror and half in amazement. The sound was plenty to jerk Gerin's head up. Splashing through the wet grass and mud came a band of eight or ten monsters.

They spied Gerin's men at about the same moment as Raffo saw them. A bulky male, evidently the leader of the band, swept out his arm to point at the warriors. He shouted something; through the rain, Gerin could not tell whether it was real words or just an animal cry. Whatever it was, the rest of the creatures got the idea. With hoarse roars, they charged the Fox's men.

In such dreadful weather, bows were useless. Gerin stooped to pick up a stone the size of a goose egg. He flung it at the oncoming monsters, then yelled, "Out sword and at them!" A moment later, his own blade slid from its scabbard.

A stone flew past his head. One of the creatures, at any rate, had wit enough to think of it as a weapon. Then the fight was at close quarters, the savagery and strength of the monsters well matched against the armor and bronze weapons Gerin's warriors carried.

With his long, heavy spear, better made for use afoot than from a chariot, Van had an advantage over his monstrous foes: he could thrust at them long before they closed with him. But when he sank the leaf-shaped point deep into the belly of one screaming creature, another seized the spearshaft and wrenched it out of his hands. He shouted in shock and dismay; long used to being stronger than any man he faced, having an opponent who could match him in might came as a jolt.

The monster dropped the spear; it preferred its natural weapons to those made by art. But when it sprang at Van, he stove in its head with an overhand blow from his mace. He needed no second stroke; the fight with the creature the day before had warned him to put all his power into the first one.

Gerin got only tiny glimpses of his friend's fight—he had troubles of his own. The monster that faced him was female, but no less unlovely and fierce on account of that. He felt as if he were fighting a wolf bitch or female longtooth, and knew none of the hesitation he might have felt against a woman warrior.

He slashed at the monster. It skipped back. It knew the sword was dangerous to it, then. The Fox went after it, slashed once more. This time the monster ducked under the blade and rushed him. He got his shield up just in time to keep it from tearing out his throat. It was very strong; when it tried to pull the shield off his arm, he wondered if his right shoulder would come out of its socket. The shield strap held, but barely.

Even in the pouring rain, the monster stank with a reek halfway between the musky smell of a wild beast and a human body that had never been bathed. Something else was there, too, a musty smell, perhaps the residue of long years—of countless generations—of life underground.

The Fox slashed again, and scored a bleeding line across the creature's rib cage. It squalled in fury and stopped trying to tear away his shield. But it did not turn and flee, as a wounded animal likely would have done. Instead, it went back to the attack, this time rushing at Gerin and knocking him off his feet, then springing on him as he lay in the mud.

Again his shield saved him, fending the monster away from his face and neck. He hissed in pain as its claws raked down his arm. But, though he was untaloned himself, his sandals had bronze hobnails to help him grip the ground. He kicked at the monster, and hurt it again.

He dropped his sword; it was too unwieldy for this work. Had he not been able to get at his dagger, or had he dropped it while yanking it from its sheath on his belt, he would have died. As it was, he stabbed the monster again and again.

It shrieked, first shrilly, then with a bubbling undertone as bloody froth burst from its mouth and nose. For once, Gerin wished he were not lefthanded; his blows to the right side of the creature's body had pierced a lung, but not its heart. Now, though, it wanted escape. He stuck out a leg in a wrestler's trick and tripped it when it tried to flee. It went down with a splash.

He half leaped, half rolled onto its back, stabbing again and again in an ecstasy of loathing, fury, and fear. The monster was as tenacious of life as any wild beast, that was certain. He'd put enough holes in it to make a sieve before it finally stopped trying to break free.

He didn't know whether it was dead. He didn't care— it was out of the fight for a good long while. He snatched up his sword again, scrambled to his feet, and hurried to give aid to his comrades.

Several of them were down, as were most of the monsters. Raffo and Parol Chickpea together battled the big male that had led the pack. It sprang on Parol. He screamed hoarsely. Gerin used the sword like a spear, stabbing the monster from behind. It wailed and tried to turn on him. Raffo's blade met its thick neck with a meaty *chunk*. Blood spurted. Head half severed, the monster pitched forward onto its face and lay still.

When their leader fell, the couple of creatures still on their feet gave up the fight and fled. Gerin's warriors did not pursue them; they had enough to do finishing the monsters on the ground and seeing to their own wounded. One man was dead, Parol's driver, a likable young fellow called Delamp Narrag's son. Several others had bites and slashes of greater or less severity. Binding them up in the rain wasn't easy.

"You're bleeding, Fox," Van remarked.

Gerin looked down at his clawed arm. "So I am. I hope we come to a village before long, so I can pour beer into those cuts and cover them over with lard. If they're anything like cat scratches, they're liable to fester."

"You're right about that." Van looked over the little battlefield. "Well, we beat 'em back. They're not as tough as armored warriors. That's something, anyhow."

"Something, aye." Now that he wasn't fighting for his life, the Fox noticed how much that arm hurt. "But I'd not want to be a peasant, even one with a mattock or scythe, and have one of those things spring at me from out of the woods. If I were lucky and hit it a good lick, it might run off. But if I missed that first stroke, I'd never get a chance to make a second one."

"You're right about that, too," Van said. After a moment's reflective pause, he added, "One of the ones that got away fled north."

"I saw it go. I was trying not to think about it," Gerin said wearily. "That's one past us, certain sure. I wonder how many more there are that we've never seen. Even the one is too many."

"And you're right about that," Van said. "If you're so bloody right all the time, why are we in this mess?" Gerin had no good answer for him.

VII

Rihwin walked mournfully through the courtyard, a bandage plastered over his left ear and tied round his head to hold it in place. "Can't you take that off yet?" Gerin asked him. "We've been back here ten days now, so you can't still be bleeding, and the wound didn't fester, or you'd have taken sick long since."

"Oh, I could, if that were all there was to it," Rihwin answered. "The sad truth is, though, that I'm uglier without the bandage than with it."

Gerin clapped a hand to his forehead. "You're vainer than a peacock, is what you are. If you hadn't worn that gold hoop in your ear, the monster down in Bevon's holding never would have had the chance to hook a claw on it and tear it out. And a torn ear's not the worst thing in the world, anyhow. I've seen plenty of men with worse, and that's a fact."

Rihwin's mobile features twisted into a dolorous frown. "But my earlobe has shriveled up and withered. In the southlands, surgeons had ways of repairing such wounds, for those who could bear the pain. Many did, as a ruined ear does one's appearance no good. Henceforward, I'm liable to be styled Rihwin One-Ear, not Rihwin the Fox. But who in this benighted country is familiar with such techniques? Not a soul, unless I'm much mistaken."

"I fear you're right," Gerin said. "Your southern surgeons may have had practice at such work, but we don't wear earrings here." He paused a moment, his curiosity awakening. "How do the southern surgeons go about their work with ears, anyhow?"

"First they ply the patient well with wine and poppy juice, to dull his senses as much as they can," Rihwin answered. "They also have his friends hold him, mind you—I've done that duty a time or two. Then they cut loose a flap of flesh from behind the ruined ear, open up what remains of the earlobe so it's raw and bloody, and sew the two together. After they grow into one—for they will, once they exchange blood—the surgeon cuts off the base of the flap and behold! One has a new ear, perhaps not so fine as the original article but far better than the miserable nub I have left."

Gerin eyed him speculatively. "Do you know, my fellow Fox, in my years up here on the frontier, I've done my share of rough healer's work: drawing arrows, stitching wounds, setting bones, what have you. The men I've treated haven't done any worse than anyone else's patients. If you like, I might try to rebuild your ear for you."

Rihwin went into a sudden and hasty retreat, holding his hands out before him as if to fend off Gerin. "I thank you, but no. Not only do you lack some of the essentials (for where will you find wine and poppy juice here in the northlands?), but, meaning no disrespect, you have neither witnessed nor essayed the procedure in question."

"But you described the procedure so clearly," Gerin said, half to alarm Rihwin, half in real disappointment. "I feel as if I could give you something better than the stub you have now. If I were to sketch in ink the shape of a proper earlobe here on the side of your neck—"

Rihwin retreated further. "No thank you," he repeated. "Now, I grant that I cannot wear a bandage forever, but if I were to let my hair grow long, in half a year it would conceal the mutilation, thus obviating the need for surgery."

"I suppose you could do that," Gerin admitted. "Why

didn't you think of it a while ago, instead of whining about how your looks were ruined forever?"

"I didn't have such incentive to devise an alternative until this moment," Rihwin answered with a sheepish grin. "Compared to the prospect of being carved upon by an inept and inexperienced butcher—again, meaning no disrespect—going through life with but one earlobe suddenly seems much less unattractive." Rihwin was self-absorbed, but not stupid. He fixed Gerin with a suspicious stare. "And you, sirrah, manipulated me into coming up with that alternative."

"I did?" Gerin was the picture of innocence. "All I wanted was to try my hand at surgery."

"I know," Rihwin said darkly. "I am certain the procedure would have been quite interesting—for you. And for me—how much I should have enjoyed it—is another matter altogether."

"If you hadn't wanted something done about it, you shouldn't have described *how* to do something about it in such loving detail," Gerin said.

"Believe me, my fellow Fox, I shall not be guilty of repeating the error," Rihwin said. "I suppose you should have been as eager to follow through had I suggested you repair the ear by thaumaturgic means."

"Now, there's an idea!" Gerin exclaimed. "You know, that really ought to be within my power, such as it is. It wouldn't involve much, just a straightforward application of the law of similarity. And you still have your right ear intact to serve as an exemplar. What could be more similar to a man's left ear than his own right? Let's go over to that little shack of mine and—"

Rihwin fled.

Selatre read, "In this year, the fifth of his reign, the Emperor Forenz, the second of that name"—she paused to sound out a word she didn't run across as often as the usual opening formula of a chronicle's annual entry; she read *that* with confidence— "increased the tribute on the Sithonian cities. And the men of Kortys gathered together and thought how best they might revel—"

Gerin blinked and leaned over to check the scroll in front of her. "That's 'rebel,'" he murmured.

She looked at the passage again. "Oh. So it is." She let out a small, embarrassed laugh. "It does change the meaning, doesn't it?"

"Just a bit." Gerin started to reach and to touch her hand in added praise, but thought better of it. Selatre made little fuss over accidental contact these days, but she remained unhappy about anything that wasn't an accident. He went on, "Even with the slip, you're doing marvelously well. You've picked up your letters as fast as anyone I've ever taught."

"Letters are simple," she said. "Seeing how they fit together and make words is harder." She looked around the room that served Castle Fox as a library. "And so many words there are to read! I'd never imagined."

Now Gerin laughed, bitterly. "When I look at them, I see how few there are. It's a good collection for the northlands—for all I know, it may be the only collection in the northlands—but it's a chip of wood drifting on the sea of ignorance. I studied down at the City of Elabon; I know whereof I speak."

"As may be," Selatre said. "When Biton abandoned me, I thought I would be empty of knowledge, of the feeling of knowledge passing through me, forevermore. This is a different sort from what the god gave directly, but it's worthy in its own way. For that I thank you."

She hesitated for a moment, then set her hand on top of his, very lightly, before she jerked it back. Gerin stared at her. Then a snarl of rage, a noise like ripping canvas, jerked his gaze to the doorway. Fand had chosen that moment to walk by. The fury on her face was frightening. Gerin waited for her to scream at him, but she stalked away instead. That worried him more than her usual firestorm would have.

"I'm sorry," Selatre said. "Your leman does not favor me, and I've gone and made matters worse."

"Not that much worse," he answered. "Things have been going, mm, imperfectly well for a while already."

She sighed and said, "I must confess, I don't altogether understand. If things between you and her have not gone well, as you tell me, why do you still seek her bedchamber?"

He felt his face heat. From anyone else, that question would have got nothing more than a sharp, *None of your affair*. With Selatre, though, he tried to be as honest as he could. Maybe that sprang from lingering awe and respect for the oracular role she'd once had, maybe just because, by her nature and not Biton's, she called forth such honesty. After a little thought, he said, "Because what goes on in the bedchamber, as you say, is one of the few good things we have left between us. Has been one of the good things, I should say."

Selatre caught the distinction. "Has been but is no more, do you mean?"

"I suppose I do." The Fox gnawed on the inside of his lower lip. "You've seen children balance a board or a branch on a rock and make a game out of going up and down, up and down?"

"Of course," she answered. "I've played that game myself. Haven't you?"

He nodded, then went on, "Van and I have played it with Fand, these past couple of years. But staying in balance, the two of us with one woman, isn't easy, any more than keeping the board in balance on a stone is.

And I seem to be the one who's falling off." He laughed, ruefully but without much anger. "I shouldn't be surprised that's happening, not when Fand has a temper like boiling oil. I ought to be surprised we've kept the balance as long as this."

"You would have kept it longer, if not for me," Selatre said. "She thinks you're out to have me take her place."

"I know she does," Gerin said. "That isn't what I intended when I brought you here to Castle Fox."

She studied him. For a moment, he thought the fathomless wisdom of Biton still looked out through her eyes. Then he realized the wisdom he saw was her own, which made it no less intimidating. "Do you intend that now?" she asked. Even if he'd intended to evade, she didn't make it easy; though she hardly had her letters, she used words with a precision the rhetoricians down in the City of Elabon might have envied.

"By Biton or Dyaus—whichever you'd rather, Selatre—I swear I do not want you to take Fand's place in my life," he answered steadily. "If you think I am in the habit of swearing false oaths, you can best judge my likely fate in the world to come."

"Only a fool mocks the gods, and whatever else you may be, lord Gerin, you are no fool," Selatre said. "For that, and for the truth you've shown me thus far, I will believe you."

"And for that I thank you," the Fox said.

"Shall we return to the chronicle?" Selatre asked. "There, with the words before us on the parchment, we have less room for misunderstanding."

"That is probably a good idea." Gerin listened to her read. Every sentence seemed to come with more confidence than the one before it. Now that she'd grasped the principle, she was showing she could apply it. Some men took years to reach the place where she'd come in moonturns. Some men gave up in dismay and never got there at all.

He was proud of her, and pleased with himself for having guessed so well where she would fit into the life of Fox Keep and the human fabric of the holding as a whole. She and Fand didn't fit; Van had foreseen that more clearly than he had himself. And Van and Fand still seemed to be getting along as well as Fand ever got on with anyone.

Under the usual busy stir of his thoughts, Gerin remembered something else as well—Selatre had reached out and taken his hand. He didn't know how much that meant; he didn't know if it meant anything. Of one thing he was sure: he wanted to find out.

Rain plashed down on Castle Fox, filling puddles in the courtyard and turning the ditch around the palisade to the muddy beginning of a moat. Harvest lay far enough ahead for the peasants to look on the storm with relief rather than alarm.

In any other year, that would have made Gerin do the same. Now a cloud-filled sky and curtains of water kicking up myriad splashes everywhere only raised his hackles; the wet weather reminded him too vividly of the storm that had rolled through the day his band of warriors fought the pack of monsters.

Planting his feet with care on the slippery steps, he mounted to the palisade and peered south. He could see the peasant village near the castle. The broad thatched roofs of the huts there would keep most of the rain away from the walls of wattle and daub, but he knew serfs would be patching them with fresh mud after the downpour rolled away eastward.

Beyond the village, at the edge of visibility through the rain, lay the woods. Gerin wished he could peer inside them, see into each windfall and cave, under each fallen tree. He feared monsters sheltered in some of them. He did not have the men he would have needed to form a cordon around his entire border, but without such a cordon, how was he supposed to hold off the creatures?

He was thinking so hard, he did not notice anyone coming up to join him until footfalls jarred the timbers beside him. Van wore a conical hat of woven straw that kept the rain off his face. "Wondering what's out there, Captain?" the outlander asked.

"I know what's out there," Gerin answered glumly. "I'm wondering how close it is and how soon we'll have to worry about it right here. But as a matter of fact, when you asked I was wishing bronze were cheaper."

"Begging your pardon, Fox, but I have to tell you I don't follow that one," Van said.

"If bronze were cheaper—if we had more copper and especially more tin—we could afford to make more weapons. Then the peasants could have 'em, and that would give them a better chance of killing the monsters instead of getting eaten."

"Mm, likely you're right." Van's features turned blunter and harder as he frowned in thought. "But even if you are, I'd lay you five to one that a lot of your vassal barons wouldn't fall in love with the idea of giving their serfs swords and spears and helms and cuirasses."

"For fear the arms would get turned on them instead of the monsters, you mean?" Gerin asked. Van nodded. So did the Fox. "Not many of my vassals need to worry overmuch, I think; they know I don't put up with some of the things that go on in other holdings. But if the idea ever spread through the northlands, I'll not deny a good many barons would have cause to fear their peasants would revolt. I can think of half a dozen I'd rise against in an instant if someone put a sword in my hand."

"Oh, aye, more than that." Van's big head bobbed up and down again. "But here's a question for you, Fox: suppose you put swords and spears in the hands of a lot of your serfs. When the time comes to pay the dues they owe you, aren't they going to go after your collectors instead of handing over the grain and ale and such? They'll be protecting themselves, so why should they go on paying you to do it for them?"

"That's—a good question," Gerin said slowly. "They all turn into villagers like the ones who tried to waylay us, is that what you're saying?"

"That's just what I'm saying," Van agreed.

Gerin thought for a while. "Do you know, it's very likely they would," he said at last. "The way of life we have here looks as it does because bronze is so scarce and costly. Peasants can't afford to get their hands on arms and armor: not enough bronze to go around. Things would be different if there were."

"Better? Worse?"

"Damn me to the five hells if I know," Gerin answered. "But different they'd surely be. Like those footholders Duin the Bold came up with a few years ago, before he died in the fight against Balamung: what with everything else that's gone on since, I haven't had the chance to explore what all they're good for, but it's plain they make riding a horse and staying on its back a lot easier than that ever was before. If you can really fight from horseback, what point to chariots?"

"Maybe *you* can fight from horseback," Van said. "You're a good-sized man, aye, but alongside me you're a stripling. The horse that could bear my weight, especially in armor" —he slapped his broad, bronze-covered chest— "hasn't been foaled yet. If it's not the chariot, I'm a foot soldier."

"That's not the point," Gerin said. "Chariots are like

any of the rest of our weapons; they're scarce and hard to come by. More men could be warriors if they just had to lay hold of a horse and some arms rather than a team and a car to go with it."

"Then you'd best start showing them those footholders and what to do with 'em," the outlander answered. "We're going to need as many warriors as we can muster, and that soon, too."

"I know—sooner than I can train them into being proper horsemen, the more so as I'm nowhere near a proper horseman myself." Gerin sighed. "If only that monster of Balamung's hadn't killed Duin when he kicked out. Our little pepperpot would have had all of us riding whether we wanted to or not."

"He rode ideas even harder than you do, and that's a fact," Van said. "You're better at picking the ones to ride, though; I give you so much."

"Such generosity," Gerin said in tones far drier than the weather. "Suppose I did teach a good many men, barons and peasants both, to ride and fight from horseback . . ." His voice trailed away. Actions had inevitable consequences; on that philosophers and historians agreed. The trick was to reason out what they might be before you acted, instead of getting caught by surprise later.

His best guess was that large numbers of warriors on horseback would prove as revolutionary as large numbers of bronze weapons in the hands of the serfs. If one lord in the northlands succeeded in forming a good-sized force of cavalry as opposed to chariotry, the rest would have to imitate him or go under. Since a man wouldn't need as many resources to maintain a horse as he would for a team and chariot, vassal barons' holdings could shrink until, after a couple of generations, it might be hard to tell a poor baron from a prosperous peasant.

Gerin had been teaching bright serfs their letters. Did

he really want to arm them, too? Was he ready to unleash more great change on a land that had seen too much too fast of late?

For the moment, the decision was out of his hands. The monsters were forcing the pace of change, not he. But if they were put down at last—

Van cleared his throat, bringing the Fox's thoughts back to the here and now. The outlander said, "Captain, what is it you've done to put Fand in such a swivet? Last night she was going on about the sheep's eyes you were casting at Selatre till I all but had to hit her over the head with an ale jar to make her leave off."

"I've done nothing of the sort," Gerin said indignantly. "I've spent time with her, aye, but I have to if she's to learn her letters and be able to go through the books in the library and find out what's in them. You hit the mark there at the start—having Selatre here hasn't set right with Fand, and she blames me, not you, that Selatre's here."

"She said you were pawing Selatre when she walked by the library the other day," Van said, doubt in his voice. "Not that I'd care to believe Fand over you, mind, but she says she saw it with her own eyes."

"She didn't," Gerin insisted. "You think Selatre would stay here for a moment if I tried pawing her? As a matter of fact, she put her hand on mine, not the other way round."

"*Selatre* touched *you*?" Van said, giving the Fox a sharp stare. "Honh!" The noise was not a word, but carried a world of meaning nonetheless.

Gerin wished his friend were not so tall; it made trying to look down his nose at Van likelier to give him a crick in the neck than to overawe the outlander. He said, "Fand's hardly speaking to me anymore. Are you going to start in and speak for her?"

"Not a chance," Van said. "Ever since I got too big for my mother to tell me what to do, I've lived just as I pleased, and I'm a great believer in letting everyone else do the same thing. But if you think I'll pretend to be blind to what goes on around me, you can think again on that, too."

The Fox rolled his eyes. "Do you know *why* she touched me? She was glad I'd taught her her letters; they fill up some of the emptiness she feels now that Biton speaks to her no more. That's all."

"That may be why she says she did it, but the fact remains—she did it, she didn't have to do it, and she hasn't done it with anybody else," Van says. "Me, I'd say that means it's not all, not even close to all."

"That's—" Gerin felt fury rising in him. He seldom lost his temper, but results were memorable when he did. But before he exploded like a tightly stoppered pot left too long in the fire, he paused to wonder why he was getting so angry so fast. When he did, the anger evaporated. "That's—possible," he said in a small voice.

Van studied him with approval. "You're honest with yourself, that I will say for you. And suppose it's not just possible but so? What will you do then?"

"You ask good questions. That's a better question than I have an answer for right now." One corner of Gerin's mouth quirked up in a wry smile. Suppose Selatre was coming to care for him? Could he come to care for her in return? After falling in love with Elise and then watching that love crumble to ashes, he wondered if he dared let himself become vulnerable to a woman again. In some ways, going into battle against the monsters was easier. There, at least, he knew what he had to do to come through unhurt.

Van said, "Mind you, Fox, I have nothing against the lass. Too quiet for my taste, but I'm a roisterer born and you're not. But I do want to know you're doing what you're doing with your eyes open."

"I don't even know," Gerin said heavily. "I tell you this much, though: just as you find Selatre too quiet, a couple of years of life with Fand have left my ears ringing, and that's the truth."

"Ah, it's not so bad," Van said. "She shouts, you shout back. After the yelling's done, you futter a couple of times and all's right till the next go-round."

"We've done that more than once, she and I," Gerin said. "Too many times more than once, as a matter of fact. That sort of thing gets wearing in a hurry, at least for me."

"Ah, Fox, you pay fancy prices for pepper and cloves and the gods only know what all else to make your food taste interesting, and you want the rest of your life dull as oatmeal porridge without even salt."

"My food won't stick a knife in me if it doesn't like the way I've cooked it," Gerin retorted. "And I wouldn't mind the rest of my life turning dull for a while. These past few years, what with one thing and another, it's been too bloody lively to suit me."

Van yawned an enormous, sarcastic yawn.

Nettled, Gerin said, "For that matter, you great barrelbrained oaf, I've never heard you speak Fand so fair. Here's a warning: if she throws me over, she'll aim her whole self straight at you. Are you ready for that?"

"I can handle her," Van said, confidence throbbing in his voice. Gerin wondered if he was as smart as he thought he was.

A peasant brought the Fox the news he'd been dreading. The fellow arrived in the back of a chariot along with Notker the Bald and his driver. He looked stunned, not only at traveling that way and faring so far from his home but also, Gerin thought, for deeper reasons: his own face might have borne that expression of disbelieving amazement just after the ground at Ikos stopped shaking.

"It's happened?" the Fox asked Notker.

"Aye, lord Gerin," his vassal returned. "This fellow here made it to my keep day before yesterday from his village next to the lands of Capuel the Flying Frog. I thought you'd best listen to his story, so I fetched him hither." His lined face made him look even more worried than he sounded.

"Monsters?" Gerin asked.

"Monsters, aye, and worse," Notker said. Gerin had not imagined there could be worse. Notker pointed to the serf he'd brought to Fox Keep. "This here is Mannor Trout, lord—he's the best fisherman in his village, which is how he got his ekename and likely why he's alive today." He nudged Mannor. "Tell the lord prince the tale you told me."

The peasant brushed a lock of dark hair back from where it had flopped down onto his forehead. "Aye, lord Notker," he said in rustic accents. His voice rang oddly flat, as if he held all emotion back from it to keep from having to remember the terror he'd known. "My village is southwest of here, you know, close to the border of your holding, and—"

"I know," Gerin said impatiently. "I rode that way not long ago, in search of my son Duren. I don't recall seeing you, though."

"You didn't, nor I you, though the talk of you going through lasted for days," Mannor said. "I was off fishing then, too." He drew himself up with pride, or at least its memory. "I bring in enough from the streams that they don't begrudge me staying out of the fields. They didn't, I mean." He shivered; that passionless tone he'd been using threatened to flee, leaving him naked against whatever it shielded him from.

"So you were at the stream the day I passed through your village, and you were at the stream this other day, the one you're going to tell me about," Gerin said, wanting to move the tale along without making Mannor face more than he could stand.

The serf nodded. That lock of hair fell onto his forehead again. This time he let it stay. He said, "I was having a day to beat all days, if you know what I mean, lord prince. Every time I stuck a new worm or a grub on my hook, I'd catch me a big tasty one, I would. Weren't much past noon when I had me 'bout as much as I felt like hauling back. Reckoned I'd eat some, trade me some to other folk, smoke me some for winter, and salt down the rest: we've a good lick close by, we do."

"All well and good," Gerin said. "So you were carrying your fish back to the village—through the woods, is that right?"

"Just like you say," Mannor agreed. "I get myself inside maybe two furlongs of the fields and hear the most horrible racket you ever put ear on in all your born days. Wolves howling, longtooths caterwauling—put 'em all together and they ain't a patch on this. I drop my fish and run up to see what I can see."

"Monsters in the village." Gerin's voice was as flat as the peasant's.

"Monsters, aye, but that's not all," Mannor said. "There was monsters, but there was Trokmoi, too, and they was workin' together to wreck and kill, Dyaus drop me into the hottest hell if I lie."

Notker nodded, his face now even grimmer: he'd already heard the tale. Gerin stared in horrified dismay. He'd imagined a great many catastrophes; he was good at it. But never in his blackest nightmares had he dreamt the creatures from the caves under Biton's temple would—or could—make common cause with his human foes.

"How do you mean, working together?" he demanded of Mannor. "Were the Trokmoi using the monsters for hunting dogs, to drive people out for destruction?" Adiatunnus was clever, no way around that. Perhaps he or one of his men had figured out a way to tame the monsters.

But the serf shook his head. "Some of the things, they was just goin' around bitin' whatever they could get their teeth into, like they was wolves or summat like that. But some, they was carryin' swords and spears and even talkin' some kind of growly talk with the red mustaches. They were uglier than the woodsrunners, but otherwise I didn't see much to choose between 'em."

"Can you confirm this?" Gerin asked Notker. It wasn't so much that he disbelieved Mannor as that he so much wanted to disbelieve him.

His vassal said, "No, lord prince. As soon as I heard the story, I figured you had to give ear, too. But do you think it's one he'd make up?" The Fox didn't, but he wished Notker hadn't made him realize he didn't.

Almost unnoticed by both of them, Mannor went on, "Two o' the things, they caught my little boy. They was squabbling over him like dogs over a bone till a Trokmê, he seen what was happening and he takes his axe and chops the body in half." Quietly, hopelessly, he began to weep.

"Here," Gerin said, tasting the uselessness of words. "Here." He put an arm around the serf's shoulder. Mannor's tears soaked hot through his tunic. He held the man, and held his own face even harder, to keep from breaking down and blubbering along with him. Hearing what had happened to the serf's son reminded him all too vividly of all the things that might have happened to Duren. That he did not know which—if any—had befallen the boy only let him exercise his ability to envision disasters.

"What do we do with him, lord Gerin?" Notker asked.

The Fox waited until Mannor had cried himself out, then said, "First thing to do is get him good and drunk." He pointed the serf toward the entrance to the long hall of the keep. "Go on in there, Mannor; tell them I said to give you all the ale you can drink." He shoved Mannor in the direction of the doorway; the man went as if he had no will of his own left. Gerin turned back to Notker. "We have to see if he can live with this now. He has to see for himself, too. It won't be easy; he'll carry scars no less than if he'd been wounded in war, poor fellow."

"You know about that, lord prince," Notker said. The Fox nodded. These days, he had no family left: his father and brother slain, his wife run off, and his son stolen.

As he'd grown used to doing, he resolutely shoved that grief and worry to the back of his mind. More immediately urgent worries took precedence. He said to Notker, "The Trokmoi and monsters didn't assail your keep?"

"No, lord," Notker answered. "First I heard of them coming over the border from Capuel's—Dyaus knows why we still call it that, with nobody in charge there these past years—was when Mannor brought word. The gods only know what's happened since, mind you, but you'd reckon raiders and yon creatures could move faster than a grief-crazy serf if they had a mind to."

"That you would." Gerin rubbed his chin in perplexity.

Notker shared that perplexity. "Not like what you'd look for from the woodsrunners, neither. The Trokmoi, when they hit you, they mostly hit you like a man going into a woman: they want to get in as deep as they can as fast as they can."

"True enough." Gerin made an abstracted clucking noise, then suddenly held up one finger. "I have it, I think. Adiatunnus is a sneaky beggar, and smart, too—though not half so smart as he thinks he is. He's cobbled up some kind of deal with these creatures, but he doesn't know how well it's going to work. So he thinks he'll try it out small at first, and if it does what he hopes, why then he'll strike harder the next time. How does that sound to you?"

"Don't know if it's true," Notker said after some thought of his own. "Makes decent sense, though."

"In a way, it does," the Fox said. "But only in a way—that's why I called Adiatunnus half-smart. Now I'm warned. He'll be gathering his forces, collecting more monsters, doing whatever he thinks he needs to do. And do you know what I aim to do in the meanwhile?"

"What's that, lord?" Notker asked.

"I aim to hit him first."

The chariot hit a bump. Gerin's legs kept him smoothly upright without conscious thought on his part. "How am I supposed to administer my holding if I'm too busy fighting to pay heed to anything else?" he asked.

Van had adjusted as automatically as the Fox. He glanced over and answered, "I don't know the answer to that one, but let me give you one in return: how are you supposed to administer your holding if the Trokmoi and the monsters swarm out and take it away from you?"

"There you have me," Gerin said. "If I can't keep it, it isn't truly mine. But if I can't run it, it's hardly worth keeping." Schooling south of the High Kirs had left him fond of forming such paradoxes.

Van cut through this one with the ruthless economy he usually displayed: "If you still hold on to it, you can always fix it later. If it's lost, it's gone for good."

"You're right, of course," Gerin said, but the admission left him dissatisfied. Endless warfare would hurl his holding back into barbarism faster than anything else he could think of. But, as Van had said, everything else turned irrelevant if he didn't win each war.

Along with his regathered host of vassals, he rolled southwest down the same road he'd taken to Adiatunnus' border after Duren disappeared. This time, he wouldn't stop and exchange polite chitchat with the Trokmê chieftain's border guards. He'd go after Adiatunnus— and his monstrous allies—with all the might he had.

Notker the Bald brought his chariot up alongside Gerin's. He pointed ahead. "There's my keep, off to one side. At our pace, we'll make the village before sunset."

"So we will, and then roll through it," Gerin said. As soon as the sun had started to swing down toward the horizon from its high point in the sky, he'd ordered a couple of chariots out two furlongs ahead of the rest. The Trokmoi were often too impatient to set proper ambushes, and he suspected the monsters Adiatunnus had taken as allies would be even less skilled in the stratagems of war.

A puff of breeze from the west brought a whiff of something sickly sweet. Raffo turned and wrinkled his nose. "Phew! What's that stink?"

"Dead meat," Van answered.

The Fox nodded. "We're coming up on the village Mannor Trout got out of, or what's left of it. Mannor didn't lie, that's certain."

The closer they got, the worse the smell grew. Gerin coughed. The stink of carrion always made fear and rage bubble up in him: it called to mind the aftermath of too many fights, too many horrors.

The serf village, though, was worse than he'd expected. He'd been braced for sprawled, bloated corpses and charred ruins, and they were there. He'd looked for the livestock to be run off or slain, and it was. He'd known the crows would rise in a black cloud and the foxes slink off into the woods when he disturbed them, and they did.

But he hadn't reckoned on so many of the pathetic corpses looking as they'd been mostly devoured before the scavengers started on them. His stomach did a slow flip-flop. He should have realized the monsters wouldn't be fussy about where they got their meat. Intellectually, he had realized it. The implications, though, had escaped him.

Van said, "I had thought to round up a hen or two here, to give to the ghosts come sundown and to cook up for us, too. But now I'm going to let that go. The gods alone know what these hens have been pecking at since the Trokmoi and their little friends went home."

Gerin's stomach lurched again. "Reasoned like a philosopher," he said. Anthropophagy, even at one remove, was worth fighting shy of. A few minutes later, a pig stuck its head out of the bushes. No one shot at it. It was even likelier than any surviving village chickens to have fed on the bodies of those who had raised it.

After making sure no life remained in the village, Gerin waved his arm. The chariots rattled on toward the border with the holding of Capuel the Flying Frog. How much of that now lay in the hands of the Trokmoi and the monsters was anyone's guess. Few men said much about what they'd seen in the clearing, but a new, grim sense of purpose informed the force. They'd collect the payment due, and more.

Just before sunset, a cock pheasant made the mistake of coming out from the woods onto a meadow to feed. Its ring-necked head came up in alarm when it saw, or perhaps heard, the chariots on the road. It began to run rapidly, then leaped into the air, its wings thuttering.

Arrows hissed toward it. One of them, either cleverly aimed or luckier than the rest, brought the bird tumbling back to earth. "Well shot!" Gerin called. "Not only will it feed the ghosts, it'll feed some of us, too."

"Aye, a pheasant's tasty, no doubt of that," Van said. "Me, though, I'd sooner hang it a while to let it get properly ripe before I cook it."

"Yes, I've seen you do that at Fox Keep once or twice," Gerin said. "I don't care for my meat flyblown, thank you very kindly. Besides, we've no time for such fripperies tonight. Bringing it down at all strikes me as a good enough omen."

"Flyblown's not the point," Van replied. "Bringing out the full flavor is. But you're right about today: we just pluck it and gut it and put it over the flames or bake it in clay."

"Fuel for the fire," the Fox agreed. "It'll help us keep going. And then we'll get into Adiatunnus' lands and set some fires of our own."

For all Gerin knew, the Trokmê guards at the border to Adiatunnus' holding might have been the same crew with whom he'd spoken when he came seeking Duren. This time, he didn't get a close look at them. As soon as they saw his force of chariotry approaching, they cried "The southrons!" in their own language and fled. They got in among the trees before any of his men could shoot them like the pheasant.

"Shall we stop and go after them, lord prince?" Raffo asked.

"No," the Fox answered. "We storm ahead instead. That way we get in amongst the woodsrunners faster than they have word we're coming."

The first village his men reached was inhabited by

Elabonian serfs who had acquired new masters in the five years since the Trokmoi swarmed south over the Niffet. When they realized the men in the chariots were of their own kind, they came swarming out of their huts with cries of exultation.

"The gods be praised!" they shouted. "You've come to deliver us from the Trokmoi and from the—things." With that seemingly innocuous word, half their joy at seeing Gerin and his followers seemed to evaporate, boiled away in the memory of overpowering fear. One of them said, "The Trokmoi are bad enough, stealing and raping and all. But those things . . ." His voice guttered out like a candle.

"If you want to go, just pack whatever you can carry on your backs and run for my holding," Gerin said. "The peasants there will take you in. The ground is thin of men these days, with so much war and plunder. They'll be glad to have you, to help bring in a bigger crop."

"Dyaus bless you, lord," the serf said fervently. Then he hesitated. "But lord, how shall we travel with these things loose in the woods and ready to swoop down on us?"

"Take weapons, fool," Van said. "Anything you have is better than nothing. Would you rather be eaten trying to get away or stay here till the monsters come into your house and eat you in your own bed?"

"Truth to tell, lord," the serf said, taking no chances on the outlander's rank, "I'd sooner not be et at all."

"Then get out," Gerin said. "Now we've no more time to waste gabbing with you. The Trokmoi and the monsters destroyed a peasant village in my land, just over the border from what used to be Capuel's holding. Now they're going to find out they can't do that without paying the price for it." He slapped Raffo on the shoulder.

The driver flicked the reins of the chariot. The horses started forward.

The Fox put himself in the lead now, with Drago's chariot right behind. The Bear would reliably follow him, and wouldn't do anything foolish. That counted for more than whatever brilliant stratagems Rihwin *might* come up with, for Rihwin might just as easily do something to endanger the whole force.

The road opened onto another clearing, this one recently hacked out of the woods. In it stood three or four stout wooden houses, bigger and sturdier than the round cottages in which most serfs dwelt. "Those are Trokmê homes," Gerin said. "I've seen enough of them north of the Niffet."

"Let's get rid of the Trokmoi in 'em, then," Van said. One of those Trokmoi came out from behind a house. He stared in amazement that might have been comical under other circumstances at the Elabonians encroaching on what he'd come to think of as his land. That lasted only a couple of heartbeats. Then he let out a shout of alarm and dashed for shelter inside.

Gerin already had an arrow in the air. It caught the woodsrunner in the small of the back. He went down with a wail. Gerin caught Van's eye. "Try doing that with your precious spear," he said.

Another Trokmê came outside to see what the shouting was about. Gerin and Drago both shot at him—and both missed. He ducked back into the house in a hurry, slammed the door, and dropped the bar with a thump Gerin could hear across half a furlong.

"Fire arrows!" Gerin yelled.

A couple of chariots had firepots in them, half full of embers ready to be fanned to life. Others carried little bundles of straw soaked in pitch. While some of his men got real fires going, others tied the bundles to arrows, just back of the heads. Still others used shields to protect them from the Trokmoi, who started shooting at them from the windows of the houses.

Trailing smoke, the fire arrows flew toward the woodsrunners' shelters. Some fell short; some went wide—their balance was all wrong. But others stuck in wall timbers or the thatch of the roofs. Before long, smoke rose up from a dozen different places. The Trokmoi inside yelled at one another. Some of the voices belonged to women. One corner of Gerin's mouth twisted down, but only for a moment. The Trokmoi hadn't cared about women or children when they struck his holding. What did he owe them?

The fires on the roofs grew and spread. The women's cries rose to shrill shrieks, then suddenly stopped. Doors came open. Red- and yellow-mustached men charged out, half a dozen in all. Some had helms on their heads; two or three carried shields. They threw themselves at Gerin's troopers with no thought for their own survival, only the hope of taking some Elabonians with them before they fell.

"You'll not have our wives and daughters for your sport," one of them panted as he slashed at the Fox. "We're after slaying the lot of them."

Van's spear caught the woodsrunner in the side. The fellow wore no armor; it bit deep. Van twisted the shaft as he yanked it out. The Trokmê coughed bright blood and crumpled.

Gerin looked around. None of the other woodsrunners was still on his feet. One of his own men swore as he bound up a slashed arm. That seemed to be the only wound his warriors had taken—they'd so outnumbered their foes that they'd dealt with them three and four and five to one, and not all of them had been engaged by a long shot.

The houses kept on burning. Drago the Bear said, "That smoke's going to give us away."

"It's liable to," Gerin agreed, "though fire gets loose easily enough, and it's bloody hard to douse once it does. Adiatunnus and his lads will know something has gone wrong, but not just what—until we show up and teach 'em. Let's get moving again."

Before long, they came to another peasant village— or rather, what had been one. Now several monsters from under the temple at Ikos stalked among the houses. More of them tore at the carcasses of a couple of oxen in the middle of the village square. They looked up, muzzles and hands red with blood, as Gerin's chariot came into sight.

Two or three monsters ran straight for the chariot, as any fierce beasts might have. Gerin shot one of them: a lucky arrow, right through the throat. That made the others hesitate, more thoughtful than any beasts would have been.

But it also gave the rest of the monsters the chance to snatch up weapons: clubs, spears, and a couple of swords. Then they too rushed toward the Fox, their cries more like words than any he had heard from the creatures before.

He had a bad moment or two there. There were a lot more monsters than he had men in the two lead chariots. He was about to order Raffo to wheel the horses around and retreat when reinforcements came rattling up.

Some of the monsters kept on with the attack, again as beasts might have done. But others must have made the calculation he'd been on the brink of a short time before: they headed off into the woods, to fight another day.

When the skirmish was done, Gerin pointed to the

deserted huts in the village and said, "Torch the place. If those things were denning here, we don't want to give them anyplace they can return to once we've gone."

More smoke rose into the sky. The Fox knew that whoever saw it would figure out something unusual was going on in the northeastern part of the land Adiatunnus had overrun. His lips skinned back from his teeth. He had reached the point where he was resigned to having a woodsrunner for a neighbor; Adiatunnus hadn't acted much differently from Capuel the Flying Frog and the other Elabonian barons he'd displaced. But if Adiatunnus consorted with monsters—

That led Gerin to another thought. As Raffo drove the chariot deeper into the Trokmê's territory, the Fox said to Van, "I wonder how the monsters came to align themselves with Adiatunnus. Most of the ones we saw in Bevon's holding wouldn't have had the wit to do such a thing."

"If I had to guess, Captain, I'd say there's smart ones and dumb ones, same as with people," the outlander answered. "Say the smart ones are as smart as dumb people: that'd make the dumb ones like wolves or longtooths or any other hunting beasts. The smart ones'd have the wit for something like banding together with the Trokmoi, and maybe even for bringing along some of their stupid friends." He laughed. "Makes 'em sound like half the folk we know, doesn't it?"

"More than half," Gerin said. Van laughed again. The Fox went on, "I wish we didn't have to waste time with all these little fights. I want to hit Adiatunnus as hard and sudden a blow as I can, but every skirmish we fight makes me slower to get to him and gives him more time to ready himself."

"Well, we can't very well say to the woodsrunners we run into—or still less to these monsters—'Sorry there, friend, we have more important things to do than slaughtering you right now. Can you hang about till we're on our way back?' "

Gerin snorted; when you put it that way, it was absurd. All the same, unease gnawed at him. Before he'd set out on this punitive raid, he'd seen it clearly in his mind: go into Adiatunnus' territory, strike the Trokmoi—and with luck kill their chieftain—and then fare home again. Reality was less clear-cut, as reality has a way of being.

Before long, his army rolled past the ruins of what had been a palisaded keep before the Trokmoi came south over the Niffet. The woodsrunners hadn't bothered repairing the timbers of the outwall; instead, they'd built a dwelling of their own in the courtyard between the wall and the stone keep, turning the place into a sort of fortified village.

A couple of Trokmoi were up on what was left of the wall, but they raised no alarm when Gerin's chariot came into sight. "Are they all asleep?" he demanded indignantly. He didn't like his enemies to act stupidly; it made him wonder what sort of ruse they were plotting.

But Van smacked one fist into the palm of his other hand. "Me, I know what it is, Captain: they think we're woodsrunners, too."

"By the gods, you're right." Gerin waved toward the distant stronghold. One of the Trokmoi waved back. The Fox frowned. "I don't fancy going in after them. They could have enough men to make that expensive—and it would cost us the speed and free movement the chariots give."

"More fire arrows?" Raffo said over his shoulder.

"Aye, and maybe a muzzle for a mouthy driver, too," Gerin answered, but he swatted the young man on the back to leave no doubt that was a joke. "We want to make sure none of them gets away, too, so what we'll do is—"

His chariot, and Drago's with it, pulled off the road a little past the keep the Trokmoi had altered. That might have perplexed the men on the battered wall, but not enough to make them cry out. Even when the first chariots of the Fox's main force came into view, they kept silent long enough to let the cars get well begun on forming a ring around the holding.

"Southrons!" The cry in the Trokmê language floated across weedy fields to Gerin's ears. "We've been cozened by southrons!"

So they had, and by the time they realized it, they were too late to do anything about it. The Elabonian warriors shot arrows at any woodsrunner who appeared on the palisade. Some of them also shot fire arrows at the wooden palisade itself and over it at the roofs of the houses it sheltered. The timbers of the palisade caught only slowly; the same was not true for the dry straw thatching of those roofs.

"Well, what'll they do now?" Van said as several thick plumes of gray-white smoke rose from the courtyard.

"Curse me if I know," Gerin answered. "I don't know what I'd do in that spot—try not to get into it in the first place, I suppose. But they don't have that choice, not anymore."

Some of the Trokmoi took refuge in the stone keep in the center of the courtyard—Gerin saw bits of motion through its slit windows. He wondered if that would save them; the door and all the furnishings within were wood, and liable to catch fire . . . and even if they didn't, so much smoke filled the air that anyone inside was liable to feel like a slab of bacon being cured.

The Trokmoi had let the ditch around the palisade alone; shrubs and bushes grew in great profusion in it. That would have made matters easier for anyone who tried to lay siege to the castle, but it helped those inside now. Some leaped off the wall—not just men but also women with their skirts flying up around them as they jumped—to land in those bushes and shelter there from fire and foe alike.

And the drawbridge thumped down. A double handful of woodsrunners in bronze armor stormed forth to put up the best fight they could. Gerin admired their gallantry even as his men thundered toward them. Fighting afoot against chariotry was like trying to spoon up sand with a sieve. The Elabonians rattled by, pouring arrows into their foes, and the woodsrunners could do little but stand and suffer.

They had one moment of triumph: an archer of theirs hit an oncoming horse in the neck. The beast crashed to the ground, dragging down its harnessmate and overturning the car the two horses pulled. Men tumbled over the ground like broken dolls. The three or four Trokmoi still standing raised a defiant cheer. Soon they were dead.

Of the Elabonians in the wrecked chariot, one also lay dead, his head twisted at an unnatural angle. Another writhed and groaned with a broken leg and other injuries besides. The third, Parol Chickpea, was on his feet and hardly limping. "By all the gods, I'm the luckiest man alive!" he cried.

Gerin was not inclined to argue with him, but said, "Whether it's so or not, don't boast of it. If you tempt the divine powers to take away what they've given, they're too apt to yield to that temptation."

He did what he could for the warrior with the broken leg, splinting it between two trimmed saplings. The fellow had to be tied aboard a chariot after that, though, which ruined the car's efficiency and made him cry out at every bump and pothole in the road—and the road seemed nothing but bumps and potholes.

"I should have brought a wagon to carry the

wounded," the Fox said as they made camp that evening in the heart of the land Adiatunnus had seized. "I didn't want anything to slow us down, but here we are slowed down anyhow by all the fighting we've done—and we haven't really come to grips with Adiatunnus yet."

"Expecting a plan to run just as you make it asks a lot of the gods," Van said.

"That's so." Gerin fretted despite the admission. He always expected his plans to work perfectly; if they failed, that reflected unfavorably on him, since he had formed them. Life being as it was, few of them came to pass exactly as designed, which left him plenty for which to reproach himself.

Pale Nothos, nearly full, was the only moon in the sky: Math was just past new, and too close to the sun to be seen, while Tiwaz was a waning crescent and ruddy Elleb halfway between full and third quarter. It had been about there in its wanderings through the heavens when the Fox and his men slew the first monster down in Bevon's holdings, though rain clouds kept him from seeing it then.

Thinking of that monster made him think of the monsters that had joined Adiatunnus. He did not expect the Trokmoi themselves to sally forth against his men at night. He still hoped, though he didn't really believe, Adiatunnus hadn't yet learned of his attack. Even if the woodsrunners did know of it, sending men out by night was not something to be undertaken lightly.

But the monsters were something else again. He'd already seen that the night ghosts held no terror for them. They might well try to fall on his warriors when they had them at a disadvantage.

That made him double the watchstanders he'd placed out away from the main campfires. The men he'd hauled from their blankets grumbled. "Go back to sleep, then," he snapped. "If you'd rather be well rested and dead than sleepy and alive, how could I possibly presume to argue with you?" Stung by sarcasm, the newly drafted sentries went out to take their places.

Sure enough, monsters did prowl the woods and fields; their yowls and screams woke the Fox several times before midnight came. He'd grab for sword, shield, and helmet, realize the creatures were not close by, wriggle around till he was comfortable once more, and go back to sleep.

Then he heard screams that came not only from the monsters' throats but also from those of his own men. He snatched up his weapons and sprang to his feet. The night was well along; Elleb had climbed halfway from the eastern horizon to the meridian. But Gerin's eyes were not on the reddish moon.

Its light, that of Nothos, and the crimson glow of the embers showed two of his sentry parties locked in battle with the monsters, and more of the creatures running toward the warriors slowly rousing themselves round the fire.

Gerin shouted to distract a monster from an Elabonian who still lay on the ground snoring. The Fox envied the man's ability to sleep through anything, but wished he hadn't put it on display at that exact moment.

The monster swerved from the sleeping warrior and rushed at Gerin. Moonlight glinted from its teeth. Its clawed hands were outstretched to rend and tear. He was acutely aware of having only helm and shield; cool night air blew through his linen shirt and wool trousers, reminding him of what the monster's teeth and claws would do to flesh so nearly naked.

Instead of slashing, he thrust at the creature, to keep the full length of arm and sword between it and him. It spitted itself on the point of the bronze blade. He twisted the sword in the wound, then yanked it free. The monster screamed again, this time with the note of shocked surprise he'd heard so often from wounded men.

As it staggered, he thrust again, this time taking it right in the throat. Blood fountained, black in the light of the moons. The monster stumbled, fell, and did not rise again.

The Fox ran to the next closest fight he could find. He stabbed a monster in the back. It shrieked and whirled to face him, whereupon the trooper it had been fighting gave it a sword stroke almost identical to the one Gerin had used.

Though the monsters were individually more than a match for unarmored men, they had little notion of fighting save by and for themselves. That let the Elabonians slowly gain the upper hand on their attackers. And, like any beasts of prey, the monsters were not enthusiastic about taking on foes who fought back hard. They finally fled into the forest, still screaming in fury and hate.

"Throw some wood on the fire," Gerin said. "Let's see what needs doing here and do it."

As the flames leaped higher, the warriors went around finishing off monsters too badly hurt to run or even crawl away. Several men were also down for good. Gerin, Rihwin, and a couple of others who knew something of leechcraft did what they could for men who had been bitten or clawed.

"Lucky they didn't go for the horses," Van said, holding out a gashed arm to be bound up. "That would have spilled the perfume into the soup."

"Wouldn't it?" Gerin said. "As is, we'll have some cars with two men in them rather than three. But you're right; it could have been worse."

"It could that," the outlander said; every once in a while, a Trokmê turn of phrase cropped up in his speech.

"Me, I'm just as glad I won't be clumping along on foot when Adiatunnus and his jolly lads come after us in their chariots. That'll be tomorrow, unless Adiatunnus is blinder than I think."

"You're right there, too," the Fox said. "We could have run into them yesterday, easy as not. I'd hoped we would, as a matter of fact. All these little fights leave us weaker for the big one ahead."

Van nodded, but said, "We've hurt them worse'n they've done to us, though."

"I console myself with that thought," Gerin answered, "but drop me into the hottest hell if I know who can better afford the hurt, Adiatunnus or me. He brought a lot of Trokmoi south over the Niffet with him, the whoreson, and these monsters only add to his strength."

"We'll find out come the day," Van said, more cheerfully than Gerin could have managed. "For me, though, the only I thing I want to manage is some more sleep." He set down spear and shield, doffed his helm, wrapped himself in his blanket, and was snoring again while the Fox still stared indignantly.

Gerin could not put the desperate fight out of his mind so easily, nor could most of his men. Some still groaned from their wounds, while others sat around the fire and chatted in low voices about what they'd just been through.

The eastern sky turned gray, then pink, then gold. Tiwaz's thin crescent almost vanished against the growing light of the background against which it shone. The sun spilled its bright rays over the land. The Fox's men scratched shallow graves for their comrades the monsters had slain, then covered them over with stones to try to keep the creatures or other scavengers from molesting their remains. The corpses of the monsters, now stiff in death, they let lie where they had fallen.

Drivers harnessed chariots. "Let's get going," Gerin

said. "What we do today tells how much this strike is worth."

The first peasant village through which they rolled was empty and deserted. Gerin thought nothing of that till his warriors had already passed the hamlet. Then he realized word of their coming had got ahead of them. If the peasants knew invaders were loose in Adiatunnus' lands, the Trokmoi would know, too.

"Well, we didn't really think we could keep it a secret this long," Van answered when Gerin said that aloud. The outlander checked his shield and weapons to make sure he could get at them in an instant. Gerin told Raffo to slow the pace. When the driver obeyed and the chariots behind came up close enough, he shouted the warning back to them. Then he thumped Raffo on the shoulder. His chariot rejoined Drago's in the lead.

Cattle, sheep, and a couple of horses grazed on a broad stretch of meadow. They looked up in mild surprise—and the herders with them in dismay—when Elabonian chariots began rolling out. The herdsmen fled for the woods, but they were a long way away.

"Shall we go after 'em?" Raffo asked. "By their red locks, they're woodsrunners."

"No, let 'em run," Gerin said. "They look like men who hardly have their breeches to call their own; they're no danger to us."

Van pointed across the meadow. More chariots, these drawn by shaggy ponies and painted with bright spirals and jagged fylfots, came rattling out of the woods there. The men in them were pale-skinned and light-haired, like the herders. Bronze shone ruddy in the morning sun. "You want folk dangerous to us, Fox, I think you've found them," Van said.

Before Gerin could so much as nod, Drago the Bear called from the other chariot: "What do we do now, lord?"

"Pull over to one side, begin to form line of battle, and clear the roadway so the cars behind us can deploy," Gerin answered. Raffo, who knew his mind well, already had the chariot in motion. Drago's driver conformed to his movements.

To Van, Gerin murmured, "Now we see how much Adiatunnus has learned from a few years of fighting against Elabonians."

"Aye, if he's brought his own army in a great roaring mass, Trokmê style, he'll swarm down on us before our friends get here," the outlander said. "Let's hope he's set out scouts the way we have, and that they're waiting for their main body, too." He chuckled. "The fighting trick'll work against him this time, not for."

Much to Gerin's relief, the Trokmoi across the meadow didn't whip their horses into a wild charge. Instead, they too sidled out onto the grass almost crab fashion, as if wondering how many cars the Fox had with him and how soon those cars would arrive.

Gerin was wondering the same thing about the woodsrunners. Adiatunnus must have done a fine job of absorbing Elabonian military doctrine, for his supporters began coming out of the woods at about the same time as those of the Fox. The two lines of chariots stretched about to equal length on the meadow. Monsters stood between the cars of Adiatunnus' battle line. Gerin wondered whether that would do the Trokmê more good than harm; the ponies that pulled the chariots seemed nervous of these fierce new allies.

Adiatunnus cupped his hands and bellowed like a bull. Gerin knew that voice. At the same moment, Gerin raised his arm and then brought it down to point toward the Trokmê line. Drivers on both sides whipped their teams forward.

Chariot battles were generally fluid as quicksilver, and

this one proved no exception. The herds in the broad field made teams swing wide to avoid them. The pounding of the horses' hooves, the rattle and thump of the cars, and warriors' hoarse, excited shouts panicked the sheep and cattle and made them run wild, spreading more confusion still.

Gerin plucked an arrow from his quiver, nocked, and let fly at Adiatunnus: if the chieftain fell, that would make his followers easier meat. Shooting from the jouncing platform of a chariot car—indeed, standing in the car without hanging on to the rail to keep from being pitched out on your head—was anything but easy, though endless practice let him do it without wondering how he managed. He cursed when the Trokmê did not fall.

An arrow hissed by his own ear; the woodsrunners were aiming at him, too. Here and there, men on both sides pitched out of chariots to sprawl in the thick green grass. Horses went down, too, and often made the cars they drew founder with them. Sometimes warriors would come up from those mishaps unhurt, and go on to fight as foot soldiers.

A monster loped toward Gerin's chariot. The creature was almost as fast as the horses, and much more agile. Unlike some the Fox had seen, it carried no weapons. Even so, it was clever enough to attack the beasts of burden rather than the men they hauled: the horses could not fight back, and if one of them went down, the chariot was apt to overturn, too.

The Fox shot at the monster from only a few yards' distance, and turned the air sulfurous when his arrow went wide. Van was on the wrong side of the chariot to attack the creature, and in any case could not reach it with his thrusting spear. The horses squealed and shied away from the monster as it came up on them.

Before Gerin could draw another arrow, Raffo lashed

the monster across its outstretched arms with his whip. The thing screeched. The driver hit it again, *craack!*, this time across its muzzle, just missing one eye. The monster clapped a hand to the wound and fled.

Along with three or four other chariots, Gerin's overlapped the end of the Trokmê line. "Come on! We'll roll 'em up!" he shouted with fierce joy, and led his men around the enemy's flank. The chaos they created was marvelous to behold—and would have been more marvelous still had the woodsrunners' line not overlapped his on the other wing. But it did, and the whole battle spun round, a mad wheel of destruction.

The Fox found himself face-to-face with Adiatunnus. The Trokmê had lost his helm somewhere in the fighting; his bald pate glowed red from exertion and sun. His eyes, though, were cold and shrewd, "Well, lord Gerin," he said with a mocking salute, "we lie athwart your way home now, don't we?"

"You do that," Gerin answered in the Trokmê tongue, "but no more than we lie athwart yours."

Fighting ebbed as the leaders parleyed. Adiatunnus scowled; perhaps he'd hoped to panic Gerin, but he'd failed. He looked over the field. "You've hurt us about as bad as the other way round," he said. "Are you fain to go on, now, or shall we say enough and have done?"

Gerin gauged the field, too. The Trokmê chief had the right of it; the battle was drawn. The woodsrunners had wrecked Mannor Trout's village, but he'd had his revenge there: he'd hurt Adiatunnus' lands worse. Fighting till only a handful of men still stood had scant appeal to him, especially with the monsters on the loose.

"Enough—for now," he said reluctantly, "if you can hold those—things—to a truce to let us separate."

"That I can, though I'll thank you for not speaking ill of my friends and allies here," Adiatunnus said. "And 'for now' indeed—we'll have at each other again, I have no doubt. Och, and when we do, I'll be after having more in the way of friends and allies, but you, Fox— what will you do?"

Gerin pondered that question as the rival forces warily passed through each other. He was still pondering it when he crossed back over the border into his own holding, and when he came home to Fox Keep. Ponder as he would, though, he found no answer that satisfied him.

VIII

"My poor ear," Rihwin moaned for what had to be the five hundredth time. Gerin prided himself on being a patient man, but when his patience snapped, it snapped spectacularly.

"By all the gods, I'm sick to death of listening to your whining," he growled, and grabbed Rihwin. The southerner tried to twist free, but Gerin was the best wrestler in the northlands. He twisted one of Rihwin's arms behind his back and started frog-marching him toward the shack where he worked his magics.

"What are you doing?" Rihwin yelped.

"I am going to fix that ear of yours, one way or the other," the Fox said. Rihwin hadn't struggled hard till then, but he started to. Gerin twisted his arm up a little higher. Rihwin gasped as he felt his shoulder joint creak.

Inside the shack, Gerin slammed him down onto the one rickety chair in front of the table where he labored at his sorcery. He'd managed to overawe Rihwin, which wasn't easy. The southerner made no effort to bolt. In a small voice, he repeated, "What are you doing?"

"What I said I'd do: use the law of similarity to build that ear of yours back to where it's the same as the other one. The spell should be simplicity itself: what could possibly go wrong?"

Now Rihwin did try to rise. "I'd really rather not find out. Given the choice between a half-trained wizard—which, you must admit, is a charitable description of your talents—and keeping silent about my mutilation, I opt without hesitation for silence."

Gerin slammed him down again. "You've said that before, over and over. You've gone back on your word, too, over and over. Now, don't be a donkey—just sit there and I'll set you right in no time. Unless you'd rather I tried that operation you described—"

"No," Rihwin said hastily. "You're sure you know what you're doing?" He had the look of a man sitting down to gamble against a fellow notorious for using loaded dice.

"I know what I have to do," Gerin answered, which was not quite an affirmative. He flipped through the vellum pages of a codex until he came to a cantrip which was a general application of the law of similarity. Then he paused a while in thought. Suddenly he smacked one fist into the other palm. "The very thing!" he exclaimed. He turned to Rihwin. "I'm going out to find something to tailor the spell to your very problem. You'd better be here when I get back."

"What are you looking for?" Rihwin still sounded suspicious.

Gerin grinned triumphantly. "Earwigs."

"Well, father Dyaus, that's ingenious," Rihwin said. "Perhaps I *shall* be here when you return."

With that Gerin had to be content. He went out and started turning over stones in the courtyard. Under one not very far from the stables, he found several of the shiny, dark brown insects. They tried to crawl away, but he grabbed them and carried them back to the shack. "Even the little pincers on their posteriors will serve symbolically to represent the ring you wore in your ear."

"Why, so they will." All at once, Rihwin went from dubious to enthusiastic. "Don't fribble away the time. Get on with it."

Gerin got on with it, but first spent more time studying the spell in the grimoire. He knew his own inadequacy as a sorcerer, and also knew he would never get the chance to make two serious blunders. Fitting a general spell to a specific application required certain adaptations of both verse and passes. He muttered to himself, planning in advance the rhymes he'd use and the passes he'd have to change. The spell was intended to be simple, which meant most of the passes used the right hand. That hindered him more than it helped. He'd overcome the problem before, though, and expected to be able to do it again.

He felt confident as he launched into the chant. His right hand was clumsy, but seemed to be doing what he required of it. He poured rose water over the earwigs he'd imprisoned in a bronze bowl. They didn't drown quite as fast as he'd thought they would, but surely that degree of exactitude wouldn't matter.

"My ear feels strange," Rihwin remarked. He brought his hand up to the ruined flap of flesh. "You've not changed it yet, but the potential for change is manifestly there."

"Shut up," Gerin said fiercely, though Rihwin had given him good news. The donkey had to know he didn't need to be distracted, not when he was coming to the climactic moment of the spell. His right hand twisted through the last pass; he grunted in satisfaction at having done it correctly. He cut a red wool thread with a bronze knife he never used for any other purpose and cried, "Transform!"

"You've done it!" Rihwin said exultantly. "I can feel the change."

Gerin turned to see what his magic had wrought. He suffered a sudden coughing fit, and hoped his face would not betray him. He had changed Rihwin's ear, but not quite in the way he'd intended. It was indeed whole, but not pink and round: it was long and pointed and hairy.

He knew what had gone wrong. He'd called Rihwin a

donkey, and then thought of him as a donkey when he'd spoken up at the wrong time. Somehow, the resentful thought had leaked into the conjuration and left his fellow Fox with a donkey's ear.

A fly buzzing around the inside of the shack chose that moment to light on the new-formed appendage. As a donkey's ear will, it twitched. The fly flew away. Rihwin started violently and clapped a hand to his head. The evidence, alas, was all too palpable. "What have you done to me, you muddler?"

"Muddled." Gerin kicked at the dirt floor of the shack, feeling smaller and more useless than the earwigs he'd drowned.

"Well, what are you going to do about it? You were going to give me an ear, you—you moldy pigeon dropping, not this—this excrescence." Gerin had never heard an unwounded man scream through three consecutive sentences before; in the abstract, the feat was to be admired.

"I'll try my best to set it right," Gerin said. "I should be able to manage a simple reversal of the spell." He reached for the grimoire.

"You said the spell itself would be simple, too," Rihwin reminded him. He wasn't screaming any more, but sarcasm sharp and sour as vinegar dripped from his tongue.

"So I did," Gerin admitted. "Look, if all else fails, I'll buy you a hat." That sent Rihwin's voice back into the upper registers.

Gerin tried to ignore him, though it wasn't easy. In theory, reversal spells were simple. Both the law of similarity and that of contagion applied and, since he'd just essayed the spell he wished to overturn, the links were temporally strong. On the other hand, given the sorcerous ineptitude he'd just demonstrated— He made himself not think about that. A magician needed to believe he'd succeed.

A magician also needs talent, part of him jeered. The rest of him made that part shut up. He plunged head-long into the first reversal spell he found. The more time he spent thinking about it, the more he'd hesitate later. If you fell out of a jouncing chariot, you needed to get back in and ride again.

By luck, most of the passes were for his left hand. He went through them with care, but not with confidence—he wondered when, if ever, he'd have confidence in his magic once more. Rihwin sat in the chair, arms folded, glaring stonily at him. Normally, having Rihwin keep quiet while he cast a spell would have been a blessing. As things were, it just disconcerted Gerin more.

He raced through the cantrip at a pace a practiced wizard would have hesitated to match. One way or another, he'd know soon. His fingers twisted through the last and hardest pass of the spell. "Let all be as it was!" he yelled.

"Something happened," Rihwin said. "I felt it." But he didn't raise his hand to discover exactly what it was. Maybe he was afraid. He asked Gerin, "Did you deck me out with an octopus tentacle?"

"I haven't even seen octopus tentacles since that Sithonian eatery I used to frequent in the City of Elabon," Gerin replied. He stared at the place where the donkey's ear had sprouted from Rihwin's head.

"That's not a responsive answer." Rihwin sighed the-atrically. "Very well, since you won't tell me, I shall just have to find out for myself." Slowly, he brought his left hand up to his head. His eyes grew as wide as Gerin's. "It's *my* ear," he whispered. Then, even more amazed, he added, "And it's whole—isn't it?"

"It certainly looks that way," Gerin said. "Does it feel so, too?"

"By Dyaus, it does. How ever did you manage that?"

"If I knew, I would tell you." Gerin cudgeled his wits for an explanation. At last, he said, "The reversal spell must have undone your wound as well as my magic—that's all I can think of."

Rihwin felt of his ear. "There's the hole through which the hoop passed. You must be right, lord Gerin; like you, I can think of no other explanation that fits." Now that his ear was restored, he started to laugh. "My fellow Fox, you are the best bad magician I have ever known."

"I'll take that for a compliment." Suddenly Gerin started to laugh, too. Rihwin's elastic features showed curiosity. Gerin explained: "If I could do on purpose what I did by accident, think of the demand I'd be in from wenches who wanted to frolic and yet be wed as maidens."

Rihwin leered. "Aye, and think of the fee you could charge, too."

"I'm surprised women don't already have a magic like that," Gerin said. "Or maybe they do, and just don't let on to us men."

"It could be so," Rihwin agreed. He felt his ear again, as if not believing Gerin had, no matter how erratically, accomplished exactly what he'd said he'd do. "Now I have to wait until Otes or another jeweler passes through, so I can have a new hoop made to replace the one I lost."

"If you get your ear torn again on account of that foolish southron conceit, don't expect me to fix it for you," Gerin said.

"If I come to you again to have my ear fixed, I deserve to wear a donkey's in its place," Rihwin retorted. Gerin mimed taking an arrow in the ribs; Rihwin had won that exchange.

One of Gerin's warriors who held the Elabon Way open through Bevon's holding brought disquieting news back to Fox Keep. "Lord prince, it's said Bevon and two of his sons have made common cause with Adiatunnus— and with the monsters from Ikos," he said between swigs from a jack of ale.

"Said by whom?" Gerin demanded, not wanting to believe Elabonians could fall so low as to align themselves with the creatures.

"By Bevander, another of Bevon's sons," the soldier answered. "He came to us calling down curses on past enmity and saying he'd sooner cast his lot with you than with a bunch of things."

"I wonder what he meant by that," Gerin said, "the monsters, or his father and brothers?" The warrior who'd brought word started, then snorted as he was swallowing, which made him choke and spray ale over the tabletop.

Gerin plucked distractedly at his beard. He'd reckoned Adiatunnus' embrace of the monsters a hideous aberration. If more and more lords proved willing to use the creatures to further their own ends, they *would* gain a permanent place in the northlands. He wondered which lord who favored them they'd first end up devouring.

"What will you do, lord Gerin?" the soldier answered.

"Do about what, Captain?" Van called from the stairway. He and Fand were coming down into the great hall hand in hand. By the foolish grins on their faces, Gerin had no trouble imagining what they'd been doing up on the second floor. Fand smirked at him, just in case he had had trouble. She wanted to make him jealous—her door stayed closed to him these days.

He knew a certain amount of annoyance at the way she flaunted what she was up to, but jealousy stayed dormant. He wondered what that was telling him. To keep from having to think about it, he turned to the trooper and said, "Tell him what you just told me."

The trooper obeyed. Van scowled and rubbed at the scar that creased his nose. Fand poked him in the ribs, indignant at being forgotten. He let go of her hand and slipped his arm around her waist. She molded herself against him, but most of his attention was still on what he'd just heard. "Good question," he said. "What *will* you do, Fox?"

"I don't know yet," Gerin answered. "I begin to think I need allies myself. I wonder if the monsters have got to Schild's lands yet. If they have, he may be more likely to remember he's my vassal. And Ricolf will fight on my side, even if he isn't fond of me anymore."

"The Trokmoi south of the Niffet will range themselves with Adiatunnus, sure and they will," Fand said.

Gerin couldn't tell whether she was trying to be helpful or to goad him further. He gave her the benefit of the doubt. "I wouldn't be surprised if you're right. All the more reason for me to look for those who will help me struggle against them." He puckered his lips, as if at a sour taste. He hated having to rely on any power but his own. It left him too vulnerable by half. But he was already vulnerable, in a different way.

"Hagop son of Hovan—" Van began.

"—Is hardly worth having on my side, for he brings little force with him," Gerin interrupted. "I want to win this fight, not have it drag on forever." As he spoke, one way to do that came to mind. "If Grand Duke Aragis would make common cause with me, now—"

Van, Fand, and the trooper all stared at him. He didn't suppose he could blame them. Ever since Elabon abandoned the northlands and the Trokmoi entered them, he and Aragis had been most successful at building from the ruins of empire. He'd taken for granted that they would clash one day, and assumed Aragis had done the same—a notion their meeting at Ikos had only reinforced. But the monsters and the lords who would use them to augment their own power were a danger to Aragis no less than to Gerin.

At last Van said, "You don't think small, Captain. That much I give you."

The more Gerin looked at the idea, the more he liked it himself. "I see two problems," he said. "One is making sure we stay allies with Aragis and don't end up his vassals. He'll have the same concern about us, no doubt. It could make working together ticklish."

"Aye, I can see that one," Van said with a sage nod. "This setup of vassalage you Elabonians have makes you so sticky about rank and honor that it's a wonder you ever get anything done. What's the second?"

Gerin made a wry face. "Simply getting a messenger from Fox Keep to the Castle of the Archer. With all the monsters loose on the land between what I hold and what belongs to Aragis, I really should send a good-sized fighting force just to see to it that he hears my offer and I hear his answer. But I can't afford to do that, not now, not with the monsters and the Trokmoi and now Bevon and his sons ganging together against me."

"Send Rihwin," Van suggested. "Ever since you got him that one ear back, he's been talking both of mine off about—what does he call it?—your natural talent as a mage, that's right."

Remembering the near fiasco in the shack, the Fox said, "That only proves he's not as smart as he thinks he is." He plucked at his beard again. "I need to ponder this a bit more before I go and do it. It's not something I can just set in motion before I try to look at the places it may lead."

"Rihwin would," Van said. "But then, you already said what needs saying about him. Not that he's stupid, mind, but that he thinks he has your Dyaus' view of things, and he doesn't."

"I don't what?" Rihwin asked, coming into the great hall from the courtyard.

"Know your backside from a longtooth turd," Fand said. Gerin and Van hadn't put it so pungently, but it did a fair job of summing up their opinion.

Rihwin looked down over his shoulder at the part of him cited. "That's what I thought I had there," he said, as if in relief. "Trying to sit down on a longtooth turd strikes me as unaesthetic."

"As what, now?" Fand said. Her Elabonian was fluent, but that was not a word used every day in a frontier castle of a former frontier province of the decaying Empire of Elabon.

"Messy and smelly," Gerin translated for her. "He's making a joke."

"Is he? Then why doesn't he up and do it?" Fand said.

"I take a certain amount of pleasure at being insulted by so fair a lady," Rihwin said, bowing, "but only a certain amount." He turned on his heel and strode out.

"A pity you gave him back his missing ear," Fand said to Gerin. "Better you should have torn off the other one." She bared her teeth and looked every bit as savage as she sounded. The Fox was sure she meant to be taken literally.

He said, "What good would that do? Rihwin didn't listen with two ears and didn't with one, so why do you think he would with none?"

Fand stared at him, then gurgled laughter. "It's not just that y'are lefthanded, Fox, but sure and you think that way as well. How am I to stay angry at you, now, when you go sneaking round my temper with such silliness as that?"

Gerin didn't answer. As far as he was concerned, he hadn't done anything to deserve Fand's anger. His thoughts were another matter, but if men—and women, too—were scourged for their thoughts, every back in the northlands—no, every back in the world—would bear stripes.

Van said, "Will you send to Aragis, then, Captain?"

"I think so," Gerin answered. "But as I said, I'll weigh it a bit more before I make up my mind. I grudge the strength I'd have to send to make sure my embassy got through."

"Fair enough, I suppose," the outlander said, "but don't go weighing overlong. My gut warns me we haven't much time to squander."

If Van was worried, the situation could not be good; Van generally saw fighting as sport. Gerin had already thought matters bleak. Seeing his friend's concern, he wondered if he hadn't been too optimistic.

Rap, rap. Knocking on Fand's door, Gerin realized he hadn't been so nervous approaching a woman since he'd gone off into the woods with a serf girl at about the age of fourteen. If she told him no again, he vowed he'd have nothing more to do with her.

The door opened. Fand eyed Gerin with the same irresolution he felt. At last, with the hint of a smile, she said, "You're not one to give up easy, are you, now?"

"If I were, I'd either be dead or living in the southlands," Gerin answered. "May I come in?"

"Sure and you'd do better with more sweet talk, not just throwing it out so, like a sausage, *splash!* into the soup pot." Fand sounded a trifle irked. She didn't close the door in his face, though, as she had so many times lately. After a moment, she stepped aside and motioned for him to join her. She closed the door behind him, barred it.

A tunic lay on the bed, bone needle and thread halfway through a rip on one sleeve. Gerin turned the sleeve
right side out so he could see how the repair would look.
"That's fine work," he said.

"For which I thank you, though sewing by lamplight
is more trouble nor it's worth, I'm thinking." Fand rubbed
her eyes to show him what she meant. After an awkward
pause, she went on, "But you didna come here to be
talking of shirts." She sat down on the bed.

"No, I didn't." Gerin sat down beside her. "I came
because I hoped we could end the quarrel between us."

"Because you wanted to futter me," Fand said. She
didn't sound angry, though, as she had so often when
she sent him away. She might have been talking about
how the wheat was doing this year. After a moment, Gerin
nodded; saying he didn't want her would have been a
lie. Fand's mouth quirked in a wry smile. "Och, you're
no seducer, are you now? But have your way this once,
Fox. We'll see what we bring to it." She pulled the tunic
she was wearing up over her head, then stood to slide
off her brightly checked wool skirt.

Seeing her naked made the breath catch in his throat,
as it always did. She was a splendid woman, and she
knew it, which only made the impression stronger. Gerin
undressed in a hurry. They got back down on the bed
together.

They did their best to please each other. The Fox tried
hard; he could tell Fand was doing the same thing. He
rolled off her quickly afterwards, not wanting her to have
to bear his weight any longer than she needed to. "I
thank you," she said, and sat up.

Gerin lay on one side. He looked over to her and said,
"It's no good any more, is it?"

She sighed. "If you're after knowing the answer, why
d'you ask the question?"

"Saying the words, hearing them, makes it seem real somehow," he answered. "Besides, I might have been wrong." He swung himself over to the side of the bed, grabbed his breeches, and put them back on. As he fiddled with the waist string, he added, "I won't trouble you that way again."

" 'Twas no trouble," Fand said. " 'Twasn't much of anything at all, if you take my meaning. And isn't that a strange thing, now? The gods know I looked for the two of us to break, but I thought 'twould be after a grand shindy we'd both remember all our days. But here we are, just—quits."

"Quits," Gerin echoed dully. He leaned over and kissed her, not on the mouth but on the cheek. "It was always lively while it lasted, wasn't it? If it's come to the point where it's not any more, as well we give it up."

"Truth there." Fand sent him an anxious look. "You'd not throw me out of Fox Keep because I'm your doxy no more, would you?"

He laughed. "And have Van come after me with that mace of his? Not likely. No, you're welcome to bide here as long as you like—provided you don't drive everyone around you utterly mad. That may not be so easy for you." He chuckled to show he didn't expect to be taken altogether seriously.

"Och, when I'm the only one right and the whole world beside me wrong, how can I not speak out plain?" But Fand laughed, too. "I ken what you'll tell me—you wish I'd find a way. Well, I'll try, indeed and I will. What comes of it we'll have to see."

He nodded and got to his feet. Walking to the doorway felt strange. He'd never parted from a longtime lover before. Elise had parted from him, and without a word of warning, but that wasn't the same thing. With his hand on the bar, he turned back and said,

"Good-bye." The word came out funereally somber.

Maybe that crossed Fand's mind, too, for she said, "I've not died, y'know, nor yet headed back to the forests. I'll be down for porridge come the dawn, same as always." But she also seemed to feel the moment. "It won't be the same any more, will it?"

"No, but it's likely better this way. If we did go on long enough, we'd have ended up hating each other." Something of that had happened with him and Elise, though there it had been quiet and one-sided till it burst out when she left.

If he stayed by the door talking, he was liable to end up talking himself out of what he'd resolved to do. He swung up the bar. Fand came over to lower it after he left. She smiled a farewell as he stepped out into the hallway, closed the door after him.

From her chamber to his was only a few strides. In the moment he needed to step between them, Selatre came down the hall, probably on her way to the garderobe. She'd seen Fand's door close. She looked from it to Gerin and back again, then kept walking without a word or another glance.

His face heated. The kindest thing Selatre could think of him was that he'd just slaked his lust. He wanted to run down the hall after her and explain that he and Fand weren't going to do that sort of thing any more, but he didn't think she'd listen.

"What's the use?" he muttered, and opened the door to his own chamber. He closed it after himself, threw off his clothes, and flung himself down onto the bed. The straw-stuffed mattress shifted back and forth on the grid of rawhide straps that supported it. The slow, rolling motion made Gerin feel as if he were on a chariot just setting out.

In a little while, Selatre's soft footsteps came back up

the hall as she returned to the chamber he'd given her.
They didn't pause in front of Fand's doorway, nor in front
of his. If anything, they sped up.

Silence returned. Outside, the moons wheeled
through their endless dance: Tiwaz full, Elleb lost in the
bright skirts of the sun, Math waxing between first quarter and full, Nothos waning from full toward third quarter. Gerin got up and stared through his narrow window
at the multiple shadows the moons cast.

Nothos had climbed almost to his high point in the
sky before the Fox finally slept.

After a couple of days of thought, Gerin did appoint
Rihwin his envoy to Aragis the Archer. He would sooner
have fared south himself, but dared not, not with so many
things poised to go wrong close to home.

"Tell him how things are here," he said to Rihwin.
"The alliance I offer is equal, neither of us to have any
claim of superiority over the other. If he doesn't care for
that, to the five hells with him. And Rihwin, my fellow
Fox, my friend, my colleague—"

"Ah, now that you've sweetened it, here comes the
gibe," Rihwin said.

"If you choose to take it as one, aye," Gerin answered.
"To me, it was just going to be a remark your nature
makes me make. What I was going to say is this: for
Dyaus' sake, don't get cute."

"I?" Rihwin was the picture of offended dignity. "What
could you possibly mean?"

"What I said. I've met Aragis. He has about as much
laughter and merriment in him as a chamber pot does,
but he's anything but stupid. Stick to the matter at hand
with him and you'll do fine. Get away from it—start telling jokes, drink too much ale, anything of the sort—and
all you'll earn from him is contempt. I don't want that to

rub off on me, because you're going there as my agent. Is that clear?"

"If you don't care for the way I do things, send Drago the Bear," Rihwin said sulkily. "He'll do exactly as you say—he hasn't the wit to do anything else."

"That's why I'm sending you," Gerin answered. "But you need to understand what's riding on this, and that I don't want any of your japes and scrapes as you fare south. You may not be able to help it; I know they're in your blood. Do your best all the same."

Rihwin's features registered anger, resignation, and amusement, all in the space of a couple of breaths. At last he said, "Very well, lord prince. I shall essay the role of a sobersided nitpicker: in short, I shall model my conduct on you in all regards." As if that were not enough, he added, "To make the impression complete, I shall seek to carry off any nubile female relative the Grand Duke may happen to have." He cocked his head to one side to see what impression that had on Gerin.

The Fox started to scowl, started to curl his hands into fists, but gave up and threw them in the air while he broke out laughing. "You, sirrah, are incorrigible," he declared.

"I certainly do hope so," Rihwin answered blithely. "Now that we've settled how I'm to comport myself on this embassy, with how large a retinue am I to be entrusted?"

"Four chariots and teams feels about right to me," Gerin said. "Any more and you'd look like an invasion; any fewer and you're liable not to get through. What say you to that, my fellow Fox?"

"It strikes me as about the right number," Rihwin said. "If you'd said I was to go alone, I wouldn't have gone. Had you put me in charge of a dozen chariots rather than a dozen men, I'd have assumed you'd gone daft— more daft than usual, I should say."

"For this ringing endorsement of my faculties, I thank you," Gerin said. "Now go ready yourself. I want you to leave before sunset. The matter grows too urgent to admit of much more delay."

"If you and Aragis together can't control what happens in the northlands, who can?" Rihwin asked.

"Adiatunnus, perhaps," Gerin said. Rihwin looked startled, then made a sour face, and finally nodded. He began a prostration such as he might have offered to the Emperor of Elabon. Had he actually got down on his belly, Gerin would have kicked him in the ribs without hesitation. But he stopped with the obeisance half made and went off to get ready to travel.

Gerin felt better now that he'd made his decision. He was doing something, not waiting on Adiatunnus and the monsters to do something to him. That desire to see something, no matter what, happen had brought others down. He knew as much. But waiting to be ruined did not sit well with him, either.

He walked back into the keep from the courtyard. He didn't know how badly his raid had hurt Adiatunnus, but at the least it must have made the Trokmê thoughtful, for the Fox had had no reports of woodsrunners on his side of the border since. Not many monsters had gone after his peasants, either. To him, that made the raid something worth doing, too.

Van and Fand were sitting in the great hall, jacks of ale in front of them. Van gnawed on a mutton shank left over from the night before. When Gerin came in, Fand pushed herself closer on the bench to the outlander, as if to say the Fox couldn't take her away from him. But Gerin was mostly relieved not to have to look forward to their next tiff. If Van wanted to stay with her, he wouldn't stand in his friend's way.

He dipped up a jack of ale for himself and sat down

across from the close-knit couple. After a pull at the jack, he told Van what he'd done.

The outlander considered it, nodded gravely. "If your pride won't keep you from working in harness with Aragis, it's probably the best move you could make."

"If it's between pride and survival, I know which to choose," Gerin said.

Fand sniffed. "Where's the spirit in that? A serf would say as much."

Gerin started to bristle, then reminded himself he didn't have to let her outrage him. "Have it however you'd like," he said. "I can only answer for myself." He drained the jack, set it down on the table in front of him, and got to his feet. "A very good morning to you both. Now, by your leave, I have other things to attend to."

As he headed for the stairway, he felt Fand's eyes on his back. She didn't say anything, though; maybe she was also reminding herself that they didn't have to quarrel. On the other hand, he thought, maybe she was just speechless that he hadn't risen to her bait.

Upstairs, he hurried down the hall toward the library. He'd been doing that ever since he came back from south of the High Kirs; when he was with his books, he could remember the scholar he'd wanted to become and forget the baron the gods had decided he would be. Had his footsteps grown quicker yet since he started teaching Selatre her letters? *Well, what if they have?* he asked himself.

She was waiting for him when he got there. She was not the sort to sit idle; she had a spindle and some wool, and was busy making thread. She smiled and put down the spindle when he came through the door. "Now for something my wits can work on, not my hands," she said, sounding as if she looked forward to the switch.

"More on the nature of the gods," Gerin said, pulling a scroll from the pigeonhole where it rested.

"Ah, good," she said briskly. "My own life was so bound up with Biton that I know less of the rest of the gods than I should, especially seeing how my circumstances have changed." She no longer sounded bitter, only matter-of-fact.

The Fox slipped the velvet cover from the scroll, worked the handles until he reached the section he and Selatre were going to read. "Ah, today we come to the god—" His voice changed. "Here, read it for yourself."

"Mavrix," Selatre said, sounding out the name. She'd caught Gerin's sudden shift of tone. "Why does the Sithonian god of wine—what's the word I want?—disturb you?"

"Raise my hackles, you mean?" Gerin shivered. "We've had dealings, Mavrix and I. I'd guess the god's not happy with them, and I know I'm not. If it weren't for Mavrix, Rihwin would still be a mage. If it weren't— But never mind all that now; I can tell it another time. Just read me what our deathless author set down on parchment." Irony filled his voice. The scroll was a thoroughly humdrum compilation of the deities worshiped by the various peoples of the Elabonian Empire. He would gladly have replaced it with a more interesting volume on the same theme, had he been lucky enough to stumble across one.

Selatre was not yet at the point where she could appreciate fine points of style. She fought her way through words and sentences, seizing meaning as best she could. " 'Mavrix, the god of wine native to Sithonia,' " she read, " 'is also widely reverenced in Elabon. His votaries are even found north of the High Kirs, although all wine in that distant province is of necessity imported.' "

"The scroll says it, but I never knew of Mavrix's cult up here," Gerin said. "Still and all, when Rihwin invoked him in a minor magic, he appeared—not to do Rihwin's bidding, but to punish him for associating with me."

"And why did the god see fit to do that?" Selatre asked. Before the Fox could answer, she held up a hand. "Tell me another time, as you said. I resume: 'The cult of Mavrix is held in chief repute by those who have little happiness in their lives. In the release they take from wine and from the orgiastic nature of his worship, they find the pleasure otherwise lacking to them.' Does *orgiastic* mean what I think it does?"

"Every sort of excess?" Gerin asked. Selatre nodded. Gerin said, "That's what it means, all right. Go on; you're doing very well."

"Thank you." Selatre started reading again: " 'The Emperors of Elabon sometimes persecuted those who took part in Mavrix's rites when Sithonia was a newly acquired province. Like much else Sithonian, however, the god's cult has become an accepted part of Elabonian life in recent years, and the cry "Evoii!" is often heard all through the Empire.' "

"I've heard it," Gerin said. "If I never hear it again, I'll be just as glad. Mavrix is a powerful god, but not one whom I care to worship. I like order too well to be easy with the lawlessness the lord of the sweet grape fosters."

Selatre clicked her tongue between her teeth. "The lord Biton is also a patron of order and reason, so I understand what you are saying, and yet—may I read on?"

"Seems you already have, if you know what comes next in the scroll," Gerin said. "You read that with just your eyes alone, didn't you? Not many can do that so soon; quite a few have to say the words to themselves no matter how long they've been reading."

"You don't," Selatre said. "I tried to imitate you."

After a few seconds, he said, "I can't think of the last time anyone paid me a compliment like that. Thank you." He let out a wry chuckle. "Not that you're likely to find the way most folks go by looking to me for a guide."

"I think you have the better way," Selatre said, which produced a longer silence, especially since, as Gerin noted, she didn't qualify the comment with *here* or any such thing. She looked down at the scroll again and read some more: " 'Mavrix is also the god who chiefly inspires poets and other artists, and is the patron of the drama. His love for beauty is well known.' " She looked up from the scroll. "Those are worthy attributes for a god, I think."

"Oh, indeed." Gerin's voice was dry. "Our chronicler here, though, is a rather—hmm, how should I put it?— a reticent man, shall we say. Among other ways, the god's 'love for beauty' manifests itself as a passion for pretty boys."

He wondered how Selatre would take that, and whether she'd even understand what he was talking about. Both the Sithonians and their gods were fonder of pederasty than the northlands peasants among whom she'd spent her life until Biton chose her for his own. But she must have figured out what he meant, for she laughed heartily. Then, sobering, she said, "Is that written down in one of your other books? If not, it may be lost."

"Do you know, I'm not sure," Gerin answered. "You've just made me sure of one thing, though, not that I wasn't already: I couldn't have found anyone better to oversee this library."

"Now you compliment me," she said. "In turn, I want to thank you once more for bringing me here to tend your books. It's not the life I had, but it's far more than I had any reason to hope for."

This time, she didn't just set her hand on his, she clasped it, nor did she pull away when he returned the pressure. He started to lean forward to kiss her, then hesitated, not from lack of desire but out of a scrupulous sense of fairness. He said, "If you're drawn to me, think on why. If it's only because I'm the one who brought you out of Ikos and helped show you how to live in the wider world, think on whether that's reason enough."

She laughed at him. She couldn't have surprised him more if she'd burst into flame. "I am a woman grown, lord Gerin, and you are not my father." As was her way, she sobered fast. "What you are with the lady Fand is something else again, especially in light of what I saw the other night."

That sobered Gerin in turn. Slowly, he said, "The thing is dead. Aye, you saw me leave her chamber." He sighed. "Aye, we'd been to bed—what point denying it when it's so? We won't do that again—no sense to it, not when it was as it was. If she and Van get along, I wish them nothing but joy. If they don't, I probably ought to wish him a hide as hard and thick as his corselet."

"So you should." She smiled again, but not for long. "And is it because what you and Fand knew is dead that you now show an interest in me?"

"Maybe in part," he answered, which surprised her. He quickly added, "But only in small part, I'd say. More— far more—is that you are as you are. Believe me or not, as you will." One of his eyebrows rose, a sort of punctuation by expression. "Besides, you were the one who took *my* hand. I wouldn't have presumed to do such a thing, not with you being who you are."

"I noticed that," Selatre said. "You'd promised as much when you took me away from Ikos, but who knows what a man's promises are worth till they're tested? When I saw you meant what you said, I—" She didn't go on, but looked down at the scroll in front of her. Unlike Fand's, her skin did not usually show much color, but she flushed now.

"You decided you wanted to take the first step," Gerin

said. Selatre kept her eyes on the scroll but, almost imperceptibly, she nodded.

Gerin plucked at his beard. What he'd known with Fand had gone beyond the pleasure of the bedchamber, but not far beyond; there was a core of himself he'd never yielded. He'd done that only once, with Elise . . . and after what came of that, he was wary—*no, frightened,* he told himself—of risking it again. But if he involved himself with Selatre, he would have to risk it; he could feel as much already.

Do you want to spend the rest of your days alone inside? he wondered. It was easier; it was safer; it was, in the end, empty.

"Are you sure?" he asked. Saying the words was almost as hard as going into battle.

Selatre nodded, a little less hesitantly. With something of the feeling of a man diving into deep water, Gerin leaned toward her. He wondered if she would know how to kiss; she'd said she'd been consecrated to Biton ever since her courses failed to start when she reached womanhood.

But her lips met his firmly; her mouth opened and her tongue played with his. It was, in fact, quite as satisfactory a kiss as he'd ever had. When at last they broke apart, he said, "Where did you learn that?"

"In my village, of course." She looked puzzled for a moment, then burst out laughing again. "Oh, I see—you expected me to be not just a maiden but ignorant as well. No. Some of the young men there couldn't have cared less that the god had set his mark on me. I knew I couldn't yield my body to them, but that doesn't mean I led an altogether empty life."

"Oh," he said in a small voice. "I hadn't thought of that. When you said Biton had chosen you, I suppose I thought you'd lived solitary from that time on."

"No," Selatre said again. "It wasn't like that, not until the god called to himself the Sibyl that was and chose me in her place—though only for a brief time." Her face clouded for a moment, then cleared. "But I must say you were right: if that time is ended, I have to live the rest of my life as best I can."

This time, she leaned toward him. The kiss went on and on. His arms closed around her. She stiffened when he cupped her breast with one hand. He took the hand away. "If you're not ready, just let me know," he said. He still wasn't sure how fast he wanted to charge ahead with her. Had he been a few years younger, lust would have overridden thought, but those days were past him, even if Van still sometimes thought more with his crotch than with his head.

Selatre said, "Having come this far, I think it's time to finish the job of returning me to the world. I've heard it can hurt the first time, but if you know hurt may be coming, it's easier to bear."

"I hope I won't hurt you, or not badly," Gerin said. "When I was down in the City of Elabon, another student there had a scroll on the proper way to deflower a maiden as gently as possible. What it said made good sense, though I confess I've never needed to use it till now."

"They write books about *that*?" Selatre said, her eyes wide. "If you had one of those in your library here, Gerin, think how many more people you could win to reading."

"You're right, I expect," he said, remembering the illustrations with which the scribe had enlivened the scroll. Then he noticed Selatre had called him by his name alone, without the honorific she'd always used before. It startled him for a moment. Then he laughed at himself. If they were about to be intimate, didn't she have the right to address him intimately?

He was never sure afterwards which of them got up first from the table in the library. They walked side by side down the hall toward his bedchamber. With any other woman, he would have slipped his arm around her waist. With Selatre, he still held back in spite of what they were going to the bedroom to do. If she wanted to touch him before then, she could.

They were three or four strides from the door when the lookout in the watchtower winded his horn. Gerin stopped dead. Grinding his teeth, he said, "Oh, a pestilence! Not *now*, by all the gods."

He couldn't read Selatre's face. Was that wry amusement there, or maybe relief? If they didn't seize the chance now, would she change her mind later? What was he supposed to do if she did? Pretend nothing had happened? Or—?

Then the lookout shouted, "Lord Gerin, Rihwin the Fox is heading back toward Fox Keep."

"What?" Gerin exclaimed, his worries about Selatre forgotten. "I only sent him out two days ago. He can't even have got out of the land I hold, let alone to Aragis' and back. Has he lost his wits? Has he lost his nerve?"

Selatre said, "You'd better go and see what that's about. Other things can wait for their own time."

"Yes," he said abstractedly. That sounded promising, even if she hadn't promised anything. He barely noticed. He was already trotting for the stairs. Selatre followed more slowly.

Gerin's trot went to a run as soon as he got down to the great hall. He dashed out into the courtyard, sprinted for the gate. Someone called from up on the palisade: "I see Rihwin and the chariot crews that went out with him, lord prince, but he's got more crews with him than just those. Not men I recognize, neither."

The drawbridge was already creaking down over the

ditch around the palisade. Panting a little, Gerin waited impatiently for it to drop far enough to let him see out. At last, it did. Sure enough, there was Rihwin's chariot in the lead, but he was bringing back twice as many crews as he'd set out with.

No sooner had the drawbridge thumped into place than Gerin walked across it. The quicker he found out what madness Rihwin was perpetrating now, the quicker he could start figuring out how to deal with it—if it could be dealt with. He was getting tired of having to clean up Rihwin's messes, especially when they were as exquisitely mistimed as this one.

Seeing Gerin, Rihwin waved. "Hail, lord prince," he called. "The business of going to Aragis' holding just got easier."

Gerin waited till Rihwin got close enough so he wouldn't have to scream, then demanded, "What on earth are you talking about, you—jackanapes? How can you be gone two days and come back claiming success? And who are these ruffians you've brought along with you?"

He hadn't had much hope of cowing the irrepressible Rihwin, but he hadn't expected him to break out in guffaws, either. "Your pardon, lord prince," Rihwin said when he could speak, though he didn't sound a bit sorry. He went on, "Allow me to present acquaintances made on the Elabon Way: Fabors Fabur's son and Marlanz Raw-Meat, envoys sent by the Grand Duke Aragis the Archer to discuss terms of alliance with you."

"Lord prince," two of the strangers said together. After they bowed, one of them added, in a voice almost as deep as Van's, "I'm Marlanz." He was young, broad-shouldered, and burly, with the look of a man for whom fighting was a favorite sport. Fabors was older and, Gerin guessed, likely to be smarter (although sometimes men who looked like nothing but bluff warriors were a lot smarter than they seemed).

"Well," Gerin said. That was better than standing there with his mouth open, but not much. He tried again, but only, "Well," emerged once more. On a third effort, he managed coherent speech: "Well, lords, I would be lying if I said I wasn't glad to see you. You are most welcome. Come into my keep, you and all your comrades. Drink of my ale; eat of my meat; you shall be my guest-friends here."

"Lord prince, you are gracious," Fabors Fabur's son said. Marlanz Raw-Meat nodded vigorously. Fabors went on, "Should you ride south, know that my keep shall be as your own for as long as you care to use it."

"And mine," Marlanz agreed.

"Come, come," Gerin said, and stood aside so the chariots—both those that had started out with Rihwin and those that had come north with Aragis' vassals— could cross over the drawbridge and into Castle Fox.

Stable boys hurried out to take charge of the horses and chariots. They gaped, big-eyed, at the newcomers. Gerin's warriors crowded round him, lest the men who'd accompanied Marlanz and Fabors had treachery in mind.

Marlanz stared at Van. "I've heard tales of you, sir," he said, "and, knowing how taletellers lie, thought to measure myself against you. I see I'm liable to have put myself too high."

"If you can fight as well as you talk, sir, you'll do well enough for yourself, I expect," Van answered. Marlanz bowed. Van bowed back. Gerin was reminded of two big dogs sniffing at each other.

"Come, lords," he said again. As he crossed the threshold into the great hall, he called to the servants: "Ale for my guest-friends. Aye, and carve some steaks from that cow we slew last night, too, and set 'em over the fire."

"Just singe mine, light as you can," Marlanz put in. "I can't abide beef cooked all gray and tough as shoe leather."

The slab of meat the servants slapped down in front of Marlanz on a round of flatbread was so red and juicy that the Fox expected it to bellow in pain when he stuck a knife in it, but he attacked it with every sign of relish. Gerin had no trouble figuring out how he'd come by his ekename.

Selatre had been standing back by the stairway. Gerin waved her forward, patted the bench beside him. Fabors Fabur's son raised an eyebrow. "Have you at last wed again, lord prince?" he asked. "Word of this had not reached the Archer's Nest."

"Good name for a keep," Gerin remarked, unsurprised that Aragis kept close track of what he did—he made it his business to learn all he could of Aragis, too. To answer the question the Archer's man had put, he went on, "Lord Fabors, lord Marlanz, allow me to present you to the lady Selatre, who was Sibyl at Ikos until the earthquake overthrew Biton's shrine there and loosed the monsters long trapped under it."

Marlanz had started to bristle at being introduced to a woman rather than the other way round, but composed himself at once when he learned who Selatre was. "Sibyl," he murmured respectfully, bowing in his seat.

"Sibyl no more," she said. "Simply Selatre . . . and who Selatre is remains in large part to be discovered." Her eyes slid to Gerin. The arrival of the envoys had interrupted part of that discovery.

That arrival had also touched off enough commotion to bring Fand down to find out what was going on. Her eyes narrowed when she saw Selatre beside the Fox; she came over and sat down next to Van. Gerin introduced her to Aragis' vassals as the outlander's companion. Van nodded at that, though he didn't seem quite certain he was pleased. Fabors Fabur's son looked thoughtful, but held his peace—here was more news that had not reached the Archer's Nest.

After the sharing of food and drink had made them his guest-friends, Gerin said to Fabors and Marlanz, "Well, lords, I know why you've come—on the same mission for which I sent Rihwin south. I daresay you'll have discussed it with him as you came here. What conclusions have you reached?"

"Lord prince, our overlord the Grand Duke Aragis sent us north with virtually the same terms for an alliance in mind as you gave to Rihwin the Fox—a fine fellow, I might add," Fabors said. "The Archer favors an equal alliance between himself and you for as long as that remains agreeable to both parties, overall command to depend on whether the fighting is north or south of Ikos."

"There's a nice touch," Gerin said approvingly. "I'd simply assumed we'd share the lead. Well, lords, as you say, I think we'll get along nicely. Since the earthquake, I've heard little from south of Ikos. Tell me how Aragis' lands fare, if you would be so kind."

Marlanz gulped down the ale in his jack before answering, "Imagine wolves in a hard winter, coming out of the woods to kill sheep and shepherds, too. Then imagine that ten times worse, and you'll have some idea of the state we're in. These cursed creatures have more wit than wolves, and they have hands, too, so nothing is safe from them. The serfs are afraid to go out into the fields, but staying huddled in their huts does 'em no good, either. I'm sure you know how that goes, lord prince."

"Only too well," Gerin answered grimly. His vassals in the great hall nodded. The Fox went on, "Have the more clever monsters joined together with any of Aragis' neighbors to make his life even more delightful?"

"No, lord prince," Marlanz and Fabors chorused. Fabors added, "When your vassal the lord Rihwin told us of their dealings with Adiatunnus—may he roast in the hottest hell forever—we both cried out in horror."

"That we did," Marlanz Raw-Meat agreed. "It speaks well of your strength here that you've held off such a dreadful combination where we faced only the monsters, yet Aragis saw the need to send us forth before you put your vassal on the road to look for his aid."

"Don't put too much into it," Gerin said. "It may just mean I'm more stubborn and less trusting of my neighbors than the grand duke."

"Meaning no offense to you, lord prince, I find that hard to picture," Fabors Fabur's son said. Marlanz nodded vigorously.

"I think you may have insulted your own lord rather than me, but have it as you will," Gerin said. "Since matters are as they are, I am going to propose that Aragis first send such chariotry as he can north to aid my forces against Adiatunnus, the monsters, and a few worthless, faithless Elabonians who have joined with them. If he can do that, how soon can he do it, and how many chariots can he spare from his own concerns?"

"Lord prince, I think he can do it, and I think he can send the cars not long after we return with word the deal has been struck," Fabors answered. "How many he can send, he shall have to judge for himself. He's spread his chariots and crews widely through the keeps of the lands he holds, and told his peasants to send up fire signals if their villages are attacked. Thus aid can reach them as soon as may be."

"That's not the worst ploy in the world for keeping the serfs safe," Rihwin said. "Why didn't you try something like it, my fellow Fox?"

"It's like covering your belly after somebody hits you,

then moving one hand to your face when he hits you there," Gerin answered. "Or, if you'll let me change my figure of speech, I'd rather dig an arrowhead out of the wound than slap a bandage on it with the point still in there."

"You're a man of sense, lord prince," Marlanz Raw-Meat said. "The grand duke himself has been thinking hard about changing the way he's fighting the cursed creatures—says it's like being nibbled to death by fleas. Between his men and yours, we ought to have a force strong enough to really do something, not just try to hit back when things get done to us."

"That's my hope," Gerin agreed. "That's why I sought alliance with him." As Marlanz had said, even though Aragis was threatened only by monsters, he'd felt the need for help before Gerin, who also had the Trokmoi to worry about. Hitting back as hard as he could had let the Fox keep his foes off balance.

"Together, we'll smash them," Marlanz said, slamming his fist down onto the table so that drinking jacks jumped. Fabors Fabur's son nodded but did not speak. When it came to negotiating terms for the alliance, he seemed to have authority; Marlanz spoke with more weight on matters strictly military.

"Are we in accord, lords?" Gerin asked. Both of Aragis' envoys nodded. The Fox said, "Then shall we take oaths to bind us to our enterprise. I will take them with you as Aragis' representatives. I know he will expect them of me, as he and I have not always been on the best of terms since Elabon pulled out of the northlands."

"And you will expect them no less of him, you're saying," Fabors remarked. "He expected as much, and authorized us to swear on his behalf, binding him to the pact in the eyes of the gods. And you are correct: he does desire your oath as well."

"Cooperation first; trust can come later," Gerin said. "And whether he authorized it or not, the laws of similarity and contagion bind you to him and him to the pact; I am mage enough to work through them at need. I hope we shall have no need. By which gods would Aragis have us swear?"

"None out of the ordinary, lord prince," Fabors answered: "Dyaus the king of heaven, of course, and Biton for foresight—that his Sibyl is here will only lend the oath more force—and, because we're fighting not least to keep our serfs safe, Baivers and Mavrix as well."

A prickle of alarm ran through the Fox. "Would not Baivers suffice on his own? Mavrix and I . . . have not got on well in the past."

"So lord Rihwin told us," Fabors said. By the way his eyes slid toward Rihwin, the tale had been juicy, too. But he took a deep breath and resumed: "Nonetheless, my suzerain was particular about wanting the lord of the sweet grape included in the oath. Baivers, said he, has power only over ale and barley, while Mavrix, along with being the god of wine, is also associated with fertility in general, and hence a protector of farmers."

That, unfortunately, made too much theological sense for Gerin to come up with a glib way around it. He remembered that he and Selatre had been reading about Mavrix when they acknowledged their attraction for each other; lust was also part of the Sithonian god's domain. Maybe that had been an omen. Gerin might not want anything to do with Mavrix, but if the converse didn't hold true, how was he supposed to oppose the god's will?

He sighed—he saw no way. "Let it be as the grand duke wishes," he said. "I have but one reservation: if he fails to send at least thirty chariots and crews, and if they fail to reach here within thirty days, I shall no longer reckon myself bound by the terms of the oath."

Fabors and Marlanz put their heads together and talked quietly with each other for a couple of minutes. At last Fabors nodded. "It shall be as you say."

Gerin and Aragis' envoys clasped hands and swore the oath, binding themselves and, through Marlanz and Fabors, Aragis to the terms upon which they'd agreed. Then the Fox called to the kitchen crew: "Slaughter us another cow. We'll burn the fat-wrapped thighbones on Dyaus' altar, that their savor may climb to heaven and make him look kindly on our cause."

"And we'll eat the rest ourselves," Van boomed.

"Remember, I'll want my portion barely cooked," Marlanz added hastily.

Gerin walked upstairs to his bedchamber carrying a lamp. He set each foot down in turn with deliberate care; he was a little drunk and very full. He opened the door, set the lamp on a chest of drawers, and started to take off his tunic. As soon as he'd undressed, he would blow out the lamp.

Someone knocked on the door. He almost got trapped in the tunic's sleeves as he pulled it back down. Fabors Fabur's son had been spinning a long, involved explanation of why Aragis insisted on having Mavrix in the oath—so long and involved, in fact, that Gerin wondered if the real reason was that the Archer knew of his trouble with the god—and hadn't wanted to stop even when the Fox yawned his way out of the great hall. If Fabors was out there now wanting to natter away some more, Gerin aimed to teach him never to do anything so foolish again.

He threw the door wide. But the load he'd planned to dump on Fabors' head turned into a coughing fit, for Fabors wasn't standing out there. Selatre was.

Listening to him splutter, she asked, "Are you all right?" in tones of real concern. When he managed a nod, she said, "Well then, shall we go on from where we were, uh, interrupted this afternoon?"

"Are you sure?" he asked; she nodded in turn. He went on, "I didn't come to your chamber tonight because—" He came to a ragged stop, not sure how to go on.

"For fear I'd lost my nerve, you mean?" Selatre said.

"That's just it," Gerin said gratefully.

"I wondered why you stayed away," Selatre said. "The only two things I could think of were that on the one hand and that you didn't really want me on the other. I thought I'd better find out which it was."

"If you don't know the answer to that—" Gerin ran dry again. After a moment, he resumed: "If you don't know the answer to that, I'll just have to show you." He took a step to one side to let Selatre come into the bedchamber. He shut the door behind her, barred it, then glanced over to the flickering lamp on the chest of drawers. "Shall I blow that out?"

"However you'd rather," she answered after her usual grave consideration. "It certainly would have been light had we come here earlier in the day, though." .

"So it would," he agreed. "Well, then—" Feeling foolish at echoing what she'd said a few moments before, he stepped forward, took her in his arms, and kissed her. As he'd discovered in the library, her knowledge of that portion of the game was enjoyably more than theoretical.

When their lips parted at last, she murmured, "Did you learn that in the book you were telling me of? If you did, I'd like to read it."

"Er—no," he answered. "And, as I said, I don't have a copy here in Fox Keep."

"That's too bad," Selatre said, quite seriously. "You really should write down what you remember of it— and what you've learned other places as well." She brought her mouth toward his again.

After some long, pleasurable time, he led her over to the bed. He was sure she couldn't be altogether ignorant of what went on between men and women—after all, she'd grown up in a peasant hut which, if it was like all the other peasant huts he'd known, would have boasted one room and in that room one bed for the whole family. But knowing how things happened and having them happen to her might be two different matters, especially when, not long before, she hadn't been able to stand a man touching her at all, let alone in her most secret places.

She hesitated with her hands at the neck of her tunic. "Do you want me to blow out the lamp after all?" he asked.

Selatre shook her head, perhaps as much at herself as toward Gerin. Almost defiantly, she pulled the tunic up over her head, then kicked off her sandals and got out of her long wool skirt and the linen drawers she wore beneath it. Gerin had known she was well made, but hadn't realized how well. If he stared too much, he might fluster her. The only way to keep from staring was to undress himself. He did that, quickly, and lay down on the bed.

Selatre hesitated again before joining him there. The soft straw of the mattress rustled as her weight came down on it. "Forgive me," she said. "I am—nervous."

"No reason you shouldn't be, and every reason you should," he said. "First times come only once."

She nodded. "What did your book say we're supposed to do next?"

"Not any one thing in particular," he answered. "If I remember aright, it says I'm supposed to kiss you and caress you for a long time to make you easy in your mind and to help make your body ready for what we'll do after that." He smiled at her. "I'd want to do that anyhow."

He embraced her, drew her to him. She started to pull back when their bare bodies met—that was touching of a different sort from what she'd known before. But she checked herself, managed a smile in return. When he kissed her, she kissed him back.

"That tickles," she said as his tongue slid down the smooth, soft skin of her neck. Then it found the tip of her right breast. "Ah," she murmured, a syllable all breath and no voice.

After some time, he let his mouth stray lower. The sound she made was half surprise, half pleasure. He'd forgotten about the book; he enjoyed what he was doing for its own sake.

"Oh, my," she said a little while later. "I'd expected one surprise, but two? Is that something you brought back with you from south of the High Kirs?"

"As a matter of fact, no," he answered. But then, who could guess what would be done in a peasant village outside of Ikos?

"Well, wherever you learned it, it's—" She didn't go on in words, but the pause and the delighted expression on her face said enough. After a moment, she added, "Could I do the same for you?"

"You could, but probably not for very long right now," Gerin said. "Let's try something else instead." He sat up on the bed. "Here, why don't you get onto my lap?"

She straddled him, which he hadn't expected quite yet; she did know the theory of what they were going to do. He took himself in hand. She lowered herself onto him, slowly and cautiously. "It doesn't hurt," she said, and then, a heartbeat later, "Wait. There."

"Yes," Gerin said. "Do you want to stop? No rush here." She shook her head. "All right, then," he said, and took hold of her buttocks, easing her down until he was fleshed to the root—that was what the racily illustrated scroll in the City of Elabon had recommended, and it seemed to work well. "Is it all right?" he asked.

"It didn't hurt as much as I thought it would," she said, nodding. "You were gentle. Thank you."

He kissed her and ran his hands over her body. When he was sure she'd meant what she said, he began to move inside her, slowly, a little at a time, not hurrying at all. His left hand slid down between her legs to add to her pleasure—or perhaps to create it, as few women were likely to find full joy from coupling itself their first time.

His own pleasure built slowly. He let that happen, rather than straining to quicken it. When at last it reached its peak, it was all the more intense because of the long, unhurried climb to get there. He closed his eyes and squeezed Selatre hard against him.

There was a little blood when she slid off him, but not much. He wondered what she'd thought. Not looking at him, she said, more than half to herself, "I'm so sorry for all the Sibyls who died without ever knowing this."

He set a hand on her bare shoulder. Instead of pulling away, she snuggled against him. He said, "I made two alliances today. This is the better one."

"Oh yes," she said. "Oh yes."

IX

Aragis' envoys rode out at dawn two days later. Gerin cordially loathed getting up with the sun, but made a point of seeing them off. He glanced up into the sky and pointed to golden Math, which, three days past full, was sliding toward the western horizon. "Lords, she makes her turn in nine-and-twenty days," he said to Marlanz and Fabors. "By the next time she reaches that phase, I hope to have the Grand Duke's chariots fighting alongside mine."

"We shall do everything in our power to make it so," Fabors Fabur's son said.

"Aye, that should give us time for travel and for gathering the men and cars," Marlanz Raw-Meat added. "I hope the Archer orders me north again. Fighting the monsters and the Trokmoi at the same time would be worth the candle, I think."

Gerin had seen a good many men, Trokmoi and Elabonians both (to say nothing of Van), who loved war for its own sake. He recognized that, but it baffled him every time he ran into it. He said, "I'd sooner not be fighting at all, but sometimes you have no choice."

Marlanz sent him a curious look. "Your hand's not cold in war, lord prince. You may not care for it, but you do it well."

He probably had as much trouble understanding the Fox as Gerin did with him—maybe more, if he didn't make a practice of trying to see into the minds of people different from him. Explaining seemed an unprofitable use of time to Gerin, who contented himself with answering, "If you don't do what needs doing, before long you won't have the chance to do anything at all." Marlanz weighed that—as Gerin had guessed on first meeting him, he was smarter than he looked—and finally nodded.

The drawbridge thumped down. Aragis' ambassadors and the warriors who had come north to protect them rolled across it and off toward the Elabon Way. The gate crew hauled the bridge back up. Visitors to Fox Keep were few in these days of disordered commerce, and who could say what lurked in the not too distant woods? For legitimate travelers, the bridge would come down again. Meanwhile, Castle Fox was fortress first.

Van came out of the keep, rubbing sleep from his eyes. "So they're on their way south, are they?" he said through a yawn. "We can use all the help we can find, and that's a fact."

"I know," Gerin answered. "I didn't like the way Adiatunnus mocked me at the fight in that clearing. We'll see how he laughs when he finds Aragis' chariots ranged beside mine."

"Aye, that'll be a good thing, no doubt about it." Van yawned again. "I want some bread and ale. Maybe they'll make my wits start working."

"The Urfa nomads in the deserts south of Elabon brew some sort of bitter drink that's supposed to keep a man awake if he's tired and wake him up if he's all fuzzy the way you are," Gerin said. He sighed. "Time was when Urfa came up to Ikos to talk with the Sibyl. We might have bought some of the berries from them. Now the oracle at Ikos is no more, and even if it were still there, the Urfa couldn't come up through Elabon to get to it."

" 'The oracle at Ikos is no more,' " Van repeated as he and the Fox walked back toward the great hall. He glanced over to Gerin. "The lady Selatre's still very much here, though."

"So she is," Gerin said. He and Selatre hadn't tried to keep their becoming lovers a secret—not that they could have even if they did try. Castle Fox had too many pairs of eyes, too many wagging tongues, for that. If he could, Gerin would have looked down his nose at Van. The outlander being considerably taller, he looked up it instead. "So what?"

"So nothing, Captain," Van said hastily. "May you and she have joy of it." He paused, then went on in a low-voiced mumble, "And may the gods grant that I keep up with Fand and don't decide to throttle her."

"There is that," Gerin observed. Fand hadn't said anything to him; one thing that had been plain to both of them was that whatever they'd had was dead. But when she looked from him to Selatre, *I told you so* gleamed in her green eyes. She *had* told him so, too, which only made the look on her face more irksome. On the other hand, Fand enjoyed getting people angry at her, so he refused to give her the satisfaction of showing his annoyance.

Van cut a chunk from the loaf of bread on one of the tables. The morning was cool; Gerin decided he'd rather dip up a bowl of barley porridge from the pot that sat above the fire on the hearth at the far end of the hall. He took a horn spoon, then set that and the bowl on the table while he got himself a jack of ale.

He'd just poured a little libation to Baivers when Selatre came downstairs. "Here, join us," he said. "Marlanz and Fabors have headed south to take Aragis word of the agreement."

"I thought it must be so when you made yourself wake so early," she answered, cutting herself a piece of bread as Van had done.

"I'm sorry," he said. "I didn't mean to wake you." He

felt guilty; he hadn't slept the night through with a woman in his own bed for a long time, and probably hadn't been as quiet as he might have been. For that matter, he hadn't slept with anyone in his own bed since Duren disappeared, and that was . . . more than sixty days ago now, he realized with a small shock, reckoning up everything that had happened since.

"It's all right," she said. "The sun was up, so I would have been awake soon anyhow. That's how it always was in my village, and that's how it was at Ikos, too." She somehow managed not to make Gerin feel bad for preferring to sleep later when he could. After she'd poured ale for herself, she sat down right beside him.

Fand came into the great hall a little later. When she saw Gerin and Selatre together, she didn't bother with breakfast. She just walked over to Van and plopped herself down in his lap.

He'd been reaching for his ale. Instead, his arms went around her. "What do you think you're doing?" he spluttered.

Her arms went around his neck. "What do you think I'm doing, now?" she purred into his ear.

Van could resist anything except temptation. He did try: "So early in the morning?" he said incredulously. Fand leaned closer still, whispered something Gerin couldn't quite catch into the outlander's ear. Whatever it was, it seemed to have the desired effect. Van snorted like a stallion and then, still holding Fand, stood up and carried her upstairs.

Gerin and Selatre stared after them. A moment later, a door—presumably the one to Fand's chamber—slammed shut. When Gerin and Selatre looked from the stairway to each other, they both started to laugh. "Oh, my," Gerin said. "She has a hook in him like a man fishing for salmon."

"Did she always act like that?" Selatre asked in a small voice. She sounded half bemused, half awed.

The Fox shook his head. "When she was with us both, she didn't—usually—try to use one of us to make the other jealous." He chuckled. "Drop me into one of the hells if she's not trying to make me jealous now that we're apart." He took Selatre's hand. "She'll have no luck there."

"I'm glad." Selatre squeezed him. *Not long ago*, he thought, *she'd have been mortally offended if I touched her at all*. Then he realized with the front of his mind that that change had of course started some days after Duren disappeared. Somehow he felt he'd known Selatre longer.

Rihwin the Fox came into the great hall for breakfast. He nodded to Gerin and Selatre as he ambled over to the pot of porridge. Though he'd formally courted Elise, he'd never made any permanent attachments since returning to the northlands with Gerin and Van, contenting himself with tumbling the occasional servant woman or peasant girl.

Catching Gerin's eye, Rihwin tugged at his left ear and brayed like a donkey. He'd done that a couple of times before, and succeeded in embarrassing Gerin. This time Gerin was ready for him. He said, "You do that very well. You must have had a good deal of ass in you even before I worked that magic to restore your ear."

Rihwin staggered, as if pierced by an arrow. That made some of the hot porridge slop out of his bowl and onto the hand that was holding it. Now wounded literally as well as metaphorically, he sprang into the air with a yelp. "See what you made me do?" he shouted at Gerin.

"I'm sorry, but I can't take the blame for that one," Gerin said. "You were a showoff long before you met me, and you've got yourself in trouble for it a good many times before, too."

As was his way, Rihwin calmed as quickly as he'd heated. "I'd be more inclined to resent that if it weren't true." He got himself a jack of ale, then bowed to Gerin and said, "May I sit by you and your lady, your supreme awesomeness?"

"Sit, sit," Gerin said, valiantly resisting the urge to throw something at him. In a way, Rihwin was like Fand: he could be infuriating, but he was never dull. Fortunately, though, he lacked Fand's flammable temper.

He threw himself bonelessly down onto the bench next to Gerin. For all his seeming insouciance, he had a keen sense of what made others comfortable; Selatre still didn't care to be touched, even by accident, by anyone save Gerin.

He took a swig from his jack of ale, then leaned forward so he could look past Gerin to Selatre. "As you are Sibyl no more, lady, let me prophesy for you now: many years of happiness. I suppose that also means happiness for this lout here" —he nodded at Gerin— "but we'll just have to put up with what we can't help."

"One fine day, I *will* throttle you," Gerin muttered. Rihwin dipped his head, as at some extravagant compliment. Gerin threw his hands in the air.

Selatre said, "I thank you for the wish, and may a god prove to have spoken through you."

"I don't think foolishness has a god, unless it be Mavrix in his aspect as king of the drunkards," Gerin said. He'd meant that for a joke, but it brought him up short once he'd said it. All he wanted was to ignore Mavrix and hope the god would do the same with him, but suddenly that didn't seem easy.

He got up and poured himself another jack of ale. He wasn't thirsty any more, nor did he want to get drunk to start the day. Maybe, though, by showing his loyalty to Baivers he could persuade Mavrix to leave him alone. But even as he quaffed the apotropaic ale, he had his doubts.

Neither the Trokmoi nor the monsters were so considerate as to wait for Aragis' men to arrive and help drive them away. Gerin's raid into Adiatunnus' holding did make the woodsrunner thoughtful, but didn't stop him. And as for the creatures, who could say whether the ones that attacked Gerin's villagers were aligned with Adiatunnus or not? Either way, the work they did was dreadful.

Herders began to disappear, along with their flocks. The monsters slew more livestock than they could eat. Wolves or longtooths seldom behaved so, but men often did. As the reports came in to Castle Fox, Gerin grew ever grimmer.

He did what he could to help his serfs cope with the new menace skulking through the woods. He ordered herdsmen to go forth in pairs, and always to be armed either with bows or with hunting spears. He gave permission for all his smiths to make spearheads and arrowheads in large numbers. With more and more serfs at least somewhat armed, they'd have a better chance of holding off the monsters when no chariot-riding nobles could come to their aid.

Some of his more conservative vassals grumbled at that. Drago the Bear said, "Who's going to take all those spears away when the monsters are gone, lord Gerin? They'll use 'em on each other, aye, and on us nobles, too, if we don't watch 'em careful—and we can't watch 'em careful all the time."

Having been through a similar argument not long before with Van, the Fox only nodded tiredly. "You're right," he said, which made Drago's eyes widen. Then he went on: "But if we go under because we didn't arm the serfs, we won't have to worry about what we do later, now will we?"

Drago chewed on that for a while—literally, for Gerin watched his jaws work beneath his unkempt mat of graying brown beard—then walked off without making any direct reply. Under his breath, though, he was muttering phrases like "newfangled foolishness" and "idiotic shenanigans." The Fox refused to let that worry him. Stones changed more readily than Drago, but the Bear did as he was ordered.

Getting spears and arrows into the hands of the serfs wasn't enough, and Gerin knew it. They might kill an occasional monster, and would be cheered no end by so doing, but they weren't fighting men. If Gerin wanted any crops brought in come fall, he and the rest of the nobles would have to ride forth and do what they could to hold the monsters away from the villages.

Leaving Selatre was a wrench. That in itself surprised him; getting away from Fand had often seemed a relief. He took his sorrow on departing as a good sign: with luck, it meant he and Selatre had more to join them together than the pleasures of the bedchamber. Fine as those were, in the end they weren't enough. You needed other bricks as well if you wanted to build something that would last.

When he'd brought Elise up to Fox Keep, he'd thought they'd made something that would last forever. One thing he hadn't yet known was that you needed to keep what you'd built in good repair. If you didn't, it would fall down on your head. He'd have to bear that in mind this time.

Such thoughts vanished from his head as the road jogged and Castle Fox vanished behind a stand of trees. "The monsters have been especially bad in the southwest," he said, grabbing for the rail as the chariot hit a pothole.

"That's no surprise," Raffo said over his shoulder. "They swarm into Adiatunnus' lands and then out against us."

"No doubt you're right," the Fox answered. "Wherefores don't much matter, though. Whatever the whys of it, we have to hurt the creatures badly enough to be sure the serfs can bring in the harvest. Fall's not that far away." He waved to the fields past which they were riding. The grain there was starting to go from green to gold.

Van dug a finger in his ear. "Am I hearing you right, Fox? You of all people saying wherefores don't matter? Either you've come down with a fever or— Wait, I have it. It must be love."

Gerin set a hand on the shaft of the war axe on his side of the chariot car. "I'd brain you, did I think you had any brains in there to let out."

"Aye, well, to the crows with you, too," Van said. Both men laughed.

As the chariots clattered by, peasants in the villages and out in the fields waved and cheered. They'd never been especially hostile to the nobles who ruled them; Gerin was a mild and just overlord. But they'd rarely seemed so glad to see armored men in chariots, either. *Worthwhile reminding them we do more than take their crops and futter their women*, Gerin thought.

Toward afternoon, one of the serfs did more than wave and cheer. He ran up to Gerin's chariot, the lead in a six-car force, shouting, "Help us, lord! Three of the creatures slaughtered our sheep, then ran back into the woods." He pointed to show the direction they'd taken, adding, "Remon hit one with an arrow, I think, but it kept running."

"Maybe we'll have a blood trail to follow, Fox," Van said. "Give us a better chance to hunt down the cursed things."

The peasant's eyes went wide. "You're lord Gerin?"

he said, and bowed when the Fox nodded. That sort of thing had happened to Gerin before. Not all serfs knew what he looked like, for years could pass between his visits to any one village.

"Aye, I'm Gerin," he answered, and alighted from the chariot. Van stepped down after him. They waved the rest of the cars to a stop. Gerin pointed in the same direction the peasant had. "Three monsters just went in there. The villagers managed to wound one, so we may have blood to follow."

"Fox, what do you say the drivers stay with the cars?" Van put in. "If there're three of the things around, there may be more, and that'll let folk properly armed fight for the serfs if monsters pop out of the woods."

"Aye, let it be as you say," Gerin answered, which drew howls of anger from Raffo and the other drivers. He glared them into submission, wondering as he did so at the urge that made men eager to risk their lives fighting and irate when they lost that chance, even with an honorable excuse.

Van pulled his mace from his belt and trotted into the woods, saying, "Come on, you lugs. The more time we waste here, the farther the cursed creatures can run."

Along with the rest of the fighting crews, Gerin pounded after the outlander. Sweat quickly burst out on his forehead. Running in armor was hard work—doubly so for Van, whose fancy cuirass was a good deal heavier than the one the Fox wore. But the outlander moved as easily as if he'd been in a thin linen shirt.

"Here, hold up," Gerin called at the edge of the woods. He was panting a little, but hadn't ordered the halt on account of that. "Let's see if we can find spilled blood. That'll give us the way the monsters took."

Less than a minute later, Widin Simrin's son exclaimed, "Over here, lord Gerin!" The Fox and the rest of the

warriors hurried to him. Sure enough, blood splashed
the grass where he stood; more painted the dark green
leaves of a holly bush.

Gerin and his men plunged into the woods. Along
with the blood the monster was losing, they also had
footprints in the soft earth to follow. They crashed
through the brush shouting at the top of their lungs,
hoping to frighten the monster and its fellows into breaking whatever cover they'd found.

"There!" Drago shouted. He used his sword to point.
Gerin caught a glimpse of a hairy body between a couple
of saplings. Parol Chickpea, fast with his bow, loosed an
arrow at the monster. It bellowed, whether in pain or
simply in rage the Fox could not tell. Along with his companions, he dashed toward the place where it had disappeared. The men spread out widely, not wanting to give
it any chance to get away.

It sprang out from behind the pale trunk of a birch
tree, almost in Van's face. The outlander shouted in surprise, but kept the presence of mind to get his shield up
and protect his bare face and arms from the monster's
claws and teeth. He smote the creature with his mace.
Blood spurted as the viciously spiked head struck home.
The monster snarled and wailed, but did not run. Gerin
sprinted to come to the aid of his friend.

The monster wailed without snarling when his sword
slash drew a red line across its rib cage. Half turning to
meet him, it left itself open to Van, who hit it in the side of its
head with all his massive strength. The creature crumpled.

"A stupid one," Van said, panting. "The ones with the
wit to wield weapons are truly dangerous."

"Even the ones without are bad enough." Gerin looked
down at the twitching corpse. "I don't see an arrow in
this one, either, so the one the peasant hit must still be
around here somewhere."

"I hadn't thought on that, but you're right," the out-lander said. "Let's get on with the searching, then." He slammed the head of his mace into the ground a couple of times to clean the monster's blood from the bronze spikes, then pushed on through the woods.

Not far ahead, two cries rang out, one from the throat of a monster, the other a deeper coughing roar that froze the Fox in his tracks for a moment, as it was meant to do. "Longtooth." His lips shaped the word, but no sound passed them.

The monster's scream rose to a high-pitched squall, then died away. The longtooth roared again, this time in triumph. Gerin rounded up his companions by eye. Ever so cautiously, they approached the place from which the roars had sounded. Twelve men were enough to drive off a longtooth at need, though doing so was always a risky business.

Gerin pushed aside the small-leaved branch of a wil-low sapling to peer out into a small clearing. At the far edge of the open space, the longtooth crouched over the monster's body.

"*That's* the one the peasant shot," Van breathed into Gerin's ear. The Fox nodded; part of an arrow shaft still protruded from the creature's left buttock. He wondered whether it had deliberately broken off the rest or the shaft had snapped as it ran through the woods.

The question was irrelevant now; the longtooth had seen to that. The great twin fangs that gave it its name were red with the monster's blood; it had torn open the creature's throat. Longtooths, fortunately, were solitary hunters—had they traveled in packs, they would have been an even worse plague than the monsters. This one, a big male, was almost the size of a bear, with massive shoulders and great taloned forepaws almost as formi-dable as its fangs.

It growled warningly at Gerin and the other warriors. The long, orange-brown hair on its neck and shoulders—not quite a lion's mane, but close—bristled up to make it look even larger and more threatening. Its little stumpy tail, the only absurd part of a thoroughly formidable creature, twitched to show its anger at being interrupted over a meal.

"Let's kill it," Parol Chickpea whispered hoarsely.

Up till then, Gerin had thought Parol's sobriquet came from the large round wen by his nose. The comment, though, made him wonder if a chickpea was what Parol used to do his thinking. He said, "No, it's done us a favor. We'll just go on our way and see if we can find the last monster."

Parol grumbled at that, but went along when everyone else moved away from the clearing. Gerin was sure the longtooth would be contentedly feeding for some time. All the same, he didn't go very far from his followers, nor they from one another. The price of being wrong about what the great hunting cat was doing was too high to pay.

Perhaps because the warriors stayed tightly bunched together, they didn't flush out the last monster. After another hour's search, Gerin said, "I fear it's got away. The gods willing, though, it won't be back in these parts anytime soon—and if it is, it may run across that longtooth."

"That would be good," Drago rumbled.

"So it would," Gerin said. "A longtooth is more than a match for one of those things, or two, or even four. But if a pack of them set out to drive a longtooth from its prey, I think they could do it."

"Best thing to happen there is that they kill each other off," Drago said. Gerin nodded at that. Somehow, though, things seldom worked themselves out so conveniently, at least not where he was concerned.

The warriors made their way back toward the peasant village. When they came out of the woods, not only the serfs but also their drivers raised a cheer. The cheer got louder after Gerin yelled, "Two of the creatures dead," and did not subside when he admitted the third had escaped.

He gave Remon a silver buckle for wounding one of the monsters. The serf, a young, well-made man, puffed out his chest, stood very straight, and did his best to act like one of the warriors who'd accompanied the Fox. Gerin thought that at best unconvincing, but it seemed good enough to impress the young women of the village. To Remon, their opinion doubtless mattered more than his.

"Sun's going down," Van observed.

Gerin glanced westward. The outlander was right. Gerin suspected his friend had an ulterior motive for the remark—several of the young women had also noticed him—but decided not to make an issue of it. "All right, we'll pass the night here," he said.

The villagers brought out their best ale for the nobles in their midst, and roasted a couple of sheep the monsters had killed. The rest, Gerin was sure, would be smoked or sun-dried or made into sausages. Nothing went to waste. He'd seen oaks in the woods nearby. No doubt the hides, however torn, would be tanned and used for winter coats or capes.

Remon disappeared from the celebration with one of the pretty girls who'd exclaimed at his prowess with a bow. There was prowess and then there was prowess, Gerin thought.

Several of his comrades also found themselves companions for the evening. As Van headed off toward one of the huts with a young woman, he turned back to Gerin and said, "You sleeping alone tonight, Fox?"

"Yes, I think so," Gerin answered. "Another cup of ale and then I'll roll up in my blanket."

"All very well to be a one-woman man around the keep, Captain," the outlander said, "but you're not around the keep now."

"I don't tell you how to live your life, and I'll thank you for granting me the same privilege," Gerin said pointedly.

"Oh, I do, Captain, I do, but if I think you're a silly loon, you may be sure I'll tell you so." Van turned back to the girl. "Come along, my sweet. I know what to do with *my* time, by the gods." She went, not only willingly but eagerly. The Fox shook his head. Van had a gift, that was certain.

Van also reveled in variety. Gerin snorted. "If I need a different woman so soon after I found one, then I didn't find the right one," he muttered to himself.

"What's that, lord Gerin?" Drago stared owlishly. He'd put his nose into the ale pot a great many times. He'd sleep like a log tonight, and likely bawl like a hurt ox tomorrow with a head pounding fit to burst.

Gerin was just as well pleased the Bear hadn't caught what he'd said. He did his best to keep his private life private. In the tight little world of Fox Keep, that best often wasn't good enough, but he kept making the effort. And Selatre, unlike Fand, did not strike him as one to relish trumpeting her affairs—in any sense of the word—to the world at large.

He glanced up into the sky. Only Elleb shone there, a day before full. Swift Tiwaz had just slipped past new, while Nothos was approaching it. And golden Math, almost at her third quarter, would rise a little before midnight.

Math was the moon that mattered now. If she returned to the waning gibbous shape she'd had when Fabors and Marlanz set out for Aragis' lands before the Archer's chariots came north—if she did that, then all of Gerin's carefully laid plans would go awry.

"In that case, I'll have to try something else," he said, again to Drago's puzzlement—and to his own, for he had no idea what that something might be.

The sweep through the southern part of his holding netted the Fox several slain monsters. More to the point, it showed the serfs—and the monsters, if they paid attention to such things—that he and his vassals would defend the villages in every way they could.

Parol Chickpea was the only real casualty of the sweep: one of the monsters bit a good-sized chunk out of his right buttock. Gerin heated a bronze hoe blade over a fire back at the peasant village from which they'd set out and used it to cauterize the wound. Parol bawled louder at that than he had when he was bitten, but the wound healed well. Then he had to endure being called Parol One-Cheek all the way back to Castle Fox.

Two days after he'd returned to the keep, Gerin was up on the palisade when a chariot came streaking up from the south. He started worrying the instant he spied it: no one bringing good news would be in such a hurry. In any case, it was too early to expect Aragis' men.

He hurried down from the palisade while the gate crew was letting down the drawbridge. "What's toward, Utreiz?" he asked when the chariot came into the courtyard.

Utreiz Embron's son was one of the leaders of the force holding the Elabon Way open through Bevon's holding: a slim, dark fellow, a better than decent swordsman, and a long way from foolish—a rather lesser version of Gerin, as a matter of fact. He scowled as he got down from the car, saying, "It's not good news, lord prince."

"I didn't think it would be," Gerin answered. "Tell it to me anyhow."

"Aye, lord." Utreiz spat in the dirt. "Bevon and two of his stinking sons—Bevonis and Bevion—came out in force against us, with monsters coursing alongside their chariots. For the time being, the road's cut."

"Oh, a plague!" Gerin cried. The outburst spent, his wits began to work. "Bevander's with us, though. That'll help. Have our men gone south to pull Ricolf the Red into the fight? Having the Elabon Way blocked hurts him no less than us."

"Lord, my guess is they have, but it would be only a guess," Utreiz answered. "I came north, thinking this something you had to know as soon as might be."

"You did right," Gerin said. "So Bevion and Bevonis are the two who went with Bevon to suck up to Adiatunnus and the monsters, eh? And Bevander is on our side, as I said. What about Bevon's fourth son?"

"You mean Phredd the Fat?" Utreiz spat again. "The gods only know what he's doing—he hasn't the slightest clue himself. He could be trying to train longtooths to draw chariots, for all I know. He's not in the fight, that much I can tell you."

"Too bad," Gerin said. "I was hoping he'd come in on Bevon's side. He'd hurt him worse by that than by joining us, believe me."

"The gods know you're right about that, lord, but so far he's sitting out," Utreiz said. "Can you send us men to help force the road open again?"

"A few, maybe," Gerin said unhappily. "I'm stretched too thin as it is. I wish some of the lordlets on the land that used to be Palin the Eagle's would do their share. No merchants will ever get to their keeps if the highway stays closed."

"I've sent men to several of them," Utreiz answered.

"Stout man!" Gerin thumped him on the back. "There aren't enough people who see what needs doing and then go ahead and do it without making a fuss and without asking anyone's leave."

Utreiz shuffled his feet like a schoolboy who'd forgotten his lessons and looked anywhere but at the Fox. Praise plainly made him uncomfortable—another way in which he resembled his overlord. "I'd best head back now," he said, and climbed into the chariot that had brought him north. "You send those men as soon as may be, lord. We could use 'em." He spoke to the driver, who got the horses going and rattled away. He hadn't even stopped for a jack of ale.

"Send those men as soon as may be," Gerin echoed, wondering where he was supposed to find men to send. If he could have conjured warriors out of the air, he would have used them against Adiatunnus. But he realized he would have to reduce the sweeps against the monsters for the time being, no matter how little he relished the prospect. He would lose a disastrous amount of prestige if Aragis had to force the road open.

Glumly, he tramped into the great hall. Selatre was in there, eating some sun-dried plums. She smiled a greeting and waved him over to her side. "Here, open," she said, and popped a prune into his mouth.

It was sweet, but not sweet enough by itself to sweeten his mood. He said "Thank you" even so; Selatre appreciated formal politeness. He studied her—she looked a trifle on the haggard side, but wryly amused at the same time. The combination tweaked his curiosity. "You've got something to tell me," he said. "I can see it in your eyes." He wondered if he was about to become a father again.

"Yes, I do," she said, and her tone made him all but sure of it. Then she went on, "Just another proof I'm Sibyl no more: my courses started this morning. I needed a moment, I confess, to figure out what was happening to me." Her mouth twisted. "One part of full woman-hood I'd willingly have missed."

"Mm, yes, I can understand that," he said judiciously. He knew a certain measure of relief that he didn't have to worry about fatherhood at such an inconvenient time, and a different measure of relief that Selatre still seemed in a reasonably good humor. At such times, Fand could often make a longtooth flinch. But then, Fand's temper was certain to be uncertain.

"I didn't know this would happen when I came into your bed, but it makes sense that it has," Selatre said. "Biton's law was that no woman who had known man could be his Sibyl. Now that we're lovers" —he admired the matter-of-fact way she brought that out— "no won-der I've lost what marked me as a possible Sibyl in the first place."

Gerin nodded. "That does make sense. And it's rea-soned as nicely as any schoolmaster down in the City of Elabon might have done—not that they're in the habit of reasoning about such things."

Selatre stuck out her tongue at him. "What about the fellow who had that endlessly entertaining book?"

"He wasn't a schoolmaster," Gerin said with a snort. "Just an endlessly lecherous student. Now that I think back on it, a lot of us were like that." He waited for Selatre to make some sort of sharp reply to that, but she didn't. For once, her ignorance of men in general worked to his advantage.

The lookout in the watchtower let go with a long, dis-cordant blast from his horn. "Chariots approaching out of the west, a pair of 'em," he bawled.

"Out of the west?" Gerin said. "I wonder who that is." He got to his feet. "Better go find out." He headed out toward the courtyard. Selatre followed.

"It's Schild Stoutstaff, lord," Parol Chickpea called from atop the palisade. "Shall we let him in?"

"Schild, is it?" the Fox said. Had he had ears like a real fox's, they would have pricked forward with interest. "Aye, by all means let him come in. I'll be fascinated to see what he wants of me."

"Why's that, lord prince?" Parol asked with a hoarse guffaw. "On account of he only remembers he's your vassal when he wants something off you?"

"That does have something to do with it, yes," Gerin answered dryly. The drawbridge lowered once more—*a busy day*, the Fox thought. A couple of minutes later, Schild and his companions rolled into the courtyard.

"Lord prince," Schild called, nodding to Gerin. He was a big, burly fellow, on the swarthy side, a few years older than the Fox, and had the air of one who trusted his own judgment and strength above any others. That alone made him less than the best of vassals, but Gerin understood it, for it was part of his own character as well.

"What brings you here?" he asked.

Schild jumped down from his chariot, surprisingly graceful for such a bulky man. He strode over to Gerin and fell to his knees in front of him, holding out his hands before him with their palms pressed together. "Your servant, lord prince!" he said, his eyes on the ground.

Gerin took Schild's hands in his, acknowledging the other man's vassalage and his own obligations as overlord. "Rise, lord Schild," he said formally. As soon as Schild was back on his feet, the Fox went on in more conversational tones: "You must need something from me, or you'd not choose to remember I'm your master."

"You're right, lord Gerin, I do." Schild didn't even bother correcting the Fox. "Those horrible things they say came up from under the ground are a hideous plague in my holding. My own vassals and I can't keep the serfs safe, try as we will. I have pride—you know that. I've buried it to beg aid of you."

"So now you'd be glad to see chariots cross from my holding to yours, eh?" Gerin waited for Schild to nod, then drove home the dart: "You wouldn't even let my men onto your land to seek my stolen son earlier this year—but you didn't need me then, of course."

"That's true. I made a mistake, and I may end up paying for it, too," Schild answered steadily. He won Gerin's reluctant admiration for that; whether you liked him or not, you had to admit he held very little nonsense. Now he let loose a rueful laugh. "I have more to tell you about that than I did then, too."

"Do you?" Gerin's voice went silky with danger. As if of itself, his hand slipped to the hilt of his sword. Schild was no mean fighting man, but he gave back a step from the expression on the Fox's face. "You had best tell it, and quickly."

"Aye, lord prince. You have to understand, I didn't know it at the time when your man came asking." Schild licked his lips. "That minstrel—Tassilo was his name, not so?—he came through my holding. You know that much already, I daresay. He didn't stop at my keep, though; he guested with a couple of my vassals before he passed out the other side of my lands. Lord Gerin, I learned not long ago he had a boy with him. If I'd known that then—"

"What would you have done, lord Schild?" Gerin asked, his quiet fiercer than a scream. "What would you have done? Sent Duren back to me? Or would you have kept him for a while, to see what advantage you might wring from him?"

"Damn me to the five hells if I know, Fox," Schild answered, formal politeness forgotten. "But I didn't have the chance to find out, which is likely just as well. Now I know, and now I'm here, and now I've told you."

"If I ever find out you lied to me about this—" Gerin let that drop. He had a score to settle with Schild even if Schild hadn't lied—but not now. Other things had to come first.

"Not here," Schild said. "I know what my life would be worth if I tried." He spoke with as much assurance as if he'd looked at rapidly approaching clouds and announced, "It looks like rain." Gerin had always done his best to give his neighbors the idea he'd be a dangerous man to cross. Seeing he'd succeeded should have been more gratifying than it was.

He said, "Duren came into your holding, then, and was alive and well when he went out again?"

"So far as I know, Fox, that's the way of it," Schild answered.

Selatre came up to Gerin, set a hand on his arm. "The prophecy Biton spoke through me said your son's fate would be mild. I'm glad we begin to see the truth of that now."

Schild's eyes widened when he realized who Selatre had to be, and then again when he realized what her touching Gerin was likely to mean. The Fox noted that without doing anything about it; his thought swooped down on Selatre's words like a stooping hawk. "Biton said Duren's fate might well be mild," he answered with a sort of pained precision he wished he could abandon, "not that it *would* be. We still have to see."

She looked at him. As if Schild—as if everyone but the two of them—had receded to some remote distance, she asked quietly, "You're afraid to hope sometimes, aren't you?"

"Yes," he answered, as if speaking to her ears alone. "Expect much and you're too often disappointed.

Expect little and what you get often looks good."

Selatre made an exasperated noise. Before she could carry the argument further, though, Schild broke in: "Well, Fox, what can I expect from you?"

That hauled Gerin back to the world of chariots and monsters and red-mustached barbarians: not the world in which he would have chosen to spend his time, but the one in which the gods had seen fit to place him. He started calculating, and did not care for the answers he came up with. He'd been stretched too thin before he'd had to commit men to reopening the Elabon Way; he was thinner now. Fixing Schild with a glare, he growled, "Why couldn't you have forgotten you were my vassal a while longer?"

"Because I need your aid, lord prince," Schild answered, more humbly than the Fox had ever heard him speak.

He suspected a great deal of that humility was donned for the occasion, but that didn't mean he could ignore it. "Very well, lord Schild, I shall defend you with such forces as I can spare," he said. "I shall not do so, though, until you furnish me this year's feudal dues, in metal and grain and ale, for your holding. You haven't paid those dues lately; I hope you remember what they are."

By the sour look Schild gave him, he remembered only too well. "I knew you were a cheeseparer, Fox," he ground out, "so I started the wagons rolling as soon as I left my keep. They should be here in a day or two with the year's dues. To try to make up for its being my first tribute in a while, I even put in a couple of flagons of wine I found in my cellars."

"Don't tell Rihwin that," Gerin exclaimed.

"The way you're using me now, I hope they've gone to vinegar," Schild said, scowling still.

"If you want aid from your overlord, you'd best give

him service with more than your lips," Gerin answered,
unperturbed at Schild's anger. He went on, "Speaking
of which, though you swore me fealty after I slew Wolfar
of the Axe, you've given me precious little."

"I've demanded precious little till now, either," Schild
retorted.

"That may be so, but the aid I send you is liable to
cost me more than this year's dues alone," Gerin said.
"My other vassals—my true vassals—pay what they owe
whether they call on me for aid or not, for they don't
know when they'll need me. Collecting all I'm due now
would break you, so I shan't try, but what I take from
you each year will go up hereafter—and if you don't
render it, you'll see my chariots in ways you won't like so
well as riding to your rescue."

Schild's expression was bright with hatred. "I wish
Wolfar had wrung your neck instead of the other way
round."

Gerin's blade hissed free. "You're welcome to try to
amend the result, if you like."

For a moment, he thought Schild would draw, too.
This once, the clean simplicity of combat looked good
to him. If he slew Schild, the other's land would pass to
him . . . and if he didn't, he wouldn't have to worry about
alliances and feudal dues any more.

But Schild took a step back. Gerin did not think it was
from fear. Few barons shrank from a fight on account of
that—and the ones who did commonly had enough sense
that they didn't go provoking their neighbors. The Fox's
reluctant vassal said, "Even if I slay you and get out of
this keep alive, I can't fill your shoes fighting the creatures, worse luck."

Gerin clapped a hand to his forehead in genuine
amazement. He sheathed his sword. "An argument from
policy, by the gods! For that I'll gouge you less than I

would have otherwise—having a neighbor who can think will pay off for itself, one way or another."

"I have to think you're right about that," Schild answered. "I've got one, and it's costing me plenty."

That crack was almost enough of itself to make Gerin like him. The Fox said, "Come into the great hall, drink some ale with me, and we'll try to figure out what we can do for you." He'd turned and taken a couple of steps before he remembered Schild had been less than forthcoming about his son. He kept walking, but resolved not to like or trust his neighbor no matter what sort of cracks Schild made.

Schild poured ale down his throat. He watched Gerin warily, too; coming to the Fox for aid could not have been easy for him. "How many cars will you send?" he demanded. "And how soon will you send them? We're hurting badly, and that's the truth. If I'd thought we'd have anything to eat this winter—" He let that hang. No, asking for help hadn't been easy.

Gerin didn't answer right away. He'd been weighing the question even before Schild asked it. "I want to say eight, but I suppose I can spare ten," he said at last.

"What, why you tightfisted—" Schild cursed with an inventiveness and a volume that had men running in from the courtyard and coming down from upstairs to see what on earth had gone wrong now.

Van said, "You don't have a moat, Captain, but shall I chuck him in the ditch for you?"

"No," Gerin answered. "He's pitching a fit because he doesn't know all the facts yet. For instance," he continued with a certain amount of spite, "I haven't told him the chariots and crew I do send will have to be back here in fifteen days' time. They can sweep his holding, but they can't stay there and fight all the way up till harvest time."

"That does it!" Schild sprang to his feet. "I'm for my own lands again, but the gods. And to the five hells with you, Fox, and a murrain on your ten stinking cars and your fifteen stinking days. We'll manage somehow, and after we do—"

"Sit down and shut up." Every once in a while, Gerin could strike a tone that produced obedience without thought. He wished he could manage it at will—it was useful. This time it worked; Schild's knees folded and he sat back onto the bench. Gerin went on, "I can't send more than ten cars because I'm sending others south to open the Elabon Way: Bevon and two of his worthless sons have struck at it and driven my garrisons back. And I'll want the chariots home soon because Aragis the Archer and I have made alliance; he's bringing his forces north so we can strike at Adiatunnus and the monsters together. I want my force of chariotry at full strength for that. Now do you understand, lord Schild?"

"I understand you're the biggest bastard ever spawned in the northlands, lord Gerin," Schild answered, but the fire had gone out of his voice. He got up again, carried his jack to the pitcher of ale, poured it full, and drained it dry. Only after he'd wiped his mouth and mustache on the sleeve of his tunic did he give his attention back to the Fox. "You set me up for that tantrum, you son of a whore. You just wanted to see how loud you could make me yell."

"If it weren't so, I'd deny it," Gerin said. "In case you're interested, you yell louder than I thought you could."

"Truth that," Van put in. "I thought one of those monsters was loose in the keep when I heard you roar."

Schild looked from one of them to the other. "To the five hells with both of you. Now, when will you send out your chariotry?"

"As soon as I can," Gerin answered. "I'll send

messengers today to my vassals who have keeps on the western side of my holding. As you'll have noticed, I haven't enough men here myself to make up ten cars, or anything close to that number. I would have, if I didn't need to order crews south against Bevon." He spread his hands. "I'm afraid that's what you get, lord Schild, for taking so long to make up your mind you're really in trouble. My men ought to be crossing your frontier about the time your tribute comes in to Fox Keep."

"Aye, I'd worked that out for myself, thanks," Schild said. "You're not an easy overlord to serve under, lord prince. I console myself by thinking you're fair in what you do."

"I'll take that," Gerin said.

The Fox lay beside Selatre, watching the lamp gutter toward extinction. Its red, dying flame cast flickering shadows on the wall of the bedchamber. He let one hand run idly down the smooth length of her torso. He'd felt sated after he made love with Fand. He felt happy now. It had been so long since he'd felt really happy after he'd made love that the difference struck him like a blow.

He wondered how he'd failed to notice when that happy feeling started to slip away while Elise shared his bed. Partly, he suspected, his own stupidity was to blame. And partly, he'd supposed it was simply part of their growing used to each other. That was probably stupid too, now that he thought about it.

When she'd bedded the horseleech after she ran off, had she felt happy afterwards? Gerin rather hoped so.

Selatre snuggled against him, which drove thoughts of Elise, if not altogether out of his head, then at least back into the dark corners where they belonged these days. She laughed a little as she said, "The time when I thought no man could touch me seems faraway now. I was foolish."

"No, you weren't." Gerin shook his head. "You were doing what was right for you then. On the other hand, I'd be lying if I said I wasn't glad you'd changed your mind." He bent his head so he could kiss the sweet hollow place where her neck met her shoulder.

"Your beard tickles," she said, and then, as if she weren't changing the subject at all, "What I'm glad of is that my courses are finally spent. I could have done without that part of becoming a woman—I think I've said as much before."

"Eight or ten times," Gerin agreed.

She poked him in the ribs. He jerked. For someone who hadn't been allowed to touch a man for a long time, she learned fast. Maybe she'd grown up with little brothers back in her peasant village. Gerin had been a little brother. He knew what pests they could make of themselves.

Selatre said, "One of the reasons I didn't care for my courses is that they kept me from having you. I've grown greedy so fast, you see."

"They don't have to keep men and women apart," Gerin observed.

"No?" Selatre sounded surprised. Her mouth twisted. "It would be messy."

"It can be," Gerin agreed. "You're apt to be dry then, too. But"—he smiled a lopsided smile—"there are compensations. I didn't want to seem as if I were forcing myself on you this first time. You're finding out about so many new things so fast, I thought I shouldn't burden you with one more. The gods willing, we have plenty of time."

"I think I am very lucky here." Selatre snuggled closer still. "I may have said that before, too—eight or ten times." She gave him a look that said, *What are you going to make of that?*

He knew what he wanted to make of it, and was hoping he could rise to the occasion once more, when someone came running up the hall toward the bedchamber. He scowled; it was too late at night for anyone to bother him without excellent reason. Then the fellow outside shouted, "Lord Gerin, there are monsters loose in Besant's village!"

"Oh, a pox!" Gerin cried, and sprang out of bed. "I'm coming!" He scrambled into tunic and trousers, buckled on his sandals and grabbed his sword belt, and unbarred the door. Selatre barely had time to throw a blanket over her nakedness.

Gerin hurried downstairs, where his armor, with that of his vassals, hung from pegs on the side walls of the great hall. He got into his corselet, jammed his bronze pot of a helm onto his head, and put his shield on his right arm. Tonight he'd make do without his greaves. He snatched up his bow and a full quiver of arrows.

Van had already armed himself. "Come on, Captain," he said impatiently. "I've missed good fighting to wait for you."

"You must have been down here, to have got into your gear so fast," Gerin said.

"Aye, so I was, drinking ale, rolling the dice with a few of the lads—you know how it goes. When the drawbridge thumped down, I figured somebody'd gone and pissed in the porridge pot, and sure enough, in came this screaming serf, babbling of monsters. I sent one of the cooks upstairs for you, while those of us who were down here got weapons and went out to fight." With that, he trotted for the door himself, the Fox at his heels.

At the gate, one of the men there handed Gerin a blazing torch. "Against the ghosts, lord prince," he bawled. Gerin was grateful for his quick thinking, but

felt overburdened as he pounded toward Besant Big-
Belly's village.

Even with the torch, the night spirits assailed him as
soon as he got outside the keep. Dark of night was their
time, their element; they sent a chilling blast of hate and
resentment down on a mortal who presumed to enter it
without better apotropaic than fire alone.

He set his teeth and ran on. Beside him, Van muttered oaths, or perhaps prayers, in a language he did not
recognize. When those had no effect, the outlander
shouted, "Be still, you cursed soulsuckers!" If any living
man could awe the ghosts, Van would have been the
one to do it. But no living man could.

Fortunately, Besant's village lay only a couple of furlongs from Fox Keep. Before the spirits could find all
the chinks in the armor of Gerin's soul and slip cold mental fingers in to drive him mad, he was among the wattle-
and-daub huts of the serfs. They'd given the ghosts the
usual gift of sunset blood, and so were not haunted
through the night. But things fiercer than phantoms
assailed them now.

A man lay sprawled in the street. His blood darkened
the dirt on which he'd fallen. His linen tunic was rucked
up; monsters had been feeding on his legs and hindquarters before the warriors came to drive them off.

Gerin threw down his bow. In the dim light, shooting
was useless. Math's crescent almost brushed the horizon, and even pale Nothos' fatter crescent, higher in the
western sky, made distances seem to shift and waver, as
if in a dream. His sword snaked free. This would have to
be close-quarters work.

Screams from inside a hut with its door flung open
told of a monster inside. Peering over the edge of his
shield, Gerin ran in. The darkness was all but absolute,
but his ears told him of the struggle there. Roaring, the

monster turned from the serf it had been attacking to meet him.

He thrust at it with his sword. He couldn't have done more than pink it, for its cries redoubled. *Crash!* Something wet splashed in the Fox's face. The monster was staggering, though—the serf, with great presence of mind, had hit it over the head with a water jar. The Fox stepped close, stabbed again and again and again. The monster stumbled, recovered, fell.

"Dyaus bless you, lord prince," the serf and his wife cried in the same breath.

"And you, for the help you gave," he answered as he turned and rushed back out into the street. No time now for polite conversation.

Fighting the monsters was not like fighting human foes. That had both advantages and disadvantages. As Gerin had noted before, the creatures fought as individuals, not as part of a larger group. In the confused brawling in the darkness, though, his own men were hardly more organized. And the creatures neither cared anything for loot nor felt any shame at running away if they found themselves in danger they could escape by no other means. Full of notions about glory and honor and courage, Trokmoi would have held their ground and let themselves be killed where they stood.

Gerin caught the reek from a monster's body—a thicker, meatier smell than came from a man, no matter how long unwashed—and threw up his shield before the creature, just another shadow in the night, closed with him. He almost dropped the shield in surprise when a sword slammed against it.

The monster gave him the first unmistakable words he'd heard from one of their throats: "Die, man!" They were in the Trokmê tongue, and snarled rather than spoken, but he had no trouble understanding them.

"Die yourself," he answered in the same language. The monster had no shield, no armor, and no skill at swordplay to speak of. But it was very quick and very strong. When it beat aside his thrust, the blow almost knocked the sword from his hand.

He wondered if it could see better in the night than he could. After it and its ancestors had spent so many generations in a troglodytic life, that seemed likely. And, though it was very awkward with its sword, something let it thwart his strokes again and again.

"Here, Captain, I'm coming!" Van shouted. His heavy footfalls got closer fast.

The monster, though, did not wait to be attacked by two at once. It turned and scampered away toward the woods, faster than an armored man could hope to follow. The fighting died away not long after that, with the rest of the creatures either down or fled. Some of Gerin's troopers had been clawed or bitten, but none of them was badly hurt.

Besant Big-Belly sought out the Fox. The serfs in his village hadn't been so lucky. As lamentations and moans of pain rose into the night, the headman said, "We've three dead, lord prince, and several more, men and women both, who won't be able to work for some while. Dyaus and the other gods only know how we're to bring in enough crops to meet your dues come fall." He wrung his hands in anxiety.

It was, Gerin thought with a flash of contempt, utterly characteristic of him to worry about the dues first and people only afterwards. "Don't worry about it," he said, "If I see the people here are making an honest effort, I won't hold them to blame for falling a bit short of what they might have done otherwise."

"You're kind, lord prince," Besant cried, seizing Gerin's hand and pressing it to his lips. The Fox snatched it back.

He suspected the headman would use his generosity as an excuse to try to slack off before the harvest or cheat him afterwards, but he figured he had a decent chance of getting the better of Besant at that game.

"Lord prince?" A hesitant touch on his arm: it was the serf in whose house he'd fought. "I want to thank you, lord prince. Weren't for you, reckon that hideous thing would've et Arabel or me or maybe the both of us."

"Pruanz is right," the woman beside the peasant said. "Thank you."

"Can't have my villagers eaten," Gerin said gravely. "They never work as well afterwards."

Rihwin would have smiled at the joke, or at least recognized that it was one. It flew past Pruanz and Arabel, a clean miss. "Words, they're cheap," Pruanz said. "Want to give you something better, show we really mean what we say."

"Pruanz is right," Arabel said. "You come back with me to the house, I'll make you feel as good as I know how." Even in darkness, he saw her twitch her hips at him.

"Lord prince, she's lively," Pruanz said. "You'll like what she does."

Gerin looked from one of them to the other. They meant it. He sighed. He'd taken his pleasure with peasant women a good many times, but he didn't feel like it now, not with Selatre waiting for him back at the keep. As gently as he could, he said, "I don't want to take your wife from you, Pruanz. I was just doing as a liege lord should, and I have a lady of my own."

Pruanz didn't answer, but Arabel did, indignantly: "Well! I like that! What does she have that I don't?" She rubbed herself against the Fox. By the feel of her, she did indeed possess all female prerequisites.

He was embarrassed enough to wish he'd left her and

her husband in the hut to be devoured. He managed to free his arm from Arabel and said to Pruanz, "The best way for the two of you to show you're glad you're alive is to bed each other."

Arabel let out a loud, scornful sniff. "Well! Maybe I should leave you to your fancy lady, lord prince, though I don't suppose she gets much use out of you, neither."

"Arabel!" Pruanz hissed. "That's no way to talk to him what saved us."

"And who saved *him*, smashing a jug over that horrible thing's head?" she retorted. "I expect that means you saved me, too." She all but dragged her husband back toward their hut. Gerin suspected his suggestion was about to be fulfilled, even if he'd given it to the wrong one of the pair.

He gathered up his troopers. They didn't have torches for the walk back to Fox Keep, but the ghosts were fairly quiet. *Why not?* he thought as he neared the drawbridge—the night spirits were no doubt battening on the new gift of blood they'd just received from the dead peasants and monsters.

Some of the warriors went off to bed right away. Others paused in the great hall for a jack of ale—or several jacks of ale—before they slept. After Gerin had put his armor and the bow he'd recovered back on their pegs, Van planted an elbow in his ribs, hard enough to make him stagger. "Fox, that's twice now lately you've turned it down when you had the chance to take some," he said. "You must be getting old."

"Oh, you heard that, did you?" Gerin looked up his nose at his taller friend, who stood there chuckling. "If you want to get much older, you'd be wise to tend to your own affairs and leave mine—or the lack of them—to me."

"Affairs, forsooth." Van drained his drinking jack,

poured it full, drained it again. Then he headed for the stairs, a fixed expression on his face. For his sake, Gerin hoped Fand was in, or could be cajoled into, the mood. If she wasn't, or couldn't, she'd throw things.

"That's the closest they've come to here," Drago the Bear said, yawning. "I don't like it, not even a little bit." By his matter-of-fact tone, he might have been talking of a hot, sticky summer's day.

"I don't like it, either," Gerin answered. "I'm stretched far too wide—seems that's all I say lately. Men and cars off in Schild's holding, more of them down in the south fighting Bevon and his bastard boys—"

"They were born in wedlock, far as I know," said Drago, who could sometimes get the letter and miss the spirit.

"They're bastards all the same," Gerin said. "Lining up with the Trokmoi is bad enough, but anyone who lines up with the monsters deserves whatever happens to him. *I* intend to happen to Bevon and Bevonis and Bevion, but while I'm dealing with them, I can't be dealing with Adiatunnus and *his* monster friends. And if my men can't push Bevon off the Elabon Way, and if Aragis' troopers fail too, what then? I can't see anything—except us losing the war, I mean."

"Never happen," Drago said, and fell asleep at the table, his head in his hands.

Gerin wished he had his vassal's confidence—and naïveté. He knew only too well how easy losing the war would be; his nimble imagination, usually an asset, betrayed him with images of blood and defeat and treachery. So many ways things could go wrong. What he had trouble coming up with was ways they could go right.

He emptied his own drinking jack and went upstairs himself. He opened the door to his bedchamber as quietly as he could, expecting Selatre to be asleep. But he found the lamp lit and her sitting up in bed waiting for him. She wasn't spending the time idly, either; she'd gone down the hall to the library and fetched back a codex to read until he returned. She put it down and said, "Biton and the other gods be praised that you're all right. Every time you go out to fight now—"

"Not a scratch," he said, turning to bar the door. "We hurt the monsters worse than they hurt the village, so that's—well, not all right, but better than it might have been." He didn't want to talk about the skirmish; all he wanted to do was forget it. "What do you have there?"

She flipped back to the first leaf of parchment. "*On the Motions of the Moons*, by one Volatin of Elabon. It was the first volume I saw in the library, the reason being that you left it out on the table there instead of returning it to its proper niche." She fixed him with the severe look of a librarian whose sense of order had been transgressed.

"I'm sorry," he said; rather to his surprise, he found himself meaning it. "So you're trying Volatin, are you? What do you make of him?"

"Not much, I'm afraid," she admitted. "Endless numbers and curious signs you didn't teach me and other obscurities and oddments. What do they all mean?"

"They mean that if I'd looked through his book five years ago I'd have known the werenight was coming, for he showed it beyond doubt in those columns of numbers. But I just thought of the book as a curiosity I'd brought back from the City of Elabon, and so it sat idle and useless on my shelf." He scowled in self-reproach.

"What could you have done about the werenight had you known of it?" Selatre asked.

"Given that I was traveling when it happened, probably nothing," he said. "But it's made me pay close attention to the phases of the moons ever since. Ten—no, eleven—days from now, Math will be full, the day after that Elleb and Nothos, and the day after *that* Tiwaz. It's not quite a dreadful werenight like the one we had before—from what Volatin says, those come less than once in a thousand years. But men with a were streak in them will come closer to changing then than on any other night for a long time to come. It's—"

"—One more thing to worry about," Selatre finished for him.

He stared at her in surprise and delight. "Well, well," he said. "I didn't know you spoke my language."

"I'm learning," she said.

X

Three days after the monsters attacked Besant's village, the lookout in the watchtower blew a long blast on his horn and shouted, "A chariot approaches from the south!" A few minutes later, he added with some excitement, "It's Utreiz Embron's son, by the gods!"

Gerin was in the stables, fitting a new spoke to a chariot wheel. He dropped the knife with which he was making a final trim of the spoke. Raffo, who was helping him, said, "Well, we'll know one way or the other."

"That we will," Gerin answered, and hurried out into the courtyard.

Men were also bustling out from the keep itself: everyone in Castle Fox—everyone in Gerin's domain—had a vital stake in learning whether the Elabon Way had been reopened. Van caught the Fox's eye and said, "Wishing you luck, Captain."

"I'll take all I can get, thanks," Gerin said.

The drawbridge seemed to be crawling down. Gerin's hands folded into fists; his nails bit into his palms. At last, with a thump, the drawbridge met the ground on the far side of the ditch around the palisade. Utreiz's chariot thumped over it. Even before the warrior spoke, a great weight lifted from Gerin's heart, for he, his driver, and the other warrior in the car were all wreathed in smiles.

"Dyaus and all the gods be praised, we smashed 'em!" Utreiz cried. He tried to go on, but a great cheer from everyone in the courtyard drowned the rest of his words. Rihwin the Fox leaped up into the car and planted a kiss on the startled Utreiz's cheek. He had no designs on the other man's body; that was just a southern way of showing joy at good news. In the rougher northlands, though, it was best used with caution. "*Get* off me!" Utreiz said, and several other rougher things the hubbub mercifully muffled.

When the din died away a little, Gerin said, "Tell us all that befell. Maybe"—he glanced around pointedly—"we'll be able to hear you now."

"Aye, lord prince." Utreiz turned as if to push Rihwin out of the chariot, but Rihwin had already jumped down. Looking foolish, Utreiz resumed: "In one way, it was just as you said: Ricolf the Red and his men came up from the south to join us and Bevander against Bevon and his other two sons. Since they held the road, we had to sneak through the woods to the west to set up a common attack on the same day. We set out right at dawn, caught 'em by surprise worse than they did when they hit us and grabbed that stretch of road. Bevonis is dead. We caught Bevion; he offered me everything in the world not to let Bevander have him. Bevon, curse him, got away and holed up in his keep."

He had to shout the last part; cheering had erupted again. Through it, Gerin said, "Well done! The road is open, we have our men back from Schild's holding—"

"What's this, lord?" Utreiz asked, and Gerin realized he hadn't heard about Schild's cry for help.

He explained quickly, finishing, "You'd have been just as glad if the men I'd sent to Schild had stayed out a few days more, seeing as Rihwin was one of them. But all we have to do now is await Aragis' troopers." *And hope they come,* he added to himself.

"This splendid news calls for an equally splendid celebration!" Rihwin shouted, which raised more cheers from the warriors gathered in the courtyard around

Utreiz. Even Gerin clapped his hands, not wanting to be thought a wet blanket. If his men felt like roistering where no fight impended, that was all right with him. But then Rihwin went on, "What say we break out the wine with which Schild was generous enough to buy our aid?"

Some of the troopers clapped again. Others—notably Van and Drago—looked to Gerin instead. "No," he said in a voice abrupt as an avalanche.

"But, my fellow Fox—" Rihwin protested.

Gerin cut him off with a sharp, chopping gesture. "No I said and no I meant. Haven't you had enough misfortunes with wine and with Mavrix, my fellow Fox?" He freighted Rihwin's ekename with enough irony to sink it.

Rihwin flushed, but persisted, "I hadn't intended to summon the lord of the sweet grape, lord prince, nor had I intended to do aught more with his vintage than sip it, and not to excess."

"No," Gerin said for the third time. "What you intend and what turns out have a way of being two different things. And I trust that gift of wine from Schild about as far as I'd trust so many jars full of vipers."

"What, you think the whoreson's out to poison us?" Van rumbled. "If that's so—" He didn't go on, not with words, but pulled his mace free and whacked the shaft against the palm of his left hand.

But Gerin shook his head and said, "No," yet again. Van looked puzzled. Rihwin looked as dubious as he had just before Gerin gave him an ass' ear in place of his own. Gerin went on, "What I mean is, I fear that Mavrix seeks a foothold in my lands." He explained how the Sithonian god of wine and fertility and creativity had repeatedly cropped up of late, finishing, "Given what's passed between the god and me—and between the god and Rihwin—these past few years, the less presence he has here, the happier and safer I'll feel. I didn't dare refuse the wine of Schild, for that would have offered Mavrix insult direct. But I shan't invite his presence by broaching those jars, either."

"I had not considered the matter in that light," Rihwin admitted after rather more thought than usual. "So far as men can, you may well have wisdom there, lord prince. But one thing you must always bear in mind: the lord of the sweet grape is stronger than you are. If it be his will that he establish himself in your holding, establish himself he shall, whether you will or not."

"I am painfully aware of that," Gerin said, sighing. "But what I can do to prevent it, I will. I'm on good terms with Baivers. Drink all the ale you please, Rihwin, and I'll say not a word. The wine jars stay closed."

"Sense, lord prince," Utreiz Embron's son said. Van nodded. After a moment, so did Drago. After a longer moment, so did Rihwin.

"Good," Gerin said. All the same, he quietly resolved to take the wine jars from the cellar—where they resided with the ale—and find a more secret place for them. Rihwin's intentions were surely good, but his actions lived up to them no more than anyone else's—less than those of a few people who crossed the Fox's mind.

The warriors trooped into the great hall, still loudly congratulating Utreiz. "It's not as if I won the fight all by my lonesome," he protested, much as Gerin might have in the same circumstances. Nobody paid any attention to him. He'd taken part in the victory and brought news of it, and that was plenty.

Seeing the invasion, servants hurried downstairs and into the kitchens. They quickly returned with ale (no wine; the Fox checked each amphora to be sure of what it held), meat from the night before, and bread to put it on. Some of the warriors called for bowls of the pease porridge that simmered in a big pot above the hearth.

The troopers made enough racket to bring people down from upstairs to see what was going on. Van caught Fand in his arms, planted a loud, smacking kiss on her mouth, and then sat down again, pulling her into his lap. He grabbed for his jack of ale. "Here, sweetling, drink!" he cried, almost spilling it down her chin. "We've beaten Bevon and his boys proper, that we have."

"Is it so?" she said. "Aye, I'll drink to that, and right gladly, too." She took the jack from his hand, drained it dry. Gerin wondered if she would have been so ready to toast a triumph over Adiatunnus—he, after all, was of her own folk, not just an Elabonian on the wrong side. The Fox shook his head. She'd never been disloyal to him that way. When Van kissed her again, she responded as if she meant to drag him upstairs in a moment—or possibly not bother with dragging him upstairs. But then she got off his lap to claim a drinking jack of her own and fill it full of ale.

Selatre came down into the great hall in the middle of that. She too got a jack of ale. Gerin stood to greet her, but hesitated to do so much as take her hand; she remained leery of publicly showing affection. Unlike many, she didn't assume her own standards applied to everyone: she watched Fand and Van with much more amusement than disapproval.

She sat down on the bench by the Fox. "I take it the news is good?" she said. Then she saw Utreiz. "Now I know the news is good, and what sort of news it is. We've beaten Bevon and his sons and taken back the full length of the Elabon Way, not so?"

Gerin nodded. "That's just what we've done." He gave her an admiring look. "You don't miss much, do you? Next time I have to ride out in a sweep against the monsters, I think I'll leave you in charge back here."

For the first time since they'd become lovers—maybe for the first time since she'd come to Fox Keep—Selatre got angry at him. "Don't mock me with things you know I can't have," she snapped. She waved to the crowd of noisy, drinking warriors. "The only use they have for women is to tumble them, or maybe to have them fetch up another jar of ale from the cellar. As if they'd pay heed to me!" She glared.

Taken aback at her vehemence, the Fox said slowly, "I'm sorry. I don't suppose I meant that altogether seriously, but I didn't mean to mock you with it, either." He plucked at his beard as he thought. "If you wanted to badly enough, you could probably bring it off. All you'd need to do is remind them that you'd once been Sibyl and give them the feeling your eye for what needed doing was better than theirs even now."

"But that would be a lie," Selatre said.

Gerin shook his head. "No, just a push in the right direction. There's a magic to getting people to do what you want that doesn't show up in any grimoire. It uses what a person has done and who he is to show that he—or she—is apt to do well, or to come up with the right answer, or whatever you like, the next time, too. That's what I was talking about here. You *could* do it. Whether you'd want to or not is another question."

"Some of me is tempted," she said in a small voice. "The rest, though, the bigger half, wants no part of it. I'm not fond of having people tell me what to do, so I don't think I have any business giving orders to anyone else, either."

"Good for you," Gerin said. "I never intended to be a baron, much less somebody who calls himself a prince. I just aimed at being a scholar, studying what I wanted when I wanted to do it." Self-mockery filled his laugh.

"What you aim at in life and what you end up with are often two very different things."

That made him think of the jars of wine Schild had sent him. They still sat down in the cellar, sealed and innocuous, and he'd move them somewhere safer yet as soon as he got round to it. But with Mavrix immanent in that wine, who could say how much his own aims mattered?

The moons coursed through the sky, Tiwaz swiftly, Nothos so slowly that his phase seemed to change but little from day to day, Elleb and Math in between. Gerin paid them close heed for two reasons: to gauge the time when the four moons would come full in the space of three days, and to see how many days Aragis the Archer had left to fulfill the promise his envoys had made.

Golden Math was two days past first quarter when word came to Fox Keep that the monsters had attacked a village near the southern boundary of Gerin's holding. Cursing under his breath—why wouldn't things ever hold still long enough for him to catch his breath?—he readied a force of chariotry and set out to sweep the countryside. He had no great hope of sweeping it clean, but refused to sit idly by and let the creatures hold the initiative.

The sweep actually went better than he'd expected. His warriors caught three monsters feeding on a cow they'd dragged down in the middle of a meadow close by the road. With joyous whoops, they sent their chariots jouncing over the grass to cut the monsters off from the safety of the woods. The creatures were slow to flee, too, staying at the carcass for a last couple of mouthfuls of meat before they tried to get away. Thanks to that, the Fox's men were able to bring them all down with no loss to themselves.

One of the monsters still tried to crawl toward the woods despite having taken enough arrows to give it the aspect of a hedgehog. Van got down from the car he shared with Gerin and smashed in its head with his mace. Then he and some of the other men began the gory business of reclaiming shafts from the bodies of the creatures.

Raffo turned to Gerin and said, "Here's another way keeping the trees well back from the side of the road did you a good turn, lord prince. If you'd let them grow up close, as other barons do, those stinking things might have made good their escape."

"That's true," Gerin said. "After a while, you sometimes get to wonder whether something's more trouble than it's worth, but when you see the work you've spent pay for itself, it reminds you that you might have known what you were doing all along."

The war party reached the ravaged village a little before sunset. The serfs there had fought back as well as they could; they'd lost a man, two women, and some livestock, but they'd also managed to kill a monster. Gerin sent his troopers out on a short foray into the forest surrounding the village, ordering them to be back in the open before night took them. That was one command he was sure they'd obey—no one wanted to meet the ghosts away from blood and fire.

A deadfall of branches and sticks caught the Fox's eye. "There's a likely place," he said, pointing.

Van and Raffo both nodded. "Aye, you're right," Van added, and probed the brush with his spear.

With a scream, a monster burst out and hurled itself at him. He held it off with his shield, though its charge forced him back two steps. Among them, he and Gerin and Raffo made short work of the creature. "Female," Gerin noted.

"Aye, so it was. Mean enough, all the same," Van said, sounding embarrassed at having to give ground. He sighed. "They're all mean enough, and to spare."

Inside the deadfall, something yowled—two some-things, by the sound. Gerin stared in dismay at Van. "It had cubs," he said, as if accusing his friend.

"Aye," the outlander answered, and then, after a moment, "No reason we should be surprised, I suppose. The creatures must have been having cubs for the gods only know how long, down in their caves. They'll have kept right on doing it now that they're aboveground. This one will have been pregnant before she got aboveground, come to that."

"So she will," Gerin said. The outlander was right, of course, but that didn't take away the startlement. The Fox dug into the deadfall, scattering brush in all direc-tions. After a moment, Van and Raffo pitched in to help.

They soon uncovered the monster cubs. Gerin stared at them in dismay. They looked like nothing so much as ugly, hairy babies. "What are you going to do with them?" Raffo asked, gulping a little. Oddly, that made Gerin feel a little easier: the driver didn't have the stomach just to kill them, either.

Van did. "Get rid of them," he said. "You know what they turn into."

"I don't know what to do," the Fox answered slowly. "Aye, I know what they turn into, but I'm still not sure how smart the monsters are. If they learn I'm slaying their cubs out of hand and understand that, it'll just make them worse foes of mine than they are already."

"Honh!" Van said, a noise of deep discontent. "How could they be?"

"I don't know, and I don't want to find out."

"Well, what will you do?" Van asked scornfully. "Take 'em home and make pets of 'em?"

"Why not? We have F and back at Fox Keep. . . ." Gerin murmured. Actually, the idea tempted him, tweaking his curiosity. If you raised a monster among men, what would you get? A monster? A pet, as Van had said? Something not too far removed from an ugly, hairy man, or, for that matter, an ugly, hairy woman? If he'd had fewer things to worry about, if he'd had more leisure, if he hadn't been certain all his vassals would scream even louder than Van had, he might have tried the experiment. As it was— "I know what we'll do."

"What's that, lord?" Raffo asked.

"Nothing," Gerin said. "Nothing at all. We killed the female in battle—well and good. We won't—we can't—take the cubs back to Castle Fox. You're right about that, Van. But I won't just slaughter them, either. I'll leave them here. Maybe beasts will get them, or maybe, if the monsters do have something in the way of family feeling, they'll take them and raise them up. I'll leave that in the hands of the gods."

He hadn't asked whether Van or Raffo approved. Now he looked to see if they did. Raffo nodded. Van still seemed unhappy, but finally said, "You have a way of looking for the middle road, Fox. I suppose you found it here. Let's go back."

When they returned to the village, they found the other chariot crews had also had good luck. They'd killed two monsters, the only serious injury they'd taken being to Parol Chickpea, who'd just recovered from his bitten buttock. Now he was gray-faced, and had a bloody rag wrapped around his left hand—he'd lost two fingers from it.

"How did that happen?" Gerin asked. "His shield should have protected him there. He's right-handed, so he doesn't have that hand out in the open the way I do."

"Just bad luck," Drago the Bear answered. "The

monster he was fighting gave a good yank at his shield, and it broke away from the handgrip and lashing. Then the thing sprang at him, and he stuck out his arm to keep from getting its teeth in his neck instead. I hope he heals; he's lost a lot of blood."

Gerin made unhappy clucking noises. "Aye, he's a good fighter, and a long way from the worst of men." He kicked at the dirt, feeling useless. "Would that the gods had never let this plague of monsters loose on us. Every warrior, every serf even, we lose is one we can't replace."

"That's all true, lord, but the creatures are here, and we have to fend 'em off as best we can," Drago said. Gerin wished he could muster that same stolid acceptance for things he couldn't help.

The warriors started back toward the main road at dawn the next day. They left Parol Chickpea behind; he'd taken a fever, and was in no condition to spend a day in the chariot. "We'll do the best we can for him, lord prince," the village headman promised. With that Gerin had to be content. The serfs' herbs and potions were as likely to help Parol as any of the fancier doctoring techniques that came from south of the High Kirs. Unfortunately, they were also as likely not to help.

When the dirt track the chariots were following ran into the Elabon Way, Van pointed south and said, "More cars heading up toward us, Captain."

The Fox hadn't looked southward; he was intent on getting back to the keep. But his eyes followed Van's pointing finger. His left eyebrow rose. "Quite a few cars," he said in surprise. "I hope Bevon hasn't rallied and driven my men off the highway again." He let out a long sigh. "We'd better go find out." He tapped Raffo on the shoulder. The driver swung his chariot south. The rest of the cars in the war party followed.

Before long, Gerin realized he didn't recognize any of the approaching chariots. He also realized his band was badly outnumbered. If Bevon somehow had managed to pull off one victory, he might be on the point of another.

Then Van pointed again. "There in the second car, Fox. Isn't that tall, skinny fellow Aragis the Archer?"

"Father Dyaus," Gerin said softly. He squinted. "Your eyes are sharper than mine." Then he let out a whoop loud enough to make Raffo start. "Aye, it *is* Aragis—and see all the friends he's brought with him."

"A great whacking lot of them, that's for certain," Van said.

The more teams and chariots Gerin saw, the more thoughtful he grew. He started to regret that whoop of glee. Measured all together, his own forces comfortably outnumbered Aragis' army. But his forces were scattered over several holdings and doing several different things, which left him in a decidedly uncomfortable position here. If Aragis should decide to take advantage of his superior numbers here on the spot, affairs in the northlands would suddenly look very different, although Gerin would be in no position to appreciate the difference.

A bold front had served him well many times in the past. He tapped Raffo on the shoulder again. "Let's go down and give the grand duke proper greeting."

"Aye, lord prince." Raffo sounded a little doubtful, but steered the car toward the approaching host. The rest of the chariots in Gerin's war party followed. He heard some of his men muttering among themselves at the course he took, but no one challenged him. He had a reputation for being right. The next few minutes would show how well he deserved it.

He waved toward the oncoming chariots. Someone

waved back: Marlanz Raw-Meat. A moment later, Fabors Fabur's son waved, too. Then Aragis also raised his hand to greet the Fox.

"Well met," Gerin called when he'd drawn a little closer to Aragis' force. "You're in good time, and here with more cars even than I'd looked for. Well met indeed. We were just out driving the monsters back from one of my villages, and slew several." *And left two to an unsure fate*, he added to himself. Aragis didn't need to know about that. He would surely have killed the cubs without a second thought.

"Good for you, lord prince," Aragis called back. "And not only have I brought my men and my horses and my cars, I have a present for you—two presents, as a matter of fact."

"Have you now, grand duke?" The Fox hoped he sounded fulsome rather than worried. An unscrupulous man, which Aragis had a reputation of being, might reckon a volley of arrows and a hard charge as presents.

But Aragis didn't order an attack. He reached down into the car and held up a large, tightly tied leather sack. "Here's one of them." Then he reached down again and lifted something else, something heavier. His lips pulled back from his teeth, partly from the effort and partly in a real smile. "And here's the other."

From his arms, Duren squealed, "Father!"

Gerin prided himself on seldom being at a loss. His pride suffered now, but he couldn't have cared less. "Duren," he whispered.

Aragis couldn't possibly have heard that, but nodded nonetheless. His driver reined in. He set Duren down on the stone surface of the road. The boy ran to Gerin's chariot.

The Fox jumped out of his car even though Raffo hadn't stopped it. He staggered a little when he landed, and then again when Duren ran into him full tilt. He picked up his son and squeezed him so tight against his own corseleted chest that he felt the air go out of the boy. "Father, why are you crying?" Duren demanded indignantly. "Aren't you glad to see me?"

"That's why I'm crying," Gerin answered: "Because I'm glad to see you."

"I don't understand," Duren said.

"Never mind," Gerin told him. Aragis' chariot had come up behind Duren. The Fox turned to the hawk-faced grand duke and said, "You know I was afraid you'd taken the boy, or rather kept him after someone else—it would have been Tassilo, wouldn't it?—took him. I never thought to get him back through you. To say I'm in your debt just shows how little words can mean."

"You've yet to open your other gift," Aragis said. He handed Gerin the leather sack without more explanation.

When the Fox undid the knot in the rawhide lashing that held it closed, a foul stench escaped. He nodded; from the weight and heft of the sack, he'd expected it would hold a head. He looked inside, nodded again, and closed it. "Aye, that's Tassilo."

"I packed him in salt for some days after I—mm—took him apart," Aragis said. "I wanted you to be able to recognize him, to be sure he was dead."

Gerin picked up the sack and threw it into the grass by the side of the road. It bounced a couple of times and lay still.

"You gave him too easy an end, you ask me," Van told Aragis.

"I thought on that," Aragis admitted. "Still, though, while he kidnapped the boy, he didn't do anything worse while he had him. That may have been because he wanted to keep his value as hostage high, but whatever the reason, it's so. I let his end be easy on account of it."

"He's dead. That's all that matters," Gerin said. "No, not all." He squeezed Duren breathless again, then asked Aragis, "When did he come to you?"

"As the gods would have it, the day after I sent my vassals to you seeking common cause," Aragis said. "So any of the men here with me will attest." His driver and the other warrior in the car with him nodded, almost in unison.

"I see," Gerin said slowly. He wondered if the grand duke was telling the truth. Had he perhaps had Duren earlier, and contemplated using him against the Fox? Aragis was not a man to cross; no doubt his own vassals would support him. Duren wouldn't know, not exactly; four-year-olds had very strange notions of time. Gerin decided to let it lie for now.

"How fare you here?" Aragis asked. "Your own men down further south were full of stories of hard fighting to hold the road open."

"That's true, but we won the fight," Gerin said, doubly glad Aragis hadn't had to try forcing his way through Bevon's men—and quadruply glad Aragis hadn't tried and failed. The Fox went on, "We've had a few other small things happening, too," and with that airy understatement explained his sweeps through his one holding and the one Schild had so urgently requested.

"You've had a busy time of it," Aragis said, a statement so self-evidently true that Gerin didn't even bother nodding. The grand duke added, "I was taking the omens before I set out, and the bird's flight warned me I'd best leave early rather than late, so here you see me now. Try as I would, I couldn't make sense of why, but I accepted the reading all the same."

"I think you did well," Gerin said, and told him of the near werenight due in a few days.

Aragis' eyes narrowed. "Is that a fact?" he said, then shook his head. "No, I'm not doubting you, Fox. Just that, with so many things closer to home to keep track of, I never thought to worry about the moons."

"Sometimes the things you most need to worry about aren't the obvious ones," Gerin said. For some reason that made him think, not of the untouchably distant moons, but of Elise, who'd given no signs—no signs he'd noticed, anyhow—of discontent until one day she was simply gone.

Aragis said, "I have a hard enough time worrying about the things that are obvious. The rest I leave to the gods and clever fellows like you." His voice rang sardonic, but only slightly. He didn't worry about the long run or the wide picture as much as Gerin did. In the short term, and over the limited space of the northlands, his methods worked well enough.

"Let's head up to the keep," Gerin said. "We'll wait out the moons there, if that suits you, and then do our best to smash Adiatunnus. If his lands aren't a sanctuary for the monsters, we'll stand a better chance of controlling them."

"I wonder if we'll ever be able to do that," Aragis said gloomily. "The damned Trokmê's lands are nowhere near mine, but the stinking creatures plague me as bad as they do you, maybe worse. After we finish up here, I'll want you and yours to ride south and help me clear my hinterlands of 'em."

"That's why we made the pact," Gerin agreed, "though as you say I don't know if we'll ever be able to clear them completely now. Sometimes that strikes me as more a job for gods than for men."

"If prayer were the answer, every monster in the northlands would have died a hundred times by now," Aragis said.

"Isn't that the sad and sorry truth?" Gerin said. "But I wasn't thinking so much of prayer. The gods hear prayer for a double handful of thousands of different things every day. No wonder most of them aren't granted—grant one and a god rejects another in the granting. What's crossed my mind once or twice lately, though, is . . . evocation."

Aragis stared at him. So did his own men. He didn't blame any of them. The last time he'd been at all involved in evoking was five years before, when Rihwin summoned Mavrix to turn sour wine back into sweet. Rihwin hadn't intended to evoke Mavrix then, only to invoke him. When you let a god fully enter the material world, you ran a tremendous risk. Summoning the god was relatively easy. Controlling him once summoned was anything but.

"You have a reputation for not thinking small," Aragis said at last, "and I see it's well earned."

"Dyaus above, it's not something I *want* to do," Gerin exclaimed. "Why do you think I so want this alliance to succeed? If we can beat the Trokmoi and the monsters on our own, we won't have to think about calling on the gods. But if it comes down to a choice between losing the fight and trying one last great stroke to win it, which would you take?"

"Damn me to the five hells if I know." Aragis shook his head, as if Gerin had made him look at something he would sooner not have contemplated. "As you say, lord prince, let us hope the choice does not come down to that. Shall we ride on to your keep now, and ready ourselves for the fighting ahead?"

"I suggested as much a while ago, but we've been standing around here talking instead," Gerin said. He picked Duren up and started to set him in his own chariot.

"Wait, Papa, I have to piddle," Duren said. He started toward the bushes off to the side of the road. Gerin and

Van both went with him, the one with drawn sword, the other with heavy spear at the ready. Wild beasts and worse dwelt in the woods these days.

When Duren was done, Van grabbed him by the feet and carried him back to the chariot upside down. He squealed laughter all the way. Hearing that laughter lifted years from Gerin's heart. He nodded to Aragis, who nodded back. It was good to know there were depths to which some men in the northlands would not sink.

Having Duren in the car with him bouncing up and down made the trip back to Castle Fox one of the more enjoyable journeys Gerin had ever taken. Even having his son ask "Are we almost there yet?" with great regularity didn't, couldn't, come close to taking the edge off his happiness, not today.

When they got back to Fox Keep late that afternoon, the castle was shut up tight against them. Gerin would have been furious to find it any other way: the lookout would have seen a great many chariots, far more than had set out the previous morning, and had better have assumed they were hostile. The Fox rode up close enough for the warriors on the palisade to recognize him and called, "We're all friends here—Aragis the Archer has brought his men north. And look!" As Aragis had before him, he held Duren high.

The men on the wall cheered themselves hoarse. The drawbridge came down quickly, heavy bronze chain rattling over the winch. Van asked quietly, "Where are we going to put all of Aragis' men? The keep won't hold the lot of 'em, and besides—"

"I won't want all of them inside at once until I have more of my own troopers here to balance the scale," Gerin finished for him. "I don't see how I can keep from feasting 'em tonight, but after that . . ." Now he let his voice trail away.

"Look sharp," Van said. "Here's Aragis coming up."

The grand duke said, "Lord prince, we are allies, but not yet certain of each other, although you've been too polite to speak much of that. We've brought canvas and such; if it please you, most of my men will sleep outside the keep. You need have no fear. We'll set a watch against monsters and such, as we did on the road north."

Gerin dipped his head. "I thank you. You've just made my life easier."

"I thought that might be so." Aragis' smile was pleasant enough, but something hard remained under the surface. "I might have made other plans, did I not need your aid in the south as much as you need mine here—maybe more."

"Indeed," Gerin said. "I understand what you're saying. Your grandson will rule mine, maybe, or mine yours, but if we fight now, we both go under. We'll be wise to bear that in mind all through this campaign."

"My grandson will have his own worries," Aragis said. "I can't untangle mine right now, let alone his. But as you say, Fox, remembering we need each other is the best way to keep from going to war too soon."

It was probably the only way that would hold Aragis in check, Gerin thought. The Archer, by all evidence, was ruthlessly effective in pursuing his own interests. Reminding him that Gerin was part of those interests seemed eminently practical. Nodding, the Fox said, "Shall we go into the keep together? You'll guest with me, of course."

"Apart from my men, you mean? Aye, of course," Aragis answered. One thing his nature made easy: Gerin didn't have to waste time with polite-sounding explanations. Aragis saw through to the essence of things and accepted them for what they were.

Some of the men on the palisade came down to greet

the Fox and his companions. Others held their posts, bows ready. Hearing the commotion, servants came out from the great hall to see what was happening. So did Fand and Selatre.

Seeing Fand, Duren jumped out of the chariot and ran to her. She scooped him up in an embrace, said to Gerin, "Och, you got him back! Good on you there."

"First thing that's gone right in a while," the Fox said. Then he glanced toward Selatre and corrected himself: "No, the second thing."

Duren wiggled out of Fand's arms. He pointed at Selatre. "Who is that lady? I've never seen her before." He looked thoughtful, which made him look amazingly like a miniature, beardless version of Gerin. "Is that my mama come back?" he asked, hope lighting his face brighter than the sun. He'd barely been toddling when Elise left Fox Keep.

"No, it's not," Gerin said gently, and the sparkle died in Duren's eyes. His father went on, "But do you know who it is? That's the lady who used to be the Sibyl down at Ikos, the one the god spoke through. Her name is Selatre. She lives at Fox Keep now."

"My vassals spoke to me of this," Aragis said, without giving any hint of how he felt about it.

Duren studied Selatre, then asked the child's natural question: "Why?"

Gerin had always tried to be as straightforward with his son as he could. That wasn't easy now, but he did his best: "Because the earthquake—do you remember the earthquake?" Duren nodded, eyes wide. Gerin continued, "The earthquake knocked down Biton's temple at Ikos, and it let loose the monsters from underground there. Van and I were afraid the monsters would kill Selatre and eat her, the way they do, so we rescued her and brought her to Castle Fox with us when we came back."

"Oh," Duren said. "All right." After a moment, he asked, "Why were you and Van at Ikos?"

"To ask the god to tell us through the Sibyl where you were," Gerin answered.

"Oh," Duren said again. "But I was with Tassilo." By his tone, that was as much a fact of nature as trees' leaves being green.

"But we didn't know you were with Tassilo," the Fox reminded him. "And even if we had known it, we didn't know where Tassilo was."

"Why not?" Duren asked, at which point Gerin threw his hands in the air.

He said, "Let's bring up some of the good ale from the cellar, slay an ox and some sheep, and rejoice that we have enough bold warriors here now to take on the Trokmoi and the monsters." *Or so I hope, at any rate*, he thought. *If we don't, we're in even more trouble than I reckoned on before.*

"Nothing finer than a good sheep's head, all cooked up proper, with plenty of ale to wash it down," Drago the Bear declared. Baron though he was, he had a peasant's taste in food.

The Fox looked to the sky. With sunset near, all the moons were up: Tiwaz at first quarter near the meridian, then Elleb halfway between first quarter and full, and then, close together and low in the east, Math and Nothos. Gerin shook his head. Five years earlier, he'd paid attention to the motions of the moons mostly to let him gauge the time by night; seeing them crawl together now sent a shiver of dread through him. This stretch, surely, would not approach the horrors of the werenight, but how bad would it be? No way to know, not yet.

He said, "The blood of the beasts slaughtered for our supper will hold the ghosts at bay. If you like, grand duke, we'll do some of the butchering outside the keep, that your men's encampment may also gain the boon of blood."

"A good thought," Aragis said. "Do it." He was so direct, he even used words like soldiers, sending forth no more than he needed to carry out his plans.

"Might we not broach even one of the jars of wine we have from Schild to help us rejoice in this alliance?" Rihwin asked.

"No," Gerin and Van said in the same breath. Gerin pretended not to see the curious look Aragis sent him for quashing the question so quickly. He was heartily glad he'd taken those jars out of the cellar and hidden them deep under straw in the stables. To Rihwin, he went on, "Ale suffices for the rest of us, so it will have to do for you, too." Rihwin's pout made him look positively bilious, but he finally gave a glum nod.

Duren kept running around the courtyard and in and out of the great hall, as if making sure things hadn't changed while he was gone. Every once in a while, his voice would rise in excitement: "I remember that!" He'd been gone a quarter of a year, no small chunk of a four-year-old's life.

Selatre came over to Gerin and said, "He's a promising boy."

"Thank you. I've always thought so," the Fox answered. "I just praise Dyaus and all the gods that he doesn't seem to have suffered badly in Tassilo's cursed hands. The minstrel must have reckoned he'd need him hale and not too unhappy as a hostage." That sparked a thought in him. He called his son over and asked, "How was it that you went away with Tassilo when he took you away from here?"

"He promised he'd teach me his songs and show me how to play the lute," Duren answered. "He did, too, but my hands are too small to play a big one. He said he

would make me a little one, but he never did do that."
And then, to the Fox's surprise, Duren started chanting what Tassilo had called the song of Gerin at his visit to Fox Keep. He did it better than he'd ever sung before he was kidnapped; in that, at least, the minstrel had kept his promise. It wasn't remotely enough.

One of the cooks came out and said, "Lords, the feast begins!" The warriors streamed into the great hall. Even with chairs and benches brought down from upstairs, it was still packed tight.

Fat-wrapped thighbones smoked on Dyaus' altar by the hearth. When a servant brought Gerin a jack of ale, he poured a libation to Baivers and the rest of the ale down his throat. A serving woman picked her way down the narrow space between benches, pulling rounds of flatbread from a platter piled high and setting one in front of each feaster in turn.

She would have gone faster had more than a few men not tried to pull her down onto their laps or to grab at her as she went past. One of them wound up with flatbread draped over his face instead of on the table before him. "I'm so sorry, noble sir," she said, very much as if she meant it.

A cook with a sheep's head on a spit carried it to the fire and carefully started singeing off the wool. "Oh, that will be fine when it's finished," Drago said. He thumped his thick middle. "Have to remember to save some room for it."

Servants with meat more quickly cooked—steaks and chops and roasted slices of hearts and kidneys and livers—came by and set the sizzling gobbets on top of the flatbreads. The feasters attacked them with belt knives and fingers. They threw gnawed bones down into the dry rushes that covered the floor. Dogs growled and snarled at one another as they scrambled for scraps.

Aragis the Archer raised his drinking jack in salute to Gerin, who sat across the table from him. "You're a generous host, lord prince," he said.

"We do what we can, grand duke," the Fox replied. "Once in a while, for celebration, is all well and good. If we ate like this every day, we'd all starve, serfs and nobles together, long before midwinter rolled around."

"I understand that full well," Aragis said. "Between war and hunger and disease, we live on the edge of a cliff. But by the gods, it's fine sometimes to step back from the edge and make life into what it was meant to be: plenty of food, plenty of drink—you brew a fine ale—and no worries, not for today." He raised his jack again, then drained it. A servant with a pitcher made haste to refill it.

Selatre turned to Gerin. Under the noise of the crowd, she said, "Surely there's more to life than a full belly."

"I think so, too," he said, nodding. "So does Aragis, no doubt, or he'd be content to stay in his castle and stuff himself. If you ask me, he'd sooner drink power than ale." But then, trying to be just, he added, "If you don't have a full belly, not much else matters. Years the harvest fails, you find out about that." He paused thoughtfully. "What civilization is, I suppose, is the things you find to worry about after your belly's full."

"I like that," Selatre said. Now she nodded. "Well said."

Van sat at Gerin's right hand, with Duren between them. He'd been talking with Fand, and missed Gerin's words. Selatre's brisk statement of approval caught his notice. "What's well said, Fox?" he asked.

Gerin repeated himself. Van thought it over—perhaps a bit more intensely than he might have at other times, for he'd emptied his drinking jack again and again—and finally nodded. "Something to that." He waved a big arm in a gesture that almost knocked a plate out of a servant's hands. "You Elabonians, you've a great many things past farming. I give you so much, that I do."

Fand rounded on him. "And what o' my own folk?" she demanded. "Sure and you're not with the southrons who call us woodsrunners and barbarous savages and all, are you now?"

"Now, now, lass, I said nothing of the sort. I didn't speak of the Trokmoi at all, just of the folk of my friend here," Van answered, mildly enough. Gerin breathed a silent sigh of relief; he'd seen trouble riding Fand's question as sure as rain rode a squall line. Then, to his dismay, the outlander, instead of leaving well enough alone, went on, "Though now that you ask me, I will say that, since I traveled the forests of the Trokmoi from north to south, I'd far sooner live here than there. More good things to life here, taken all in all."

"Would you, now?" In the space of three words, Fand's voice rose to a screech that made heads whip around. "Well, have some fine Elabonian ale, then!" She picked up her drinking jack and poured it over Van's head, then got up from the bench and started to stalk off.

Snorting and cursing and blinking because the stinging stuff ran down into his eyes, Van reached out a meaty hand and hauled her back. She squawked and swung at him. He blocked the blow with his other arm, slammed her down into her seat hard enough to make her teeth come together with a loud click. "Here, see how you like it," he said, and drenched her with his jack of ale.

She cursed him in Elabonian and the forest tongue, loudly and ingeniously. He just sat there grinning, which fanned the fires of her wrath.

"Go on, both of you, and dry yourselves off," Gerin said, uncomfortably aware a common role for a would-be peacemaker was taking arrows from both sides. "Van may say what he thinks—"

"I'd like to see anyone stop me," the outlander put in.

"Shut up, will you?" Gerin hissed at him before continuing, "—and you, lady, may agree or not, as you judge best. But if you drench someone, you shouldn't be surprised or even angry to get drenched in return."

He waited for her to flare back at him, but every once in a while logic reached her. This proved one of those times. "Aye, summat to that," she said, tossing her head so little drops of ale flew from her coppery hair. She looked warily at Van. "Quits for now?"

"Aye, for now." This time, the outlander got up first. Fand followed him. Gerin wondered if they'd look for a towel or the nearest bedchamber. He laughed a little. Even if Fand wasn't his woman any more, he still got involved in her quarrels.

After a while, Duren said, "Why aren't Van and Fand coming back?"

"I think they're probably making up their quarrel," Gerin answered, smiling.

"Seldom dull around this place, is it?" Aragis said. He was smiling, too, more than half in bemusement. "My keep is more, mm, sedate."

By which you mean anyone who doesn't think like you had best not let you know it, Gerin thought. But how the Archer ran his holding was his business. Duren curled up in the space Fand and Van had vacated and went to sleep. Gerin ruffled his hair and said, "Somebody finds it dull, anyhow." He stared down at the little boy, still hardly daring to believe he had him back again, then raised his jack to Aragis in salute. Returning Duren made up for a multitude of the grand duke's sins.

Presently Van and Fand did return. Fand looked rumpled. The outlander looked smug. They both looked surprised when they found Duren stretched out where they'd been sitting.

"Don't worry," Gerin said. "You can have your places back. I'll take him up to bed." He scooped up his son, who wiggled and muttered but did not wake.

Selatre drained her drinking jack, set it down, and brought a hand up to her mouth to cover a yawn. "I'm for my own bed," she announced. "I'll walk up with you, if that's all right."

"Your company is better than just all right, as you know very well," Gerin said. He lifted Duren up as high as he could, to keep the boy's dangling legs from catching any of the feasters in the head, and made his way toward the stairs. Selatre followed.

Duren sighed again when Gerin put him down in the bed they both used. Duren muttered something, but Gerin couldn't make out what it was. "He has the look of you," Selatre said.

The Fox nodded as he straightened up. "He has my coloring, certainly. I suppose his features are mostly mine, too." Gently, he pulled off his sleeping son's shoes and tossed them by the side of the bed. "After what happened, I hate to leave him alone, even for an instant."

"I don't blame you," Selatre said. "But if he's not safe here in your bedchamber, where can he be safe?"

"The way the world wags now? Maybe nowhere," Gerin said bleakly. "None of us is really safe these days." He took a couple of steps over to Selatre, put his arms around her, and kissed her. "We just have to do the best we can, that's all."

She nodded. "Do you think you could leave him alone long enough to come with me to my little chamber?"

He paused in some surprise before he answered: she hadn't invited him to her chamber before. After he'd given it to her, he'd stayed out of it, not wanting to infringe on the privacy he knew she craved. On the other hand, the two of them would need privacy from Duren now.

She'd grown up with everyone sleeping and doing everything else in one big bed, but he hadn't. He slipped an arm around her waist. "I think I'll take that chance."

Afterwards, though, he quickly dressed and returned to his own room. Wanting to make sure Duren was safe was only part of that. Selatre's chamber lay on the south side of the hall, and its window faced south. Light from the moons streamed into the chamber and cast multiple shifting shadows. With what lay ahead, Gerin wanted to think about the moons as little as he could.

Golden Math came full first. That night passed well enough: Tiwaz was two days before full, ruddy Elleb and Nothos both one day before. All three of them had risen earlier than Math, and so their rays did much to diminish the one full moon's effect.

From the werenight of five years before, Gerin knew which of his men were vulnerable to taking beast's shape. The two he worried most about were Widin Simrin's son—who'd been just a boy at the time of the werenight—and Parol Chickpea. He wondered how Parol was, down in the serf village. Widin he locked away in the cellar with the ale; the youngster came through that first night unchanged.

He fretted more over Aragis' men than over his own, for they were an unknown quantity to him. He asked the Archer which of his men had the were taint, but Aragis was vague: "Lord prince, that's hard for me to answer, for my vassals were most of 'em at their own keeps the night of the werenight. The Trokmoi hadn't reached my lands yet, so we were still at ease. Afterwards, I had more urgent things to worry about than finding out which of my warriors had donned beast shape. I just didn't see the need."

Gerin looked down his nose at the grand duke. "Which

means we're vulnerable now," he said in reproof as mild as he could make it. No, Aragis wasn't forethoughtful enough; when something had gone, he assumed its like would return no more.

As the next evening approached, the one on which Elleb and pale Nothos would be full and swift-moving Tiwaz and Math but one day to either side of it, he sent all of Aragis' men save the Archer himself, Marlanz Raw-Meat, and Fabors Fabur's son out to the tented encampment they'd made. If trouble broke out, he wanted it well away from the keep. To his relief, the only comment Aragis made was, "A sensible precaution, lord prince."

The Fox sent Widin Simrin's son to his shelter and mewed him up, saying, "If you don't change tonight, you probably won't tomorrow. But better safe—we'll enclose you then, too." Widin just nodded; he knew necessity when he saw it.

Tiwaz came up over the eastern horizon first, a day before full and not far from round. Then, as the sun set, Elleb and Nothos rose side by side. Gerin watched them from the palisade. No cries of alarm rent the air the instant the two full moons appeared, for which he gave hearty thanks. Golden Math soon followed. Because she moved through her phases more slowly than Tiwaz, her bright disk was even closer to a perfect circle than his.

When all four moons were in the sky and no screams of horror had come from within the keep or from the tents where Aragis' men sheltered, the Fox decided he could safely descend and eat supper. He'd been sensible enough to have plenty of ale brought up before he closed Widin in the cellar, so washing down his meat would not be a problem.

Aragis, who was already gnawing on beef ribs basted with a spicy sauce, greeted him with a wave and something not far from a sneer. "All quiet as the tomb here, lord prince. Seems to me you fretted over nothing."

Gerin shrugged. "Better to be ready for trouble and not have it than to have it and not be ready, as happened at the werenight of the four full moons."

"Can't quarrel hard with that, I suppose," Aragis admitted. He took another big bite from the rib he was holding; grease ran down his chin. "Your cooks do a fine job indeed; I give you that without any argument."

"Glad something here makes you happy," Gerin answered. He waved to one of the kitchen servants for some ribs of his own.

"Only thing that bothers me about sitting here some days eating your good food is that we could have been out campaigning already, striking at the Trokmoi and the monsters," Aragis said.

"They'll be there, grand duke, never fear," Gerin said. The servant plopped a round of flatbread on the table in front of him, then set atop it several steaming ribs. He tried to pick one up, scorched his fingers, and stuck them in his mouth. Aragis hid a chuckle behind a swig of ale.

"I thought you were the patient sort, lord prince," Fabors Fabur's son said slyly, a gibe enough to the point to make Gerin's ears heat.

"I don't know why everyone is praising the food to the skies," Marlanz Raw-Meat grumbled. "They've cooked it to death, and that after I told them and told them I like it with the juice still in it."

Gerin stared over toward the gobbet of meat Marlanz was attacking. It might have been lightly singed on the outside, but juice and blood from it soaked the flatbread on which it lay. If Marlanz wanted it cooked less, he should have torn it off a cow as the beast ran by.

Before he could say as much, Gerin looked from the

dripping chunk of meat to Marlanz himself. His beard seemed thicker and bushier than it had moments before, his teeth extraordinarily long and white and sharp. His eyes gave back the torchlight with red glints of their own.

"Meat!" he snarled. "Rrraw meat!" The backs of his hands grew hairier by the heartbeat.

"Your pardon," Fabors Fabur's son said, his voice rising to a frightened squeak as he slid down the bench away from his friend. Aragis' eyes were wide and staring. Van started to draw his sword, then slammed it back into its sheath. Gerin understood that; he'd stopped his own hand halfway to the hilt of his blade. Unless struck with silver, werebeasts knit as fast as they were cut. He'd seen that, to his horror and dismay, during the werenight.

"Rrrraw meat!" Marlanz said again, and growled deep in his throat. His voice was hardly a voice at all—more like an angry howl.

"Give him what he wants," Gerin called quickly to the frightened-looking cooks. "Raw meat, and lots of it."

The men used that as an excuse to flee the great hall. Gerin hoped one of them, at least, would be brave enough to come back with meat. If not, Marlanz was going to try getting it from the warriors and women with whom he'd sat down to supper.

A cook, staggering under the weight of the haunch he carried on a platter, came slowly out of the kitchens. He did not bring the meat out to Marlanz, but set it down between the hearth and Dyaus' altar and then retreated much faster than he'd advanced. Gerin found himself unable to complain. That the fellow had come back at all was enough.

The Fox rose and edged past Marlanz, whose tongue lolled from jaws that had stretched remarkably to accommodate the improved cutlery they now contained. "Good wolf," Gerin said in a friendly way, as if he were talking to one of the keep's dogs. He looked around for those dogs, and did not see them—they'd all run outside as Marlanz began to change. They wanted no part of him. Gerin didn't, either, but he had less choice.

Grunting, he picked up the platter and carried it over to Marlanz. He bowed over it as if he were an innkeeper serving up an elaborate repast at some splendid hostelry in the City of Elabon. Indeed, his concern for his client's satisfaction was even more pressing than such an innkeeper's: none of their guests was likely to devour them if displeased with his proffered supper.

Marlanz looked from the dripping haunch to Gerin and back again. He bent low over the meat and sniffed it, as if to make certain no flame had ever touched it. Then, not bothering with the knife that lay on the table by the platter, he began to feed. That was the only word that seemed appropriate to Gerin—Marlanz tore off bite after bite with his teeth, worked his jaws briefly, and gulped down the barely chewed chunks. Meat vanished from the bone at an astonishing rate.

Gerin hurried back to the kitchens. "That haunch may not be enough," he warned. "What else have you?"

A cook pointed. "There's but half a pig's carcass, lord prince, that we were going to—"

"Never mind what you were going to do with it," Gerin snapped. Some of the doctors down in the City of Elabon reckoned eating raw pork unhealthy. That, as far as the Fox was concerned, was Marlanz's lookout. He grabbed the split carcass by the legs and lugged it out into the great hall.

As he came up to Marlanz, he realized that the offal from the carcass would have served just as well in the noble's present condition. He did not, however, have the temerity to haul the meat back from the kitchens. Instead, he set it on the table in front of Marlanz, who began destroying it with the same wolfish single-mindedness he'd shown on the chunk of beef.

"He can't eat all that," Van said as Gerin cautiously sat back down.

"You have my leave to tell him as much," Gerin said. "Go right ahead." Van sat where he was; he was as bold as any man ever born, but a long way from a fool. Fand set a hand on his arm, as if to congratulate him for his good sense. That surprised Gerin, who would have expected her to urge the outlander into any fight that came along.

"I'd have tried fighting him, lord prince," Aragis said, his eyes shifting back and forth from Gerin to Marlanz. "Your way is better, though. You're sorry to lose so much meat, no doubt, but you'd be sorrier losing men hurt or killed against a werebeast that can't be slain—and one who's a good vassal when in his proper shape."

"That last weighed heaviest on my mind," Gerin said.

"For which I am in your debt," Aragis said, "and Marlanz will be when he comes back to himself."

Marlanz wasn't quite in full beast shape, as he would have been during the werenight of five years before; he seemed rather a man heavily overlain with wolf. That made Gerin wonder if he possessed the full invulnerability werebeasts had enjoyed then. Some experiments, he'd found, were more interesting to think about than to try. And, as Aragis had said, Marlanz was a good fellow—and certainly looked to be a good warrior—when fully human.

The Fox wondered if he was going to have to get more meat still to set before Marlanz. As a werebeast, he ate like a wolf. Little by little, though, Marlanz slowed. He glared around at the unchanged men and women watching him, then picked up what was left of the pig carcass with mouth and pawlike hands and carried it over to a

dark corner of the great hall. There he set it down while
he heaped up rushes beside it into a sort of nest. He lay
down in that nest, turned himself around a couple of
times to accommodate its shape to his, and fell asleep.

"I hope he sleeps well," Gerin said sincerely. "Come
sunrise tomorrow, he'll be a man again."

Selatre giggled. "And wondering mightily, too, how
he happened to end up on the floor beside half—no,
less than that now—a dead pig."

"Maybe we'll call him Marlanz Pork-Ribs," Rihwin
said blithely.

Fabors Fabur's son sent him a serious look. "Van of
the Strong Arm might possibly do that and have it taken
in good part. For anyone less imposing, such chaffing is
liable to be unwise."

"I think you're likely to be right," Gerin said. He too
gave Rihwin a severe look. Sometimes Rihwin paid
attention to such signals, sometimes he didn't. Gerin
hoped this was one of the times he did, because he might
end up very sorry if he got Marlanz angry at him.

"I hope that will be our only excitement for the night,"
Selatre said. Even Van, an incurable adventurer, nodded; the horrors of the werenight must have burned
themselves into his memory for good.

Gerin said, "I'll check and see how Widin is doing."
He went down to the door of the cellar, rapped on it,
and asked, "Are you all right in there, Widin?"

"Aye, and still in my own shape, too," his young vassal
answered. "May I come out now?"

"I don't see why not," Gerin answered. "Marlanz Raw-
Meat's long since gone were; if the fit hasn't hit you by
now, I don't expect it will tonight." He unbarred the door
and released Widin.

"What sort of beast is he?" Widin asked.

"Wolf, like most northern werecreatures," the Fox said.

"Actually, he's about half wolf and half man right now. He's gone to sleep in the rushes, guarding some meat like a hound. Come upstairs to the great hall, and you can see him for yourself."

He led Widin upstairs. Widin gave the sleeping Marlanz a wide berth, and did not turn his back on him even for a moment. That struck the Fox as eminently practical. A trooper who'd drawn palisade duty came to the entrance to the great hall and said, "Lord prince, a warrior of Aragis' wants us to let down the gate so he can have speech with you."

"Is he in his own proper shape, with no beasts with him?" Gerin asked after a moment's thought.

"Aye, lord, he is," the sentry answered. "The moons are so bright, nothing could hide, neither."

"We'll let him in, then," Gerin decided. He walked out to the gate and told that to the men who worked the drawbridge, adding, "but we'll raise the bridge again as soon as he's across it into the courtyard here." That would mean more work for the men, but he did not want to leave the keep open and vulnerable to whatever lurked under two full moons and the other two nearly full.

Down rattled the drawbridge. As soon as Aragis' warrior had crossed it, the gate crew hauled it back up again. The fellow came over to Gerin and sketched a salute. "Lord prince, I'm Rennewart Forkbeard, one of Aragis' vassals, as your man said." He was middle-aged, solid-looking, and wore his beard in the old-fashioned style his ekename described.

"What's toward in your camp out there?" Gerin asked. "You've had a man take beast shape, is that it?"

To his surprise, Rennewart shook his head. "No, it's not that. Oh, a couple of the lads are hairier than they have any business being, but they're all still their own selves, if you know what I mean. We aren't worried about 'em. No, the thing of it is, just a little bit ago we had a man walk into camp naked as the day he was born, and a deal bigger. He's not one of ours. We were wondering if he came from the keep here some kind of way, or maybe from your peasant village not far off."

"Why do you need to ask me?" Gerin said. "Why not just ask him?"

"Lord prince, the thing of it is, he won't talk—won't say a word, I mean," Rennewart answered. "Won't or maybe can't—I don't know which. We figured you'd know him if anybody did."

"Yes, I suppose I would," Gerin said, puzzled: his holding had a couple of deaf-mutes, but they lived in distant villages and had no reason to show up at Fox Keep in the middle of the night, especially naked. He plucked at his beard; his curiosity was tickled. "All right, Rennewart, I'll come out and look at him."

The walk from keep to camp was short enough that the ghosts did not much afflict him before he came to the area protected by the sacrifices Aragis' men had made. Most of them were awake, either on watch or aroused by word of the strange newcomer.

"We brought him into my tent, lord prince," Rennewart said, leading Gerin to it and holding the flap wide. "Here he is."

Gerin drew his sword before he went in, wary of a trap. But the inside of the tent was brightly lit by several lamps, and held only some blankets and, as promised, one naked man sprawling on them.

"I've never set eyes on him before," Gerin said positively. "I'd know him, were he from my lands." The fellow was almost Van's size, and just as well-thewed as the enormous outlander. He was swarthy and hairy, with a beard that came up almost to his dark eyes and a hairline that started just above them. "Who are you?" the Fox asked. "Where are you from?"

The naked man listened with every sign of attention—mute he might be, but he wasn't deaf—but didn't answer. Gerin tried again, this time in the Trokmê language. The fellow stirred on the blankets, but again gave no answer and no real sign he understood.

"We tried that, too, lord prince, with no better luck than you just had," Rennewart Forkbeard said.

"Go fetch my companion, Van of the Strong Arm," Gerin said. "He knows more different languages than any other man I've met."

Rennewart hurried away, and soon returned with the outlander. Listening to the drawbridge go down and up, Gerin spared a moment's sympathy for the gate crew. Van stared at the naked man with interest. Like the Fox, he started off with Elabonian and the Trokmê tongue, and failed with both. Then he used the guttural language of the Gradi, who lived north of the Trokmoi, and after that brought no response he spoke in the hissing tongue used by the nomads of the Shanda plains. Those, at least, Gerin recognized. Van tried what must have been a dozen languages in all, maybe more. The shifting sounds of his words interested the naked man, but not enough to make him say anything past a couple of grunts. After a while, Van spread his hands. "I give up, Captain," he said, returning to Elabonian.

"Come to think of it, I have one other tongue," Gerin said, and addressed the naked stranger in Sithonian, a language he read more fluently than he spoke it. He might as well have saved his breath.

"He can hear," Rennewart said. "We saw that."

"Aye, and he's not altogether mute, anyhow," the Fox agreed. "But—" He paused, a suspicion growing in him, then said, "Maybe what he needs is a jack of ale. Could you bring him one, please?"

Rennewart sent him a first-rate dubious look, but brought the jack as asked. He handed it to Gerin, saying, "Here, you want him to have this, *you* give it to him."

Gerin took the couple of steps that brought him over to the naked man. He held out the leather jack, smiling invitingly. The stranger took it, gaped at it, but did not raise it to his lips. Quietly, Van said, "It's like he never saw one before."

"I'm beginning to think that's just what it's like," Gerin answered. He took back the jack, drank from it to show what it was for, and returned it to the naked man. The fellow drank then, clumsily, so ale trickled through his beard and dripped on the ground. He spent a moment thinking over the taste, then smacked his lips and gulped down the rest of the ale. He held out the jack to Gerin with a hopeful expression.

Gerin pulled him to his feet. "Here, come along with me," he said, and eked out his words with gestures. The naked man followed him willingly enough. So did Van and Rennewart, both looking curious.

The naked man jumped when the drawbridge thudded down, but went across it with the Fox. The feasters in the great hall stared at the newcomer; Gerin hoped Van didn't notice Fand's admiring glance. He gave the fellow another jack of ale, then took a pitcherful with him as he led the naked man down to the cellar from which he'd but lately released Widin.

Lured by the prospect of more ale, the stranger again accompanied him without protest. Gerin set the pitcher on the ground. As the stranger made for it, the Fox hurried out of the cellar, shut the door behind him, and dropped the bar. Then he went back up to the great hall, poured a jack of ale for himself, and gulped it down in one long draught.

"All right, Captain, what was that all about?" Van demanded when he thumped the jack down on the table. "You know something; I can see it in your face."

Gerin shook his head. "Come morning, I'll know something. Now I just suspect."

"Suspect what?" several people answered in the same breath.

"I suspect I just locked a werebeast in the cellar," Gerin answered.

Again several people spoke at once, Aragis loudest and most to the point: "But that was no beast—he was a man."

"And quite a man he was, too," Fand murmured, which drew her a sharp look from Van.

"When men go were, they take beast shape," the Fox said, filling his drinking jack again. "If a beast goes were, though, what would it become? A man, unless all logic lies. And look at this fellow—not just at how hairy he was, either. He had no idea how to be a man. He wore no clothes, he couldn't speak, he didn't know what a cup was for till I showed him. . . . As I say, we'll know for certain come morning, when we open the cellar door after moonset and see who—or what—is down there."

Aragis shook his head, still doubtful. But Selatre said, "I like the notion. It might even explain how the monsters came to be: suppose a female beast turned woman long years ago, and a farmer or hunter found her and had his way with her and got her with child. Come morning, she'd be an animal once more, but who knows what litter she would have borne?"

"It could be so," Gerin said, nodding. "Or men as werebeasts might have mixed their blood with females of their beast kind. Either way, you're right—the get might be horrific. It's a better guess at how the monsters began than any that's crossed my mind." He raised his jack in salute to her cleverness.

"If you conceive by me, you'll know what you'll have, lass," Van said to Fand.

"More trouble than I'd know what to do with, I expect," she retorted.

"How d'you put a viper's tongue in such a pretty mouth?" he asked, and she looked smug.

The ale ran out not long after that, and no one seemed enthusiastic about going down to the cellar for more, not with the stranger down there. No one seemed enthusiastic about staying in the great hall, either, even if Marlanz had plenty of raw meat by his side as he slept. The kitchen helpers went to their quarters and barred the door. Everyone else went upstairs.

Gerin made sure the sun was well up—which meant full Elleb and Nothos would be well down—before he went downstairs the next morning. Even then, he went not only armed but ready to beat a hasty retreat.

He found Marlanz Raw-Meat back in fully human form, and just sitting up in the rushes, looking mightily confused at how he'd got there and even more confused at the pile of well-gnawed pig bones beside him. "How strong *do* you brew your ale, lord prince?" he asked. "Funny, though—it must have been a mighty carouse, but my head doesn't hurt."

"It wasn't ale—it was the moons," Gerin answered, and explained what had happened the night before.

Marlanz stared, then slowly nodded and got to his feet. "I'm told the same fit came over me, only stronger, at the great werenight five years gone by. I remember nothing of that night, either."

Van came downstairs then, also armed. He grunted in relief to see Marlanz without visible traces of lycanthropy, then said, "Shall we go down to the cellar and see what your wereman's become?"

That required more explanations for Marlanz. When they were through, Aragis' vassal pulled out his own sword and said, "Let's slay the appalling creature."

"If we can get it out of the keep without fighting, I'll be just as happy to do that," Gerin answered.

Marlanz stared, then realized he meant what he said. "You are the lord here," he said, in tones that implied he was willing to obey even if he wouldn't have gone about things thus himself.

"Take a shield off the wall and carry some of those bones of yours in it," Gerin told him. "Maybe they'll make the thing in the cellar as happy as they made you—and you didn't quite get all the meat off them."

Marlanz's stare turned reproachful, but he did as he was asked. Van said, "What if it's still a man down there?"

"We'll find him something else for breakfast," Gerin replied, which had the virtue of making both his companions shut up.

They went down to the cellar together. Gerin unbarred the door and pushed it open. "Father Dyaus above," Marlanz said softly—a medium-sized black bear sprawled on the dirt floor. The beast looked up at them in absurd surprise.

It did not growl, nor did the hair on its back rise. It didn't jump up and flee into the dark recesses of the cellar, either. "What's wrong with it?" Van demanded, as if he assumed Gerin would know.

And, for a wonder, Gerin did. "It's still got ale coursing through it from last night. That was a good-sized pitcher, and who knows when in man-shape it might have finished?" He paused, then chuckled. "I'm glad it's a friendly drunk."

Luring the bear upstairs with bones proved easy,

though it wobbled as it walked. "I still say we ought to kill it," Marlanz grumbled as the gate crew let down the drawbridge and the bear staggered off toward the forest.

"We didn't try killing *you* last night," Gerin reminded him.

"Lucky for you that you didn't," Marlanz said, drawing himself up with prickly pride. Gerin agreed with him, but wasn't about to admit it.

XI

The next night, only Tiwaz was full, with Elleb and Nothos a day past and Math two. This time, Gerin sent Marlanz Raw-Meat down to the cellar and locked Widin Simrin's son in the shack where he worked on his magics. To his great relief, neither Marlanz nor Widin changed shape, so he released them both when all four moons had risen into the sky.

The bear that walked like a man did not return to the camp of Aragis' warriors, either in man's form or its own. Gerin had wondered if a taste for ale would draw it back.

"Just as well it's staying away," said Drago, a Bear himself, when Gerin remarked on that. "We don't need a thirsty bear when we have a thirsty Fox." He sent Rihwin the Fox a sly look. Rihwin ostentatiously ignored him.

Late the next afternoon, Parol Chickpea came into Fox Keep, riding in the back of a peasant's oxcart. "By the gods, I'm glad to see you," Gerin exclaimed. "When I left you behind there, I feared you'd never come out of that village again."

"I feared it myself, lord, but I went were night before last, and here, look at this." Parol thrust the hand from which he'd lost a couple of fingers under Gerin's nose.

"I see what you mean," Gerin said. The wound, instead of being festering and full of pus, looked as if he'd had it for years. The rapid healing werebeasts enjoyed hadn't been able to restore his missing digits, but had done the next best thing. Somehow, the Fox doubted it would ever become a popular part of medicine all the same.

"The bite on my arse is better, too," Parol said

confidentially, "but I don't suppose you want to see that."

"As a matter of fact, you're right," Gerin said. "I wasn't interested in your hairy bum before you had a chunk bitten out of it, and I'm not interested in it now, except to see if it makes you sit at a tilt."

"It doesn't, by Dyaus!" Parol was the picture of indignation till he noticed the smirk Gerin was trying to hide. He laughed sheepishly. "Ah, you're having a joke on me."

"So I am." Gerin felt embarrassed; jokes at the expense of Parol were too easy to be much fun. To make amends, he told the warrior something about which he'd just made up his own mind: "Now that we've passed through the little werenight, we'll start the move against Adiatunnus and the monsters come sunrise tomorrow."

Parol beamed. "Ah, that's very fine, lord. I owe those horrible creatures something special for all they've done to me, and I aim to give it to them."

"Stout fellow!" Gerin said. Parol was not the best fighting man he had, lacking both Rihwin's grace and cleverness on the one hand and Drago the Bear's indomitable strength on the other. But he was not in the habit of backing away from trouble, and that covered a multitude of sins.

The tents in which Aragis' men had passed the nights since they reached Fox Keep came down. The warriors stored most of them inside the keep, bringing along only a few in which they could crowd together in case of rain. Gerin was less worried about Aragis' men coming into Fox Keep than he had been when they first arrived. Not only had the grand duke shown he didn't intend treachery, but enough of Gerin's troopers had come into the area to put up a solid fight if Aragis suddenly changed his mind. The force that rolled southwest against Adiatunnus and the monsters had more of Gerin's men in it than Aragis'.

Leaving Fox Keep stirred mixed feelings in Gerin: hope that this fight, unlike the ones that had gone before, would yield decisive results; sorrow at leaving Selatre behind; and a separate mixture over Duren: sorrow at leaving him, too, but also joy that he was there to be left.

Aragis brought his chariot up alongside the Fox's. "You have a good holding here," he said. "Plenty of timber, streams where you need them, well-tended fields—you must get a lot of work out of your peasants."

Gerin didn't care for the way Aragis said that: it brought to his mind a picture of nobles standing over serfs with whips to make them sow and weed and harvest. Maybe such things happened on Aragis' land—he had a reputation for ruthlessness. The Fox said, "They work for themselves, as much as they can. I don't take a certain proportion of what they raise, whether that's a lot or a little. I take a fixed amount, and they keep whatever they produce above that."

"All very well in good years," Aragis answered, "but what of the bad ones, when they don't bring in enough to get by after you've gathered your fixed amount?"

"Then we dicker, of course," Gerin said. "If my serfs all starve giving me this year's dues, I'm not likely to get much out of them next year."

Aragis thought that over, then saw the joke and laughed. "I don't dicker with peasants," he said. "I tell them how it's going to be, and that's how it is. As you say, starving them is wasteful, but I always remember I come first."

"I believe that, grand duke," Gerin said, so innocently that Aragis again paused for a moment before sending him a sharp look. Smiling inside, Gerin went on, "I haven't had a peasant revolt since I took over this holding, and we've been through some lean years, especially the one right after the werenight. How have you fared there?"

"Not well," Aragis admitted, but his tone made that seem unimportant. "When the peasants rise up, we knock them down. They can't stand against us, and they know it. They've no weapons to speak of, and no experience fighting, either."

"But if they're going to fight the monsters, they'll need more weapons than they have, and if they spend a good deal of time fighting the monsters, they'll get some experience at that, too," Gerin said.

Aragis gave him a look that said he hadn't thought so far ahead, and wished the Fox hadn't, either. After a long silence, he answered, "You must be of the view that solving one problem always breeds another."

"Oh, not always," Gerin said blithely. "Sometimes it breeds two or three."

Aragis opened his mouth, closed it, opened it again, and finally shook his head without speaking. He tapped his driver on the shoulder. Gerin was not surprised when the grand duke's chariot dropped back behind his own. Van laughed a little and said, "Here you went to all the trouble of making an ally of the Archer, and now you do your best to drive him away."

"I didn't mean to," Gerin said. He sounded so much like Duren after he'd dropped a pot and broken it that he started to laugh at himself.

When the dirt road went through the woods, it narrowed so that the chariots had to string themselves out single file. It was wider in the cleared lands between the forests; the cars bunched up again there.

The peasants working the fields paused to stare as the chariots rolled by. Some of them cheered and waved. Gerin wondered what Aragis thought of that. From all he'd said, and from all the Fox had heard, he ruled his serfs by force. He was a hard and able man, so he'd got away with it thus far, but was his heir likely to match him? Only time would answer that.

Gerin noted that a fair number of peasants cultivated their wheat and barley and beans and peas and turnips and squashes with full quivers on their backs. As one of them moved down a row, he bent, picked up his bow, carried it along with him, and then set it down again. Herdsmen also carried bows, and spears in place of their staves. What they could do against the monsters, they were doing. But an unarmored man, even with a spear in his hands, was not a good bet against the speed and cleverness the creatures showed.

The Fox saw only one monster that first day of the ride southwest. The thing came out of the woods a couple of furlongs ahead of his chariot. It stared at the great host of chariotry rattling its way, then turned and swiftly vanished back between the beeches from which it had emerged.

"Shall we hunt it, Captain?" Van asked.

Gerin shook his head. "We'd be wasting our time. If we can beat Adiatunnus, we'll take their refuge away from the creatures. That'll do us far more good over the long haul than picking them off one and two at a time."

"Sometimes you think so straight, you cook all the juice out of life," Van said, but let it go at that.

As sunset neared, Gerin bought a sheep from a village through which he passed. That provoked fresh bemusement from Aragis, who, like a large majority of lords, was accustomed to taking what he needed from his serfs regardless of whether it was properly part of his feudal dues. The grand duke also seemed surprised when the Fox told some of his warriors to cut firewood rather than taking it from the serfs or putting them to work. But he did not question Gerin about it and, indeed, after a few minutes ordered his own men to help those of his ally.

With all four moons now past full, the early hours of the night were unusually dark. Although the evening was warm and sultry, Gerin ordered the fires kept burning brightly. "The last thing I want is for the monsters to take us unawares," he said, after which he got no arguments.

The dancing flames kept more men sitting around them and talking than would have happened on most nights. After a while, Drago the Bear turned to Van and said, "What about a tale for us, to make the time pass by?" To several of Aragis' men sitting close to him, he added, "You've never heard a yarnspinner to match him, I promise you."

"Aye, give us a tale, then," one of those troopers said eagerly, and in a moment many more—and many of Gerin's men as well—took up the cry.

Van got to his feet with a show of shyness Gerin knew to be assumed. The outlander said, "I hate to tell a tale now, friends, for after Drago's spoken of me so, how can I help but disappoint?"

"You never have yet," one of Gerin's men called. "Give us a tale of far places—you must've seen more of 'em than any man alive."

"A tale of far places?" Van said. "All right, I'll give you another story of Mabalal, the hot country where they teach the monkeys to gather pepper for 'em—some of you will remember my tale about that. But this is a different yarn; you might call it the tale of the mountain snake, even though it's really about the snake's head, as you'll see.

"Now, they have all manner of snakes in Mabalal. The plains snake, if you'll believe it, is so big that he even hunts elephants now and again; the only time the natives go after him is when he's fighting one of those huge beasts."

"What's an elephant?" somebody asked. Gerin knew about elephants, but had his doubts about serpents big enough to hunt them—although he'd never managed to catch his friend in a lie about his travels. After Van explained, the warrior who'd asked the question was loudly dubious about the elephant's snaky trunk, though Gerin knew that was a genuine part of its anatomy.

"Well, never mind," the outlander said. "This story's not about elephants or plains snakes, anyhow. Like I said, it's about mountain snakes. Mountain snakes, now, aren't as big as their cousins of the plain, but they're impressive beasts, too. They have a fringe of golden scales under their chins that looks like a beard, and a crest of pointed red scales down the back of their necks almost like a horse's mane. When they're burrowing in the mountains, the sound their scales make reminds you of bronze blades clashing against each other."

"Are they venomous?" Gerin asked; unlike most if not all of his companions, he was in part interested in Van's stories for their natural—or perhaps unnatural—history.

"I should say they are!" Van answered. "But that's not why the men of Mabalal hunt them—in fact, it'd be a good reason to leave 'em alone. The snakes sometimes grow these multicolored stones in their heads, the way oysters grow pearls, but these stones are supposed to make you invisible. That's what they say in Mabalal, anyhow.

"There was this wizard there, a chap named Marabananda, who wanted a snakestone and needed an axeman to help him get it. He hired me, mostly on account of I'm bigger'n any three Mabalali you could find.

"Marabananda wove gold letters into a scarlet cloth and cast a spell of sleep over them. Then he carried the cloth out to one of the mountain snakes' nests. The snake heard him coming—or smelled him, or did whatever snakes do—and stuck its head out to see what was going on. He held the cloth in front of it, and as soon as the mountain snake looked, it was caught—snakes can't blink, you know, so it couldn't get free of the spell even for a moment.

"Down came my axe! Off flew the head! The snake's body, back in its burrow, jerked and twisted so much that the ground shook, just like the earthquake that knocked down the temple at Ikos. And Marabananda, he got out his knives and cut into the head—and damn me to the five hells if he didn't pull out one of those shiny, glowing snakestones I was telling you about.

" 'I'm rich!' he yells, capering around like a madman. 'I'm rich! I can walk into the king's treasure house and carry away all the gold and silver and jewels I please, and no one will see me. I'm rich!'

" 'Uh, lord wizard, sir,' says I, 'you're holding the stone now, and I can still see you.'

"Well, Marabananda says this is on account of I'm just a dirty foreigner, and too unenlightened for wizardry to touch. But the Mabalali, he says, they're more spiritually sensitive, and so the magic will work on them. He wouldn't listen to me when I tried to tell him different. But I did talk him into not trying till dead of night, in case he was wrong.

"Around midnight, off he went. He would have had me come with him, but I'd already shown the magic didn't work on me. He got to the treasure, and—" Van paused for dramatic effect.

"What happened?" half a dozen people demanded in the same breath.

The outlander bellowed laughter. "Poor damned fool, the first guard who spied him going in where he didn't belong struck off his head, same as I did with the mountain snake. I guess it goes to show the snakestone not only didn't make old Marabananda invisible to the guard, it let the guard see something even the wizard couldn't."

"What's that?" Gerin got the question in before anyone else could.

"Why, that he was a blockhead, of course," Van replied. "When he didn't come back from his little trip after a bit, I figured it had gone sour for him and I got out of there before the royal guardsmen came around with a pile of questions I couldn't answer. I don't know what happened to the mountain snake's head after that. Just like life, stories don't always have neat, tidy endings."

By the way the warriors clapped their hands and came up to chatter with Van, they liked the story fine, neat, tidy ending or no. Aragis told him, "If ever you find life dull at Fox Keep, you can stay at my holding for as long as you like, on the strength of your tales alone." When Van laughed and shook his head, the grand duke persisted, "Or if you decide you can't stomach staying with your Trokmê-tempered ladylove another moment, the same holds good."

"Ah, Archer, now you really tempt me," Van said, but he was still laughing.

"I'm for my blankets," Gerin said. "Any man with a dram of sense will do likewise. We may be fighting tomorrow, and we will be fighting the day after."

Off in the distance, a longtooth roared. Some of the horses tethered to stakes and to low-hanging branches snorted nervously; that sound was meant to instill fear. It had made Gerin afraid many times in the past. Now, though, he found it oddly reassuring. It was part of the night he'd known all his life. The monsters' higher, more savage screeches he found far more terrifying.

✦   ✦   ✦

Morning came all too soon, as it has a way of doing.
The sun shining in Gerin's face made him sit up and try
to knuckle sleep from his eyes. Where all four moons
had been absent at sunset, now they hung like pale lamps
in the western sky. Soon they would draw apart again,
and Gerin would be able to stop worrying about their
phases for a while—although he promised himself he'd
check their predicted motions in the book of tables from
time to time.

Drivers gulped hasty breakfasts of hard-baked biscuits, smoked meat, and crumbly white cheese, then hurried to harness their horses to their chariots. The warriors who rode with them, generally older men of higher
rank, finished their breakfasts while the drivers worked.
The food was no better, but time could be a luxury, too.

As soon as the chariots rolled out of Gerin's land into
the debatable ground south and west of his holding, the
troopers saw more and more monsters. The monsters
saw them, too; their hideous howls split the air. The Fox
wondered if they were warning their fellows—and
Adiatunnus' men.

In the debatable lands between Gerin's holding and
the territory Adiatunnus had taken for himself when the
Trokmoi swarmed over the Niffet, brush and shrubs and
saplings grew close to the road. The barons who'd owned
that land before had been less careful of it than the Fox
had with his. Now most of them were dead or fled. Gerin
claimed much of their holdings, but the woodsrunners
made his possession too uncertain for him to send woods-
men onto it.

The first arrows came from the cover of the roadside scrub a little past noon. One hummed past his head,
close enough to make him start. He snatched up his
shield and moved up in the car so he could hope to
protect himself and Raffo both. "Keep going," he told

the driver, and waved the rest of the chariots on as well.

"What?" Van said indignantly. "Aren't you going to stop and hunt down those cowardly sneaks who shoot without showing their faces?"

"No," Gerin answered, his voice flat. The unadorned word made Van gape and splutter, as he'd thought it would. When the outlander fell silent, the Fox explained, "I am not going to slow down in any way, shape, form, color, or size, not for monsters, not for Trokmoi. That's what Adiatunnus wants me to do, so he'll have more time to ready himself against us. I don't aim to give it to him."

"It's not manly, ignoring an enemy who's shooting at you," Van grumbled.

"I don't care," Gerin said, which set Van spluttering again despite their years of friendship. Gerin went on, "I am not fighting this war to be manly. I'm not even fighting it for loot, though anything I take from the Trokmoi helps me and hurts them. The only reason I'm fighting it is because I'll have to do it later and on worse terms if I don't do it now. Fighting it now means moving as fast as we can. We weren't quite quick enough the last time we struck at Adiatunnus. This time, the gods willing, we will be."

Van studied him some time in silence. At last the outlander said, "Me, I've heard you call Aragis the Archer ruthless a time or three. If he wanted to hang the same name on you, I think it'd fit."

"And what does that have to do with unstoppering the jar of ale?" Gerin asked. "I do what I have to do, the best way I can see to do it. You'd better pass up the little fight if you intend to win the big one."

"Put that way, it sounds good enough," Van admitted. He still looked unhappy, like a man forced to go against his better judgment. "When somebody shoots at me, though, I just want to jump down from the car, chase him till I catch him, and leave him as pickings for the crows and the foxes—no offense to you—and the flies."

"That's what the Trokmoi want us to do," Gerin answered patiently. "When you fight a war, you're better off not doing what your foe has in mind for you."

"You'll have your way here with me or without me," Van said, but then relented enough to add, "So you know, Captain, you have it with me—I suppose."

With that Gerin had to be content. By the time his army drew out of range of the archers, they'd had two horses and one man wounded, by luck none of them badly. *A small enough price to pay for avoiding delay*, he thought, relieved it was not worse.

He kept the chariots rolling almost up to the moment of sunset before stopping and sacrificing some of the hens he'd brought from Fox Keep. "Adiatunnus may know we're coming," he said, "but with luck he doesn't know we'll be in his lands so soon. We should start hitting him early tomorrow; we've made fine time coming down from my keep."

When the sun set, the night was very dark, for none of the moons would rise for more than two hours. That stretch of evening blackness would just grow over the next several days, too, till swift-moving Tiwaz sped round to the other side of the sun and began to illuminate the night once more. It worried Gerin. Because of the ghosts, his men could do little in the night, but he'd already seen that that did not hold for the monsters.

He took such precautions as he could, posting sentry squadrons all around the main area where his men and Aragis' rested. The Archer's troopers were inclined to complain about having their sleep interrupted. Gerin stared them down, saying, "When my warriors come south to your lands, we'll be under the grand duke's commands, and he'll make the arrangements he thinks best. Now the worries are mine, and I'll meet them in my own way."

He did not look to Aragis for support; this too was his worry. Had the Archer chosen to argue with him, he'd been ready to lose his temper in as spectacularly dramatic a way as he could. When he was through dealing with the grand duke's men, though, Aragis got up and said, "The prince of the north is right—he leads here. Anyone who doesn't fancy that will answer to him here and then to me after we go south." Out went the sentries without another word.

Gerin bundled himself in his bedroll and soon fell asleep. What seemed like moments later, shouts of alarm rang out from the sentries, and mixed with them the monsters' screams. The Fox had his helm on his head, his shield on his arm, and his sword in his hand and was on his feet and running toward the fighting before he fully understood where he was.

As soon as the situation did sink in, Gerin realized whoever led the monsters—whether that was Adiatunnus or some of the more clever creatures—knew how best to use them. Instead of attacking the troopers, who were armed and at least partly armored and could fight back, the monsters turned their fury on the long lines of tethered horses.

There dreadful din and chaos reigned. The horses screamed and kicked and bucked under the savage teeth and claws of their attackers. Some of them tore loose the lines by which they were tethered and ran off into the night. Every one that got away would have to be recaptured later—if Gerin and his men could manage that. At the same time, though, every horse that fled drew monsters away from the main point of the assault, which left the Fox unsure how to feel about the flight.

He had little time for feeling, anyhow—nothing to do but slash and hack and keep his shield up to hold fangs away from flesh and pray that in the darkness and confusion he didn't hurt any of his own men, or Aragis'. The fear-maddened horses were as appalled to have men close by them as monsters. Someone not far from Gerin went down with a muffled groan as a hoof caught him in the midsection.

He stabbed a monster that was scrambling up onto a horse's back—and leaving long, bleeding claw tracks in the beast's flanks. The monster howled and sprang at him. He slashed it. It screamed in pain and fled. The hot, coppery smell of its blood and the horse's filled his nose.

Pale Nothos was the first moon over the eastern horizon. By the time he rose, the warriors had managed to drive the monsters back into the wood from which they'd come. "Put more wood on the fire and start another one over here," Gerin shouted. "We have a lot of work to do yet tonight."

His army was still at it when Tiwaz, Elleb, and Math rose in a tight cluster a couple of hours after Nothos appeared. The men went out by squads to bring back the horses that had bolted, but that was the smaller part of what they needed to do. Treating the animals' wounds—and their panic—was a far bigger job. The drivers, men who dealt most intimately with their teams, did the greater part of the work. The rest of the troopers lent what help they could.

"I mislike everything about this," Gerin said gloomily. "Who knows what the beasts will do when they next face the monsters, or even smell them?"

"I'd not yet thought past this night," Aragis said. "Did we bring enough spare animals to make up for the ones we lost and those hurt too badly to pull a car?"

"I think so," the Fox answered; he'd been trying to run his own mental count, but confusion didn't make it easy. He looked at the hairy corpses scattered over the grass. "We hurt the monsters badly here; I don't think they'll try anything like that again. The question is, was the once enough?"

"We'll know come morning." Aragis yawned. "I don't know if we'll have any wits left by then, though. I'm dead for sleep, and I'm for my blanket."

"And I," Gerin said with a matching yawn. "One more thing for Adiatunnus to pay for—and he shall."

When the sun rose, Gerin stumbled over to a nearby stream and splashed cold water on his face to give himself a brittle semblance of alertness. Then he examined the horses the monsters had attacked. They looked worse by daylight than they had in the night, with blood dried on their coats and matted in their manes, with gashes the drivers had missed by the light of moons and fires, with mud slapped on the wounds the men had seen. He wondered how they would fare when they had to draw the chariots, but had no choice. He waved for the drivers to harness them.

Because the animals were sore and nervous, that took longer than it might have. But once they were hitched to the chariots, they pulled them willingly enough. Van drew a clay flute from a pouch on his belt and began a mournful, wailing tune that sounded as if it had come off the plains of Shanda. He assumed an expression of injured dignity when Gerin asked him to put the flute away for fear of frightening the horses.

The border post Adiatunnus had set up in imitation of Elabonian practice was empty and deserted; he must have got wind that Gerin was moving against him.

"We move straight on," the Fox commanded. "No stopping for loot anywhere. Until we run up against

Adiatunnus' main force and smash it, we haven't accomplished a thing."

But when the army came to a peasant village, Aragis ordered his chariots out of the road to trample the wheat and barley growing in the fields around it. After a moment's hesitation, Gerin waved for his warriors to join the Archer's. "I hate to hurt the serfs," he said, "but if I strike a blow at the Trokmoi thereby, how can I keep from doing it?"

"You can't, so don't fret yourself," Van answered. "You go to war to win; you said as much yourself. Otherwise you're a fool."

The peasants themselves had vanished, along with most of their livestock. The army took a few chickens and a half-grown pig, set fire to the serfs' huts, and rolled on.

Perhaps the next village they came to had planted earlier than the first; the wheat and rye growing around it had already turned golden. That meant the crops were nearing ripeness. It also meant they would burn. The warriors tossed torches into the fields near the road, watched flames lick across them. The serfs would have a hungry winter. Gerin vowed to himself to work enough destruction in Adiatunnus' holding to make their Trokmê masters starve, too.

Every now and then, a red-mustached barbarian would peer out of the woods at the invaders. Gerin ignored those watchers; every man afoot was one he wouldn't have to face in a chariot. "I want to reach Adiatunnus before the sun sets," he said grimly. "Spending a night in his lands with the monsters prowling about sets my teeth on edge."

"Ah, but Captain, does he want you to reach him?" Van said. "You ask me, that's a different question altogether. If he can get the monsters to come out and soften us up again, you think he won't do it?"

"No, I don't think that," Gerin said. "But he pays a price if he hangs back, too. The deeper we penetrate into his lands, the more harm we do him, and the hungrier his warriors and serfs will be come winter. It's a nice calculation he has to make: can he afford what we will do to him for the sake of what the monsters might do to us tonight?"

"You think he'll weigh the odds so—this much on this side, that much on the other?" Van shook his head vehemently. "That's what *you'd* do, certain sure. But Adiatunnus, he'll be watching the sky. As soon as he sees so much smoke there that his fighters start screaming at him louder than he can stand, he'll yell for them to jump into their chariots and come at you. Whether that's today or tomorrow morning we won't know till we see the woodsrunners drawn up in a meadow athwart our path."

"Or, better yet, till we catch them trying to get across our path," the Fox said with a ferocious smile. "But you're likely right; if you try to judge what the other fellow would do by what you'd do yourself, you'll be wrong a lot of the time."

The army moved past the small keep Gerin had burned out in his earlier raid. The castle at the keep's heart had burned; the roof was fallen in, and soot covered the outer stonework. No one moved on the walls. Gerin grinned again. He'd struck Adiatunnus a blow there.

To his surprise, the Trokmê chieftain did not sally forth against him while the sun remained in the sky. He'd pushed close to the keep Adiatunnus had taken for his own and to the woodsrunners' village that had grown up around it by the time failing light at last made him halt. Behind him, all the way back to the border of Adiatunnus' lands, lay as broad a swath of devastation as the Fox could cut. Gerin's eyes were red with the smoke he'd raised; his lungs stung every time he breathed.

When he encamped, he treated the horses as if they were pure gold come to life. He placed them and the chariots in the center of the camp, with the warriors in a ring around them and sentries out beyond the main force. That meant spreading his men thinner than he would have liked, but he saw no other choice. Without chariotry, what good were the warriors? The Trokmoi would ride circles around them.

Rihwin the Fox said, "The first of the moons will not rise tonight until even longer after sunset than was so yestereven."

"I know," Gerin said dolefully. "And the other three, moving more swiftly in their rounds than Nothos, will have gone farther still and will rise later still." He pronounced the words with a certain amount of gloomy relish; every now and then, he drew perverse enjoyment from imagining just how bad things could be.

Few men sought their blankets right after they ate. No one put weapons out of arm's reach. After one attack on the horses, another looked too likely to take lightly.

Twilight still lingered in the western sky when, in the black shadows of the woods, a monster screamed. Warriors who had tried to sleep snatched up swords and shields and peered about wildly, waiting for a sentry or perhaps a horse to cry out in agony.

Another monster shrieked, and another, and another. Soon what sounded like thousands of the creatures were crying out together in a chorus that sent icy fingers of dread running up Gerin's back. "Damn me to the five hells if I see any way to sleep through this," he said to Van, "not when I'm already on edge looking ahead to battle tomorrow."

"Ah, it's not so bad, Captain," the outlander said. When

Gerin stared at him in some surprise, he explained, "I don't care how loud they scream at us. Last night, we taught 'em something they hadn't known before, else they'd be running out of the woods at us with slobber dripping off their fangs. Now with all the moons down'd be the best time for 'em to try. Me, I think they don't dare. They're just trying to make us afraid."

Gerin considered. All at once, the hellish cries seemed less terrifying than they had. "You may well be right," he said, and managed a laugh. "They aren't doing a bad job of it, either, are they?"

"It's nothing but a great pile of noise." Van refused to admit fear to anyone, most likely including himself.

"We won't stop staying ready for a fight, whether you turn out right or wrong," Gerin said. "That's the best way I know to make sure we don't have one."

The hideous chorus kept up all night long, and got louder as the moons rose one by one. By then, though, most of the troopers had concluded the monsters were screaming to intimidate rather than as harbinger to an attack. Those not on sentry did manage to drop off, and their snores rose to rival the creatures' shrieks.

Gerin didn't remember when he dozed off, but he woke with a start at sunrise, having expected to pass the whole night awake. Most of the men were in the same state, complaining of how little they'd slept but grateful they'd slept at all. The horses seemed surprisingly fresh; an attack like the one of the night before might have panicked them, but they'd resigned themselves to the monsters' screams faster than the warriors who guarded them.

"Will we fight today?" Aragis asked rather blurrily; his mouth was so full of smoked sausage that he looked like nothing so much as a cow chewing its cud.

"We will," Gerin said with grim certainty. "If we don't, we penetrate to the heart of Adiatunnus' holding before noon, and torch the big Trokmê village that's grown up around the keep he's taken for his own. He won't let that happen; his own warriors would turn on him if he did."

"There you're right," Aragis said after a heroic swallow. "A leader who won't defend what's his doesn't deserve to keep it. My men will be ready." Gerin had the feeling the Archer primed his vassals for battle by making them more afraid of him than of any imaginable foe, but in his own savage way the grand duke got results.

Not half an hour after the chariots rolled out of camp, they passed the meadow where Gerin's forces and Adiatunnus' had dueled fewer than fifty days before. Some of the ruts the chariot wheels had cut were still visible; grass had grown tall over others.

Gerin had wondered if the Trokmê chieftain would pick the same spot to defend his lands as he had in the last fight. When Adiatunnus didn't, the Fox's anxiety grew. Fearing an ambush when the road went through the next stand of woods, he dismounted several teams of fighting men and sent them in among the trees to flush out any lurking woodsrunners. That slowed the rest of the army, and the searchers found no one.

Past that patch of forest, a broad stretch of clear land opened up: meadows and fields that led to Adiatunnus' keep, the Trokmê village, and the meaner huts of the Elabonian peasants who still grew most of the holding's food. Mustered in front of them was a great swarm of chariotry: Adiatunnus, awaiting the attack.

The Fox was lucky—he spotted the Trokmoi before they spied his car in the shadow of the woods. He ordered Raffo to a quick halt, then waved the chariots of his force up as tight together as they could go without fouling one another. "We'll need to be in line before the woods-runners can sweep down on us," he said. "The gods be praised, they don't look all that ready to fight, either. My men will form to the left when we burst out into the open, Aragis' to the right. I expect we'll all be mixed together before the day is done— that's just a way of keeping us straight when we start. May fortune roll with us."

"May it be so," several troopers said together. Gerin thumped Raffo on the shoulder. The driver flicked the reins and sent the horses forward onto the meadow. A great shout rose from the Trokmoi when they caught sight of the chariot. They swarmed forward in a great irregular wave, hardly bothering to shake out into line of battle in their eagerness to close with their enemies.

"Look at 'em come," Van said, hefting his spear. "If we can get ourselves ready to receive 'em, we'll beat 'em to bits, even with the monsters running between their cars there."

"They don't care much for tactics, do they?" Gerin said. "Well, I've known that a great many years now. The trouble with them is, they have so much pluck that that's too often what decides things."

He nocked an arrow and waited for the Trokmoi and the monsters to come within range. Behind him, ever more chariots rumbled out of the woods to form line of battle. Each one drew fresh cries of rage from the woodsrunners. Gerin saw he had more cars than the woodsrunners did. Whether they'd all be able to deploy before the fight opened was another question.

When the Trokmoi closed to within a furlong, Gerin waved his arm and shouted "Forward!" at the top of his lungs. Chariots depended on mobility; if you tried to stand to receive a charge, you'd be ridden down.

Raffo cracked the whip above the horses' backs. The beasts bounded ahead. A chariot wheel hit a rock. The car jounced into the air, landed with a jarring thump. Gerin grabbed the rail for a moment; his knees flexed to take the shock of returning to earth.

He'd pulled all the way to the left, to be on the wing of his own force. That also meant he was far away from the track that led toward Adiatunnus' keep. The horses galloped through ripening rye, trampling down a great swath of grain under their hooves. The Fox's lips skinned back from his teeth in a predatory grin. Every stride the horses took meant more hunger for his foes.

An arrow hissed past his head. Adiatunnus' hunger was distant, something that would come with winter. Had that arrow flown a couple of palms' breadth straighter, Gerin would never have worried about it or anything else, again. Planning for the future was all very well, but you had to remember the present, too.

Gerin loosed the shaft he'd nocked, snatched another from his quiver, and set it to his bowstring. He shot once more. The Trokmoi were packed so closely, the arrow would almost surely do them some harm. He shot again and again, half emptying his quiver as fast as he could. The rest of the shafts he thriftily saved against more specific targets and urgent need.

His men had followed him on that wide sweep to the left, encircling the Trokmoi on that wing. Had Aragis taken the same course on the right, the woodsrunners would have been in dire straits. But Gerin's deployment order had left the Archer with fewer chariots there, and he commanded that wing with a blunter philosophy of battle than the Fox employed. Instead of seeking to surround the enemy, he pitched straight into them. Some of his men kept shooting at the Trokmoi, while others laid about them at close quarters with sword and axe and mace.

A monster ran at the chariot in which Gerin rode. It

came at the horses rather than the men, and from the right side, where Van with his spear had less reach than the Fox with his bow. But the creature reckoned without Raffo. The driver's long lash flicked out. The monster howled and clutched at its face. Raffo steered the car right past it. Van thrust his spear into the monster's vitals, yanked it free with a killing twist. The monster crumpled to the ground and lay kicking.

A Trokmê driver whipped his team straight for the Fox. His car bore two archers, both of whom let fly at almost the same time. One arrow glanced from the side of Van's helmet, the other flew between the outlander and Gerin.

Gerin shot at one of the archers. His shaft also failed to go just where he'd intended it, but it caught the Trokmê driver in the throat. The reins fell from his fingers; he slumped forward over the front rail of the car. The team ran wild. Both of the archers grabbed for the reins. They were past before Gerin saw whether either one managed to seize them.

"Well aimed, Fox!" Van cried.

"It didn't do what I wanted it to do," Gerin answered. Uncomfortable with praise, he used bitter honesty to turn it aside, like a man trying to avert an omen he didn't care for.

"Honh!" Van said. "It did what it needed to do, which is what matters." That left Gerin no room for argument.

His hopes built as the battle ground on. The Trokmoi were ferocious, but not all the ferocity in the world could make up for a bad position—and, this time, he'd brought more men into the fight than Adiatunnus had. The monsters helped even the odds, but not enough.

He spied the Trokmê chieftain, not far away. "Well, you robber, you asked what I'd do next," he shouted. "Now you see."

Adiatunnus shook a fist at him. "To the corbies with you, you black-hearted omadhaun. You'll pay for this." He reached for his quiver, but found he was out of arrows.

Gerin jeered at him. He pulled out a carefully husbanded shaft, set it to his bow, and let fly. Adiatunnus realized he had no time to grab for his shield, so he threw up his arms. The arrow caught him in the meaty part of his right upper arm, about halfway between elbow and shoulder. He let out a howl any monster would have envied. The wound wasn't fatal, probably wasn't even crippling, but he would fight no more today.

Van swatted Gerin on the back, almost hard enough to pitch him out of the chariot onto his head. "Well aimed!" the outlander boomed again.

And again, the Fox did what he could to downplay praise. "If that had been well aimed, it would have killed him," he grumbled.

The Trokmoi tried to slam through Aragis' men. Had they succeeded, they'd have regained their freedom of movement. But Aragis' chariots were grouped more tightly than Gerin's, and the woodsrunners could not force a breakout. When they failed, they began falling back toward the cover of their village.

"We'll roast 'em like mutton!" Aragis' fierce, exultant cry rang over the battlefield, though the Trokmoi still fought back with fierce countercharges—they were beaten, but far from broken.

Gerin waved several chariots with him, trying to get between the Trokmoi and the haven they sought. Bad luck dogged the effort. An arrow made one of the Elabonian drivers drop the reins, and the horses, freed from control, chose to run in just the wrong direction. A pair of monsters sprang into another chariot; the mad fight that ensued there kept the car from going as he'd hoped it would. He never did find out why a third car failed to follow, but it did.

That left him with . . . not enough. The Trokmoi did not have to slow down much to get around the handful of chariots with which he tried to block their path, and then he was the one in danger of being cut off and surrounded. Cursing, he shouted to Raffo, "We can't go back, so we'd best go on. Forward!"

Like an apple seed squeezed out from between thumb and forefinger, the Fox and his followers fought their way free from the far side of the fleeing Trokmê force. Now he was on the right wing of the attack, and most of his vassals on the left. He'd foretold that things would get mixed up in the fight; being of an uncommonly orderly turn of mind, though, he hadn't expected the mixing to include himself.

He still had arrows left, and shot them at the retreating Trokmoi. Some of the woodsrunners had their cars pounding down the narrow lanes between their homes. "Uh-oh," Van said. "Are you sure we want to go after 'em in there, Fox?"

Whenever Van urged caution, he had to be taken seriously. "Looks like a good way to get chewed to bits, doesn't it?" Gerin said after he'd taken a long look at the situation.

"Doesn't it just?" Van agreed. "We'll get a good many of 'em, and do the rest real harm, if we set the place afire. But going in there after the woodsrunners, you ask me, that's putting your prong on the block for the chopper."

Had Gerin been undecided before, the wince from that figure of speech would have been plenty to make up his mind. He waved his arms and shouted for his men to hold up and ply the Trokmê village with fire arrows. A good many Trokmoi, though, were thundering into the village between him and his vassals, so only a few of those vassals heard. And, while he was supposed to be in command of Aragis' men as well, they ignored him when he tried to keep them from pursuing the Trokmoi.

"Now what, lord prince?" Raffo asked as the chariots streamed past.

Gerin looked at Van. The outlander's broad shoulders lifted in a shrug. The Fox scowled. The only thing he could do that would let him keep his prestige among the Elabonian warriors was also the thing he'd just dismissed as stupid. "Go on," he shouted to Raffo. "If that's where the fight is, that's where we have to go."

"Aye, lord prince," Raffo said, and cracked the whip over the horses' backs.

It was as bad as Van had predicted, as bad as Gerin had thought it would be. Foundered chariots blocked several of the village lanes, robbing the Fox's force of mobility, the essence of chariotry. Some of the Trokmoi fought afoot, side by side with the monsters. Other men ran into the houses and shot arrows at the Elabonians from windows and doors, ducking back into cover after they'd shot.

And quite as fierce as the men were the Trokmê women. It was like fighting dozens of berserk Fands. They screamed and shouted. Under their pale, freckled skins, their faces turned crimson with fury and the veins stood out like cords on their necks and foreheads. Some threw stones; others used bows and swords like their men. They weren't merely unnerving; they were deadly dangerous.

"Back, curse it! Back and out!" Gerin shouted, again and again. "We'll throw everything away if we get stuck in this kind of fighting. Out and back!"

Little by little, his men and Aragis' began to heed him. But pulling out of the battle was harder than getting into it had been. Turning a chariot around in the crowded, bloody alleyways of the village was anything but easy; too often, it was next to impossible. Gerin wondered if going forward would have cost less than the withdrawal did.

A lot of the chariots had lost the firepots with which they'd begun the day's fighting. Still, before long, fire arrows sent trails of smoke through the air as they arced toward the thatched roofs of the Trokmê cottages. The weather had been dry. Before long, the straw on the roofs was blazing.

More chariots rampaged through the fields outside the village, wrecking the crops that still stood after the battle had gone through them. Through thickening smoke, Gerin saw Trokmoi fleeing into Adiatunnus' keep.

"Do you aim to lay siege to 'em?" Aragis the Archer asked. The grand duke's helmet was dented, maybe by a stone. The edge of the helm had cut him above one eye; when he healed, he'd have a scar like Gerin's.

"We can't take the keep by storm, however much I wish we could," Gerin answered. "We don't have the numbers, we don't have the ladders, and they'd be fighting for their lives. We can't starve them out, either. Adiatunnus will have more in his storerooms and cellars than we can draw from the countryside. We can send in fire arrows and hope to start a big blaze, but that's just a matter of luck."

"Aye, but we should try it," Aragis said. Nonetheless, he showed relief that Gerin did not intend to linger in Adiatunnus' country.

The Fox understood that. "You'll want to campaign against the monsters in your own lands as soon as may be, won't you?"

"As a matter of fact, that's just what's in my mind," Aragis said. "Harvest won't wait forever, and I'd like the woods cleared of those creatures before then . . . if that can be done. I'd not care to harm your campaign by pulling back from here too soon, but—"

But I will, if you don't pull back on your own hook soon enough to suit me. Aragis didn't say it—Gerin gave him credit for being a good ally, a better one than the Fox had expected—but he thought it very loudly.

"If it suits you, we'll spend the rest of the afternoon lobbing fire arrows into the keep in the hope of sending it all up in smoke, and then—then we'll withdraw," Gerin said. "We'll ravage more of Adiatunnus' lands as we go. By your leave, we'll stop at Fox Keep for a few days, to let me set up the defenses of my own holding while I'm in the south, and then I'll meet my end of the bargain."

"Couldn't ask for fairer than that," Aragis said, though his eyes argued that any departure later than yesterday, or perhaps the day before, was too late. But again, he held his peace; he recognized necessity, and recognized that against it any man struggled in vain.

The charioteers rode rings around Adiatunnus' keep, howling and shouting louder than the Trokmoi on the walls as they sent more fire arrows smoking through the air. Up on the walls of the keep with the woodsrunners were several monsters. Gerin hoped they and the Trokmoi would quarrel in the tight quarters, but had no way to make that happen.

Two or three times, thin columns of black smoke rose from within the keep. Whenever they did, Gerin's men, and Aragis' too, cheered themselves hoarse. But each time, the smoke thinned, paled, died. At last, as the sun sank ever lower in the west, the Fox called off the attack. He and his followers drew off toward the northeast, back in the direction from which they had come.

Wounded horses and men and monsters still thrashed and groaned and screamed on the battlefield. Now and again, an Elabonian chariot would halt so its crew could cut the throat of a horse or a monster or a Trokmê, or so the troopers could haul an injured comrade into their car and do for him what they could once they stopped to camp. Some of the injured cried out louder in the jouncing chariots than they had lying on the ground. Their moans made Gerin grind his teeth, but all he could do was keep on.

"One thing," Van said as they entered the woods from which they'd emerged to fight: "we won't have to offer much in the way of sacrifice to the ghosts tonight."

"That's so," Gerin agreed. "We gave them blood aplenty today. They'll buzz round the bodies the whole night long, like so many great carrion flies round a carcass—gloating, I suppose, that all those brave men joined their cold and gloomy world."

The chariots came out of the woods bare minutes before sunset. Gerin led them out into the middle of a broad meadow. "We stop here," he declared. "Van, I leave it to you to get the first fire going." He told off parties to go back to the forest and chop down enough wood to keep the fires blazing all through the night. Nothos would rise with a third of the night already passed, and the other three moons later still.

That accomplished, the Fox turned his hand to giving the wounded what help he could. As always in the aftermath of battle, he was reminded how pitifully little that was. He splashed ale on cuts to help keep them from going bad, set and splinted broken bones, sewed up a few gaping gashes with thread of wool or sinew, bandaged men who had ignored their hurts in the heat of action. None of what he did brought much immediate relief from pain, although some of it, he made himself remember, would do good in the long run.

More horses were hurt, too. He helped the drivers

doctor them when he was done with the men. The men, at least, had some idea why they'd been hurt. The horses' big brown eyes were full of uncomprehended suffering.

He didn't know who'd ordered it, but the men had made the same sort of circle of fires they'd built the night before. He chose warriors who'd slept through the previous night undisturbed for sentry duty, and made himself one of them. He was tired down to the marrow of his bones, but so was everyone else.

"Did we win?" Van asked as he replaced the Fox for midwatch. "Did we do all you wanted done?"

"Aye, we won," Gerin said, yawning. "Did we do enough?" Yawning again, he shook his head and made for his bedroll.

"Wait, Captain." Van called him back. The outlander pointed to the woods, from which monsters were coming forth.

Sentries' shouts roused the camp. Swearing, men snatched at weapons and armor. Gerin found his sword in his hand. It wasn't magic; he just didn't remember drawing the weapon.

The monsters approached to the edge of bowshot, but no closer. "There aren't that many of them," Gerin remarked as the creatures began a chorus of their dreadful shrieks. Shriek they did, but they made no move to attack. After a while, the Fox said, "I think they're trying to put us in fear, nothing else but. A plague on 'em, says I. No matter how they scream, I'm going to get some sleep." He raised his voice: "All save the sentries, rest while you can. We'll have warning enough if they truly aim to come after us."

He rolled himself up in his blanket. The monsters' hideous outcry kept him awake a little longer than he would have been otherwise, but not much. Not even Mavrix the god of wine appearing before him would have kept him awake for long, he thought as sleep swallowed him.

He woke wondering why he'd worried about Mavrix, but shook his head at the pointlessness of that: sleepy minds did strange things, and there was no more to say about it. The monsters were gone. That didn't surprise him; with sunrise, the Elabonians could have started shooting at them with good hopes of scoring hits.

Not all the warriors had been able to sleep. Some of them shambled about as if barely alive. How they'd be after another day in the chariot was something about which the Fox tried not to think.

No help for it. After breaking their fast on hard bread and sausage and ale, they rolled northeast, back toward the Fox's holding. Knowing no large force lay directly ahead of them, they spread out widely over the countryside, doing as much damage to Adiatunnus' lands and villages and crops as they could with fire and their horses' hooves and the wheels of their chariots.

A victory, but not a perfect one. Gerin had hoped to smash Adiatunnus utterly; he'd hurt the Trokmê chieftain, literally and metaphorically, but not enough to seize much of his territory with any assurance of keeping it. Maybe the monsters had learned not to attack large bands of armed and armored men, but they hadn't been exterminated—and Adiatunnus' lands still gave them haven.

"Not enough," Gerin said under his breath. Van glanced over to him, but did not venture to reply.

Some of Gerin's vassals peeled off from the main force as they reentered his territory, off to their own castles and to protect their own villages. Most, though, stayed on the road to Fox Keep. Before long, they'd be riding south to help Aragis and fulfill Gerin's part of the bargain.

He'd wondered if the serfs would ask him whether he'd rid their villages of the monsters for good, and dreaded having to tell them no. Then the army passed through a village the creatures had attacked while he was deep in Adiatunnus' territory. That made him feel worse. He'd hurt the Trokmoi and the monsters, but he'd been mad to think he could root them out with a single victory.

He also wondered how much he and his men would accomplish down in the holding of Aragis the Archer. He feared it would be less than Aragis hoped, but kept that fear to himself. Whatever the grand duke's misgivings, he'd come north. The Fox saw no way to keep from reciprocating, not if he wanted to keep his good name.

The return to Castle Fox was subdued. The victory the army had won did not outweigh the men who would not come back, the complete triumph that had eluded the Elabonians.

Seeing Selatre again, squeezing her to him, was wonderful, but she quickly sensed that, past having come home alive and unhurt, Gerin had little to celebrate. That made her shrink back into herself, so that she seemed to stand aloof from the chaos in the stables although she was in the middle of it.

Van and Fand got into a screaming fight over what business the outlander had had going off to fight the Trokmoi. He clapped a hand to his forehead and bellowed, "You tell me not to tangle with them when the only reason you're here is that you stabbed the last woodsrunner daft enough to take you into his bed?"

"Aye, I did that, and I had the right of it, too, for he was of my own folk, for all that he was an evil-natured spalpeen to boot," she said. "But you, now, you're the Fox's friend, but you're after being my lover. So you see!"

Van shook his head—he didn't see. Gerin didn't see,

either. If being Fand's lover turned Van into some sort of honorary Trokmê, by her own argument that gave him a special right to go to war against the woodsrunners. Fand was seldom long on logic; the gods seemed to have given her extra helpings of all the passions instead.

Duren hopped around, saying, "May I go fight too next time, Father? May I, please?"

"You're raising a warrior there," Aragis said approvingly.

"So I am," Gerin answered. He wasn't altogether pleased. Aye, any holding on the frontier—any holding in the northlands—needed a warrior at its head. But he hoped he would also be able to raise a civilized man, lest barbarism seize all the land between the Niffet and the Kirs and hold it for centuries to come.

The castle cooks dished out mutton and pork and bread and ale. The warriors ate and sought their bedrolls. Gerin stayed down in the great hall, hashing over the fight, till Duren fell asleep beside him. Then, as he had a few nights before, he carried his son upstairs to his bedchamber.

When he went back out into the hall, he found Selatre waiting there. She said, "If you were so worn you'd gone to bed with your son, I'd have walked back to my room, but since you're not—"

He caught her to him. "Thank you for being here when things don't look as good as they might." Even as he spoke the words, he realized he was doing his best to put a good face on the campaign from which he'd just returned. Things looked bloody awful.

Selatre ignored all that. She said, "Don't be foolish. If you hadn't been there for me, I'd be dead. Come on." She led him back to her chamber.

He took her with something approaching desperation. He hoped she read it as passion, but she wasn't one to be easily deceived. That she stayed by him when he needed her most was a greater gift than any other she could have given him.

Afterwards, he fell into a deep and dreamless sleep. When he jerked awake, Nothos' light streamed through the window, but not yet golden Math's: past midnight, then, but not far past. Beside him, Selatre was also sitting bolt upright.

"Something is amiss," she said. Her voice sent chills through him. For the first time in many days, she sounded like the Sibyl at Ikos, not the woman he'd come to love.

But no matter how she sounded, she was right. "I heard it, too," Gerin said. He stopped, confused. "Heard it? Felt it? All's quiet now. But—" He got out of bed and started to dress.

So did she. "I don't know what it was. I thought for a moment Biton touched me." She shook her head. "I was wrong, but it was more than a dream. I know that. And if it woke you, too . . ."

"We'd better find out what it was." Gerin held his sword in his left hand. How much good the blade would do against whatever had roused him and Selatre, he had no idea, but it couldn't hurt.

All seemed quiet in Fox Keep as he and Selatre tiptoed down the hall to the stairs. Van's snores pierced the door to Fand's chamber. Gerin smiled for a moment at that, but his lips could not hold their upward curve. A few warriors had fallen asleep in the great hall, maybe too drunk to seek their proper beds. Gerin and Selatre walked by. He looked this way and that, shook his head in the same confusion Selatre had shown. Whatever was wrong, it lay outside the castle proper. He didn't know how he knew, but he did.

Outside, sentries paced their rounds up on the palisade. The courtyard seemed as still as the keep. Gerin began to wonder if worry and nerves hadn't played tricks on Selatre and him at the same time. Then he heard footfalls—slow, erratic footfalls—coming up from the stables toward the entrance to the great hall.

"Stay here," he whispered to Selatre, but when he trotted round to the side of the keep to see who—or what—approached, she followed. She was not so close to him as to cramp him if he had to fight, so he bit down his annoyance and kept quiet.

He rounded the corner and stopped dead with a strangled snort of laughter. No wonder the footfalls had been as they were: here came Rihwin, gloriously drunk. Gerin wondered how Rihwin managed to keep up his footfalls without falling himself. His face bore a look of intense concentration, as if putting one foot in front of the other took everything he had in him. It probably did.

Gerin turned to Selatre in mingled amusement and disgust. "We might as well go back to bed, if this poor sot's the worst menace we can find."

"No. We stay," she said, again sounding like the Sibyl she had been. "More is here than we yet know. Can you not feel it?"

And Gerin could: a prickling of the hairs at the nape of his neck, a tightening of his belly, his mouth suddenly dry as dust. He'd felt like this in the instant when the ground began to shake at Ikos, when his body gave alarm but his mind hadn't yet realized why.

The ground wasn't shaking now, though he wouldn't have bet Rihwin could have told whether that was so. Nevertheless, the feeling of awe and dread built inside Gerin till he wanted to run or scream or smash something just to get relief. He did none of those things. Forcing himself to stillness, he waited for Rihwin's staggering progress to bring his fellow Fox to him.

Rihwin was so intent on walking, he didn't notice Gerin till he almost ran into him. "Lord pr-prince!" he said thickly, and gave such a melodramatic start that he nearly tumbled over backwards. "Mercy, lord prince!" he gasped, and then hiccuped.

Now Gerin drew back a pace, his nose wrinkling. "Feh!" he said. "Your breath stinks like a vineyard in pressing season."

"Mercy!" Rihwin repeated. He swayed as he stared owlishly at his overlord; standing in one place seemed about as hard for him as walking. His face was slack with drink, but alarm glittered in his eyes.

Then Gerin looked through him instead of at him, really hearing for the first time what he himself had said. "You've been at the wine Schild brought us, haven't you, my fellow Fox?" he asked softly. He'd let his sword trail to the ground. Now it came up again, as if to let the wine out of Rihwin.

"Mercy!" Rihwin squeaked for the third time. "I found it buried in the hay when we brought our—*hic!*—horses to the stables. I broached but two jars. Mer—*hic!*—cy!"

"That is it." Selatre's voice was firm and certain. "That is what we felt: the power of Mavrix loosed in this holding."

Gerin wanted to scream at Rihwin. Even in his fury, though, he remembered the hour, remembered the warriors and women and cooks and servants asleep inside Castle Fox. But although he hissed instead of shrieking, his fury came through unabated: "You stupid, piggish dolt. Thanks to your greed, thanks to the wine you're going to piss away over the course of the next day, you've made Mavrix notice us and given him a channel through which he can enter this land—and he hates me. What shall I do to you for that? How could Adiatunnus serve me worse than you just did?"

Tears ran down Rihwin's cheeks; they glistened in Nothos' pale light. "Lord prince, you're right," he mumbled. "I don't know what came over me. I shaw—saw—the jars there in the straw, and it as as conshu—consuming fire blazed all through me. I had to drink, or die." Even sozzled, he spoke with elaborate southern phrasings.

"That's the fanciest way to call yourself a no-account, worthless drunkard I ever heard," Gerin said in disgust.

Selatre set a hand on his arm. She still used that gesture seldom enough to command attention when she did. "Wait," she said. "There may be more truth in what he says than you hear. Perhaps Mavrix inflamed his soul, as he put it, to open the way for the god to make his presence felt in the northlands once more."

"It could be so, lord prince," Rihwin exclaimed eagerly. "Though the lord of the sweet grape expunged all sorcerous ability from my spirit, he left intact my knowledge."

"Not that you haven't tried to drown it in ale—and now wine," Gerin snarled, still anything but appeased.

"I deserve that." Rihwin's voice was full of drunken earnestness. "But it is as your gracious lady said. Were Mavrix to seek entry to your holding, I am just the sort of insht—insh—instrument he would employ." He smiled in triumph at finally forcing out the difficult word.

"All right, it could be so," Gerin said grudgingly. "Shall I thank you for it? Great Dyaus above, I'm still trying to figure out whether we can survive it. As I said, as you know, the god loves me not, nor you either."

Rihwin hung his head. "That is true."

"The god has his purposes, and we have ours," Selatre said. "He will accomplish his come what may. We can't say the same, worse luck. What we have to seek is a way in which the god's purposes are met, and ours as well, and, having found it, coax him into accepting it."

Gerin looked at her gratefully. "Put that way, it might almost be done." But in the back of his mind, he heard, or thought he heard, the god laughing, laughing.

XII

Red-eyed and yawning, Gerin told the tale over breakfast the next morning to those who had been lucky enough not to sense the coming of Mavrix in the night. Beside him sat Selatre, also yawning. He was glad to have her there, for without her confirmation he doubted whether Aragis or Van, to say nothing of the rest, would have believed him. But at the same time he worried, for she sounded once more like Biton's Sibyl, not like his woman. He shook his head, bemused. Having lost Elise to a horseleech, would he lose Selatre to a god?

Aragis snapped him out of his reverie. The grand duke might not have been much for the long view, but he had a supremely practical grasp of the moment. "All right, lord prince, Mavrix is here among us, whether we like it or not," he said. "What do we do about it? Can we turn it to our own purposes?"

"I" —Gerin glanced at Selatre— "we, that is, think we may have found a way." One reason he was red-eyed was that he and Selatre had spent the last part of the night talking over that very question. He sighed. He didn't like the answer they'd come up with. "We are going to evoke the god, to bring him fully into the world here and bargain with him."

"Are you daft, Fox?" Van burst out. "Mavrix, he hates you. Bring him fully here and you just make it easier for him to squash you flat."

"This is the course of which you spoke when we met in the southern marches of your holding. A desperate one, if you ask me," Aragis said. But past that, he did not

421

try to dissuade Gerin. Mavrix was not angry at *him*. And if the Sithonian god of wine did destroy the Fox in some lingering, interesting, and creative way, no one would be better positioned to take advantage of it than the grand duke.

Gerin tried to answer both men at once: "Mavrix will come, whether we want that or not. If we try to stand against it, he'll find more reasons to be angry. If we aid his path, we may satisfy him and still accomplish what we want. If not, we still may be able to control him." He looked at Selatre again.

She nodded. Voice hesitant at first, she said, "At the same time as lord Gerin evokes Mavrix, I—I shall try to bring into the world Biton, my former patron, my former—bridegroom." Even with her swarthiness, her cheeks darkened in embarrassment. But she went on, "Biton the farseeing is a god of order, of forethought, the opposite of most things Mavrix stands for. And Biton is old in the northlands, old. His power is rooted here, not new-come like Mavrix's. It may be that he can keep the lord of the sweet grape from the excesses that can accompany his rite."

"But, lass," Van said gently, "after what befell at Ikos, will the god hearken to your evoking?"

Selatre bit her lip. She'd asked the same question, just as morning twilight began to paint the eastern horizon with gray. "I don't know," she answered. "The only way to find out is to make the attempt."

"What if Biton won't come when you call him?" Aragis said. "What then?"

"Then we're left with Mavrix—undiluted," Gerin said after a moment seeking the right way to put it. "We'd be no worse off than if we didn't try to evoke Biton at all." *No better off, either*, his mind jeered, but he resolutely ignored his own gloomy side.

Aragis stuck out his chin. "I insist that you don't seek to bring the gods into the world until you fulfill your half of our agreement. If they wreak havoc on you, I'll also suffer on that account."

"But if we can persuade them to do as we'd like, we might be able to rid the land of monsters without any more fighting," Gerin said. "Have you thought on that, grand duke? Not just driving the creatures back into the woods so they're a lesser nuisance, but actually being rid of them for good and all. We can't make that happen; we're mere mortals. But the gods can do it, if they will. A risk, aye. But if things go as we design . . ."

"Besides which, thanks to Rihwin, Mavrix is already loose in the land, remember," Van said. "He can make mischief any time he chooses. Sometimes the best way to keep someone from moving on you is to move first your own self."

"Rihwin!" Aragis eyed Gerin. "With your name for being clever, lord prince, I can't believe you sent that sot to me as ambassador. Where is he, anyhow?"

"Still drunk asleep in his bed, I suppose," Gerin answered. "As for the other, there's something in what you say, but less than you think. He's brave and clever enough when he's sober, if short sometimes on common sense. But every now and then, things—happen—with him." He spread his hands, as if to say Rihwin's vagaries baffled him, too.

Aragis' hawk face was not made for indecision. Scowling, he said, "All right, Fox, I don't see how I can stop you short of war here, but this I tell you now: it had better work."

"That I already know," Gerin answered. "For my sake, for your sake, for the northlands' sake, it had better work—which is no guarantee it will."

"All right," Aragis said heavily, as if with his warning

he washed his hands of whatever might result from the evocation. "When do you begin your wizard's work?"

"At noon," Gerin said, which made the grand duke gape.

"Noon is Biton's hour," Selatre added, "the time when the sun sees farthest. Mavrix is strongest by night, when his impassioned votaries cry 'Evoii!' Whatever chance his lesser strength by day gives us, we'll gladly take."

"Besides," Gerin said, "by noon Rihwin will be up— or I'll drag him out of bed, one. We'll need him in this business, too."

"The gods help you," Aragis said, a sentiment with a multitude of possible meanings.

Even by noon, Rihwin the Fox was not a happy man. His face was pasty and his eyes tracked with red; by the way he kept blinking in the sunshine, he found it much too bright to suit him. "I don't see why you're making *me* carry the jars of wine to your shack," he grumbled petulantly.

"Because if it hadn't been for you, we wouldn't have to be trying this," Gerin answered, his voice hard as stone. "Since the fault is yours, you can bloody well play the beast of burden." He brayed like a donkey. Rihwin flinched.

Selatre had laid an assortment of growing things on a makeshift stone altar in the shack: flowers, fir cones, duck's eggs. "We won't want to summon Mavrix solely as god of wine, but also as the god of increase generally," she said. "That may make him more restrained—or, of course, it may not." Among the flowers, she set the scroll that held a book of the Sithonian national epic by the great poet Lekapenos. "Mavrix also inspires the creation of beauty, as we've noted."

"As you've noted, you mean," Gerin said. "Most of

this was your idea; you're the one who's studied Mavrix of late. Till that wine came into the holding, I was happy pretending he didn't exist." He turned to Rihwin. "Set that last jar down over there—carefully! Don't crack it."

Rihwin winced. "When you shout like that, you make my head feel as if it's about to fall off." After a reflective pause, he added, "I rather wish it would."

"Remember that the next time you try to drown yourself in a wine jar, or even one full of ale," Gerin said without much sympathy. He drew his dagger, cut through the pitch that sealed the stopper of one of the wine jars, and then worked in his knife blade and levered out the stopper.

The sweet bouquet of wine wafted from the jar. Gerin sighed with relief. He'd worried that the wine jar, or even both surviving jars, might have gone to vinegar. Had they been bad, he didn't know what he would have done. Drawing some of Rihwin's wine-soaked blood didn't seem like the worst idea in the world.

Gerin dipped up two cups of wine, one for himself, the other for Rihwin. "Don't drink yet," he growled as he handed Rihwin his. He looked over to Selatre and went on, "I still think we might be wiser to call on Biton first. Then his presence will also serve to check Mavrix."

But she shook her head, as she had ever since they began planning the evocation. "Biton has little reason now to hear any summons from me. But if I call on him with Mavrix already here, simple jealousy may help to lure him. Whatever the lord of the sweet grape seeks, the farseeing one is likely to want to thwart."

"You served the god; you know him best," Gerin said, yielding yet again. He, and after a moment Rihwin with him, approached the altar and poured a small libation, being careful not to mar the scroll of Lekapenos. "Thank you for your bounty of the sweet grape, lord Mavrix,"

Gerin declaimed in halting Sithonian, and sipped from
his cup of wine.

Rihwin also drank. His eyes widened; he suddenly
seemed several years younger, or at least less worn.
"*Thank* you for the sweet grape, lord Mavrix," he said,
and then to Gerin, in more ordinary tones, "Nothing
like letting a small snake bite you to ease the venom of a
big one."

"Rihwin, your trouble is that you don't know how to
keep any snakes small," Gerin said. Just to irk Rihwin,
he waved the southerner to silence, not giving him a
chance for a sharp retort. "Be still. I am going to summon the god."

He walked over to the altar, raised his hands high,
and said, "I summon you to my aid, lord Mavrix, I who
have drunk your wine, I who have met you in days past,
I who am but a mere mortal imploring your assistance, I
who am weak—" He humbled himself without shame.
Measured against the might of a god, any mortal was
weak.

The litany went on and on. Gerin began to wonder if
Mavrix would let himself be evoked. The Sithonian god
of wine had some of the deviousness of the principal
folk that worshiped him. He might appreciate the irony
of forcing Gerin to summon him and then refusing to
appear. If that happened, the Fox intended to drink as
much wine as he could hold and then ride south with
Aragis.

But just when he became certain Mavrix had indeed
set him up to fail, the god appeared in the crowded little
shack, somehow without making it more crowded—gods
had their ways. Mavrix's features were regular, exceed-
ingly handsome, and more than a little effeminate. The
god wore sandals and a fawnskin robe, and had a
leopardskin tunic draped over his shoulders. In his right

hand he carried a green, leafy wand tipped with ivory. A faint odor of grapes and of something else, harsher, ranker—perhaps old blood—rose from him.

His eyes were not like a man's eyes. They were two black pits that reflected nothing. When Gerin looked into them, he felt himself falling through infinite space, down and down and down. He needed a great effort of will to pull his senses back from those twin pits and say in a shaken voice, "I thank you for granting me your presence this day, lord Mavrix." He knew he'd just made a hash of the Sithonian grammar, which was likely only to win the god's contempt, but it couldn't be helped, not now.

Mavrix looked at—and through—him. He felt himself pierced by the god's gaze, almost as if by a sword. In a voice in perfect keeping with his appearance, Mavrix said, "Pleased, are you? Pleased? The vengeance I owe you, you should be quaking like an aspen leaf in a gale. I moved Schild Stupidstaff to give you wine in hope it would let me come here and take that revenge. And you are *pleased?*"

Selatre started her petition to Biton then. Gerin heard her speak of her own unworthiness to summon the god who had abandoned her, and then forgot about her. If he didn't give Mavrix all his attention, he would be ruined past any hope of Biton's redemption.

Gesturing toward the altar and the various gifts it contained, Gerin said, "If you so badly wanted your revenge, lord Mavrix, these would have brought you here. Did you truly need the gift of wine?"

"Aye, for two reasons," the god replied. "First, now that you have summoned me into the world at this place, I can act here more fully than I could otherwise. And second, while first fruits and such are mine, wine is *mine*, if you take my meaning. When I am called by wine, I am more truly myself than if evoked in any other way."

"By which you mean you can be vicious without regretting the consequences, blaming them instead on the strength of the wine," Rihwin said. "You—"

"Silence, worm," Mavrix said, and, although Rihwin's lips continued to move, no more sound came from them. It was an effect Gerin had often wished he could achieve. To Gerin, the lord of the sweet grape said, quite conversationally, "You'd think he'd learn his lesson, wouldn't you? And yet, having fallen foul of me once, he persists in risking my wrath yet again. As do you, I might add, and you are less a fribbler than he. Why is this?"

Gerin did not directly answer that. Instead, he pointed to the book of Lekapenos he had set on the stone. "You are not god of wine only, lord Mavrix. You are also patron of beauty and cleverness. Is this not so?" He was remembering more Sithonian than he'd thought he had in him.

Mavrix drew himself up to his full height, which was much more than a man's, yet somehow did not break through the ceiling of the shack. "No one would deny it, little man. But you did not answer my question, and not answering a god is yet another capital crime to set against you." He gestured with his wand. It looked innocuous, but in his hands it was a weapon more fell than any spear or sword in the grip of the boldest, fiercest fighter.

Gerin's mouth went dry; he knew the power of that wand. Forcing his voice to steadiness, he replied, "Lord Mavrix, I had to answer in a roundabout way. Truly I know your role in inspiring the folk of Sithonia to the peak of artistic endeavor they once enjoyed. The reason I summoned you, lord, is that ugliness now blights the northlands. If you look about here, if you see it, I pray you to banish it for aesthetic reasons if no others."

"Seldom have I seen a fish wriggle on a hook as you do," the god said petulantly. "Very well, I shall look." His eyes lighted for a moment. Gerin saw in them shifting scenes of the monsters' depredations. Then they became deep pools of blackness once more. He sneered at Gerin. "Ugly they are, but what of it? You savages in these cold, grapeless lands treat each other as vilely as the monsters use you. Why should I care what they do?"

Before Gerin could answer, Selatre let out a gasp of startlement and delight, and Biton manifested himself in the shack. Again, it somehow accommodated him without growing and at the same time without seeming crowded. Gerin had wondered how the farseeing god would appear, whether as the handsome youth of the pediment reliefs on his overthrown shrine or the more primitive image that was mostly eyes and jutting phallus. To him, Biton seemed now the one thing, now the other, depending on which was uppermost in his own mind at any given moment.

Selatre gasped, "Thank you, farseeing one, for hearing the prayer of your former servant who reveres you still."

"Loyalty is rare enough to deserve notice," Biton answered in a voice that held the same slight rustic accent as Selatre's, "the more so when it is retained even after it can no longer be returned."

Mavrix stared at Biton with undisguised loathing. His features shifted with divine celerity to suit his mood. Turning to Gerin, he sneered, "If you think summoning this boring backwoods bumpkin of a deity will somehow save you, I urge you to disabuse yourself of the notion."

"That's not why I called on him," Gerin answered. He bowed to Biton and said, "Farseeing one, the Sibyl begged your presence here for the same reason I evoked Mavrix lord of the sweet grape: to beg you to help rid the land of the monsters now infesting it. As they sprang from the caverns beneath your fallen fane, I dared hope you might consider them in some small measure your responsibility."

"Lord, I beg you to look about," Selatre added, "and see the destruction and disorder these monsters spread wherever they go."

As Mavrix had, Biton looked. Sometimes Gerin saw his head revolve on his neck in a manner impossible for mere flesh and blood, while at other instants what he perceived was a basalt stele spinning. In either case, though, Biton unquestionably had eyes—or at least an eye—in the back of his head.

When his image settled, he said, "This is most distressing. It seems the sort of chaos this foreign mountebank might favor." With an arm or with that phallus, he pointed at Mavrix.

"I?" Mavrix twisted in indignation, so that his leopardskin cape swirled gracefully about him. Gerin could not imagine him doing anything ungraceful. But he'd seen in previous encounters with Mavrix that the god had a temper. Mavrix's smooth voice turned into an angry screech: "Mountebank, is it? I'd think these monsters more your style—barbarous creatures they, fit only for a barbarous land. And after all, they haunted the caverns under your shrine. If you despise them so, why didn't you get rid of them? I suppose you lacked the power." He sneered dismissively.

Biton suddenly seemed wholly human to Gerin; perhaps the stone pillar that was his other guise could not properly express his wrath. "They are not my creatures!" he bellowed in a voice that reverberated through Gerin's head like the deep tolling of a great bronze bell. "My temple blocked them from coming forth and inflicting themselves on the upper world. In the caverns, they were part of nature, not a blight upon it. But when I saw the shrine would fall—"

"Farseeing one indeed," Mavrix interrupted, sneering still. "If it took you so long to notice that, you aren't much of a god."

"At least my senses aren't blinded by drunkenness, adultery, and incest," Biton retorted primly. "Half the time, you don't even know what you see; the rest of the time, you don't care."

Both gods started screaming. Gerin clapped his hands to his head, but it did no good. He was hearing Mavrix and Biton with his mind, not his ears, and they kept on dinning just as loud as before.

"Father Dyaus protect us," Rihwin mouthed silently.

"Don't invite him, too," Gerin exclaimed. "Aren't two squabbling gods enough to satisfy you?" He wanted to run, but he didn't think that would do any good, either. If Biton and Mavrix went at it with everything they had, the whole of the northlands might not be big enough to hold a safe haven. He'd hoped evoking both of them at once would help keep them under control. Instead, it seemed to be inflaming them.

"I thought this scheme mad from the outset." Rihwin moved his lips exaggeratedly and eked out his words with gestures, so Gerin could not mistake what he meant. "You are sorcerer enough to evoke the gods, but not enough to make them do your bidding once here. Better you should never have tried!" He clapped a hand to his forehead.

At that moment, Gerin would have been hard-pressed to argue with him. Mavrix thrust his ivory-tipped wand at Biton. Faster than thought, the farseeing god was stone again, and knocked the wand aside with his phallus. Mavrix howled in pain. Biton, anthropomorphic once more, laughed in his face. Mavrix stuck out a tongue longer and pinker than a human could have had.

Some philosophers called the gods men writ large.

Gerin was reminded of nothing so much as small, squabbling boys writ large—but these small boys had superhuman strength and power.

"I should have listened to Aragis and waited," Gerin groaned.

"You should have listened to someone," Rihwin mouthed. With Mavrix distracted, he was faintly audible. "You're always so splendid at deducing what everyone else should do, but when anyone makes a suggestion to you, do you heed it? Ha!" In case his fellow Fox hadn't caught that, he repeated himself: "Ha!"

That held enough truth to sting. Gerin had always relied on his own judgment because he'd found none consistently better. More often than not, his judgment had served him well. But when he made a mistake, he did not commonly content himself with a small one.

"Oh, shut up," he growled nonetheless. "As if you've proved yourself worth listening to over the years." Rihwin gave back a gesture much used by street urchins in the City of Elabon.

Next to the way the gods were behaving, the argument between the two men seemed downright sedate. Mavrix used the same gesture Rihwin had, and stuck out his tongue again to boot. Still in human guise, Biton lifted his robe and waggled the phallus whose stone version had parried the fertility god's wand.

Mavrix laughed scornfully. "I've seen mice with more than that."

"For one thing, you're a liar. For another, who cares what you've seen?" Biton retorted. "I'd sooner look at things of consequence than the private parts of mice."

"I'd sooner look at things of consequence than *your* private parts," the lord of the sweet grape said. With another nasty laugh, he went on, "Some seeker after consequences you are, too, if you couldn't even tell your own chief temple was about to be overthrown."

"What is the blink of an eye against the great sweep of time?" Biton said. "The temple at Ikos stands for centuries yet to come; am I to be condemned for failing to notice the brief interval in which it is downfallen?"

Under less harrowing circumstances, Gerin might have found that interesting, or even hopeful. If Biton's temple at Ikos was to be rebuilt, that argued some sort of civilization would survive in the northlands. His own survival, however, seemed too problematic at the moment for him to take the long view he usually favored.

"Now that you mention it, yes," Mavrix answered. "Perhaps your true image should have a patch over that third eye—and one of the other two, as well."

"I'd almost welcome such," Biton snapped, "if it meant I did not have to see all the hideous things your monsters are working and shall work in this land."

"They're not my monsters!" Mavrix screeched. "Are you deaf as well as blind? They're not my monsters! Not! *Not!* They're hideous and ugly and revolting, and what they do is enough to make anyone with a dram of feeling puke right onto his shoes, thus." What Mavrix spewed forth had a bouquet richer than that of any wine Gerin had ever known—another area where gods enjoyed an advantage over men.

Not long before, Mavrix hadn't cared what the monsters were doing in—and to—the northlands. Gerin, though, hadn't blamed the god for them. Now that Biton had blamed him, he resented that more than he enjoyed making Gerin squirm. And if Gerin could bend Mavrix's course, even a little . . .

"Lord Mavrix, if you despise the monsters so, you could easily show lord Biton they have nothing to do with you by driving them out of the northlands," he said.

"Be quiet, little man," Mavrix said absently, and Gerin

was quiet, as Rihwin had been before him. He had no choice in the matter. He exchanged a look of despair and alarm with Selatre. It had been worth a try, but not all tried succeeded.

Biton said, "Ah, lord of the sweet vomitus, so you do claim the creatures for your own."

"I do *not!*" Mavrix screamed in a voice that should have knocked Fox Keep flat. "Here, I shall prove it to you." He sucked in a theatrically deep breath, puffed out his cheeks, and turned purpler than any man could: Gerin thought of a divine frog with skin the color of wine. After that tremendous effort, the god exhaled hard enough to make Gerin stagger. "There! They're gone. Look all over the northlands, unseeing one, and you shall find not a single one of the disgusting creatures."

"Coming from you, drunken fool, any assertion requires proof," Biton growled. As it had before, his head began to spin independently of his body—or, alternatively, the stone pillar that was his body turned round and round. Suddenly he stopped and stared contemptuously at Mavrix. "You're as slovenly a workman as I might have guessed. Look there."

Something glinted for a moment in Mavrix's fathomless eyes. "Well, so I missed a couple of them. What of it?" He gestured. "Now they are here no more. Do you see? They are not mine!"

Biton continued his surveillance. His whirling head abruptly halted once more. "And again! You must in truth be the god of drunkenness, for you're sloppy as a drunkard. Look over yonder now."

Gerin wondered what sense Biton used to find the monsters, how he indicated to Mavrix where "over yonder" was, and how Mavrix turned his own senses in that direction, whatever it was. He also wondered just how Mavrix was getting rid of the monsters, and where they were going. Were he a god, he supposed he would know. As a man, he had to go on wondering.

"All right, those are gone, too." Mavrix stuck out his froggy tongue at Biton again. "*Now* do you see any more, lord with the eye in the back of your bum?"

Biton spun and searched. A moment later, he said triumphantly, "Aye, I do, you sozzled ne'er-do-well. What of those?"

Mavrix must have stretched his senses in the direction the farseeing god gave him, for he said, "And they are vanished, too, and so am I. Even with these few drops of wine to ease the path for me here, the northlands are a place I'd sooner leave than come to." He fixed his black, black eyes on Gerin. "Clever man—you were right. There are things uglier than you and your kind. Who would have thought it?" With that, he vanished.

Gerin found he could speak again. Being a politic man, the first thing he said was, "I thank you, lord of the sweet grape, and bless you as well." Then he turned to Biton. "Farseeing one, may I ask a question of you?" When the god did not say no, he went on, "Did Mavrix truly rid the northlands of the creatures that dwelt so long under your temple?"

He waited nervously, lest Mavrix hear him and return in wrath at having his power questioned. But the lord of the sweet grape evidently had been only too glad to leave the northlands for good.

Biton started to nod, then searched once more. When he stopped, he looked annoyed. "That wine-soaked sponge of a Sithonian god is too inept to deserve his divinity," he said.

The Fox took that to mean a monster, or a handful of monsters, still survived somewhere in the northlands. He wondered if Mavrix had left behind the cubs he'd spared—and if he would ever find out. In his humblest tones, he went on, "Lord Biton, would you be generous enough to complete what the lord of the sweet grape began?"

To his dismay, Biton shook his head. "I do not see myself doing that," the farseeing one said. "It is a task for men if they so choose. No, my duty now is to restore Ikos to what it was before the earth trembled beneath my shrine. Everything there shall be as it was—everything. The temple shall stand again without the agency of man, and the Sibyl shall be restored to her rightful place there, to serve as my instrument on earth." He gazed fondly at Selatre.

She looked from the god to Gerin and back again. Her voice trembling, she said, "But lord Biton, I no longer qualify to serve you in that way. In your last prophetic verse, you yourself called me an oracle defiled. Since that day, I have known the embraces of a man" —she glanced nervously toward Gerin once more— "and my courses have begun. I am no longer a fit tool for your work."

"Everything shall be as it was—everything," Biton repeated. "If I can rebuild my fane from tumbled stones, do you think I have not the power to restore your maidenhead, to make you a fit vessel for my voice?"

Selatre looked down at the ground. "I am certain you have that power, lord Biton," she murmured.

Gerin wished desperately for some way to attack Biton, but could imagine none. Unlike Mavrix, the farseeing god could not be duped into losing his temper, not by a man; he was far less vulnerable to earthly concerns than the earthy lord of the sweet grape. The Fox stared over at Selatre. Of course she would choose to go back to the god. How could she not? She had been consecrated to him since she became a woman, had served him as Sibyl since her predecessor died. Sibyl was all she'd wanted to be; she'd resented being rescued from her residence by the temple after the earthquake; she hadn't been able to abide even the touch of a man for a long time after she was rescued.

True, she'd come to love him and he her, but what was that brief brightness when measured against the course for which her life had been designed? Now that she had the chance to return to that course, how could he blame her if she chose to take it?

Truth was, he couldn't. Having her go back to Ikos would tear him worse inside than he'd been torn when Elise left him. No matter what he'd felt about Elise, she'd no longer cared for him, else she'd not have gone. But he knew Selatre loved him still, as he'd come to love her. Only being certain she would be happier back at Ikos let him bear up under the thought of losing her. Even with that certainty, it was hard, hard.

Biton turned his farseeing eyes on Selatre. "You say nothing. Are you not honored, are you not pleased, that all shall be restored? Even as I speak to you, the shrine at Ikos returns to its proper state. It awaits your coming."

"Of course I am honored, lord Biton," she answered, very softly. "Whether I am pleased ... Lord, have you the power to see what might be as well as what shall be?"

For a moment, Biton seemed a stone pillar to Gerin, and altogether unfathomable. Then he resumed his human appearance. "Even for me, a god, this is difficult," he replied, his voice troubled. "So many paths branch off from the true one, and then from one another, that losing oneself grows quickly easier the farther ahead one seeks to see. Why do you ask?"

"Because I would have you look down the path I would choose for myself," Selatre said. "You are a god; if you wish your will to be done, done it shall be. How can I, who shall live for a little and then die, oppose it? But—" She did not go on. Even thinking of declining an honor a god would confer on her took something special in the way of courage.

It also filled Gerin with hope as wild and desperate as his despair had been a moment before.

Biton's head began its boneless spin. This time it did not just revolve, but also grew misty, so Gerin could see the far wall of the shack through it. The farseeing god searched for what seemed a very long time; now and again, he would almost disappear altogether. Gerin started when Biton fully returned.

"You may live your life as you will," the god told Selatre. "My Sibyl is my bride, not my slave. I shall mark another, one who will be willing to serve me. I shall not tell you what may spring from your choice, but I say this: as with any other, make the best of it. And a word of warning— for mortals, there is no such thing as living happily ever after."

"I know that, lord Biton. Thank you. I will try to make the best of it." Selatre started to prostrate herself to the god, but Biton disappeared before her knees could touch the ground.

She and Gerin and Rihwin stared at one another, dazed. "I think we may have won," Gerin said in a voice that sounded disbelieving even to him. Then he remembered something more important to say than that. He turned to Selatre. "Thank you. I'll try never to make you sorry for choosing me over, over—" For one of the few times in his life, words failed him. She'd known what she was giving up. At last, huskily, he managed, "I love you."

"I've noticed that," she said, and smiled at his startled expression. "It's why I chose to stay with you, after all.

You love me, while for Biton I'd just be—oh, not a tool, not quite, maybe something more like a favorite pet. It's not enough, not now that I've known better." Her own voice went soft. "And I love you, which did, mm, enter into my thinking." She smiled again, this time with a touch of mischief.

Rihwin said, "We have two jars of the blood of the sweet grape here, waiting—indeed, all but crying—to be drunk in celebration of our triumph."

"How right you are, my fellow Fox." Gerin picked up the jar they'd opened to summon Mavrix—and poured it out over Rihwin's head. The red-purple wine splashed him and Selatre, too, but it drenched Rihwin, which was what he'd had in mind. The southerner spluttered and squawked and flapped his arms—which just splattered the wine more widely—and rubbed at his eyes. Gerin didn't doubt they stung fiercely—and didn't regret what he'd done, either.

"A waste, a criminal waste," Rihwin said, sucking at his mustache so as to swallow every precious drop he could. "Had it not been for my wine-bibbing, we would not have seen the northlands freed from the vicious and horrible curse of the monsters."

"Had it not been for your wine-bibbing," Gerin said grimly, "we wouldn't have had to put our fate in the hands of two gods, one of whom was already angry at me and the other ready to get angry because I'd taken his voice on earth as my woman. Aye, it turned out well. That's not why I gave you the one jar of wine as I did—it was for forcing us to take such a dreadful chance." He picked up the other, unopened jar. "Because we succeeded, this one is yours to do with as you will."

Rihwin bowed, dripping still. "You are a lord among lords, my fellow Fox."

"What I am is bloody tired of having to worry every

moment of every day," Gerin said. "The gods willing" —
a phrase that took on new and urgent meaning after the
evocation— "I'll have maybe three days of peace now
before the next thing, whatever it is, goes horribly wrong.
Come on, let's tell Aragis and the rest what we've done
here today."

Along with Van and Fand and Drago and Marlanz
and Faburs, Aragis the Archer stood at what Gerin
thought of as a "safe" distance from the shack. The word
was a misnomer, of course. Had the gods truly released
their wrath, nowhere in the northlands would have been
far enough from Fox Keep to escape—as the monsters
had discovered.

Everyone pointed and exclaimed when they came
forth. Fand's voice pierced through the rest: "Did the
sot spill the wine and wreck your magic, now?"

"Not a bit of it," Gerin answered. "We summoned
the gods, and the monsters are no more."

That raised the hubbub quite a bit higher than it had
been. Van said, "But how can it be, Captain? You only
just went in there."

"What? Are you witstruck?" Gerin demanded. "We
were in the shack an hour at least, more likely two." He
looked to Selatre and Rihwin for confirmation. They both
nodded.

Without a word, Aragis pointed up into the sky. Gerin's
eyes followed the track of the grand duke's finger toward
the sun. He had to look away, blinking, but not before
his jaw dropped in astonishment. By the sun's place in
the sky, a couple of minutes might have passed, but no
more.

"I don't understand it," he said, "but I was telling the
truth, too. I suppose the bigger truth is, when you treat
with gods, you can't expect the world they know to be
the ordinary one we usually live in."

Aragis said, "I think you had better tell me in detail all that came to pass in there. I warn you, I am not satisfied with what you have said so far. It strikes me as likely to be a ploy to keep from having to honor your share of our terms of alliance. Are you saying the monsters are simply gone, thus?" He snapped his fingers.

"Let's go into the great hall and broach some ale, and I'll tell you everything I remember," Gerin said.

Rihwin held out the jar of wine Gerin had given him. "No, let's share this," he said. "As Mavrix is part of the tale, so should he also be part of the explanation." That made sense, but hearing it from Rihwin surprised Gerin. For his fellow Fox to share wine he could have kept for himself was not far from a revolution in human nature, and confirmed that something extraordinary had indeed happened inside the hut.

Divided among so many—and with a libation to the lord of the sweet grape—the one jar of wine did not go far, but Gerin savored every sweet drop; when he'd evoked Mavrix, he'd hardly tasted what he'd drunk. Aided by Selatre and the wine-soaked Rihwin, he explained everything that had passed in the hut.

When he was done, Van said, "Some of the yarns I've told are wild, but I hand it to you, Captain: that beats 'em all."

"Thank you—I think." Gerin could rely on his friend to believe him. Aragis the Archer was something else again. Gerin eyed the grand duke with some concern, wondering how he would react.

Aragis' jaw worked, as if he were chewing over the tale Gerin had told. At last he said, "It fits together well enough; I give you so much. But how am I to know whether it's the truth or just a clever tale to get me out of your hair?"

"Send a team down to Ikos," Selatre suggested. "If

they find no monsters on the way and discover Biton's shrine restored, you'll know we have not lied. It's not a long journey; four days, five at the most, will get your men to the temple and back. Then you won't have to guess—you will know."

Aragis' jaw went up and down again. After a moment, he dipped his head to Selatre. "My lady, that is a fine thought. We would not have left here much before my men could return from Ikos in any case. I'll do as you say, though I'll send more than one team south, on the off chance you're . . . mistaken." He was too courteous to suggest straight out that she was lying, but left the implication in place.

Once his mind was made up, he was not a man to waste time. Four chariots fared south toward Ikos that afternoon. Gerin gladly gave them supplies for the journey; he was confident about what they'd find there. He went to sleep that night wondering where the last of the monsters, the ones Mavrix had missed, still lurked in the northlands. Were they the cubs he'd spared? Solve that riddle and you'd deserve undying praise. The world being what it was, you probably wouldn't get it, but you'd deserve it.

Two days later, the lookout in the watchtower blew a long blast on his horn and shouted, "Lord prince, chariots approach out of the southwest." Gerin frowned; it was too soon for Aragis' men to be coming back, and the southwest . . . The sentry's voice cracked in excitement as he added, "Lord prince, they're Trokmoi!"

The Fox cupped his hands and called up to the sentry, "How many chariots? Are we invaded?" That would be a mad thing for Adiatunnus to try, but just because a thing was mad didn't mean it couldn't happen.

"No invasion, lord prince," the sentry answered, much

to his relief. "There's just a handful of them, and they're showing the striped shield of truce."

To the gate crew and the men on the palisade, Gerin called, "We'll let one crew into the courtyard; the rest can wait outside. If they try to follow, they'll never go home again."

The Trokmoi uttered not a word of protest when Gerin's troopers passed them those conditions. At the Fox's nod, the gate crew let down the drawbridge, then grabbed for bows and spears. A single chariot rattled and rumbled over the bridge into Fox Keep. Gerin recognized one of the woodsrunners in it. "I greet you, Diviciacus son of Dumnorix," he said.

"And I'm after greeting you as well, lord Gerin, though I met some of your men closer than I cared for, these few days past," the Trokmê answered. A long, ugly cut furrowed his left arm and showed what he meant. He got down from the car and bowed low to Gerin. "Lord prince, in the name of Adiatunnus my chieftain, I'm come here to do you honor. Adiatunnus bids me tell you he'll be your loyal vassal for as long as you're pleased to have him so. Forbye, there're tribute wains waiting to come hither so soon as your lordship is kind enough to tell me you accept his fealty, indeed and there are."

Gerin stared at Van. They both stared at Aragis. All three men seemed bewildered. Gerin knew he was. He turned back to Diviciacus. "What accounts for Adiatunnus' . . . change of mind?" he asked carefully. "A few days past, as you said, we were all doing our best to kill one another."

"Och, but that was then and this is now," Diviciacus answered. He sounded bewildered, too, as if he'd expected the Fox to know exactly what he was talking about. When he saw Gerin didn't, he went on, "Himself was chewing things over with one of the monsters—one o' the smart ones, y'ken—the other day when lo! All of a sudden the creature turns to smoke before the very eyes of him, and then it's gone! All the others gone with it, too; not a one left, far as we can tell. Will you say that's none o' your doing, lord prince?"

The Fox didn't say anything for a moment. Now Aragis bowed to him, almost as low as Diviciacus had. "Lord prince, I think in your own way you have met the terms of the alliance to which we agreed, which is to say, I doubt the monsters now threaten my holding."

"Thank you, grand duke," Gerin said vaguely. He'd known what Mavrix had said he'd done, of course, but knowing in the abstract and being confronted with actual results were two different things. Pulling himself together, he told Diviciacus, "Aye, the god worked that at my urging." In fact, the gods had worked that because they'd been quarreling with each other, but some things the Trokmê didn't need to know. "And so?"

"And so, lord prince," Diviciacus answered, "Adiatunnus has the thought in him that he'd have to be a raving madman to set himself against your honor, you being such a fine wizard and all. 'Diviciacus,' he tells me, 'not even Balamung could have magicked the creatures so,' and I'm after thinking he's right. If he canna stand against you, he'll stand wi' you, says he."

"So he'll stand with me, will he?" Gerin said. "I mean him no disrespect, but he's shown he's not to be trusted, that chieftain of yours. When he says he'll stand with me, he's more likely to mean he'll stand behind me, that being the best place from which to slide a dagger between my ribs."

Diviciacus sighed. "Himself feared you'd say as much, there being bad blood betwixt the two of you and all. He gave me leave to say this if you didna trust him: he'll give you his eldest son, a boy of twelve, to live with you here at this keep as hostage for his good behavior. The lad'll leave with the load of tribute I spoke of earlier."

"Will he?" Gerin pondered that. Adiatunnus could hardly offer more to show his sincerity. The Fox added, "Did your chieftain give you leave to take the oath of homage and fealty in his place?"

"He did that, lord prince, and I know the way you southrons do it, too." Diviciacus went to one knee before Gerin and held out his hands, palms together. Gerin set his hands to either side of the Trokmê's. Diviciacus said, "Adiatunnus my chieftain owns himself to be your vassal, Gerin the Fox, Prince of the North, and gives you the whole of his faith against all men who might live or die."

"I, Gerin, Prince of the North, accept the homage of Adiatunnus through you, Diviciacus son of Dumnorix, and pledge in my turn always to use him justly. In token of which, I raise you up now." The Fox did just that, and kissed Diviciacus on his bristly cheek.

The Trokmê beamed. "By Taranis, Teutates, and Esus I swear my chieftain Adiatunnus' fealty to you, lord prince."

Any oath less than the strongest one the Trokmoi used would have made Gerin suspicious of the chieftain. With it, he bowed in return, satisfied. "By Dyaus the father of all, Biton the farseeing one, and Mavrix lord of the sweet grape, I accept his oath and swear in turn to reward his loyalty with my own."

Diviciacus eyed him keenly; Adiatunnus had not dispatched a fool as his ambassador. "You Elabonians are always after swearing by Dyaus, but the other two aren't usually the gods you name in your frickfullest aiths. They'd be the ones who did your bidding for you, I'm thinking."

"That's my affair," Gerin said. The Trokmê was right and wrong at the same time: Gerin had indeed summoned Mavrix and Biton, but the gods did their own bidding, no one else's. If you were clever enough—and lucky enough—you might make them see that what you wanted was also in their interest. That once, the Fox had been clever and lucky enough. He never wanted to gamble on such bad odds again.

Aragis' chariot crews returned with word of Ikos miraculously restored and not a sign of monsters anywhere, and seemed miffed when everyone took their report as a matter of course. The day after they got back to Fox Keep, Aragis and his whole host set out for his holding in the south.

"Perhaps we'll find ourselves on the same side again one day," Aragis said.

"May it be so," Gerin agreed. He didn't quite care for the grand duke's tone. Had he been in Aragis' sandals, he would have worried about himself, too: with Adiatunnus as his vassal, his power and prestige in the northlands would soar . . . maybe to the point where Aragis would go looking for allies now, hoping to knock him down before he got too powerful to be knocked down. In Aragis' sandals, Gerin would have tried that. To forestall it, he said, "I almost wish I didn't have the Trokmê as my ally. He'd be easier to watch as an enemy than as someone who claimed to be my friend."

"There is that." Aragis rubbed his chin. "Well, we'll see how you do with him." With that ambiguous farewell, the Archer turned and went back among his own men. Gerin knew he would bear watching, too, no less than Adiatunnus. This once, his interests and the Fox's had coincided. Next time, who could say?

Gerin sighed. If he spent all the time he should watching his neighbors, where would he find time for anything else?

Not long after Aragis and his warriors left for the grand duke's lands, Duren came up to Gerin and asked, "Papa, are you angry at Fand?"

"Angry at Fand?" The Fox frowned. He often thought Fand counted any day where she didn't make someone angry at her a day wasted, but he didn't say that to his son. Duren liked Fand, and she'd never been anything but gentle with him. "No. I'm not angry at her. Why did you think I was?"

"Because you never go to her chamber anymore. It's always Van."

"Oh." Gerin scratched his head. How was he supposed to explain that to his son? Duren awaited a reply with the intense seriousness only a four-year-old can show. Slowly, Gerin said, "Fand has decided she likes Van better than she likes me. You remember how she and I would quarrel sometimes, don't you?"

Duren nodded. "But she quarrels with Van, too."

"That's true," the Fox said, "but it's—usually—a happy sort of quarreling. She doesn't treat you any differently now that she's just with Van instead of with him and me, does she?"

"No," Duren said.

"That's good." Gerin meant it; he would have quarreled with Fand, and in no happy way, had the boy said yes. He went on, "Now that Fand is with Van, Selatre is my special friend. Do you like her, too?" He waited anxiously for Duren's answer.

"Oh, yes," Duren said. "She's nice to me. She doesn't treat me like a baby, the way some people do just because I'm not big yet. And do you know what else?" His voice dropped to the conspiratorial whisper reserved for secrets. "She taught me what some of the letters sound like."

"Did she?" Gerin said. "I'll bet I know which ones, too."

"How can you know that?" Duren demanded in the tone children use when, as frequently, they assume their parents can't possibly know anything.

"Were they the ones that spell your name?" Gerin asked.

Duren stared at him. Every once in a while—not often enough—a parent will redeem himself by proving he does know what he's talking about after all. "How did you know?" the boy said, his eyes enormous. "Did you use magic?" Now that his father had got away with summoning two gods, he assumed Gerin was a mighty mage. The Fox, who knew how lucky he'd been, wished that were so but made a point of bearing firmly in mind that it wasn't.

He said, "No, I didn't need any magic for that. The letters of a person's name are almost always the ones he learns first, because those are the ones that are most important to him. Do you know what else?"

"No, what?" Duren breathed. He liked secrets, too, and was good at keeping them for a boy of his years.

"When Selatre came to Fox Keep—that was just a few days after Tassilo stole you—she didn't know her letters, either," Gerin said. "I taught them to her myself. So she should know how to teach you, because she just learned."

"Really?" Duren said. Then he looked doubtful. "But she reads so well. I can only read the letters in my name, and find them in other words sometimes. But I don't know what the other words say."

"It's all right. It's nothing to worry about," Gerin assured him. "You're still very little to know any letters at all. Even most grown people don't, you know. Selatre learned hers quickly partly because she's smart—just like you—and partly because she's a woman grown, and so when she reads something she understands what it's talking about.

You can't always do that, because a lot of things that are in the words on the parchment haven't happened to you yet. Do you understand?"

"No." Duren's face clouded over. "I want to be able to do it now."

Gerin picked him up, tossed him in the air, and caught him as he came down. Duren squealed. Gerin spun him around and around and around. He squealed again. When Gerin set him down, he took a couple of staggering steps and fell on his bottom. Gerin was dizzy, too, but tried not to show it. He said, "Could you throw me up in the air and spin me around and around like that?"

"Don't be silly, Papa." Duren tried to get up, but seemed to have as much trouble walking as Rihwin had the night he broached the wine.

"Why not?" Gerin persisted. "Why can't you do that?"

"You're too big."

"That's right, and you're too little. When you're bigger, you'll be able to do things like that, and you'll be able to read easier, too."

Duren considered that, then said, "Spin me again!" Gerin happily obeyed, and enjoyed listening to the happy sounds his son made. This time, Duren didn't even try to stand up when Gerin put him on the ground. He lay there staring up at the sky; Gerin would have bet he saw it going round and round. Finally he made it back to his feet. "Again!" he demanded.

"No," the Fox said. "If you do too much of that, you can make yourself sick."

"Really?" Gerin watched his son think that over; the process was very visible. Duren obviously decided that was an interesting idea, and one worth exploring further. He spun away, laughing out loud.

Gerin laughed, too, but only for a moment. Duren could afford to live for the present—indeed, at his age, he could hardly do anything else. Gerin did not enjoy that luxury. His son was the only good thing he had left from his shattered marriage with Elise, and he loved the boy without reservation. But what would happen to Duren when he wed Selatre and had children by her? Minstrels sang songs about stepmothers, but how would he blame Selatre for wanting her own blood to advance? Who would end up whose vassal, and after how much hatred and strife?

With such unpleasant thoughts in his mind, he was almost embarrassed when Selatre came out of the great hall and walked over to him. "Why so grim-faced?" she asked. "The monsters are—wherever Mavrix sent them. They're not here, anyway. Ikos is risen again, I suppose with a new Sibyl. Adiatunnus is lying low, at least for now. You should be happy."

"Oh, I am," he said, "but not for any of those reasons."

She frowned, looking for the meaning behind his words. When she found it, she looked down at the ground for a moment; sometimes a compliment could make her as nervous as being touched once had. Then she said, "If you are so happy, why haven't you told your face about it?"

He clicked his tongue between his teeth. "I was trying to look into the future, and I don't have a god to guide my sight."

"Biton didn't guide me," Selatre said. "He just spoke through me, and I had no memory of what he would say. What did you see that troubled you so?"

Gerin wondered if he should have kept his mouth shut. But no: Selatre prized truth, partly from her own nature and perhaps partly also because so much raw truth had washed through her as the god's conduit. So, hesitantly, he explained.

"Yes, those are troubling thoughts," she said when he was done. "Much will depend on what sort of man Duren becomes, and on any other children who may appear." She glanced over to him, her head cocked to one side. "So you aim to wed me, do you? This is the first I've heard of it."

He coughed and sputtered; his ears got hot. "I did intend to ask you formally," he said; hearing how lame his voice sounded only made his ears hotter. "But yes, it has been in my mind, and it just—slipped out now. What say you to that?"

"Oh, I say yes, without a doubt," Selatre answered. He hugged her, glad past words that he hadn't been too clumsy for her to bear. But she still had that—measuring—look on her face. She said, "As long as you are looking into the future, what makes you bold enough to think *I* won't want to run off with a horseleech someday, as Elise did?"

"Oof!" he said, the air rushing out of him; she couldn't have deflated him any more thoroughly if she'd kicked him in the belly. "And we men like to think we're the cool and calculating sex." But he saw she wanted a serious answer, and did his best to give her one: "I've learned some things since I wed her, or I hope I have, anyhow. I know better than to take a wife for granted just because we've given each other pledges. Marriage is like, hmm, the palisade around this keep: if I don't keep checking to make sure the timber stays sound, it'll fall to pieces one day. That's most important. The other thing is, you suit me better than she did in a lot of different ways. I don't think the two of us will rub each other raw. And if we start to, I hope I'm wise enough now to try to make sure that doesn't get too bad. And I hope you are, too." He waited to see what she'd say to that.

Once more to his vast relief, she nodded. "Those are

good reasons," she said. "If you'd given me something like, 'Because I think you're lovelier than the stars in the sky,' then I'd have worried."

"I do," Gerin said. "Think you're lovelier than the stars in the sky, I mean."

Selatre glanced away. "I'm glad you do," she answered quietly. "But while that's a fine reason to want to bed someone, it really isn't reason enough to wed. One fine day, you'd likely see someone else you think is lovelier than the stars in the sky—and then, what point in having married?"

"The one and only good thing about growing older that I've found is that I don't think with my crotch as much as I used to," he said.

"As much, eh?" Selatre stuck out her tongue at him. "I will put up with a certain amount of that, I suppose . . . depending on whom you're thinking about."

He slipped an arm around her waist, drew her to him. Not very long before, even trying that would have got him killed by the temple guards at Ikos. Even more recently, she'd have pulled away in horror, still thinking a man's touch a defilement. Now she molded herself to him.

As if to prove he hadn't been thinking entirely with his crotch, he said, "Duren tells me you're starting to teach him his letters."

"Do you mind?" Her voice was anxious. "I didn't think I had to tell you; you've always been one to want people to be able to read. And he's a good boy, your son. I like him. If he has an early start on his letters, they'll come easier for him. Learning them once I was all grown up, I sometimes thought my head would burst."

"Did you?" Gerin said. "If you did, you hid it very well. And you learned them very well, too—better than most of the people I've taught when they were younger.

No, I don't mind. You're right—I'm glad he has a start on them. And I'm glad you like him."

Maybe he gave that some slight extra emphasis, or maybe Selatre was getting better at fathoming the way his mind worked. She said, "Aye, I can see how you might be."

She made a face. "I don't intend to act like a wicked stepmother in a tale, I promise you that." She paused for a moment, her expression thoughtful. "I wonder what the stepmothers in those tales intended. Is anyone ever wicked in her own eyes?"

"Do you know," Gerin said slowly, "there's a question that would keep the sages down in the City of Elabon arguing for days. When I first opened my mouth, I would have said of course some people seem wicked, even to themselves. But when I try to see through their eyes, I wonder. Balamung the Trokmê wizard set the northlands on their ear a few years ago, but he thought he was taking just revenge for slights he'd got. And Wolfar of the Axe—" He broke off and scowled; remembering Wolfar made him remember Elise, too. "Wolfar was out for his own gain, and didn't see one bloody thing wrong with that. You may be right."

"They probably saw you as wicked for trying to stop them," Selatre said.

"So they did," Gerin said. "Which didn't mean I didn't judge them wicked, or that they didn't need stopping."

"And you stopped them," Selatre said, nodding. "Did I rightly hear that you slew Wolfar in the library?" She gave him a different sort of sidelong look this time, as if to say that was not the proper use to which to put a chamber dedicated to preserving books.

"If I hadn't killed him there, he certainly would have killed me," Gerin answered. "That he didn't wasn't for lack of trying." His neck throbbed at the memory; Wolfar had come within an eyelash of strangling him. But he *had* strangled Wolfar, and in so doing won what passed for Schild's loyalty.

Selatre said, "If you hadn't slain him then, I probably wouldn't be alive today—the monsters would have caught me the day of the earthquake." Her laugh came shaky. "Strange to think your own being depends on something that had happened years ago to someone you didn't know then."

"Aye, that is a curious thought," Gerin agreed. "Some Trokmê—or maybe more than one of the woodsrunners; I've never known for certain—twisted my life out of the path I'd planned for it when he—they—killed my father and my brother and left me baron of Fox Keep. If you dwell on the might-have-beens, it's like wandering through a maze."

"Might-have-beens strain even the powers of the gods," Selatre said. "Remember how Biton had to strain to see what might come from my going back to Ikos and my staying here with you?"

"I'm not likely to forget it," Gerin said with feeling. "I thought I'd lost you forever."

"Biton was kindly, perhaps in memory of how I'd served him before," Selatre answered. "But even if he hadn't been, how could you hope to set your will against a god's?"

"I couldn't," Gerin said, and let it go at that. The god's will had not been his principal concern; Selatre's had. With a lifetime devoted to Biton and bare days to him, she was only too likely to have chosen to return to what she'd always known. That she hadn't left made him grateful every time he looked at her. Most seriously, he said, "I'll do my best to make sure you're never sorry about your choice."

"You needn't worry about that," Selatre said. "The

farseeing one will have made his own selection by now; with the temple at Ikos restored, he would not leave it without a Sibyl. I'm here because I wanted to be, and not because I have no other choice open to me."

Again Gerin kept part of his thoughts to himself. There was always another choice: the one Elise had taken. What he had to do now—what he had to do forever—was to make sure Selatre was too content at Fox Keep ever to want to leave it.

He hugged her again, but didn't think, as he had a little while before, of taking her up to his chamber and barring the door. Simple affection had its place, too. Maybe after all he could say some of what he'd thought: "If we work at it, it *will* turn out all right."

"Are you making prophecies now?" Selatre asked. "Perhaps I should have worried about whether Biton would take you back to Ikos and set you on the throne of pearl."

"Thank you, no," Gerin said. "I'm right where I belong, not doing what I'd hoped to be doing, maybe, but doing something that needs doing—and I'm just happy you think you belong here, too."

"That I do," Selatre agreed. "And now, if you're not going to drag me upstairs, I'll go up by myself and wade through that scroll on Kizzuwatnan hepatomancy I was trying to make sense of the other day."

"That one doesn't make much sense to me, either," Gerin said. "My guess is that it either didn't make much sense to the Sithonian who wrote it in the first place or to the Elabonian who put it into our language. I've tried foretelling a few times from livers of cows or sheep we've slaughtered, but what I divined had nothing to do with what ended up happening. Something's been lost somewhere, I think."

"Maybe it will come clear if I keep studying it," Selatre said, and headed back into the great hall.

Gerin smiled as he watched her go. Though she didn't put it the way he had, she also believed in working at something till you got it right. Even without hepatomancy, he knew a good omen when he saw one.

The way she'd teased him about dragging her upstairs he took for a good omen, too. With Elise, anything involving the bedchamber had been a deadly serious business. With Fand, he'd never known whether he was in for a grand time or a fight. Making love with someone neither earnest nor inflammatory was new to him, but he liked it.

Drifting after Selatre, he walked into the great hall himself. Van sat at one of the tables there, a roast chicken—mostly bones now—in front of him, a pitcher of ale within easy reach. He nodded to the Fox and said, "Grab yourself a jack, Captain, and help me get to the bottom of this."

"I don't mind if I do." Gerin sat down across from the outlander, who poured him a full jack.

Van raised his own and said, "To the Prince of the North—maybe one day to the King of the North!" He poured the ale down his throat, then stared sharply at Gerin. "You'd better drink to that."

"So I should," Gerin said, and obediently drank. He smacked his lips, partly tasting the ale, partly Van's words. King of the North? "If I'm lucky, my grandson may wear that title."

Van plucked at his beard. "I don't know, Fox. All's topsy-turvy here, and you're a young man yet. If you live, you may do it."

Gerin shifted uncomfortably on the bench, as if he'd got a splinter in his backside. "I don't know that I *want* to do it. A title like that . . . It'd be an open invitation to all the other lords in the northlands to gang together and pull me down."

"I don't know," Van repeated. "Me, I don't think Aragis

would lift a finger against you, for fear you'd call down the gods and turn him into a lump of cheese, or some such. Same with Adiatunnus. And without them, who'd raise a proper fight?"

"They're wary of me now, aye," Gerin said, "but that'll fade by the time the first snow falls. I can't make myself king before then; I'm too weak. And taking the title when I haven't the strength to back it up—" He shook his head. "Aragis wants to be king. I think he'd fight for pride's sake if I went and put on a crown."

"Have it your way—you generally do," Van said. "From where I sit, looks like you could bring it off." He poured the last of the ale into his jack, drained it, got up, and headed for the stairs.

He'd left one of the wings on the roast fowl uneaten. Gerin pulled it off the carcass, gnawed on it thoughtfully. He shook his head after a little while, still convinced he was right. All the same, he sent a resentful look toward the stairway: Van had kindled his ambition, and he'd known just what he was doing, too.

"Not yet," Gerin said. His lands had suffered too much from the monsters, and from the fights with Adiatunnus. He wanted time to wed Selatre and to enjoy life with her (though the calculating part of his mind said being married to the former Sibyl of an Ikos now miraculously restored would also foster his prestige among his neighbors). No, not yet.

But who could say? The time might come.